Critical Acclaim for Kame
Bel Dame Apocry

"Hurley's world-building is phenomenal... (she) smoothly handles tricky themes such as race, class, religion, and gender without sacrificing action."
—*Publishers Weekly*

"...where some writers might focus on high-tech weapons or explosive battles in space, Hurley brings things down to a personal level, recalling more the toughminded realism of Chris Moriarty's *Spin State*..."
—*New York Review of Science Fiction*

"*God's War* was part slow burn, part explosive action... in the end the novel was utterly compelling."
—*Tor.com*

"*God's War* is one of the most thought-provoking debuts I've read so far this year."
—*Locus Magazine*

"Hurley indeed creates in her lead character a thoroughly unlikeable, but wholly independent, female Conan. Actually, that's wrong: Nyxnissa would quite clearly kick Conan's ass. In her own words, 'Women can fight as well as fuck, you know' (p. 64). Coarse and inelegant, but bold and pungent: Nyx's retort might be this punchy, refreshing, and imperfect novel's grating, gutsy epigram. Just what the genre ordered."
—*Strange Horizons Magazine*

"An aggressively dark, highly original SF-fantasy novel with tight, cutting prose and some of the most inventive world-building I've seen in a while."
—*Fantasy Literature.com*

"*God's War* is a clever reinterpretation of the war novel. Hurley takes on issues of gender roles, violence, and religion and does it all with a deft hand."
—*Staffer's Musings*

Critical Acclaim for Kameron Hurley's Bel Dame Apocrypha

(continued)

"*God's War* is a violent tale set against the backdrop of a centuries-old holy war. But beyond all the blood and violence, it's a beautifully crafted work of art that keeps astonishing you when you least expect it."

—*Pat's Fantasy Hotlist*

"Hurley belongs in the new class of Sci-Fi authors we've been waiting for to invigorate the genre along the sides of Rajaniemi, Bacigalupi, and Yu..."

—*The Mad Hatter's Bookshelf & Book Review*

"This beautifully crafted novel is truly a work of art—bloody, brutal, bug-filled art."

—*The Ranting Dragon*

"Are you frustrated with Mary Sue heroines? Well, here comes *God's War* to rock your face off... If you like rough, battle-scarred women who know how to regulate, you're going to love Nyx... She makes Han Solo look like a boy scout."

—*i09.com*

"*God's War* is a fine piece of writing, and not one that its readers will easily forget."

—*Escape Pod*

"The ostensibly ground-breaking, jaw-dropping ultra-progressive newness of *God's War* is remarkable not because it pushes the boundaries of science fiction, but because it is a novel in which those boundaries are already gone."

—*Pornokitsch*

"If you want a down-and-dirty book that takes a hard look at the consequences of religious intolerance and the idea of what 'feminine' is, read *God's War*."

—*SFF Divas*

"Budding authors take note: you want to know how to do that 'show me don't tell me' trick? Read this book. Read every sentence. Hurley's writing is full of descriptive wonder, of an almost M. John Harrison-y, Jeff VanderMeer-y appreciation for intense color, smell, and sound."

—*The Little Red Reviewer*

RAPTURE

Other books by Kameron Hurley

Bel Dame Apocrypha

God's War

Infidel

Rapture

RAPTURE

KAMERON HURLEY

NIGHT SHADE BOOKS
SAN FRANCISCO

Cover art by David Palumbo
Cover design by Rebecca Silvers
Interior layout and design by Amy Popovich

Edited by Ross E. Lockhart

First Edition

ISBN: 978-1-59780-431-8

Night Shade Books
www.nightshadebooks.com

For Jayson
Thanks for the meat suits.

"Then We which are alive and remain shall be caught up together with them in the clouds, to meet the Lord in the air: and so shall We ever be with the Lord."

(Bible, Thessalonians 4:16–17)

"Whoever works righteousness, man or woman, and has faith, verily, to them will We give a new Life, a life that is good and pure, and We will bestow on such their reward according to the best of their actions."

(Quran, Chapter 16, Verse 97)

1.

Every time Nyx thought she'd gotten out of the business of killing boys, she shot another one.

He lay bleeding at her feet as the spectators for the weekly fights streamed past, muddying the dusty street with his blood. She had not meant to shoot him, but she was drunk, a common condition during her exile. The boy had grabbed clumsily at the knot of her dhoti where she kept her currency. Her response had been unthinking, like breathing. She had pulled the scattergun from her hip and shot him in the chest. It was the only weapon she carried, these days, because she was generally such a poor shot. After nearly seven years in exile without incident, she hadn't expected she'd ever use it. What a boy his age was doing on the street instead of at the front, she didn't know. He was likely a deserter anyway.

As he squealed in the dirt, trailing blood as he scrabbled away from her, a few curious passersby raised their brows, but no one interfered. This was Sameh, a scaly, contaminated, know-nothing little Nasheenian town bordering the vassal state of Druce, populated mainly by speculators and mad magicians. People stayed out of each other's business here. It was why she'd come.

Nyx worried someone might call an order keeper, but the boy had already turned into a neighboring alley, spitting and cursing and bleeding. The pop of the organic rounds in the gun hadn't been loud enough to get much attention, so in a few minutes the incident was forgotten, one more anonymous Nasheenian shooting among a crowd of spectators hoping to see a far more dramatic show of violence inside, in the ring.

A passing woman shook her head at the blood and said, "He's one of those surplus boys just come home from the front. They're stealing us blind. Wondered who'd do him in."

Nyx hadn't heard much about any "surplus boys," but then, she preferred to avoid the belchy, misty images spouting from the local radios whenever possible. The present and the past mixed together too much. Muddled her head.

Nyx did what she always did after she shot a terrorist or garroted a deserter. She carried on. She stepped inside the fight club. She ordered a drink, and sat down to watch the fights. Among this bloodthirsty crowd, she was just another touchy, trigger-prone spectator.

Throughout Nyx's exile, she didn't think much about all the men and women she'd beheaded, or the mullahs she'd pissed off, or the mines she'd planted, or the battles she'd lost. She thought about the ring. A bad left hook. Poor footwork. Blood in her eyes. Hornets on the mat. Because everything that happens after you climb out of a boxing ring, one-half of your face ballooning into a waxy blue-black parody of death while you spit bile and blood and some fleshy bit of somebody's ear on the mat, slowly losing sight in one leaky eye, dragging your shattered, roach-bitten leg behind you… is easy. Routine. Just another day breathing.

After the fights, she sobered up a little on the three-hour drive back to her mercenary buddy Anneke's homestead, just across the Drucian border. Anneke and her family had picked up house when Nyx was exiled from Nasheen and moved across the border. They gave her a place to stay and built up a new life from scratch. They never once complained about it.

The homestead site had been Anneke's pick, a seaside compound with whitewashed walls and tangled, sandy gardens. The sound of the wailing ocean kept Nyx up at night and the contagion sensors sounded off more times a day than the muezzin in Mushtallah. They usually lost everything in the garden to giant beetles and blight. It'd been a season since she ate a green vegetable.

Nyx turned off the rutted main road and onto a logging trail half-covered over in massive evergreen branches. The trees here before the land turned to dunes were tall as a Nasheenian tenement building. They made Nyx claustrophobic. A single fallen branch had pulverized one of Anneke's kids two years before. Just like that, and Anneke's baker's dozen had been culled to an even twelve.

Nyx drove through the towering seaside grove and down the long drive to the house. Eight-foot walls squared the compound.

As she pulled around the circular drive, Nyx saw a foreign bakkie parked in the yard. It was a sleek blue-black hybrid. The whole front end pulsed purple as it sucked up the sun, feeding the bugs in the cistern that powered it. She'd seen fuzzy images of bakkies like this one playing in the background on the radio at a bathhouse in Sameh. They were some new thing out of Tirhan. Expensive, but efficient. No need for juice. The bugs had chlorophyll that fed on solar. At any rate, the tags were foreign on this one. Foreign to Druce, anyway… Familiar to Nyx.

Nasheenian tags.

Government.

Nyx slowed her bakkie to a crawl and killed the juice to the cistern. She pulled her scattergun from behind her seat.

Nobody drove a Nasheenian government bakkie over the border, not unless they were part of an armed caravan of politicians headed for the interior. That said, even caravans didn't cross the border at the coast—it was too contaminated. They would have come down the Sunskin Way E., from Mushtallah. Fifty kilometers from here.

Nyx pulled on her hat and slid out of the bakkie. She held the scattergun at waist height. The big white compound fence gave her some cover. She got close enough to the foreign bakkie to make out the footprints scuffed across the soft, sandy ground.

Three sets of prints. Two heavy folks, and somebody a lot smaller. Heavy bel dames—the Nasheenian government's preferred assassins—didn't use vehicles with government tags. So the little one had to be some government official—and young. All the old ones were soft and fat.

Most Nasheenian politicians were First Family matriarchs—snobbish, inbred, smooth-skinned folks with a taste for languages and distrust of anything that hadn't passed through an organic filter. They wouldn't be caught dead inside a shoddy seaside compound in a backward Nasheenian vassal state.

Nyx circled around to the back of the house and listened for the kids. They were always up to some shit in the garden or on the grounds. But out here, behind the fence and filter, she didn't hear a damned thing but the thrashing sea.

She crouched next to the rear gate. She didn't see any footprints around the back. No sign of anything being tampered with.

The gate was coded for her and Anneke's family. They'd invested in the filter and the codes first thing. Trouble was, you exiled yourself long enough and you started to get comfortable. You started getting drunk and going to fights. You started bringing women home. Nyx should have known somebody would find her.

She pressed her palm to the faceplate. There was a brief prickling as the plate extracted and verified her blood. Then the gate clicked.

Nyx shoved the door open with the end of her scattergun. She waited a half breath before chancing a look into the compound, gun first.

Anneke was waving her arms around like a woman on fire, caught up in some animated conversation with a Ras Tiegan woman. It took Nyx a minute to recognize the foreigner.

The Ras Tiegan was Mercia sa Aldred, a diplomat's daughter who Nyx had been charged with keeping alive six or seven years before. Mercia was a slim young woman now, with the flat face and tawny complexion of a Ras Tiegan. Her eyes were big and dark, half-lidded. As she turned to Nyx, the corners of her wide mouth moved up. Paired with her flat forehead, the broad nose, and strangely delicate frame, she was not a handsome woman. Mercia kept her hair uncovered now, but Nyx noted the scarf wrapped around her neck, stitched with the little x-shaped symbol that marked her as a follower of the Ras Tiegan messiah. No doubt she'd prayed to some minor god of diplomats before coming here. Ras Tiegans had minor gods for everything.

Behind Mercia stood two government-issued bodyguards. Nyx recognized their type. Former vets—underworked and overpaid. They wore loose, dark trousers and matching tunics. Their burnouses were less somber. Smoky gray instead of black. Both women had cropped hair and the peculiar hyper-awareness about them that came from spending too much time at the front. Veterans were always the first pick for government security.

A delighted smile lit up Mercia's face. She made the leap from unremarkable to handsome when she smiled. Mercia stood in one clean movement, and even if Nyx hadn't known her, the polite, easy way she stood to greet her with that plastered-on smile would have given her away as some kind of diplomat or politician.

Nyx hated diplomats and politicians almost as much as she hated babysitting their kids.

"Mercia sa Aldred," Nyx said.

The smile broadened.

"You remember," Mercia said.

"Where is everybody?" Nyx asked Anneke.

"How the hell should I know?" Anneke said. Her dark little face was scrunched up like a cicada husk. "It's fight night. You don't think the kids are going to hang around here with a couple old women, do you?"

"Anybody follow you?" Nyx asked Mercia. "Or can I take out you and your nannies and be done with it?"

Mercia's smile vanished. "I—"

The bodyguards moved forward.

Nyx cocked the gun and leveled it at them. "Who's first?"

"Lay off," Anneke said. "She's got something worth hearing."

"There are a good many people back in Nasheen who'd pay for my head," Nyx said. "I like it just where it is, thanks."

"You've been taken off the lists," Mercia said, quickly. Her hands were up now, gesturing rapidly as she spoke. "They're even sending Chenjan terrorists home. Mhorian spies. Mercenaries, too. And bel dames. Anyone who moved against the Queen during the war has been pardoned. It's part of the armistice."

"Catshit," Nyx said. "There have been ceasefires before. One of them lasted twenty years. The war's not ending. No such thing as peace. Somebody's paying for my head. Who?"

"There's no bounty, Nyx. And the war *is* ending."

Anneke grimaced. "Ease off. Eshe sent a message and vouched for her." Anneke reached for an empty glass sitting on the sandy stone of the yard and poured a drink. Nyx hadn't noticed the drinks before. How long had this sweet-tongued diplomat been lapping at Anneke's ear?

"Oh, Eshe the Ras Tiegan rogue called, did he?" Nyx said. "Well, let in every wandering creeper who caught his eye, then." Then, to Mercia: "Who sent you? Bel dames? Queen? Your slick diplomat mother?"

"My mother's dead," Mercia said.

"Well, sorry about your mother," Nyx said. She wasn't sorry at all, in fact. She had never liked Mercia's mother, but the old cat bitch's death likely put Mercia next in line on someone's hit list.

"You don't listen to the news?" Mercia asked.

"Not if I can help it," Nyx said. She hadn't sought out news of home in three years. All the news was the bloody same. "I'm not in Nasheenian security anymore. I don't give a cat's piss for politics. So tell me why you're here or go home."

"I'm Ambassador sa Aldred until my mother's replacement is appointed," Mercia said. "Things in Nasheen are very bad."

"Things in Nasheen have always been bad."

"And there is good money to be made when things are bad."

Anneke thrust a glass of whiskey at Nyx. Nyx considered it. She eyed the bodyguards again. "You want to talk? Send them back outside." She nodded to the guards.

"No way in hell," the smaller of the two guards said.

"I could shoot you now," Nyx said.

"Please wait in the bakkie," Mercia said.

"I have to respectfully—" the bigger one began.

"I said wait there."

The bodyguards mulled for a bit. Then started for the gate. Nyx kept her gun trained on them. The bigger one eyed Nyx as she passed, said, "We'll burn this place down you do anything to her."

"It'll be a little late then, won't it?"

The woman bared her teeth.

When the gate was closed behind them, Nyx lowered her gun.

"Nasheen is on the brink of revolution," Mercia said. "There are discharged boys with nothing to do but start fights and steal bread. Women are running raids on their own into Chenja, in defiance of the ceasefire. The bel dames… I have never seen them so openly hostile to their own people. The streets are bloody. Bloodier than I've seen them, and I spent half my life in Nasheen. I've had three bodyguards murdered in as many months."

"What does this have to do with me?"

"I remember you saving my life when it was yours they wanted," Mercia said. "I'd pay you for it again."

"Honey pot, you came all this way to offer me a *job*?" Nyx snorted. "I think that's enough talk. Take your women out of here and go home." She started toward the house, said over her shoulder, "And next time you come banging on a wanted woman's door, think up a better story."

"Wait, please," Mercia called after her.

Nyx trudged up the steps. She should go out front and kill the bodyguards. She wasn't too keen on killing Mercia—she was a diplomat after all—but there were plenty of places in Druce to stash a body. Thing was, she wasn't so certain it was only Mercia and the bodyguards who knew where she was now. How long until some other bakkie full of women came along and bombed out the house? How many more of Anneke's children would blister and bleed to death before it was done? Seven years. She thought she might just die out here, forgotten, presumed dead. But once they found you out, there was no turning back. She would have to kill a dozen people to keep this place quiet and safe now. Kill a dozen people… or go back to Nasheen with Mercia.

"You know how long it took me to find you?" Mercia said. "Finding Eshe took many months, and I had to tell him the fate of the world was at stake before he'd even give me the name of the nearest town. I wouldn't be here if it wasn't important."

Nyx got to the top of the steps. She heard two of Anneke's kids—Avava and Sabah—arguing inside about which of the three squads of kids was making dinner that night. Anneke's remaining dozen were almost thirteen years old now, and there were few things more mentally aggravating than a house full of hot-and-bothered thirteen-year-olds. Most of them were wickedly good shots and passable at putting together mines, thanks to Anneke and Nyx, respectively, but more and more these days, Nyx was asking herself what the hell they were doing teaching kids to fight a war that everybody said was supposed to be ending.

"Nyx!" Mercia pleaded.

Nyx started to push through the filter that kept the worst of the bugs and contagion from the house.

"Fatima sent me!"

Nyx stopped cold in the door. Turned back.

Mercia had followed her to the edge of the porch. Mercia's look was less composed now, on the edge of panic. Why? Why was it so important to bring a bloody anachronism back to Nasheen? Weren't there enough bel dames and mercenaries to keep the streets running red?

"And what does Fatima have to say?" Nyx asked.

"She has… a job for you."

"And you couldn't say that up front?"

"She didn't think you would come. And if it had been her or another bel dame at your door, you would have killed them outright. But she said that if you wouldn't come… She said she has a job for you. She wants you to be a bel dame again. She says now that the Queen's pardoned you and she's leading the council, she has the authority to redeem you."

Nyx felt something flutter inside of her, something that had been dead a good long time.

"She must be very desperate to send you here with an offer like that," Nyx said. "Or she must think I'm very stupid."

"Things are bad, Nyx."

"How do you profit from this?" Nyx knew enough about politicians to know that even Mercia was likely a fine one at this point, and fine politicians didn't do anything unless they stood to profit from it.

"It's not about me, exactly, it's about… saving Nasheen."

"Of course it is," Nyx said.

She raised her gun and aimed it directly into Mercia's face. The little diplomat had the sense to tremble. The color bled out of her face.

"Get the fuck off my porch," Nyx said.

✚

"You going to fuck her or kill her?" Anneke asked when Nyx sent Mercia off with her bodyguards. "You never look that close unless it's one or the other."

Nyx stood with Anneke in the prayer room on the second floor, watching Mercia and the bodyguards get into the bakkie. Downstairs, the rest of the kids had come home and joined Avava and Sabah, still arguing about who was going to make dinner. Nyx supposed their choices would be fried locusts, yam noodles, or something unsavory that they had fished out of the ocean. They had pulled some globular one-eyed monster out of that seething, viscous sea the week before, and the thought of it still gave Nyx the dry heaves.

"Not sure yet," Nyx said.

Anneke sighed. She had a stooped way of walking now, something to do with the degeneration of her spine. Genetic, the magicians had told her. Shouldn't have hauled around forty kilos of gear for twenty-five years of mercenary work, either. But what was done was done, and though bone regeneration was possible, eliminating the root cause of her disease was not, and no matter how often Anneke went in to get it fixed, her body would just fail again. Anneke's hair was shot through with white now, and her pinched, Chenjan-dark face was the face of an old woman, though she wasn't much older than Nyx.

"You gotta make a decision sometime," Anneke said.

Nyx said, "She upstairs?"

"Who? Oh. Yeah."

"Mercia see her?"

"No."

"You tell Mercia about her?"

"Fuck no, why'd I do that?"

"Mercia's got a pretty story," Nyx said. She watched Mercia's bakkie roll off down the rutted drive. "I just don't know that I believe it."

"Believe her or not, they know where we are now," Anneke said.

"I got that."

"You going to risk it?"

And Nyx heard the real question behind that. It wasn't fear for Anneke's own life, no—Anneke knew she didn't have long left—it was fear for the kids, and for everything and everyone they had come to care for here. It was a mistake to let her guard down, to let anyone close, even after all this time.

"Just got to tear it all down," Nyx muttered.

Anneke pursed her mouth. "She'll understand. She knew what you were before you hooked up with her."

"Nobody really knows what I am," Nyx said. "Not until I put a bullet in their head."

Nyx went upstairs. Opened the bedroom door. There sat her lover, Radeyah, sketching the view of the sea from the balcony on a foolishly expensive slide that devoured each stroke. She was joyously lit up in that moment like a woman at peace with God.

Radeyah turned as Nyx entered, and the light went out of her face.

"It was one of them, wasn't it?" Radeyah said.

"They've asked me to go back to Nasheen."

Radeyah and Nyx had grown up together in Mushirah, a farming settlement on the Nasheenian interior. Friends first, lovers later. Then they fell apart when the boy Radeyah fancied came home from the front with half his body missing. Radeyah stayed on in Mushirah, and Nyx went to war.

Nyx thought that was the end of it, until a boozy night in Sameh, now thirty years later, when she saw Radeyah sitting out on the levee sketching the sea. Nyx had known her immediately. Radeyah was older, and plumper, but her face was still warm and her body, if anything, more inviting. Nyx knew it could only end badly.

It's why she was so shocked when Radeyah came to her two weeks later at the local tea house and said, "I've been wondering all week why you were staring at me. But you're Nyxnissa so Dasheem, aren't you? Do you remember me?"

In answer, Nyx had ordered her a fruity drink, and asked if she had finally bought the seaside house she always talked about. Radeyah laughed, and it was a liquid laugh that stirred something long since dead and buried inside Nyx—some whole other life that she had to forget in order to lead this one.

Radeyah ceased her sketching. "Tell them no," she said. Nyx admired the nimble way she held her stylus. She imagined Radeyah would have been a fine swordswoman, if she ever had a mind to pick up a sword. But Radeyah had spent her entire life on a farmstead in Mushirah. After her family died, she said she came to Druce to paint the sea, but when Nyx saw her moth-ridden flat with the leaky tub, moldy ceiling and surplus of drugs in the bathroom, she suspected Radeyah had not come to Druce to retire. She had come here to end it all.

Nyx didn't like that idea. When she was with Radeyah, she dreamed less of the ring.

"I have to go," Nyx said.

Radeyah's jaw tightened. "I suppose we've been playing at being lovers a year now. Like children. It was bound to end soon enough."

"You know what I am. What I've done—"

"That was all a long time ago—"

"The Queen has a very long memory."

"Just tell them—"

"They know I'm here now. They'll come for you. All of you. They'll burn it up and scatter your corpses. That's who I deal with. That's the kind of person I am. If I don't go with them now, you're dead."

"How long?" Radeyah said.

"Could be two or three months. Could be a year. I don't know."

Radeyah wasn't good at hiding her emotions. She never had to. The pain that blossomed on her face made Nyx's gut clench. She had to look away.

Had to start cutting out that part of herself again, the one that cared about a thing because somebody else did. I've gotten soft, she thought. This woman made me soft.

"I waited for a man most of my life, and when he returned, he was little more than a hunk of charred meat. Is that what you'll come back as? Or something worse? I have spent my whole life waiting to live, Nyx. I'm too old to wait."

"I'm not asking you to wait."

Radeyah closed her slide and stood. "I should go."

"Stay for dinner."

"I should have known you would go."

Nyx walked up to her. Took her by the arms, leaned in. "If I didn't give a shit about you I'd tell them to fuck off. I'd wrap you up and cart you off to some other house and fuck you on the porch all day until they burned it around us. But I do give a shit. And I'm too fucking old to see everything me and you and Anneke and the kids built destroyed because I couldn't do one last job."

Radeyah wrapped her arms around Nyx. Nyx pulled her close. They made love there on the floor as the light purled through the billowing curtains. Nyx traced Radeyah's scars from her two births, all dozen children lost to the war. When Radeyah came, she bucked beneath Nyx's hand, revealing the twisted collection of scars on her backside where the magicians had pulled shrapnel from her after a commuter train accident north of Mushirah. There were more scars, more blemishes, a lifetime of Nasheenian living mapped out on her body. Nyx loved her for it, a little. And feared for her—far too much.

Radeyah stroked her hair, after. "I won't wait for you," she said.

"I know," Nyx said.

Even as they lay together in the cool breeze, Radeyah soft and comforting next to her, Nyx felt herself pulling away, boxing herself back up, until soon she was nearly numb, and the spidery tattoo on Radeyah's ankle that still bore Nyx's name no longer gave Nyx the same flutter of affection. It was easy to become everything she hated again. Remarkably, maddeningly easy.

Nyx closed her eyes, and stepped into the ring.

2.

Eshe put his shotgun down on the battered table between him and the priest. The priest was a fastidious little man, clean and neat, with long limbs and balding head that put Eshe in mind of a dung beetle. He was Ras Tiegan, flat faced and broad nosed, with a pale as piss complexion that was a little ruddy in the nose and cheeks. He was already halfway through a pint of hard ale, and Eshe guessed he'd started drinking well before Eshe showed up.

The priest's eyes bulged at the shotgun. Eshe figured the old guy had never seen a gun up close. Eshe was prepared to get him a good deal closer to it.

"You have a license for that?" the priest asked, hissing around his drink like there was anyone else in the tavern who cared about their business.

The sticky sweet smell of opium seeped in from the bunkhouses upstairs. A woman wearing a muslin habit with the back torn out slipped into the front door and scurried into the kitchen on bloody, swollen feet. Someone cried out from the gambling room in back. The distant gong of church bells called the faithful to midnight prayer. Just another dark Ras Tiegan night at the edge of the protected territories.

"You think I'd need a license here?" Eshe said.

The priest mopped his brow with a yellowed handkerchief. "There's no need for that, boy. I came here, didn't I? What kind of whore's dog are you, to throw weapons around at a holy man? I need another drink."

The priest had come wearing the long brown robe and tattered cowl of his order. His was one of the less popular sects, populated by cowardly little men instead of the more fit, robust types Eshe was used to. He had a golden cord looped about his waist and neck, fashioned into a crude X at his collar, but the garb didn't mean much out here. In the larger cities, the less contaminated ones, maybe, a priest's robe was enough to save a pious man's life. But when bugs crawled through your filters every night to lay eggs in your flesh and noxious air killed off your babies if you kept them too close to the ground, there was less reverence for a man of God who did not also wear the bloody apron of a magician. Magicians saved lives. You only called on a priest when you knew your life was over.

Eshe leaned toward the priest. "Tell me what I need to know or your next drink will be leaking out a hole in your gut."

"I only meant—"

"It's my people in this place, old man. I could skin you alive right here and they'd help me chop you up and feed you to the flesh beetles."

The priest swallowed. "They're moving her next week, before the Feast of the Blood. I don't know where they're keeping her, but I know where she's going." His gaze lingered on the gun, darted away. "It's Jolique so Romaud's house. You know it? He has a… collection… of those like her. He felt that, with her mutation, she would be an excellent addition to his collection."

Eshe should have known. Jolique was cousin to the Queen of Nasheen, and all but untouchable in Ras Tieg. No magistrate or God's Angel would dare raid his house looking for captive shifters. Abuses committed by the rich and powerful were overlooked in Ras Tieg, just as they were in every country.

"What road?" Eshe asked.

"Rue Clery. She should arrive around fifteen in the morning."

"Staff?"

"Four men and a wrangler."

Eshe leaned back in the chair and lifted the gun off the table.

The priest sighed. The shadow of a smile tugged at his lips. He didn't know that he'd been dead from the moment he sat down.

Eshe pointed the shotgun into the priest's mealy little face and pulled the trigger.

The gun popped. The priest's head caved in. Black, bloody brains splattered the wall behind the priest.

Eshe stood and wiped the blood from his face with his sleeve. The mostly headless torso of the dead priest slumped sideways. Eshe expected he'd feel happier about it, after all this man and his kind had done.

The bar matron, Angelique, *tsked* at him. “Did you need to do that?” she said. “That’s four priests in as many weeks.”

“That’ll keep them from coming around, then, won’t it?” Eshe pulled on his hat and pushed toward the door.

“Godless heathen,” Angelique muttered.

“I know all about God,” Eshe said. “These men don’t. Or did you forget what they did to Corinne?”

“It’s just… you Nasheenians—”

“Nasheenians don’t murder their own people for being born shifters. They don’t kill their own babies. And they sure as fuck don’t—”

“Shut it, Eshe,” a man at the end of the bar said. Eshe had seen him around, but couldn’t place him. Angelique’s hired muscle, ever since the Madame de Fourré started using the place for meetings for her rebel shape shifters. Angelique’s son was a member of the Fourré, but it didn’t mean they liked Eshe’s half-breed face. Sometimes he wondered if his heritage was more offensive to them than his ability to change into a raven.

Eshe bristled. “Sorry about the mess,” he said to Angelique. “It won’t happen here again.”

He would find a new tavern.

Outside, the Ras Tiegan night was cool. It was a rare clear night in the city of Inoublie during the rainy season. He could already smell the promise of more rain on the wind, mingling with the scent of curry and dog shit. As he hustled through the narrow streets, swarms of mayflies and cockroaches choked his path. A ragged, mewling desert cat in a cage whined at him from a high balcony.

Along the edges of the horizon, just visible through the occasional break in the buildings, was the swampy jungle—a dark, ragged stain. Odd hoots and cries and drones muttered at the edge of the city, barely muffled by the spotty filter that kept out the worst of it. What Ras Tieg had managed to build out here had been hacked out of contaminated jungle—a jungle that ate cities nearly as quickly as the Ras Tiegans could put them up. He passed the hulking wreck of a former church, now a recreation hall. Old, twisted slabs of metal protruded from the exterior—corroded, half-eaten. Metal was not known to last long on Umayma, but the Ras Tiegans had been entrenched there only twelve hundred years or so. Even their poorly put-together, non-organic ship skins took a while to break down.

He climbed up into the clotted, ramshackle district tenement he called home; swung down into the guts of his apartment. It was a tight little room: raised bed, mud-brick oven. Most of the important stuff he kept in the walls or in the pockets he'd burrowed out in the floor.

He took off his coat and stowed his gun. Then he unrolled his prayer mat, faced north, and went through the salaat for evening prayer. There was no call to prayer here, only the bells for midnight mass and the weekly call to services every ninth day. It was a lonely thing, to pray alone, to speak to God alone. Salaat always calmed his nerves, though, and when he finished the final recitation, he remained on his knees for some time, breathing deeply. If someone had asked him seven years before what he thought he would miss most about leaving Nasheen, he would not have thought about the call to prayer. Mostly, he missed the sense of being part of something larger than himself. Praying alone every day just reminded him of how different he was here.

As he settled into bed, he heard a soft whistle. He reached below the bed to where his shotgun lay, and waited. The whistle came again. Then a scrabbling on the roof. He remained still until he saw a familiar, scruffy-headed outline in the entry.

"Get in here before I shoot you on accident," Eshe said.

Adeliz climbed down into the room, slender and quiet as a shadow in her baggy trousers and coat. The first time she'd come into his room, he hadn't noticed her until she had her hands on his shotgun. Why they hadn't killed each other then, he wasn't so sure.

She crouched near the stove. "Cold in here," she murmured. She talked softly, slip of a voice, just like she moved. "I think you should come to mass tonight," she said

"I thought I wasn't invited anymore."

The last time he went to midnight mass, he'd been roughed up and escorted out by three priests. Adeliz was one of the first members of the Fourré he had met, and it was she who led him to the first sorry cell of defeated shifter rebels. She was only seven or eight back then, but could pick a pocket like the most hard-assed kid in Mushtallah. Her fierce little face and fast fingers reminded him of himself, some days. That meant he liked her—but he knew better than to trust her.

"Sometimes they forget," she said. "What about the puppets tomorrow?"

"No, I have a wake to go to."

"Another priest? Not the one you killed tonight?"

"You heard about that?"

"I hear about everything."

"Yes, it's the wake for a different priest."

"The Madame will not be pleased."

"When was the last time she was pleased with me?"

"True, true." Adeliz hopped from foot to foot. "Are you taking the girl with you? Your new partner? She was very angry you didn't take her out tonight."

"Isabet is always angry."

"It's why you get along so well," Adeliz said, and beamed.

"What the fuck is that supposed to mean?" Eshe said.

"Language, language," Adeliz said. "Did you find out where they took her? The Madame's missing operative?"

"Jolique so Romaud's house. They'll be coming at fifteen in the morning, taking the Rue Clery. Four men and a wrangler."

"Good news, good news," Adeliz said. She hopped back up the ladder.

"Adeliz?"

"Yes?"

"Get her back. Don't let them do to her what they did to Corinne."

"The Madame will see to it."

"That's what she said about Corinne."

Adeliz shrugged. "Just the messenger."

And I'm just the pawn, Eshe thought. He thought of Corinne, and the way she laughed the first time he reached out to adjust the crumpled wimple that covered her tangle of curly black hair.

He could murder as many Ras Tiegan priests as he liked, but it was the Madame who decided what to do with the information he got from them. She decided who lived, and who died.

And he wasn't sure how much longer he could put up with it before he took the Madame's little rebellion into his own hands.

"Do you need anything for the wake?" Adeliz said. "Weapons? Explosives?"

"No," Eshe said. "When the dead come back, I know exactly what to do with them."

3.

Rhys stood on the carved stone balcony of his tenement house in Khairi, smoking a sen cigarette and watching the blue dawn touch the desert. This far north, the desert *moved* at night, like maggots writhing on the surface of some rotten beast. In the garish red light of the moons, the desert was a bloody carcass shot through with splinters of wind-worn stone towers that predated the beginning of the world. Some natural configuration, maybe, or remnant of a civilization that had come before? It had been a long time since he questioned what had come before his people descended from the moons to remake the world. What had it been before? Barren and bloody, like this?

Rhys pulled his burnous close against the bitter cold of the desert night. Out here, the difference between daytime and nighttime temperatures was extreme. Despite nearly a year in this quiet desert outpost, he still was not dressed properly for it.

Behind him, inside the two rooms he shared with his wife and children, his son squalled. He had been wailing since midnight prayer. Rhys had given up on sleep even before his wife had, and retreated to the balcony to watch the suns rise.

The boy had been unplanned, as had the two girls before him. When his wife told him she was pregnant for the second time in as many years, he had not greeted the news as a good man should have. They wouldn't have had the first one at all if Elahyiah hadn't been four weeks pregnant the night the bel dames murdered their other children. When he found out about this third pregnancy, he yelled at her, questioning why the old methods they had used to prevent pregnancy were no longer working. She had wept and told him she did not know.

"I had no choice! Do you think a woman has a choice? The old ways don't always work. That is God's will. We must bear the consequences of our actions. And it is my burden and blessing more than yours."

He suspected some deception on her part until the day his son was born. It was a long, painful labor lasting nearly two days. After, she begged him to allow one of the magicians to put a hex on her—semi-permanent sterilization. He had refused. He refused because a moment before she asked he held his son for the first time. When he did, some great unknown emotion rose up in him, something he had not felt since the bel dames came and mangled his wife and killed his children. He nearly lost everything that night. He badly wanted to rebuild. As the years passed, and his eldest daughter grew without either of them talking about more children and his wife became more and more distant, he had stopped believing rebuilding was possible.

But now he had a son. It was as if anything were possible again, as if he himself had been reborn with a second chance at life.

As if to punish him for his decision, the boy squalled day and night. Elahyiah no sooner put him down than he started screaming again. Rhys once insisted they simply leave him in the house while they went to dinner—he, Elahyiah, their eldest daughter Mehry and the younger girl, Nasrin. When they came back three hours later, the infant was still screaming. Elahyiah thought there must be something wrong with him. They brought him to hedge witches and even the local Khairian midwives, but they all came back with the same answer. If you want him to sleep, give him a bit of whiskey.

This part of Khairi was a dry town—it was a Chenjan-occupied settlement called Shaesta, and had been for some time. Whiskey was nearly impossible to find, and came with a sentence of six lashes for possession. Some nights, Rhys thought the lashes might be worth it.

Rhys tried to listen for the more soothing sounds of the settlement, the susurrus of the massive sand caterpillars in the pen opposite their building as the creatures chewed their leafy breakfast, and the singing of a caravan member in Khairian, her voice high and warbling. He knew it was a Khairian because no Chenjan woman would dare sing in public.

She emerged from a tent posted next to the caterpillar pen. Like most Khairians, she was tall and wiry, her hair bound up in a scarlet turban.

As he watched, her voice drew a swarm of wild insects, mostly harmless—desert fireflies and grasshoppers. They emerged from the sand, scurrying toward her like a locust to a body. Rhys saw her two husbands step outside after her and begin collecting them in jars. As the jars filled, the men took them back into the tent, presumably to throw the bugs into the cook pot for breakfast. Rhys had asked these strange singing Khairians if they were magicians—he had not gotten any sort of sense of talent from any of them, which was highly unusual. But each one he asked laughed and said it was just something their people had always done, as if conversing with insects was as natural to them all as breathing.

The call to prayer sounded from the settlement mosque just as the Khairian ended her song. He leaned over the stone rail and listened. The call to prayer was the only sound that could drown out his son's cry.

He took another pull on his cigarette. He had prayed at midnight prayer, and though joining the throng of other men headed toward the mosque was tempting, he refrained. If he wanted to keep food on the table, he needed to be at the tea house before the end of prayer.

"Rhys?"

Elahyiah's voice. Tired. Strained. She sounded the way he felt.

He quickly dropped the hand with the cigarette below the balcony rail, hoping she could not see the burning glow of its tip in the dawn light.

Elahyiah stepped onto the balcony. She cradled their son, Rahim, in her arms. At six months old, he was still a slip of a thing. Rhys worried he was underfed. Elahyiah insisted she fed him all he would eat. She herself was terribly thin for a woman so recently in child bed. Only the fullness of her chest gave any indication that she was the mother of this child. Her stomach had flattened in time with their dwindling funds. Most nights, they ate fried grasshoppers.

"I'm going out to meet Payam for a job," Rhys said.

"Can you bring back coconut milk?"

"If they have some, certainly." And if they allowed him to take out any more credit.

She wrinkled her nose. He suspected she could smell the cigarette smoke. But she said nothing.

The supplies at the local trade house varied considerably by the day.

It depended on what caravan had come in. Many had been delayed by early spring sandstorms. Others were diverted by the mine cleanup efforts now that the ceasefire had begun. Chenja had issued the ceasefire first. They were also the first to pardon their deserters and criminals, a full two years before Nasheen. It was why he agreed to come out here to a Chenjan-held Khairian outpost—that and the promise of fast money. He hoped it would be like coming home again. He hoped that maybe, away from Elahyiah's family and the bad memories in Tirhan, things would be easier.

He had been very wrong.

"Have you asked the mullah if he needs help during prayer days?" Elahyiah said.

"There's no money in that."

"I thought you would enjoy teaching the Kitab to children. It has been… many months since we sat and read together as we once did."

"I have been busy, Elahyiah." Trying to make sure they didn't starve.

Elahyiah averted her eyes. "I understand," she said. "I just thought it may soothe your nerves more to read the Kitab than… other things." She ducked back inside.

Rhys put out his cigarette on the rail and followed her. The girls were awake. Mehry was nearly seven now, and far too precocious for a girl growing up in a Chenjan settlement. Always full of questions. Her sister Nasrin was two, and sat up in her basinet watching Mehry pray. Rhys saw nothing of himself in either of them. Like the two girls he and Elahyiah had raised before, these resembled their mother. But now he could not help but compare them to their dead sisters as well.

Elahyiah paced back and forth with Rahim, admonishing Mehry to finish prayer, though by all counts Mehry was still too young for anyone to insist that she observe so many of them. Mehry studied at the madrassa at the end of the street, one of only six girls. They learned from the same teacher as the boys, a balding old mullah who had not, blessedly, asked that Mehry learn her lessons from behind a screen. But she did have to go to school in a uniform that was becoming less modest as she grew, tall and lanky as a mantis. The madrassa and uniform were not cheap. Nor was the two-room flat that stank perpetually of cabbage and peppercorns from the Heidian family on the floor beneath them.

Rhys washed his face and hands at the kitchen sink; just a sluice set in the wall above a chipped clay basin. They shared a privy down the hall with the rest of their floor. He avoided it as much as possible. Someone had found a dead infant there not three weeks past, cold and unmoving in a pool of blood and afterbirth. Insects had already eaten out the eyes and hollowed the placenta. The bugs were worse out here than even the Tirhani wilderness. After they heard about the baby, Elahyiah insisted that Rahim sleep beside them. There was no more talk of leaving him on his own for hours to scream out his frustrations.

Rhys pulled on his burnous. He leaned toward Elahyiah to kiss her, but she turned her head away.

"Remember the milk," she said.

"We may not have enough for milk."

"We seem to have enough for your filthy habits. I expect you can find something for milk."

"Don't presume to tell me what to spend."

"It is our money. Our family's money. We used to decide everything together, Rhys. Now you shut me out like I'm some stranger."

The anger came then, unbidden. "Isn't this enough? Selling myself into servitude? What else can I do for you and this family? Bleed all over your shoes?"

"It was your idea to come here to the edge of nothing," Elahyiah said. "I believed we would do better in Chenja itself, not this terrible outpost."

"I've told you why I can't go back to Chenja."

"Things have changed. We can do much good there. Have you heard about the women's initiatives there?"

"What we don't need is Chenja becoming another Nasheen."

"It won't be Nasheen. It can be another Tirhan. I want to help them, Rhys. They're our people."

"The decision has been made."

Rahim began to squall again.

Rhys threw up his hands. "Enough. You want him to eat, let me do my work."

He shut the door behind him without waiting for a response. He knew what Elahyiah wanted. What he could not tell her was that going home to Chenja terrified him. Being this close had given him many sleepless nights, but what she wanted was to go home to Chenja—her parents' country more than hers—and teach women to read. He had to tell her, gently, that only the very poorest Chenjan women did not know how to read. Some of the gross generalizations he heard in Tirhan about how Chenjans treated their wives often offended him. Yet after many years abroad, he could not help but hope for a future for his daughters that looked a little more like a Tirhani one than a Chenjan one. Why couldn't his daughters have good marriages to men who honored and protected them but retain the freedom to vote and speak in matters of governance, so long as they did so modestly?

Outside, the second dawn touched the world. A blaze of fiery red scorched the eastern sky, banded in deep purple along the horizon. He made his way to the settlement's only tea house, a squat mud-brick building set with cracked amber tiles that spoke of better days. As he walked, an arthropod as long and thick as his leg uncurled from the nearest ditch and moved across the road in front of him. His skin crawled. Khairians called them *mauta kita*, and killed them at every opportunity. They were purported to grow large enough to swallow a wagon of goods whole, further north. Most of the wagons in this desert were pulled by native armored caterpillars instead of sand cats—both because the *mauta kita* were more likely to eat the cats and because the caterpillars lasted longer on the open sand without water.

As he walked, he paused at the window of a clothier. Displayed there were two headless mannequins wearing brilliant red and amber burquas. The burquas themselves were not strange. What made him stop was that he noticed that the mannequins had hands. In his childhood, mannequins were sexless, formless things—the less lifelike, the better. Most store windows simply put clothing on vaguely human-shaped leather hangers. The few mannequins he did see were just torsos. No legs. No hands. But these had hands, and as he got closer, he saw something like feet and legs as well.

Elahyiah had told him for many years that things in Chenja were changing. Her parents still had family there. Words were one thing, yes, but seeing these mannequins and their hands was quite another.

Rhys turned away from the window, and ducked into the tea house opposite. There were prayer wheels hung at each of the windows. He heard the sound of someone reciting from the Kitab, voice low and beautiful, almost musical. It calmed him.

Payam already waited for him at a far table. He dressed like a Tirhani businessman in a long white khameez and somber bisht, but his scarlet turban was a more local affectation. Payam was younger than Rhys by nearly a decade, with a fleshy face and soft hands that marked him as a Tirhani, not just a Chenjan in Tirhani garb. Most Chenjans bore bodies that had seen the war.

He was speaking to a swarm of red beetles at his left elbow—not something he had called but sent to him by one of his caravans. He concluded whatever his message was and waved the bugs away. The swarm buzzed past Rhys and out into the dawn.

"Punctual as ever," Payam said.

Rhys sat opposite him and ordered green tea with honey from a woman wearing a creamy burqua.

"What do you have for me today?" Rhys asked.

"I have exciting news today," Payam said, and he grinned so broadly Rhys thought his head might split in two. "No more one-off translations or bacterial infusions. Oh no! I have something quite fine. Something perfectly suited to your skills. You came and God brought you!"

That meant it was something that would make Payam a lot of money. It didn't always mean it made Rhys much. He had come out here not just because of its remoteness to Chenja itself but also because he heard that magicians and translators were making obscene money working with the Khairian nomads. That, more than anything, finally persuaded Elahyiah. The ceasefire meant more traffic coming down from Khairi—safer trade routes were good for everyone's business but the black marketeers. But when he arrived, he found that most jobs were taken, or involved joining up with a caravan for a year or more, or indenturing himself to some middleman like Payam. By the time Rhys realized he was going to be spending most of his days begging for work, his family was already settled, and they did not have enough currency to get them back to Tirhan.

So Rhys waited. Payam kept grinning. Rhys began to feel uneasy. "Are you going to tell me about the job?" Rhys asked.

"The pay is remarkable. It will solve all your little… problems. All four of them." Payam winked. He was unmarried, by all counts, and spent far too much time harassing Khairian girls who came in with the caravans. But his time among the Khairians had tempered his speech, at least. He talked more like a Khairian than a Tirhani. Rhys found he appreciated the straightforward—though often pleasantly deceptive—speech to the Tirhani practice of false politeness.

"Doing what?"

"Doing what you do best. Translation work."

"Why does it pay so well?" Everyone in Khairi spoke four or five languages. That was the part Rhys had not counted on. There was little need for a translator if everyone spoke multiple languages.

"Well, that's the truly *exciting* part," Payam said. He leaned closer. "It's just a little further north. Fewer people up there know Chenjan or Nasheenian. You're a much more prized property. And a man who has some talent with bugs! That goes a long way, too."

"How much further north? I have a family."

"It's… not far. A few weeks' travel. But you'll have room and board and a fine salary. A signing bonus today and another the day of the journey if you agree. Something to tide you over. A taste of what's to come."

"Who is this job for?"

"A man you've not heard of. Has some renown further north, beyond the Wall. Doing a fine job bringing order to the nomads up there. Name of Hanife. He speaks Khairian all right, and whatever his bastard native tongue is, but nothing else. When I heard he needed somebody he could trust, I thought of you. Who better than a devoted Chenjan family man who has worked for the Tirhani government?"

Rhys showed his teeth—more grimace than smile, but he had never seen a Khairian smile. Just the grimace. "How much?"

"One thousand Tirhani notes. That's three hundred now, and the seven hundred when you get there. Another five thousand at the end of the job."

The serving girl brought Rhys's tea. He hardly noticed. He had never seen that much money in his life. "Is that with or without your commission?"

Payam laughed. "My friend, I am pleased to tell you that that is after my commission."

Rhys felt the knot of anger and worry that he had been harboring all morning begin to ease. He did not trust the feeling, though, because he did not entirely trust Payam. For all he knew, it was one of Payam's conquests that left her child to die in the privy in Rhys's tenement. Such an immoral man could not be trusted.

"Why didn't anyone else take this job?"

"I have four translators out on jobs. The other two don't know Nasheenian. And he was very specific that the translator speak Nasheenian."

Rhys wrapped his hands around the teacup. The warmth was soothing, familiar. The last time someone wanted him to translate Nasheenian, bloody bel dames hacked off his hands and murdered his children. But the money…

"Did he say why Nasheenian?"

"He does dealings with them. Not sure if you've kept up with Nasheenian politics, but there's a big rift over there. The Queen, First Families, bel dames, all looking to take over if it turns out the war's really ending. But the magic has turned against them. His man tells me Hanife does quite a lot of black market business with Nasheenian First Families."

"First Families? Not bel dames?"

Payam shrugged. "He said nothing to me of bel dames. Why? Have some trouble with them?"

Rhys stared at his hands. The long sleeves of his burnous covered the scars at his wrists where he had lost his hands. The ones fixed to his body now were not his, but some dead laborer's. Short, thick fingers. They had been rough and calloused when he first got them. He had not been able to touch his wife without cringing for more than a year.

"Three hundred now?"

"Yes. I know I have two-thirds of your mind. You'll do it?"

"You knew I would." Payam also ran the local trading post. He would have seen how long Rhys's credit list was, and how desperately his family needed to eat.

Payam grinned. "Of course I knew you would. Have some more tea! This commission will finally send me on my haj to Chenja. Birthplace of the martyr, may she bless this transaction. A fine day for both of us!"

Rhys stumbled outside into the warm dawn. The rest of the settlement was back from prayer, and the streets were alive with the hiss of cats and the song of Khairians. He had three hundred notes in his pocket. He went immediately to the trading post and paid two hundred and eighty five of it toward his tab, and used some of the rest to buy coconut milk, lizard eggs, protein cakes, rye flour, and a packet of sen-laced tobacco. He hid the tobacco deep in the pocket of his burnous and walked home.

Inside, Nasrin played at the center of the main room with a dead grasshopper. He heard Elahyiah singing softly to Rahim in the other room. Mehry would be at school by now.

"Da!" Nasrin said, and held out her arms. He stared blankly at her for a moment, because she suddenly reminded him so strongly of his dead daughter Souri that he experienced a moment of dissonance.

His body went through the expected motions. He reached for his daughter. Picked her up. She patted his face with her little hand. But he was still numb. Disconnected.

"Rhys?"

He turned. Sometimes it surprised him how easily he answered to that name. It was not his given name, Rakhshan, the name that marked him as a Chenjan deserter. He wondered if he would ever hear his given name again.

Elahyiah came to him. Her abaya was stained with spit up. She had a rag in one hand. Her skin was sallow, lusterless, and her tangle of dark hair was knotted back from her dark, gaunt face.

"I brought groceries," he said, setting Nasrin back down. The girl cried out in protest and waved her arms at him.

"You received a job?"

"Yes, of course." He pulled back the curtain from the set of shelves they used as a makeshift pantry. Four cockroaches the size of his thumb dropped from the curtain to the floor.

"What is it?"

"It's a translation job. It's not local, though. We'll need to pack our things and go north with the next caravan."

He carefully put away all of the groceries. When he was finished, she still had not said anything.

He turned.

Elahyiah's face was stricken, as if he'd just said that her father died. He watched her crumple. She leaned against the wall for support. She pressed the rag to her face and choked back a sob.

"Elahyiah?" he said. He reached for her, but she smacked his hand away.

"No," she said. "No more. No more of this."

"It's just one more move. A few weeks' travel."

"A few weeks? Weeks? God be merciful, are you mad? Have you seen the state of your children? Have you seen me at all since we arrived here? We are in no state to go anywhere. We're dying here, Rhys."

"The money is good, Elahyiah. It will get us all the way back to Tirhan, once the job is done."

"Good? For *us*? You mean for *you*. I don't understand any of this. We were going to Chenja to do good work in this world, but I hardly have the energy to care for our children. We can afford no help. I miss my family. I miss the housekeeper. I cannot do this on my own, Rhys. Remember when we were partners? I have not felt that for some time."

"We'll sort this out. You need to trust me, Elahyiah."

"Trust you? The way I trusted you to bring us out here? I have prayed long about this, Rhys. I am a good wife. A good mother. And I know my rights."

"I know it's been very difficult..."

"One year has turned into two, then three, now seven. And you keep turning away from me. We keep going farther and farther, and getting nowhere—"

"Think this through."

"I have. I have asked God and prayed often. I am not a woman to forget my prayers. It's my right to ask for a divorce, if I feel my husband is unworthy."

Rhys stumbled. He caught himself on the shelf behind him. It was like a blow—a blow he had known was coming. "Elahyiah, please," he said. He pressed his hand to hers. "I know I've been a poor husband. I won't pretend it's been easy for any of us. But... not yet."

Elahyiah began to cry. "I'm sorry, but I cannot honor a man who cannot care for us. My father has agreed to help us get home. Me and the children."

"The children are mine."

"Rhys, please don't—"

But his resolve was firm. He knew his rights, too. "You take your right, Elahyiah, and I will take mine. I will take the children, and you'll have nothing."

"Rhys, please—"

"One chance," Rhys said. He took her hands. "I can't lose you all. Not now. Don't let them take you from me now."

"It's not the bel dames I fear anymore, Rhys," his wife said. "It's *you*."

From the next room, his son began to wail.

4.

Nasheen smelled different. It was the first thing Nyx noticed as they crossed the border. She expected to get a lungful of tar and ashes, even this far from the front, but instead the air had the tangy lemony flavor of some nearby red crix beetle colony, the same bug used in many com consoles to translate and transmit communications.

They met the patrol escorting Mercia and her entourage just twenty kilometers out of Sameh. The three armored bakkies felt like overkill to Nyx, but then, she hadn't been in Nasheen for a long time. Mercia assured her things were much changed. To Nyx, that sounded ominous.

Nyx sat up front in the lead bakkie with the patrol leader and a driver. Mercia followed in the second bakkie with her bodyguards.

"All this just to escort a diplomat?" Nyx asked. Not that she could judge. She wore a baldric bristling with weapons—a short sword sheathed at her back, the hilt sticking up through a slit in her burnous; a scattergun secured horizontally just beneath that; a pistol at her right hip and a dagger at her left thigh. She had also tucked three poisoned needles in her hair and slipped on a pair of sandals with razor blades in the soles. She hadn't worn her old sandals in so long that she'd had to customize a new pair just for the trip.

The driver spit sen out the window. Clouds of pale dust spewed behind them. "There are boys on these roads," she said. She was narrow-waisted, slim in the hips, with a bony hacksaw of a face. Her wiry arms were visible—her black organic slick was cut off at the shoulder, and again at the calf.

"There are..." Nyx tried rolling that around on her tongue, "*boys* on these roads?"

"Yup."

"Since when are we afraid of boys?"

"Since they came back from the front, woman. What, you think they all put down their guns for babies?"

All the women in the caravan wore standard-issue military gear—organic black slicks and boots and utility belts. They were heavily armed for a patrol, too. Nyx had noted two side arms apiece, assault rifles, and acid rifles—the sort more often used to scare off bugs than melt people. It was gear she should have seen on folks at the front, not women patrolling Amtullah.

"How long you been away from Nasheen?" the patrol leader asked. The leader sat in the back, a broad, muscular woman who wore the simple green stripe of an officer on her arm.

"Six or seven years," Nyx said. "Never thought stuff in Nasheen changed that fast."

"It's been changing fast since the boys started coming home. Everything's a big shit pile. The breeding compounds at the coast are the worst. Nobody's sure what to do with them now that we're not churning out a war. Can't even fit what we've got in the cities, and there's still more boys out there stationed in remote posts."

"You say there are all these boys," Nyx said, "but where? I've been riding with you since the border, and I haven't seen boys in the numbers you're talking about."

The patrol leader regarded her coolly for a long minute, then looked back at the road, toward Amtullah. "You will."

✚

When Nyx was growing up, people talked about Amtullah like it was a shining pillar of wisdom and learning, a haven for com technicians, hedge witches, and paltry magicians of all sorts with a desire to concoct potent war potions to decimate the Chenjans. Back then, it was a sprawling, well-kept city of organ galleries, state-sponsored theaters, historical facades, and the oldest mosque in the country. But over the years it had become a raucous mass of humanity, full of half-breeds and chained cats and corrupt order keepers and organ hawkers and gene pirates. It was also a hive of corrupted First Family heretics, half-breed laborers who barely spoke Nasheenian, and a peculiar native organic grit that ate the flesh between your toes if you didn't clean up regular. That wasn't to say the city wasn't clean as a Tirhani kid's ass, aesthetically speaking. The pretty streets in the good parts of town were impressive, as Nyx recalled—etched in geometric designs and prayer script. The gaudy theaters with their domed roofs took up a whole district, and most public buildings were still faced in detailed stained-glass windows that threw rainbows of light across the streets. Foolish, all those windows, but the interior could get away with having some finery on display. Nyx wondered how much of that had changed.

As they approached in the darkness, Amtullah rose up from the hilly white plain like a thorny, blackened crown capped in a giant soap bubble that wavered and shimmered in the ruddy light of the moons. The filter went red, then pale purple, then black, colors mixing and swirling like a captured aurora.

But it wasn't the city itself that drew her attention. It was the conspicuously bright light in the sky. It did not shimmer like starlight, and it was no planet she recognized. No, this was something else. Something she generally only ever saw over Punjai.

Stragglers appeared along the road as they got closer, long-legged boys and men swathed in turbans that covered their heads and faces. Most carried duffle packs and some still wore government-issue slicks. Two boys about Mercia's age lunged at the caravan as they passed. One of the patrol women shot off a few rounds in their direction. Nyx was surprised the woman let the bullets go wide, then remembered these men weren't deserters. They were, by rights, discharged and full citizens. Watching the boys spit and swear at them as the caravan coughed along, Nyx found the idea that these vagrant squatters now had full independent personhood and voting rights rather appalling.

The entrance to the city was worse.

Up close, the filter was a shimmering curtain. They pulled up at the bakkie barn outside the main entrance, the one opposite where the train pulled up, and it was teeming with dark figures. Asleep? Some of them. A few boys stirred and offered open hands. Others padded after the bakkie, pulling tattered coverings from baskets of bread or saffron or locusts for trade or sale. The cry and stink and closeness of the men made Nyx think of the front, and her nostrils were suddenly filled with the smell of lavender. She coughed.

The patrol alighted from the caravan and took up an immediate defensive posture around Nyx and Mercia. Around them, the horde of boys stared back.

"How bad is it inside?" Nyx asked the patrol leader.

"It's been worse," she said. "First few weeks we thought they were going to riot. Once they coded the filter to keep boys out, though, it settled down. Some."

There were more enlisted women posted immediately outside the city's filter, and some boys too, clad in full combat gear more appropriate to the front—shiny, body-hugging organic slicks, acid sprayers, fully automatic contagion guns, polished boots, and machetes. They held the line in groups of three and five, small but intimidating squads that gave Nyx the impression that there was some ravaging Chenjan horde waiting outside the gates, not a rag-tag stir of discharged Nasheenian boys.

The squad ushered them to the edge of the filter. Nyx slid through. Her skin prickled. The dog-leather thong on her left wrist crackled and smoked. Sand fleas turned to gray dust and dropped off her flesh.

They waited a few minutes for another bakkie, this one armed by a smaller patrol of three women.

"We'll be going to the diplomatic residences on the south side of the city," Mercia said, "in Nafisa Square."

"Thought all the dips were living in Mushtallah," Nyx said to Mercia as they waited. "You have places for them out here?" She had assumed Mercia was just renting a place near Fatima's.

"The bel dames made them," she said. "They purchased some of the old Family houses."

"How'd the Families feel about that?"

"They bought them legally. I'm not aware of any political motive."

Nyx doubted that.

"How about that ship in the sky? You know anything about that?"

"The aliens? No more than what I hear on the radio. They've come to parley with the Queen of Nasheen. What about, I've no idea. They have been here before, though. Have you heard of New Kinaan?"

Nyx's chest tightened. "Sure have," she said. She stared up at the light, and wondered just what it was Fatima had in store for her this time.

The new driver took them through a long, circuitous route across the darkened city. Inside the filter, the streets of Amtullah were paved in smooth, colored stones. It was quiet. Nyx had expected a young, drunk crowd of arty types or spoiled kids, but aside from the occasional creeper or order keeper patrol, there was nothing.

"You put in a curfew?" Nyx asked.

"Six weeks ago," the driver said. "Had a lot of trouble with the boys who were let in early, after the ceasefire. Lots of rioting. Looting. There were too many to lock up all at once. It's been quieter, last few weeks."

They came to a ten-foot wall marking the border between the city proper and the private residences beyond. Even from this distance, Nyx could see how large the residences were, all of them carved neatly into the side of a hill overlooking the city. Beyond the wall, Nyx saw another filter. The guards at the gate had to code Nyx into the filter for safe passage into the district.

They drove through. The filter wasn't nearly as sticky as the one that prevented the bugs, organics, and contagions of the rest of the world from entering Amtullah. This one just kept out the dangerous plague that was the Nasheenian underclass. Going through two tight filters in quick succession made Nyx's skin itch.

Twisted thorn trees and hardy butterstalk hybrids with plate-sized leaves lined the roads. The compounds here were all walled. The tops of the walls were lined in hanging gardens of yellow spiderstalk, magnolia vine, amber grass, and lilac. The streets were clean as dinner plates. It put Nyx in mind of Tirhan and their blinding sidewalks and gratuitous parks. She even saw a wasp swarm patrolling a narrow alley.

"Have you been up here before?" the driver asked.

"My clients meet me on my turf. I don't go to theirs," Nyx said.

The driver eyed her over. "Yeah, I imagine that's true."

They pulled up to an amber-colored compound at the far end of the hill. Most of it was built into the hill itself, so all Nyx saw as she climbed out inside the compound wall was the main floor. But even from the ass-end of the place, she caught a striking view of the city.

"Your mom knows how to pick them," Nyx said.

"I picked it," Mercia said. "Fatima had a dozen houses to choose from."

Nyx wondered just how deep Mercia had put herself into Fatima's pocket.

A small staff met them at the gate. The on-site magician introduced herself as Yah Rafika. The others were a half-breed servant and a housekeeper, and nobody bothered telling Nyx their names.

"This is Nyx," Mercia told the housekeeper. "She is our guest. Please, see her in."

The housekeeper took in Nyx's full measure with an accusing stare. "This way," the housekeeper said.

The house was some petty First Family's place from back in the Caliphate days. Building into the hill helped cool the house, and so did the constantly running water pumped through the latticed walls of the compound's interior. There was a central courtyard that everything else wrapped around, and on the side, a long, sloping yard with a ten-foot mud-brick wall topped in friendly poisoned needles.

Nyx bided her time in the living quarters downstairs. She faced a wide, tiled fireplace etched in fanciful geometric designs inlaid with gold. Most of the floor was bare stone, but there were carpets in every room—clean ones.

The housekeeper entered. "I have a meal prepared, if it would please you," she said. "When you are clean and rested, Ambassador sa Aldred would like to see you."

"Thanks," Nyx said. She followed after the housekeeper and had a seat in the warm little kitchen. She asked for liquor, but the housekeeper said they had none. Mercia didn't permit it. Nyx ate a late supper of curried locust rotis. As she ate, she watched where everybody ended up. The magician didn't live at the house. She made nice with the housekeeper and said goodbye for the evening. When Nyx's supper was done, the housekeeper dismissed the additional servant, as well, leaving just the housekeeper, Mercia, and the two bodyguards Mercia had brought with her to Druce still in the house.

The housekeeper led Nyx to the bathhouse downstairs to get washed up. They had clean clothes ready. She dressed. Everything was soft. Organic. Expensive.

When she was ready, the housekeeper took her upstairs. They followed a large, winding stairway made of burnished bug secretions. The housekeeper gestured to a door just across the hall, and Nyx went through the soft arch of the doorway. The bedroom was long and thin, running along the whole north side of the house. The room was dominated by a stone slab where a mattress draped in red and white held court. Mercia was unpacking her case on the bed. A giant tapestry above the bed was spun up in a dozen colors; a swirling Ras Tiegan garden surrounding a broken forest bathed in blood.

"That's subtle, isn't it?" Nyx said, nodding to the tapestry.

"My mother's," Mercia said. "I suppose she thought there wouldn't be any Nasheenians in here. She forgot about the servants of course."

As Nyx moved closer to her, she noted that Mercia had bathed and changed as well, even combed out her hair.

"Saw you don't have any filters in the house. What is this, the year 1200?" Nyx said.

"I've never had need of it." Mercia tucked a loose curl of dark hair behind one ear. She truly was unremarkable in nearly every way. Nyx had to admit she had a soft spot for plain folks. There was something to be said for finding beauty in the rough.

"Might be time to start," Nyx said. "All those dead bodyguards and all."

Mercia shrugged. "Yah Rafika has a swarm set out on patrol. It's enough. You know Fatima will want to see you." She went to her desk and palmed open a drawer. She removed a green envelope and passed it to Nyx. "That's the official invitation, and her address."

"I hope she paid you well," Nyx said, slipping the invitation into the band of her trousers.

"I'm sorry," Mercia said.

"I'm sure."

"No, I am," she said, and Nyx heard shame in her voice, like some little kid caught telling a lie.

"If you weren't a diplomat, I'd kill you," Nyx said.

"They said they wouldn't hurt you. I didn't let them follow me. We doubled back three times to make sure. I wasn't followed."

"You seem very sure of that."

"You're a bel dame. Aren't you supposed to be able to know things like that?"

"People keep saying I'm a bel dame, but I'm not. Haven't been in over twenty years. I'm just a woman, Mercia. And you lied to me."

"I didn't lie… all right, at first I lied, but I was doing a favor for the Queen."

"In return for what?"

"It's politics. It's not personal."

"Everybody says that when they're the ones doing the shitting, not when they're being shat on."

"I'm sorry."

"You've said that already."

Mercia flexed her fingers. Nyx wondered if there was a weapon in the case she was unpacking on the bed.

"I wanted to find you," Mercia said. "They just gave me a good reason to do it."

"But you found me all on your own?"

"Eshe helped."

"You better not have mixed Eshe up in this."

"I didn't. When he learned I was trying to find him, he contacted me on an untraceable pattern. Well… the bel dame said it was untraceable."

"And you found Anneke's place the same way?"

"I didn't use any of Fatima's agents to find the house. Only me and Khanaya and Ayah—my bodyguards—know where the house is."

"You're making this a very easy interrogation."

"Is that what it is?" Mercia's voice was light.

Nyx realized she still didn't get it. "You just told me that there are only three people in this country who know where Anneke and her kids are. Who know where my safe house is. Three people."

"I don't want—"

"Doesn't much matter what you want, does it?" Nyx crossed to the bed in three long strides and took Mercia firmly by the chin, leaned into her. She smelled of cinnamon and cocoa butter. Her skin was incredibly soft, like some First Family kid.

"Leave me alone after this. All of us. I see you again… I hear something's happened to them…"

"I didn't go out there for them," Mercia said. She raised her eyes, met Nyx's look. "I went out there for *you*."

Mercia kissed her.

Nyx wasn't sure which of them was more surprised.

Mercia grabbed her by the collar of her vest and pulled her into the bed. Her leg slipped between Nyx's thighs. Warmth bloomed through Nyx's body, as if she'd been soaked in warm honey.

My God, she's soft, Nyx thought, tangling her fingers in Mercia's dark hair.

Mercia tugged Nyx's vest open. Suckled her breast with her warm, wet mouth.

"Fuck," Nyx said.

Mercia drew her head up, eyes glassy, cheeks flushed. "You'd better," she said.

And that was the end of the interrogation.

For a time.

✚

The sheets were still damp, tangled around their feet. The darkness clung to them like another lover, hot and close. Nyx watched the long rise and fall of Mercia's chest. Gorgeous breasts. She had never seen such perfect breasts. She slid her hand up Mercia's thigh. Mercia sighed and smiled, caught up her fingers with Nyx's.

"That was worth going to Druce for," Mercia murmured.

The floor rumbled softly.

Nyx raised her head. Heard a *pop-pop* sound outside, distant. It was almost dawn.

"What is that?" Mercia asked.

Nyx pulled herself out of bed and walked naked to the window. Opened the shutters. Gazed out over Amtullah. The view from the bedroom was even more spectacular than the one from the front courtyard. Orange, yellow, green, and lavender lights blazed across the city. The filter above caught the light, reflected it back, made the world glow softly even in the deepest part of the night.

Nyx listened.

The *pop-pop* sound came again, closer this time. Another rumble. From the east. She turned and saw a flickering flare of fire, and a smoky haze over the lights. The floor trembled again.

Mercia padded over to the window, pulling on her robe. She took Nyx's arm, pressed against her. Nyx wondered just how attached Mercia wanted to get. "Chenjans?"

"No," Nyx said. "It's coming from inside the city."

"You think they've infiltrated the city?"

"No. It's the *boys*." Nyx pulled away and started getting dressed. "Stay up here. You'll be safe in this district."

"Where are you going?"

"It's a good time to see Fatima. She'll be all riled up." Nyx holstered and stowed her weapons. It always took longer to get them back on than it did to get them off.

Mercia took a breath. "Nyx?"

"What?"

"Fatima promised me information I could use against our ruling Patron. I've long suspected that he has worked with Nasheen to repress our people. She said that if I went after you, she would give me that proof."

"And you believed her?"

"It cost me nothing."

Nyx felt her expression harden. "Didn't it?"

Mercia pulled her robe closed. "That's what you wanted to know, isn't it?"

"This is *business*, Mercia. This is all just business. You mistake it for something else, you get killed. You understand? Bodies are my *business*."

Mercia raised her chin. "I understand," she said.

"Good."

Nyx walked to the door, looked back once. Mercia stood in the dim light of the window, robe slightly open, long, pale legs visible. Her expression was a little stricken. She'd be fine. Neither of the bodyguards had checked in on them, and they hadn't exactly been quiet, which meant her people were used to her bringing lovers home. Nyx wondered if all the others Mercia dragged home were like her—scarred and twisted, something to gossip about back home over high tea. Going to bed with a Nasheenian was about as exciting a time as a rich dip could hope for. Not for the first time, Nyx wasn't so sure that one of her impulsive fucks was a good idea. Especially knowing what she was about to do.

Nyx shut the door.

She stood a moment in the hall, trying to get her bearings. The radio was on downstairs, coming from the kitchen. The housekeeper's rooms were out back, further down the lawn.

Nyx pulled her dagger. Not her preferred weapon, but it was quiet.

She padded down the stairs. Peered into the kitchen. The smaller bodyguard, Ayah, was there, feet on the table, listening to the radio as it wafted out misty images of some story from the Kitab. She was sipping a malty beverage. She was alone.

Nyx killed her quickly and cleanly. Ayah barely had time to turn her head before Nyx bared her throat. Ayah kicked back, spastically jerking her legs. Her chair clattered across the floor.

Nyx left the bodyguard in a pool of blood and went into the yard searching for Khanaya. She found her peering up toward Mercia's room. Mercia had just closed the shutters.

At Nyx's age, she had learned to move fast. Surprise and experience were her only advantages.

Khanaya turned as the knife came down. Caught the blade with her forearm. They grappled.

Khanaya fumbled for a pistol, too hasty, panicked. Nyx drove her knife into Khanaya's eye and punched her in the throat to stifle the scream. She held Khanaya down until she bled out. Then Nyx gritted her teeth, hooked her arms under the body's, and hauled the still-warm corpse back into the kitchen. She slopped it next to Ayah's.

She sniffed at Ayah's forgotten glass. The malty stuff gumming up the bottom was bad bootleg liquor. Nyx kicked the body's leg away from the chair and sat down with the glass to wait. Sipped the liquor. Not bad. She listened to the *thump-thump* of explosions in the city center, and the low grumble of angry humanity. Blood congealed on the floor. Tiny blood mites began to appear along the edges of the room and scurry their way across the bare stone to the pooling blood.

That made two less people who knew where Anneke and Radeyah and the kids were. And a very simple message to Mercia. It should have been the most relaxed Nyx had been in years. She should have enjoyed killing this cleanly, and fucking a smarmy young diplomat. Instead, she found herself thinking of another woman back home, and a house full of kids, and Anneke's crumbling back.

She finished her drink, and went out into the rumbling dawn to find Fatima.

5.

Ahmed traded his face for a ticket out of Sahar. It seemed a fair enough deal at the time—the butchers told him it was a pretty face, and they had a fair number of mutilated veterans coming off the front who'd have use for it. As it was, he could use a new face himself. It was harder for bel dames to hunt down faceless men.

But when he woke on the butcher's block, his vision a gray haze, a dull throbbing in his swollen mouth—like it had been stuffed with gauze—and he pressed his fingers to his engorged face and lips and tried to speak… he knew something was terribly wrong.

They had not taken his face.

They had taken his tongue.

A tall woman entered. Her hands were bloody crimson, her gaunt face a hallowed mask. In her fingers she held a strange creature—half worm, half beetle. It was flat and smooth, with savage hooks at one end.

"Open," the woman said. He did not recognize her. Someone else had made the deal with him, and another woman had taken him here. She gripped his chin firmly in one hand, presented the worm-bug with the other. "Open," she said, "Or did you never want to speak again?"

He opened. The worm fell into his mouth, wriggling and lashing. The morphine had taken the edge off, but he felt it when the worm jabbed itself into the stub of what was left of his tongue.

Ahmed retched.

"Don't fight it," the woman said. She slapped his shoulder. Left a long red smear of blood. "Just let it settle. In a week you won't even notice it."

He choked and drooled and finally, painfully, mumbled something like a curse. The worm waggled on the stub of his tongue. His words felt mangled, mushy. He gagged again.

"It'll conform to you," the woman said. "It's a proper parasite. Just give it time."

A tongue was a cheap organ, he knew. Not at all worth a trip out of Sahar. He bled all over the paperwork and collected his small sum and would have cursed the woman who'd taken him here, but the thought of speaking made his stomach churn. If he spent another day in Sahar, he would be dead. It didn't matter much what he had to sell to get out.

So he slogged back into the fleshpots, and traded his right kidney for the remainder of what he needed for his train ticket. Still drooling and stumbling, he picked the first train headed to the interior. The woman at the counter spent twenty minutes reviewing his discharge tattoo and accompanying paperwork, then asked for an additional personal fee.

"I don't understand that request," he said, his words coming out garbled, sloppy, as if he were chewing on the worm with every word. He gagged again.

The ticket agent smiled, brazenly, the way all the women did who weren't at the front. She told him men weren't permitted on the interior without a special pass. "You won't get past the filter, even with a face like that."

He had no interest in being reminded of his fucking face.

"I'm not aware of that law," he said, and spit blood and some yellow-pink mucus on her counter.

"You are now," she said. "One hundred notes, or you stay here at the front with the rest of the boys." She leaned away from the ticket counter, still grinning. "I suppose you could walk across that desert. Plenty of other boys have, I hear. Mushtallah looks like some magician's slab, bunch of pretty boys all standing around waiting to get put in jars."

He had spent far too many nights on the sand already. His slick was going bad, starting to stink, and they had relieved his entire platoon of weapons before getting their discharge tattoos. Aside from the slick and his other kidney, he had little left of any value. If only they'd taken his face.

Ahmed took a deep breath. He started to recite the ninety-nine names of God, the way he had the time he saw his first squad torn apart by a hornet burst. It was the calm that kept you whole, when a hornet burst started biting. He had spent an hour in perfect stillness as his squad screamed and died around him, their faces and hands swelling and bursting, bloody foam at their mouths.

He thought, again, of his face. Tried to tame his new tongue. "Is there some other arrangement we can come to?"

It was easier to make the proper words this time, but it still felt grotesque, as if he were swallowing some live meal with every word.

The woman laughed. A big laugh, full and fearless, like the rest of her. "I have plenty of those offers, thanks." She waved at the packed platform beyond the station, filled with boys and men, many of them still in their tattered standard-issue slicks, just as he was. "I work for currency. Blood, bugs, or notes. No exceptions."

Ahmed considered that. "I can pay you a pint of blood and three locusts."

"What kind of locusts?"

"Khairian."

"Deal. Come here in the back and Samara will take care of you."

He had no locusts, but it took him only a few minutes to call some. She was no magician. It wouldn't be until she presented the locusts to a buyer that she would discover they were just some local variety. He had promised not to use his skill again after leaving the front, but it was like trying to put down any other weapon—once you became accustomed to it, you picked it up again, easy as breathing.

Samara, the woman waiting for him in the back, was a pleasant sort of woman, beefy and generous. A quick glance behind the ticket counter told him there were no magicians there either. Samara happily took his locusts, and more. Despite her colleague's insistence that no other services were of value, her friend Samara had other ideas. Not even his wormy little tongue would dissuade her.

She seemed only mildly disappointed his cock wouldn't cooperate, but did not ask why. He wondered how many others she had brought back here, and how many had been in any state to satisfy her with something other than a tongue or a hand.

She pushed his ticket at him when she was finished, and he gripped it closely and hurried away. Thrust it at the first platform manager he saw. She directed him to a waiting train. He stepped in, found a seat in the crowded third-class cabin, and wept for the first time since the end of the war.

+

Ahmed stepped out of the train ten hours later and into a hot, chalky evening. He was hungry and light-headed, but full of hope that the interior cities he remembered would be significantly more welcoming than the border towns.

He had bunched up his ticket and jammed it in one of his slick's pockets. Now he fished his ticket out, but the drugs and exhaustion meant he had trouble reading it. When the morphine had worn off on the train, he switched to siva, the military-issued version of sen, but it still left him muzzy-headed and aching. He doubted the vet he got it from was entirely honest about what it was. Siva had never left him feeling this disoriented.

A few passengers disembarked around him, and he finally mustered up the gall to ask one of the nearby women, "Excuse me, matron, what city is this?"

She looked startled. Then something like disgust tore at her face. It was a reaction he was becoming accustomed to. But it still cut at his heart. He had hoped the interior was different.

She kept moving as she said, "You're in Amtullah, boy."

It was never anything but that—boy. Not sir, not patron, not "What's your name?" Just... boy. As if he had walked off his house mother's stoop just yesterday.

Ahmed had never heard of Amtullah. That in itself wasn't odd, he supposed. He grew up in the southeast, near the Drucian border. There weren't a lot of people there, or proper schools. His first squad thought his accent was a laugh, and it had taken him two years to suppress it.

He gazed over the stir of women, toward the city proper. In the south, there were still some green things, so he expected the rest of the interior would be like that too, but no—even on the train, all he saw of the interior was dry and desiccated, just like the front. Yet, unlike the border towns, this city was intact. He saw elegant minarets in the distance rising from a cluster of domed public buildings and upscale tenement houses, all of it surrounded in a massive filter that blanketed the stir of the city like some kind of membrane. It was the most massive filter he'd ever seen, and he spent a long time working out how to deal with it. Outside, the boys and men who had come with him were headed toward customs, already arguing with the armed women who he assumed would carry the city's only passkeys.

He found a call box inside the station and dialed the only civilian pattern he still remembered.

After the line stirred and chittered and spat for some time, a thin voice rose from the darkness and rasped, "Who is this?"

"Amtullah. Filter. You done one before?"

"Who is this?"

"You said to call if I ever came home."

He heard something clatter on the other side of the line. "Been a long time, friend."

"Have you done that filter or not?"

"Call this pattern. Oval. Square. Circle. Circle. Triangle. Hex. Got that?"

He repeated it.

"Good. She'll hook you up." There was some noise in the background. Ahmed wondered if the man had a proper family now, someone he had to hide Ahmed from. "Don't call again."

"I won't."

"Ahmed?"

"Yes?"

The man's voice broke. "Everyone has his fate, but I asked God, the compassionate, the merciful, at each prayer for your safe return. May God preserve you."

Ahmed hung up. Stared at the filter. His commanding officer had told him once that fear in the ranks was rampant, yes, but it was fear that kept people in line. "They need to fear me more than the enemy," she told him. "That's the secret to any great command."

He had put a knife through her three years later. But even in that instant, he wasn't sure who was more terrified—him or her. Worse, he wasn't sure what any of that proved.

Ahmed had worked for a lot of smart, sadistic fucks. They had hidden the sadism behind military intelligence badges and security protocols, but their arrogance and lack of compassion were harder to tuck up under a prayer rug. They had taught him everything they knew, and he had used it ruthlessly, relentlessly. It had kept him alive, yes. But his reward for fifteen years of service and putting a knife in the eye of every good soldier he knew was *this*.

Six weeks ago, he'd known very little about the world outside the military. Now he knew enough to be certain that the man he was at the front no longer existed. Assholes lived a long time, but if that was living, he wanted none of it. It was time to let go of all the catshit, and learn how to be a man on his own terms, in a new world that had no idea what to do with him.

6.

Eshe wore somber colors to the wake, darkened by the warm rain. He stood well back from the gravesite, now clogged with mourners and pall bearers and swordsmen. The whole steaming, chanting, incense-heavy affair reminded him of just how stubbornly conservative many parts of Ras Tieg still were. All the rest of the people on Umayma had learned not to bury their bodies three millennia ago, back at the beginning of the world. They cut off their heads and burned them, no matter the prescriptions set down in any holy book. Those instructions were for people on some other world.

But Ras Tiegans on the frontier thought differently. Cutting up a body and burning it was still sacrilege, desecration. It had something to do with ashes and dust and prophets who didn't stay dead, and how that was holy. Eshe didn't really follow it. But it meant that this crowd waited for something far more dramatic than just seeing a man's body covered over in dirt.

The priest's grave was about as deep as Eshe's arm was long. The body was covered in a white muslin shroud that trembled and shook. Beetles and midges skittered along its surface. The trembling and writhing beneath the shroud was likely still just the bugs, doing what bugs on Umayma did—devouring, destroying—transforming.

Three priests walked around the edges of the fresh grave garbed all in their silver-and-gilt finery. The robes, by now, were soggy and just a little transparent. Many Ras Tiegan priests had some talent with bugs, having been conscripted as soon as their talent emerged. They also tended to be lean, muscular fighters in their youth. So even after an hour walking around in the mud swinging pots of incense and flogging themselves with strings of holy beads while intoning the same monotonous prayer about resurrection, they were holding up pretty well. The little red dots drawn onto their foreheads with ink—the symbolic eye of god donned by this particular sect—had begun to tear and run, leaving crimson rivulets dripping into their faces like bloody tears. Only the very rich could afford this many priests for a wake. Most folks got an anonymous beheading by some underpaid graveyard swordsman. Eshe watched a man of just that sort trekking down the far side of the graveyard, long sword over one shoulder. A shimmering trail of bloody entrails sloughed off the sword as it bounced along.

Eshe stood on a low rise well behind the funeral party with his reluctant partner, Isabet Softel. She was pensive in the gray morning. Some of her dark hair had escaped her white wimple. Her loose hair clung in delicate tendrils to her pale face—pale even for a Ras Tiegan. He once asked her if she was part Mhorian, and she'd been offended. Most things he did or said offended her. Why it was the Madame de Fourré kept pairing them together was beyond Eshe. He had caught her without her wimple once, and the spill of her hair reminded him so strongly of Corinne that his heart ached.

But Isabet was not Corinne. Isabet had a head full of honey and strong convictions, and where he was from, being pretty and haughty didn't get you a promotion. It got you your head chopped off by some woman who was less pretty but had a better sense of humor.

Now, after half the night on watch, she appeared sodden and exhausted. Her dark eyes were shadowed.

Putting her on watch hadn't been fair, he knew, but he had last night's priest to take care of, and he didn't want her there for that. Not like last time. So far as he knew, she wasn't a shifter, just one of the handful of sympathizers who'd come over to their side. In some ways, it meant she was safer than any of them, no matter what task he gave her.

"Shouldn't be much longer," he said.

Isabet rubbed her eyes. "I'm fine. Did you learn anything last night?"

"It's like I expected. It's Jolique."

"At least we can finish what we started now."

"You mean what *I* started," Eshe said. She was always trying to take credit.

"We had an assignment. One with clear goals. Those goals did not involve killing a priest. Or attending his wake. It would have gone more smoothly without you."

"And you'd be dead," he said. "Sounds like a success all around."

Isabet pursed her mouth. Though he resented the soft, pale skin she presented to the world, he admitted that it gave her a striking appearance. Someone only got skin that soft by spending most of their life behind a filter, away from the harsh light of the suns. He hadn't spent enough time around rich people to get used to it. Seeing her wealth in her face was... distracting.

As he gazed at Isabet now, Eshe wondered if anyone had ever forced her to do anything, or if she'd just run off to join the Madame's little shape shifter rebellion to get back at her mother for refusing her some trinket. No one had asked her to join the war for God. Or farmed her out to strange women to raise. Or sold her body to war vets.

Memories of his less than pleasant Nasheenian childhood stirred. He tried hard to focus on the present. The present was always better than the past. He thought of Corinne again.

"Would you stop staring at me?" Isabet said. He saw her cheeks color.

Eshe turned away. "I can't help it if you're distracting," he said. He would have never looked at a Nasheenian woman the way he often looked at Isabet. He would have gotten a fist in the face, or a lewd offer.

"Perhaps I should wear a burqua like some Chenjan. Would that dissuade you? No, I'm sure. You'd mishandle a Chenjan woman just the same. I know your type."

"Don't insult me."

"It's no matter. The half-formed opinions of half-breed boys do not concern me, no," she said.

"You get that mouth in etiquette class?"

Her look was all oily fire. He wondered if that was the look he'd get for asking her to bed. He half-thought to find out, but saw movement from the corner of his eye.

A wave of black roaches burst from the lip of the grave and streamed into the crowd. Mourners clutched at one another. They joined the priests in a new prayer, one about being nearer to God. The priests took up positions around the grave and raised their hands. The sword-bearer jerked out of his doze and stepped forward.

An ear-piercing scream came from the grave—too high-pitched to be human. It was something bordering on the edge of a cicada's whine.

The muslin-draped body shuddered and rolled up from the grave. Bloody muslin fell from the corpse, revealing a spiny, bloated torso clothed in a white habit. It flung out pale, meaty arms and shook away the flesh of the head, revealing a shiny carapace. Black roaches escaped the sleeves of the habit, spraying across the crowd. The body jerked and thrashed, sloughing off flesh. Long strings of mucus oozed from the gaping wounds in the chest—the ones Eshe had put there. One for each shape shifter the priest had killed.

Eshe took half a step forward, his whole body taut. He was more than ready to kill the priest again, even if this was just a bug clothed in a dead man's skin.

As the sword-bearer swung, the giant beetle opened its gaping maw, and a cloud of flying black larvae escaped.

Isabet gasped.

The swordsman swung. The body juddered. A hunk of raw flesh and juicy white beetle ooze was exposed. It took three more swings to sever the beetle's head from what remained of the priest's body. The body dropped, and the beetle's bloody, flesh-smeared head rolled neatly next to it. The cloud of larvae droned and circled the remains.

Eshe let out his breath. Moved his hand away from his knife.

The crowd broke into a hymn.

Eshe turned his back on the grave. "Let's go," he said. He started back to the church, pushing the weeping fingers of spiny widows' tree branches away from his face.

Isabet hurried after him. "Is that all? That's everything?"

"That's all."

"I—" She adjusted her wimple. In all the rain, the stiffness was beginning to give way, and the wings were starting to droop.

"I've heard about it, of course," Isabet said. "But that was the first one I *saw*."

"Sometimes they shamble on for a while longer. They only last three days like that before the body rots out, but its long enough to scare the hell out of people."

"Why would God—"

"It's the bugs," Eshe said. "And stupid Ras Tiegan stubbornness. Not God."

"But if that was so, bodies on a battlefield—"

"Bodies on battlefields aren't buried. They're carted home and burned. Because of… that. The bugs live in the dirt."

He escorted Isabet as far as the edge of the graveyard where a long stand of incense burners flickered and sputtered in the heavy rain. From there, they were to take separate routes home. On the street, they were too obviously unmarried and unrelated to be seen together. It was another reason Eshe didn't understand why she had been partnered with him.

"Well," he said once they reached the tiled street, "you saw it through to the end. Satisfied?"

"I'm glad he's dead," she said. A rickshaw clattered past, draped in colors as somber as what Eshe was wearing. Outside a wedding or non-shifter birthing celebration, Inoublie was a colorless sort of place during the day. The buildings here were squeezed close together, bucking up against the massive grated storm drains that kept the streets clear during the rainy season. Tangles of trees lined the roads, many of them twice as tall as the buildings, their broad canopies bowing in the rain. Ancient root systems jutted from cracks in the tiled sidewalk. Mourners often draped wreaths of white and gold flowers over them during a funeral procession. The old, rotting flower chains had broken and tumbled to the sidewalk, forming a fine, slick skein of rot on the tile.

"Remember that next time you get the chance to kill somebody," he said.

"You don't have to kill everyone." She enjoyed bickering for bickering's sake, like a child. He was nearly twenty-one now, and her shrill, seventeen-year-old fury felt like something half-remembered from a lifetime ago.

"Yeah, next time we'll try your way."

"I know why you do it," she said. "The Madame told me about your mother."

"My… mother?"

"The bloody Nasheenian assassin."

"She's not… that's a complicated story."

"Did you hear they're pardoning assassins now, in Nasheen?"

"Where did you learn that?"

"It was in the papers, of course." The radios in Ras Tieg were all censored, so most people held up the less rigidly enforced papers as truth. Eshe knew better.

"Well, you're wrong. They'd never do that."

"I know what I heard."

"I'll see you tomorrow," he said. He had no interest in discussing his… mother with her. Or Nasheenian politics. But he knew who he *should* talk to about it.

Isabet huffed off down the street, slipping and sliding on the rotten flowers. He paused a moment to watch her go. Her habit was mostly shapeless, but he had seen her in trousers before, the first few times he bumped into her at the Madame de Fourré's place, and it was hard to get the shape of her legs and ass out of his mind now as he watched her slide along.

He shook his head and went off in the opposite direction, sticking to the center of the street where the way was less precarious. Some days the women here drove him to drink. But mostly, he just prayed harder that God would help him untangle what it was he really wanted from them.

✣

"When were you going to tell me?" Eshe asked.

Inaya was never alone these days, and, it seemed, never free of Eshe's sudden and dramatic entrances. She looked up from her glowing table slide, and quickly tapped out the obfuscation code that turned the correspondences and schematics into an imperceptible gray haze. In the hall beyond Eshe, she watched runners, agents, and two hooded bodyguards move through her headquarters with bug casings and supplies. Never alone, and never a quiet moment here.

Michel, her second, perched on her right shoulder in his blue-gray parrot form. She felt his one good claw tighten painfully on her shoulder at Eshe's voice. The floor stirred with feathers and dog hair, and the air was heavy with the smell of cooking meat from the makeshift kitchen a level below. The stink of meat and feathers and damp dog hair turned her stomach, but this was the most secure room in the compound. For all the good it did at dissuading Eshe.

"I see someone finally told you," Inaya said. She reached out and slid open a schematic of the district around the southern edge of Rue

Rosalie, the city's main thoroughfare. "Perhaps it will encourage you to read the papers more often."

Eshe stepped further into the room and closed the door behind him. Michel squawked.

"Those rags are full of lies. Sorting out the half-truth from the catshit isn't worth the time," Eshe said.

"Then perhaps you will make time," Inaya said.

Eshe put on his little pout, the one that made her want to smack him. She had never considered herself a violent person, and she had not raised her hand to even one cadre here, but the sight of this capable young man playing at being a child sometimes enraged her. Of all the people in her circle, she had come to rely on him the most, at least in the beginning. She expected more of him.

"If they're pardoning political criminals," Eshe said, "it means..." He shot a quick glance at Michel. "It means they're pardoning us, too."

Inaya waved her hand over the slide. The misty images flickered and dispersed, filling the room with the faint smell of burnt lemon. "It was my understanding that you came here to save Ras Tiegan shifters from genocide," she said. "That's what I came here to do."

"I—" He hesitated. "I did. But it would be nice to know—"

"I have other responsibilities, Eshe. As do you. I'm far more concerned about you murdering priests in taverns. What would you think of it if I went around Nasheen murdering mullahs without cause?"

"That's a different thing entirely."

She had never been partial to these backwater priests, herself, but she had not liked his mullahs, either. She had sense enough to know that shooting a religious leader or teacher in the face would do the cause no favors.

"It's not," she said. "We worship the same God and we carry the same sins. Every time you walk into a tavern and kill one of our contacts without provocation, you soil that. Senseless death may be what she taught you in Nasheen, but that's not how I do things here."

"I forgot. You just let your priests fuck you and abort your babies."

Inaya stiffened. She remembered young girls she had nurtured after they were cut open and their shifter children smashed. And the others, the terrified twelve-year-olds raped by priests and forced to bear non-shifter children. It was a helpless feeling, to know you could not protect the women you cared for. To know that women's bodies here were co-opted so fully and completely that they had ceased to be fully human in the eyes of the priests.

"I had hoped that Isabet's influence would soften you," she said coolly.

"Soften me? That rich snot? It's like trying to teach a tax clerk to be a bel dame. She isn't meant for this work. You should have her doing intelligence."

"I do," Inaya said.

"On who?"

Inaya waved away Michel at her shoulder. He squawked and flapped away, settled onto a perch at the corner of the room.

"Come with me," Inaya said.

She led him down another level into the cramped quarters she had called home the last six months. There was a single cot, two three-legged stools, some storage bins. She had hung a large red tapestry inscribed with the mark of the martyred messiah above the cot. Her quarters had gotten narrower and narrower over the years as God's Angels and government enforcers had hounded them further and further outside the primary cities. Her nom de guerre, Madame de Fourré, was on the list, but her face wasn't. Nor was her true name—Inaya il Parait. She had gone to elaborate lengths to change her blood code in every city they settled in, smoothly taking on a different pattern in each one. She supposed she could have changed her face as well, but there was only so much she was willing to give up. Eshe and the others in the Fourré had risked much to allow her to keep her face. And killed a lot of priests. She reminded herself of that as she prepared what she had to say.

"Please sit, Eshe," she said.

He sighed and sat on the edge of the bed.

Inaya sat next to him. From this close, the smell of him was stronger—bitter red wine laced in milky hybrid oak and stale sweat. He wore a simple habit like hers, calf-length instead of ankle length, and he sported a spotty beard and long hair, as was the fashion in Ras Tieg.

Michel once told her that she and Eshe had aged faster in Ras Tieg than he expected. The face she saw in the polished mirror each evening was different than the one she had brought with her nearly seven years ago. Fine lines creased her face now, and she felt as if her body had already begun to bend and sag in all the wrong places. Her muslin habits had become baggier as the stress and low rations had taken their toll. Eshe, for his part, was a young man, lean and well-muscled, and a head and shoulders taller than her now—a very Nasheenian build that made him stand out more in crowds. His height was even harder to hide than his half-breed complexion, so he stooped more, even in her headquarters among his own kind.

Inaya reached out and took his hands. His were nearly as rough as hers, darker, though she was part Nasheenian, too. The Nasheenian part of him had not balanced well with the Ras Tiegan features, and he had a typically flat Ras Tiegan face with a bold Nasheenian nose and broad cheekbones. When she looked at him, it reminded her all too often of how imperfectly the two of them tried to straddle the line between one world and another.

"I asked Isabet to report back to me about your methods," Inaya said softly. She watched him carefully as she said it.

He immediately pulled his hands away. "Her? You asked *her* to spy on *me*?"

"I'm worried about your violence, Eshe. I'm worried—"

"You're worried I'm going to be like *her*," he said.

"It is a fine line we walk, Eshe. Not all of our goals can be accomplished by violence. The more violent shifters are, the easier it is to dismiss our cause—"

"And the easier it is to roll all over you," Eshe said. He stood, color blazing on his face. "These people were a bunch of bloody cowards before we came here. Bloody kittens. I taught the younger ones to fight, just like you asked. Now you want to rein us in?"

"Not them," Inaya said. "*You.* I know you are not like her at all, not really, but you try so hard to be. It puts our people in danger. And the cause."

"I'm saving—"

"You are *killing* people for crimes long done and buried. I need the support and voices of these men, Eshe, and you are making that… difficult."

"When did we stop getting things done and start licking priests' asses?" Eshe spat.

Inaya stood. "That priest whose wake you just attended has a family, and they've asked for blood debt. God's Angels rounded up a dozen shifters in retaliation. Now your face and local name are on the list.

Those Angels will be coming for you next, and none of us can afford that. All killing gets us is more killing."

"They're thugs, not angels. Call them what they are."

"It's what the people call them. It's who will come for you if you don't listen to sense."

"It's what *Ras Tiegans* call them," Eshe said.

"Aren't you Ras Tiegan?" She hated the way it came out—pleading. She had wanted to believe they were alike, in some ways. And more—she wanted to believe he could be saved. But her hardships were not like his. A dead brother, murdered parents, broken family—these were small things to a Nasheenian-raised street boy who had been grown in some coastal compound and farmed out to a dozen different house mothers as a source of cheap labor and cheaper sex.

"I wanted to be," he said.

"Eshe...."

"You know how that priest died?"

"The one *before* the one you killed last night? Yes. You stabbed him. Repeatedly."

"I walked in on him and Isabet. You know, the one you sent in to do some *talking*. One rich person to another. Trouble is, she's just a girl to them, not anybody with clout, and they treated her like it. He was so fast on her she didn't make a sound. When I got there he'd wrapped a bag around her head and started beating her. Tell me *words* would have fixed that, Inaya."

Inaya felt something inside of her harden. It was a twisted game she played, and some days, she felt terrible guilt over it. "I have seen horrible things here too, Eshe."

"Tell me words would have fixed it!"

"The right words would have."

"You're full of shit."

"Maybe so. I just don't think Nasheen's way of doing things is going to work here."

"We *are* Nasheenian."

"I'm not," Inaya said. She was many things, but not... like those women.

"Nyx got things done."

"She's just a killer."

"So am I."

Inaya slapped him.

It happened so suddenly she didn't realize she'd done it until she pulled her hand away. The color drained from his face. He stared dumbly at her. She wasn't certain which of them was more shocked.

"Go back to that bloody place then," she said. "And see what mercy God will grant you."

"You'll lose your war if you fight it nice," Eshe said. She saw his eyes fill.

Her heart broke.

He turned away, and opened the door.

She immediately regretted it. All of it. The words, the violence. "I'm sorry, Eshe. Don't go. Let me explain."

He rubbed at his eyes with his sleeve. His face was red and wet. "You'll lose and you'll all die here."

"God bless you, Eshe."

"Fuck you. And fuck your maggoty little parrot, too. You're a married fucking woman, Inaya."

He slammed the door behind him.

She thought to call Michel, or Adeliz, someone who could talk some sense into him. He needed to lie low now, preferably in shifter form, until the blowout from the priests' murders was done. But Adeliz had gone out, and Eshe had never listened to a word Michel said, not since the rumor started that he spent nights in Inaya's quarters. She had denied those rumors, but they persisted.

She walked back into her communication room and opened the slide. She needed to decide what to do with Isabet if he left. Putting her with Eshe had been the safest place, the one least likely to result in anyone discovering who Isabet was. Eshe knew little of what happened at the higher levels of Ras Tiegan politics. What motivated Eshe was nurturing a woman he still believed needed saving. Isabet was a fine choice to play that role. But now God's Angels would round him up, and Isabet would need another protector. Because if Inaya had to choose between the Nasheenian boy shifter who had loyally stood by her side for seven years or the renegade rich girl who could win her people the revolution… she would choose the rich girl. She had been in Ras Tieg so long now, making so many choices just like this one, that the guilt was easy to suppress. She tucked it into that part of her where she kept the memory of her children, and all that she had given up to see this through.

They were sacrifices she did not intend to make in vain.

"Inaya?"

One of her cadre commanders waited in the doorway. "We're ready to start the recovery of the missing operatives."

Inaya nodded. "Let's begin."

7.

Nyx had saved a lot of women in her time. Killed a few, too. But most of the people she killed were men. That was the way of the world. Or at least the one she remembered.

Until after morning prayer, the streets were strangely quiet. She saw a few in doorways and alleys and heard the far-off scuff of order keeper boots on cobbles. The soft buzz and whir of bakkies puttering off through the city. Saw a spotlight searching the skyline.

But as the suns rose, the streets filled, and Nyx stepped into a heaving mass of men the likes of which she hadn't seen since her days at the front. The roads further inside Amtullah were too narrow for bakkies or rickshaws, so Nyx walked.

The crowds for the time of day were unexpected. The warm morning air was invigorating, but the potential threat was more so, especially with the tarry stink of the night's riots still in the air. Boys and young men clotted the sidewalks. Most were just making their way to tea houses or bars or pushing back home from the mosque after morning prayer. But others had made the street their permanent home, and they lurked in doorways, slumped in alleys, begged for handouts, or talked up passersby in the hopes of selling grapes or prayer rugs or bootleg whiskey. Nyx wondered where all the itinerants went at night. The stink of them as she passed hinted that they took up residence in the sewers.

Nyx raised a hand to push a boy out of the way, but he darted back before she could touch him. Old women who walked like bel dames had always put Nasheenian boys on guard. It was good to know some things hadn't changed.

Someone was yelling from the direction of the mosque. Nyx rolled her shoulders and glanced to her right. The crowd stirred. A few heads turned. She rested a hand on her pistol.

Then she moved down another street, the main way running outside the square, and some of the noise died down. Nyx waited another breath before pulling her hand away from her pistol. Ahead of her, she saw a dozen blue-clad order keepers swarming the sidewalk. She was close to the address Mercia had given her.

She turned down another thoroughfare. There were more order keepers here, and something else—women dressed in deep brown and crimson burnouses who had the arrogant stance of bel dames. She couldn't ever remember seeing bel dames and order keepers congregating together. Order keepers hated bel dames, and bel dames thought order keepers were a bad joke.

She stepped up to the banded gate bearing Fatima's address and presented the invitation Mercia had given her to the bel dame at the gate.

The bel dame keyed Nyx into the filter and opened the gate. "Sorry for the filter. Three boys got in last week. We've had to tighten it a lot. No more boys get in, though." She gestured for Nyx to go in. "Welcome to Blood Hill."

"Blood Hill, huh?" Nyx said. Bel dames were never much for creativity. She'd bet her left lung Fatima had named the place. Bloodmount in Mushtallah was mostly abandoned now, she heard. Kept on for show, but the real shit went down here, far from the Queen's most supportive city.

The bel dames who moved through the halls were all hard-bitten, straight-backed women with ropy muscles and keen stares, but for all their mental maturity, they were—physically—young, including the four escorting Nyx to Fatima's office. They passed strutting sixteen-year-old novices and bitter veterans with scarred twenty-year-old faces. The cranky weapons teachers and protocol specialists—the ones Nyx always thought looked like the desert had eaten them up and spit them out—were a ripe old thirty.

Nyx was painfully aware that she was the oldest person in every room by nearly a decade. Every room but the last.

The one Fatima waited in.

Fatima sat at a deep mahogany desk of real wood. Her backless chair was padded in deep umber brown. The name of God was scrawled along the top border of the room, repeated endlessly like something from a Chenjan prayer wheel. No windows in this room—not surprising. It was nicer, but smaller than the bel dame's former quarters on Bloodmount.

"Have a seat," Fatima said, gesturing to one of the padded, backless chairs. There was a large slide hung against the far wall, blank now. Nyx wondered what they planned and plotted on that monstrosity. She had never seen a slide so big, and wondered how many new magical gadgets and super weapons had been pushed through production in her absence.

Watching Fatima's savage, skinny frame easily inhabiting the space behind the desk where she picked over government policy made every muscle in Nyx's body tense. Fatima had done well for herself, she'd give her that. Sucking at the government's tit was a good way to make a living. But Nyx liked to think that remaining a free agent helped preserve what little honor she had left.

Nyx nodded at her bel dame escorts. "You want to keep them around?"

"I think we'll be all right. Won't we?"

"You tell me."

Fatima dismissed the bel dames. They shut the door.

Nyx sprang across the table.

It was not the action of a young woman, and as soon as she leapt, she regretted it. She had expected to move a lot faster.

But then, Fatima wasn't young either.

Fatima ducked left, twisted right, and snapped her elbow back. Nyx dodged. Fatima's elbow glanced off Nyx's brow instead of her temple. Nyx slammed her full weight into Fatima's torso. The two went down together.

Nyx pinned Fatima between the desk and the wall, one knee pressing hard into the small of her back. She got a good grip on Fatima's free hand and twisted her arm behind her, pulled it taut.

Fatima made a strangled sound, somewhere between a bark and a snarl. She tried kicking at the back of Nyx's head, but Nyx caught her leg and pinned it with her own.

"Give me a reason," Nyx said.

Fatima hissed in a breath. "I could have sent a dozen bel dames after Mercia."

"Not good enough." Nyx yanked Fatima's arm back sharply. Felt it pop out of the socket. Fatima shrieked as her arm went limp.

"Cat bitch, I'm not here to kill you!" Fatima said.

"And I'm not here to get used again. What the fuck do you want, and why did you pay Mercia to get it?"

"Talk, just talk. Goddammit, Nyx."

"Bel dames don't talk," Nyx said. "And you've gotten slow."

"I'm a high councilwoman. All we fucking do is *talk*. I could call half a dozen women in here."

"If that was true you'd have done it."

"Let me speak—"

"I haven't cut your throat yet. Talk."

"The Queen asked for you. Not to kill you! In case you haven't noticed we have some… issues here. We need someone not associated with the bel dames or the monarchy. Your name always comes up when we have those jobs. If it was up to me, I'd let the exile stand and let you wither away in whatever shitty hole you crawled into."

"This better be good."

Fatima nodded to the door. "Haven't you *seen* them out there? The Queen asked for you by name. I don't fucking know why. She pardoned all criminals and made sure your name was on the list. Rumor is she's dying, and that's the only reason she did it."

"Catshit."

"It's the truth."

"Swear to God."

"I swear to God—the compassionate, the merciful. I swear on my oath as a bel dame. You hear that?"

Nyx heard it. There were a lot of things Fatima would do for the Queen, but shitting on God or her oath wasn't one of them. Nyx released Fatima's arm and stood. Went back around the desk. She waited while Fatima struggled to her feet, useless arm dangling.

"Some assistance?" Fatima said, motioning to her bad arm.

"Gladly." Nyx took hold of her arm and popped it back into place.

Fatima cried out and cursed. "Sit," she barked.

"No more orders," Nyx said. "I don't work for you. Never did. You didn't sit on the bel dame council till long after you stripped my title."

Fatima winced. She settled back into her chair, favoring her injured arm. "Fine. I didn't ask you here, Nyx, and it wasn't my idea. I'd just as soon people forgot about you."

"Me too."

Fatima pulled a wad of sen from her desk drawer, and took a pinch, offered some to Nyx. Nyx shook her head. She wasn't stupid enough to eat or drink anything in this kill hole.

"Before I tell you the details, we have some unfinished business," Fatima said. She reached into the desk drawer with her good hand. Nyx recognized the chittering click of an organic lock tailored to Fatima's blood.

Fatima pulled out a piece of red organic paper. As she did, glittering silver words appeared on the page. She pushed it toward Nyx.

Nyx leaned back, as if the red paper emitted some terrible heat. Her heart beat a little faster.

"That looks… official," Nyx said. The words were in a flowery script that was nearly impossible to read, but she didn't need to read it. She'd seen one before.

"We finally got around to processing the Queen's request to reinstate your bel dame status," Fatima said.

"What, twelve years later?"

"Bel dames are not known for the efficiency of their paper pushing."

"Why now?" Nyx said. She raised her gaze from the letter. She had been played often by her sisters. Promised much. Given nothing. "I saw the ship in the sky. Is that our friends from New Kinaan again, come to talk war and weapons and negotiate deals?"

"It has nothing to do with them. There are certainly disagreements between the Queen and the Families about what the aliens are proposing, but that is not your concern."

"Aliens aren't my concern? So what is?"

"This is a job bel dames need to be… involved in."

Nyx raised a brow. "I thought the Queen wanted someone not associated with either. That's why she called me."

"What is best is not always…" Fatima sighed. "The Queen is set to abdicate. Those rumors are true. There will be a… different kind of government after her. You know me Nyx, and you know the bel dames. You've seen those men out there. We need to ensure that the bel dames become a part of whatever new government entity is built out of this mess. I need one of our own to do this."

"But why me? You have hundreds of younger, faster women."

"Young, fast, and stupid," Fatima said. "And they do not know the man I need you to bring in the way you do."

Nyx tried to parse that. She fixed her gaze on the letter again. What man did she know that needed bringing in? The first face she saw was Rhys's—it was a face she had tried hard to forget. People said you forgot faces after a while, and maybe she had forgotten his, but the feeling she got when she thought of him was the same—a fierce protectiveness that left her with some mixture of anger and regret. But why would they want Rhys? What other man had she worked with who was still alive? Khos was off making babies in Tirhan. He wasn't dangerous. There were a few more—men she had served with at the front, old partners, but most of those were dead now.

"Tell me his name," Nyx said.

"Not until you agree to come back."

Nyx stared hard at the page. It was everything she had wanted just a handful of years ago. To become an honorable bel dame again. But that was before she blew up a dozen bel dames in Tirhan. Before she let go of Rhys for the last time. Before Radeyah.

"My last day as a bel dame, you stripped my title and sent me to prison," Nyx said. "Nobody puts bel dames in prison. You know what they do to us there? Not a great time. Then I ate dead bugs and dog shit for a year while I hauled in debtors and shoplifters. I slept in doorways and in trash heaps. Also not a great time. Everything I built since then, Fatima, I did without you and the bel dames. I'm not so sure I need you."

Fatima's mouth was hard. "If you knew what this job was, you would change your mind," she said.

"There were a lot of other things you needed to take care of, Fatima. How about Alharazad? You ever take care of that, or did you fuck that up as well as you did the rest of the country?"

"You think I could get anybody to go after her? I know what I promised you, Nyx. But this is a delicate time. Have you heard some of the men talk? They make it out like we're mindless monsters, and every lunatic that ever walked across the sand has it out for the Queen, or the diplomats, or the creepers, or the magicians, or the First Families. Now the Queen's about to dissolve the entire monarchy—against all advice to the contrary. The people will elect a governing body, led by a minister elected by the body. It's complicated. A bit like what the Mhorians do, only with less self-flagellation.

"Nyx, we're so close to ending this war. But any little thing can fuck it up. Murdered Queen. Crazy bel dames. Mobs of unhappy boys… anything."

"You really think Chenja's going to abide by this ceasefire?"

"There's a weapon on the table. Something we used against them that got them to talk."

"Talk? Not retaliate?"

"They have the same weapon and blew up one of our northern outposts."

"Let me guess. Is Yah Tayyib in the country?"

"He turned up in Mushtallah three years ago. Him and a bunch of the broederbond. It's why I couldn't touch him. Why?"

"Broederbond? Isn't that the oath boys take to watch each other's backs after they graduate from combat training?"

"Yes. They've… co-opted it as the name of their ridiculous men's advocacy movement. They were just flics before, but they have numbers now. Don't know what they find to natter on about. It's not as if we treat them like animals the way Chenjans treat women."

Nyx had her own opinions about that. "We're done here, Fatima."

Fatima scrambled up. She grabbed the paper, shoved it toward her. "Just bleed on it and you're a bel dame again, Nyx."

"And you can control me."

"Nyx, if you knew who we were after—"

"Fuck you. And fuck the Queen."

"The bel dames made you, Nyx. They can unmake you."

Nyx started to the door, only half expecting to get a knife in her back.

"It's Raine al Alharazad," Fatima said. "Your old boss."

Nyx stopped in the doorway.

"He's head of the broederbond now. He went missing three weeks ago. Raine's always been a disgruntled activist. You knew that. But he showed up here five years ago calling himself Hamza Habib and growing a far larger following than ever before. We think he'll be elected to the ruling council after the Queen forms the new government, if the boys have their way."

Nyx let out a long breath, like she'd been punched in the gut. "Raine is dead. I put a sword through him and left him to die in a ditch in Chenja. A long time ago."

"People don't stay dead in Nasheen," Fatima said. "You know that better than most of us."

"Who has him?"

Fatima sighed. "That's the trouble, isn't it? We don't know, but we do have some idea where they've taken him. Could be bel dames, certainly. But not likely. Between your… theatrics in Tirhan and our cleanup here of the rogues, the bel dames are more united than ever before."

"But you people sure do have a dog in the fight, don't you?"

"Everyone does, Nyx. Anyone with a vested interest in Nasheen is about to get fucked. The Tirhanis aren't happy. The Ras Tiegans aren't happy. The Families aren't happy. And no, not all of the bel dames are terribly happy either, I admit."

"You have to have some idea of where he's gone."

"I thought you weren't interested."

"I'm not interested in working for *you*. But I'm interested in Raine."

"Make no mistake, Nyxnissa. If you go after this man without bel dame authorization, you'll receive no support from me. You become a bel dame or we do not back you. Do you really want to go up against a hundred bel dames or the most powerful families in Nasheen? *Alone?* I can give you an entire team if you're one of us. Our best. Good, fast, fierce women."

"And whoever took him will see that coming, won't they?"

"Don't do this alone, Nyx. I've seen plenty of assassinations backfire. You kill the leader of a revolution instead of bringing them home alive because you think it all just dies with them. That might work when you kill somebody who doesn't have many followers yet, but you take a man like Raine who easily has the sympathy of two hundred thousand men, and you know what you get? A man made into a martyr. It'll spur those men out there to start some violent regime and new, repressive government that puts bel dames and all other women back under some archaic law they carve out of the Kitab. No, we'll have no martyrs here. Not while I'm serving on any council. He needs to come back alive. Dying is the absolute worst thing that could happen to Raine al Alharazad. You understand?"

"That's why I let his mother live, Fatima. And look how well that turned out. Sometimes I wish I had come in here and blown up the whole bloody lot of you."

"A proper bel dame only kills when she knows the kill will make a difference," Fatima said. "That is where you always had trouble. You never believed in anything."

"No. And I never pretended otherwise."

"Let me help you with this. I can't have you do this on your own."

"I won't be on my own," Nyx said. "I have old colleagues, and you said yourself there are plenty of boys out of work."

"And wouldn't that be lovely?" Fatima said, biting. "Hauling along some men's sympathizer with you?"

"Better than letting them all think it's a bel dame job. You ever consider that giving this to a bel dame would send a message to those boys that we don't intend to bring Raine in alive?"

Fatima frowned. "It's more dangerous to send someone who's not one of us."

"I disagree," Nyx said. "I've worked with a lot of boys, and they fucking hate bel dames. They hate what we do and they hate what we stand for. You want a chance at this, you let me run it my way."

"No."

"You're the one who called me back," Nyx said. "Tell me what you know."

Fatima gritted her teeth. She proffered the paper again. "Sign it."

"No."

"Don't make me play this card, Nyx."

"I'm not going to be owned again."

Fatima sighed. She pulled a gun from beneath her desk.

Nyx raised a brow, interested.

Fatima laid the gun on the table. "You said something to me, once. When I was torturing you, admittedly. But I'll never forget it. You said you'd take everything from me, the way you had from Raine. My face, my license, my lover, my daughters. You know what I did after that? I joined the high council, so if I lost my bel dame license, I wouldn't lose my livelihood. I stopped taking serious lovers, so there was no one to care about. And I happily sent my daughters off to war, so you could not take them from me. Last year I got word that the last of my children had died on the frontier, defending some mealy little outpost in Khairi."

"That's not my—"

"I'm not finished. Now I'm telling you the same. You will work for us this final time, Nyx, or I will take everything from you. I know where your house is. I had Mercia tailed, though the sorry little kitten thought us beat. You bleed on this page or I hunt down Anneke and her militant brats one by one and burn that place to the ground. The woman, though, I'll save for you. Did you really think I wouldn't find out about your little lover? Your little happy home? I'm a fucking bel dame. I can sense one of ours going soft on sight."

Nyx stared at the gun. Then the paper. She felt as if she was watching everything from a great distance. There was a story, she knew, about bargaining with Iblis, and how the promises made meant nothing.

She had a choice. Die here, now, trying to murder Fatima. Or take the job, and see how deep this well went.

Fatima tapped the paper with the gun.

8.

The cell was dirty, bare, and dark. The withered husk curled against the wall had been a person at some point in the hazy past, though it did not often recall it. Once, the world had been full of light—blazing, blistering, blaring light—like a chorus of angels burning in the sun. It had showered the world in stars, and danced on the graves of a thousand screaming points of life, and been content.

They fed it oranges in the mornings and rice and saffron at night, year upon year. The tainted food made the world even more muted, as if covered in a soft, gray shroud. Time yawned and stretched and twisted back in on itself, meaningless. The blinking syringes wielded by pleasant, humming Plague Sisters pinched and measured. Weighed and calculated. Plague Sisters only cared for the best and the worst of Nasheen's monsters. But it did not remember which it was.

Time drifted. Ate itself.

And then, one day, they opened the door.

It garbled at them and laughed, the way it did whenever it conversed with those misty-honey illusions it summoned up for company.

Memories always flickered, just there, at the edges of the gray world. Brief images. Fighting. Blood. And that blazing, ethereal light. She… yes, *she* remembered a world eaten by plague and contagion and rebuilt into some other world's image. Whether it was the world outside her cell anymore or if that world had become something else, she did not know.

"Not this time," they said, and clawed at her.

She twisted and fought. Dug fingers and teeth into flesh. But they pricked her, doped her, and her body went limp, like a fresh caught mock parrot. She tried to snarl—but that, too, had left her, so she snarled at them silently.

I had a name, once. *Fear me.*

I.

They dragged her into the light.

✚

After a few days of detox, they lashed her to a chair in a dim, dry room. There was a large devotion mounted in a scarab carapace on the wall. No windows. Just the door. When the door opened this time, the world was not quite so gray, and she had a sense of herself. Knowledge.

I have a name. *The bitches took my name.*

Two slim women entered. Bug women. They wore long, shapeless tunics, aprons, and hijabs of the same off-white color. One had a soft smear of blood on her apron. She could smell it. The women had three sets of blinking butterfly syringes peeking out from the front of their aprons. She flinched at the sight of them. A shadow moved through the door behind the women.

She lifted her head, regarded the shadow. "You're not like the others," she said. Her voice came out broken and raspy, not at all the way she remembered. When she once spoke, so long ago, people thought the sun was singing.

The new woman was slender at the waist, but broad in the arms and shoulders; top heavy. She wore dark trousers, tunic, burnous, but no weapons. They wouldn't have allowed it here. She stood a little closer than the women who held the syringes, easily confident. No fear. What she was was written in the lines of her face. The tautness of her body.

"What can I do for you, bel dame?" she asked the shadow.

"I heard you were a woman," the hunter said. "And a powerful magician… once."

"I've been a lot of things," she said. "Once." Her memories suddenly stretched and flexed, unfolded—delicate as a locust's wings. It was an overwhelming vista, a gasping, stomach-knotting glimpse into blood and darkness and absolute power. Power that blotted out the sun.

She gasped.

"You bloody fucking bitches!" she screeched, and jerked at her bonds. The chair rattled.

The Plague Sisters reached for the syringes.

"You bitches!"

The bel dame waved the sisters away. "I'm searching for a bug," the bel dame said. "Someone willing to go back into the desert. Someone not afraid of my kind."

She hissed and bared her teeth at the bel dame. "No. You want someone's head. A bloody fucking impossible one, if you're willing to wake me up."

"It's not yours I want. If anyone wanted your head, we'd have taken it a long time ago."

"It's not your kind that captured me," she said. "I was far too clever for *you*."

"Nor my kind who keeps you," the bel dame said, cocking her head at the sisters. "So you've nothing to revenge yourself on with me. No... you have another group all together to revenge yourself on, yes?"

"Who do you want?"

"We'll come to that. But first I need to know if you're capable of protecting us again."

"You know I am."

"Good. I have a target for you." The bel dame rubbed her hands together, opened them. A grainy blue-gray mist appeared between her hands, and took the shape of a woman. In that moment, she wondered if her impression of this bel dame was correct. There were no bel dame magicians. Shifters, yes, but no magicians. I still have no sense of her, she thought. The blindness was crippling. Like being half a person. Demimonde, the Ras Tiegans said. She had had a Ras Tiegan lover once, hadn't she? A bitter girl with a fragile heart.

"You see this woman?" the bel dame magician said.

"I've seen many women."

"I want her dead."

"That's all?"

"That's all. She exiled herself sometime after her... retirement. Few know where, but with the pardoning of so many criminals, there are a good many powerful ones on their way back to Nasheen. They will have old scores to settle with her. I have it on good authority that she's conspiring to make trouble for the Families."

She laughed. "What is she, a mutant? A rogue conjurer?" She leaned forward, bared her teeth. "Tell me something nasty came down from the moons. One of those organic demons, or a blood djinn—"

The bel dame shook her head. "She's just a woman."

"You would wake me for… a woman? Just a woman?"

"There is far more than one head at stake. But I must see if your… rehabilitation has been effective."

"To see if you can control me?"

The bel dame did not answer.

She laughed. "Does she have a name?"

"Do you?"

"I suppose I must."

"And does it matter?"

"Not now."

"I'm counting on it." The bel dame slapped her hands together, and the mist cleared.

"I'll get you more information after your deprocessing. You and her will have some things in common. Hard to catch. And powerful. Far too smart for your own good. You understand?"

"Send a monster to kill a monster."

"Something like that. One more thing. She will not show herself easily. You will have to root her out. Exploit those with an interest in her—and those she has an interest in. They may not be trustworthy, but they will be skilled. Can you kill her?"

"You know why I'm here?"

Some emotion passed over the bel dame's face. Something like dread or fear. Finally. "Of course. Everyone knows why you're here."

"Everyone who remembers."

"Yes. Though all the ones who were there when you did it are good and dead now. Only you mutants live on."

"Then you know what I can do."

"Good," the bel dame said.

"I have a name," she said.

The bel dame regarded her. The Plague Sisters were tense. One of them stepped forward, fast, and plunged a syringe into her thigh. The bloody thing bit into her, and blinked up at her dumbly. She hated live syringes.

"I have a name," she repeated as the gray haze covered her mind again, dampened the world.

"You do," the bel dame murmured. "But no one out there remembers it. Praise be to God."

9.

Nyx did not go back to Mercia's that night. She made a few calls and got drunk on cheap whiskey at a bar with a name she couldn't pronounce, and slept it off in a gutter somewhere. She woke to find a grizzled war vet trying to steal her sword. She ran him through with it and left him wailing there in the street as she stumbled off to find a cheap room for the night.

She needed to put together a team. But it had to be a team of strangers, people she could run through as easily as she had that war vet. Everyone was in danger, now. Everything was on the line. Fatima promised that more information about Raine's whereabouts would be forthcoming. She was going to need the whole scenario—where he disappeared from, who last saw him.

In the morning, she cleaned her weapons and herself and rented a storefront from a venom dealer in one of the less pristine parts of Amtullah, close to a rank of rickshaws and makeshift Ras Tiegan eateries. Most war vets developed a taste for curry at the front. Ras Tiegan expatriates living in Chenja always did well during skirmishes when the border switched. Both sides ate their food, and harbored little animosity for them as a people. Nyx knew it would be a good place to find men and women who knew how to shoot straight.

Putting up a sign in the door saying you were looking for mercenaries generally wasn't done, even in Nasheen. You told people you were looking for magicians and "bug killers" or "precision bug hunters." Using that language would dissuade the order keepers for a while, but it wouldn't fool anybody trying to track Nyx's movements. She kept a watch on the street, looking for anybody paying too much attention to her business.

When she put up the sign, she expected to get a fair number of hedge witches and venom-addled tissue mechanics knocking on her door, but those could be weeded out pretty quickly.

What she didn't expect was the long line of boys standing outside.

Nyx spent the morning interviewing boys between the ages of seventeen and thirty-six, most of whom should have been mixing up burst shells and developing contagions at the front. There were some real surprises, though—two or three were actual, God-fearing, certified magicians. When she turned them away, it wasn't for lack of skill—she just didn't respect them. If you were going to hump a team into the desert after some group of reckless rogues, you had to respect that team.

As she sat in the storefront memorizing names and faces—she learned most things by rote—she thought about how much it was like being at the front. When they sat down, she had a knee-jerk impulse to ask them for their orders, like she was back in Sharifa screening sappers.

There were fresh-faced young boys not a day over sixteen who hadn't been at the front six months when they got pulled home. There were bug-addled twenty- and thirty-year-old veterans with missing eyes, severed limbs, poorly patched-together heads that barely kept their brains in, and worse; boys wearing long sleeves who twitched and jittered in their seats, trying to hide signs of venom addiction; young, bearded men with eyes deep and empty as dry wells; and the hardened ones, the distant ones, the ones who did not look at you but through you, off just beyond your left shoulder where the war still raged, where their best friends bled out, where a buddy took a bullet or a burst they were too scared to take themselves. Boys who had pushed their friends into fire, or abandoned them during a surge, listening to their cries as the Chenjans tore them apart; and there were the soft-spoken, matter-of-fact heroic boys, the few who had lived. They talked the least, said "sir" the most. They were the ones who'd done what she hadn't, and what most living folks never would—they lost their limbs, their skins, their sanity to take a burst or a bullet for a friend, for a squad, to save a mission.

Those were the ones she worried about most. The heroes. Heroes were unpredictable. They'd be the most likely to die in the desert, throwing themselves to some unnecessary death to save some damn fool. When you hired a mercenary, you didn't want to hire a hero. You wanted men and women with guns who liked living enough to use them.

She took a break for midday meal, which suited the men in the queue just fine, as they dispersed for noon prayer. She ate up on the roof, watching the men wander off. She noted that one of them did not—a hunched beggar sitting against the cracked tile of the building across from hers. She resolved to keep an eye on him.

That night, discouraged, she settled into the bare office, and lay under the desk in case the bursts started again and the roof fell in. Habit.

Tomorrow would be a long day. If Fatima knew she was back in Nasheen, other people would too. They would come searching for her. She needed to move quickly, before too many people found out she was back in the country.

Nyx slept lightly.

When she heard a scraping at the door, she woke instantly. The pale blue dawn had turned the world gray. Nyx saw the light cutting through the slats of the shuttered windows. She listened.

More scraping, scrabbling at the front door, like somebody was trying to circumvent the security. Nyx came up in a crouch. She drew her scattergun and padded into the reception room. She waved her hand in front of the door before remembering it was the old-fashioned solid kind, not a smart door like her store in Mushtallah.

She unlatched the door and yanked it open. Pushed her scattergun out ahead of her.

The scattergun snapped a young man right in the center of his forehead. The man flailed back, grabbing at his face.

"Get going before I put a bullet in it!" Nyx said.

The man stumbled off the stoop, peering at her through splayed fingers. He snorted something. Like a laugh.

"You couldn't hit a bakkie at that distance," he said, and snickered again. She recognized him then—the petulant mouth, the slightly bent spine.

"Eshe?" Nyx said.

He pulled his hands away.

"Shame you didn't get prettier," Nyx said, holstering her pistol.

"You aren't exactly beddable either," Eshe said.

"I know some folks might argue that point." She glanced left, right, down the misty street. The stink of munitions was still heavy in the air. "Get the fuck inside before some other old woman shoots you."

✚

Eshe woke to the pungent aroma of frying dog meat. The smell was intoxicating. Getting over the Nasheenian border meant shifting, and he was still starving for meat. There was never enough protein in the world after a few days in form.

He rubbed his eyes and rose from the hard pallet in the reception room of the storefront. He saw Nyx standing at a hot plate on the other side of the room. There was a wash basin next to the plate, with actual running water. In Ras Tieg, he could never afford that kind of luxury. All the water came from barrels on the roof. He pulled his knees to his chest and watched Nyx. There was something comforting about her muttering at the frying pan, shifting her generous weight back and forth on her bare, scarred legs. She had put on a lot of weight since the last time he saw her, so if he didn't know how powerful she was under all that flesh, he might think to call her soft or fat. But it wasn't the sort of fat he saw on rich people. It was the bulk of an aging boxer who had long since stepped out of the ring.

"You gonna sit there and stare, or eat?" Nyx asked.

Eshe grinned and got up to help her.

The meat was tough and stringy, barely edible, probably something she had bought and rehydrated for the occasion.

"How much you pay to rent this storefront?" Eshe asked. They sat in the reception room as the sun came up. The floor was covered in bug carapaces. Eshe saw two cracked windows and a broken flesh beetle skin that filtered the worst of the sun's rays—a cheaper solution to getting an operational filter. It wasn't random chance that brought him to her. He had contacted her house in Druce before he left Ras Tieg, and Anneke said she was heading to Amtullah with some diplomat. Nyx in the company of a diplomat was strange enough. He half thought Anneke was using some kind of code that meant Nyx was going to prison.

Once he knew where she'd gone, she was easy to find. The boys on the street knew where to find all the most dangerous women in town. When he told Nyx how easily he found her, she hadn't looked pleased.

"Too much," Nyx said. "But I'm not staying long."

"This about the job? The one you talked about last night?"

She nodded, but didn't look at him.

As they ate, the call to prayer sounded, long and oddly mournful this morning. Eshe stilled for a long minute to listen. It tugged at something inside him. He had missed that sound. He set his food down and unrolled his prayer rug.

It was good to be back.

When he finished praying, he saw Nyx staring at him. "What?" he said.

"I don't know I'm going anywhere you'll like," Nyx said.

Eshe shrugged. "I got tired of Ras Tieg. I like our work better. Come on, Nyx. I can help. I have a lot more experience now." She had told him about the job the night before, but it wasn't until now that he realized she hadn't invited him to join her.

"Experience with what?"

"Just… everything. You'll need a shifter on your team, won't you? Somebody good with a knife? You know that's me."

She stared into her bowl. Something twisted in her face, something like resolve.

"Yeah, I've gotta have somebody I can trust."

"You can trust me."

"That's what I'm afraid of."

"I don't get it."

"Fatima's sending some people with me. A magician and a bel dame. Best intel she's got says Raine is being taken north, into Khairi. The magician's supposed to act as a guide through Khairi. But I can't trust her magician. Or her bel dame. I need my own team."

"Call Suha then. Aren't there other people you've worked with, too?"

Nyx shook her head. "It's bad enough taking you."

"So you're taking me? I mean, hiring me?"

"You negotiating now?"

"Are you paying?"

"We'll see. Listen, lots of boys think the bel dames took Raine. If that's so, he's probably dead. I heard the monarchy's on the way out, but what comes after that?" Nyx said. "Electing some man to the low council? The high council? That's as close as they're getting."

Eshe shook his head. "From what I heard, the Mhorians have had some influence. Might be nice for something fresh, though, you think?"

Nyx snorted. "There's no new thing. Just the same old shit in different clothes."

He had forgotten just how grim Nyx could be. Inaya was lively and optimistic by comparison.

"Well, it's not like things can go on the way they are," Eshe said. "The Queen's got no heirs, and her successor isn't around anymore."

"That was an accident," Nyx said.

"Yeah, well, tell Nasheen that," Eshe said.

"You pissed at me?" She peered at him.

Eshe started. "No. I just… It's just strange to be back." She hadn't asked him yet about Ras Tieg, or Inaya, or anything that had happened to him since they parted. He knew she didn't like to ask questions outright. She said it was rude to ask personal information from trusted people because it implied you didn't trust them. But he wanted to tell her about Inaya and the Fourré, and the priests he had killed and how crazy the Ras Tiegan bordels were compared to Nasheenian brothels and how much he had missed the wild swagger and careless confidence of Nasheenian women.

He wasn't sure what he expected to come back to, but now he found himself watching Nyx hopefully, like a kid. He knew better than that. He wasn't a kid anymore. But he felt safer and more wanted around her than he had with anyone else in a long time.

She left her dirty dishes on the floor, and stood. "You in, then?"

He tried to sound casual. "As long as there's work to do."

"Always work to do," Nyx said.

"You never turned down a job, right? I never have either."

He got to his feet. When they stood next to each other, he was nearly as tall as her, which made him tall in Ras Tieg. It was strange what a few years could do. Despite the height, and the extra bulk, she was smaller than he remembered, and a lot older. The hair braided back against her scalp was long and thick—not the sort of hair you wanted to drag with you into a fight, unless you wanted to give your attacker a handhold—and he could just make out a few silver threads. But her ragged face, scarred throat, and mismatched skin said volumes about who and what she was—and why nobody should fuck with her. He half hoped he would look that ravaged at her age. Maybe people would take him more seriously.

Nyx rubbed her eyes. “Good. I’m kinda tired of exile. Maybe you are too.”

“Yeah,” Eshe said, but it wasn’t the rioting, tar-tasting streets of Nasheen he was yearning to get back to. For once, he wanted to feel like he was needed somewhere, like he actually fit. Being with Nyx was the closest thing to feeling like he was home. Like somebody gave a shit.

Nyx said, “Let’s get started then.”

+

Three hours and twelve candidates later, Nyx was ready to close up shop. The sun was low in the sky, and evening prayer would be coming on soon. Fuck having her own magician. She would rely on Fatima’s and take her fucking chances.

Eshe escorted the next one in. When Nyx looked up, she saw a tall, lean man fill her doorway. That in itself was not remarkable. But his face was. He might not yet have been thirty—hard to tell. He had the aspect of a good boy made old by war. His skin was puckered with wind-scoured creases—fine lines at the edges of his eyes, his mouth. Unlike the ravaged bodies she’d been processing all day, he was whole. She saw the tail end of some broad scar peeking up from his collar, but that was it. His eyes were hazel-gray—shifty, she thought—set in a dour, handsome face with a strong jaw. His dark hair was sun-kissed a deep brown, dusty, and unkempt—it just brushed the nape of his neck. Nice hair, for a war vet. Most shaved it clean or had it all burned off.

If Mercia was attractive for her plainness, this man was remarkable for his beauty—particularly in a place where smooth skin and supple limbs didn’t last long.

“Have a seat,” Nyx said.

He hesitated, one hand on the back of the chair. She figured out the reason for the hesitation, or thought she did. “No need to salute,” she said. “I haven’t served in a long time.”

He bowed his head slightly as he sat, like some Tirhani businessman. “I am Ahmed al Kaidan.” His voice was soft, but she caught the hint of a speech impediment; gentle slurring that turned the end of his words to mush.

"Did you have a rank?" she asked.

He passed a token to her. A black scarab in tailored resin. "I've been told I can bleed on this, and it will verify my service," he said.

Nyx had seen a few of these tokens from other hopefuls. Some new thing the government was doing to help discharged boys find jobs without a lot of paperwork.

"Important stuff first," she said. "You know Chenjan?"

"Yes."

"How much?"

He immediately switched languages, and said something mostly unintelligible in Chenjan. All she could make out was "prisoners" and "desert."

Nyx shook her head. "That's fine."

"I worked interrogation," he said, in Nasheenian. The tone he said it in was flat, the way he would have said, "I worked in bakkie repair." That explained the soft tone, and unmarred face. He was intel.

"You speak enough, then."

"Enough." Same flat tone. His gaze, too, was unemotional. A man used to putting on faces.

"Good with any other languages?"

"I know Khairian. Training camps were up there. We all picked up some."

"You have a knack?"

"I can tell Tirhani from Chenjan. Order food in Ras Tieg, Heidia, and Mhoria. I learn quickly."

"Lot of translating in my line of work. Anything else?"

"I also know Drucian," he said, grudgingly.

"Where you learn that?"

"From Drucians," he said.

Nyx took in the full measure of him again. Nothing special, she supposed, no different than the others. She liked the color of his eyes, now, though. It was growing on her.

"Former intel guys can be unpredictable," she said. She tapped the beetle casing. "That going to tell me you're mad as a violet-gassed magician?"

"I was processed through psych before discharge."

"What's your talent level with bugs?" She knew magicians ranked their own. He wouldn't have been able to handle munitions without a higher than average talent. If they just stuck him in intel instead of R&D, he was likely no more skilled than a com tech.

"I had a strong rating," he said. "But I moved to intel my first year. I was… better at it."

"Better at torture than bugs?"

"It was my preference."

"I suppose a talent with bugs makes for a good torturer," Nyx said. She had the scars on her legs to prove it. "Why you want *this* job?"

"It's what I'm good at," he said.

"What's that? Bugs?"

"Using bugs to get a job done."

There was a fine line between madness and intelligence, and she still wasn't certain which he was. "What makes you think I need a magician for killing?"

"Some of the other men had heard of you. I know you kill bel dames."

"You have a grudge against bel dames?"

He shook his head. "I'm just looking for a job, matron." He said "matron" instead of "sir." No hero, then. That, at least, was promising.

"If you're intel, you can handle a com, right?"

He nodded.

"Let's prove it, then. I need you to sort out some transcriptions and hack some information for me on a politician. I need some work done on an old bakkie, too. Call it a test run."

He hesitated. The words that came out were gravelly, a bit broken. "If I do it, can I get a meal?"

Something tugged at her, some errant emotion that had been building all day as she processed one starving, mangled, bug-ridden boy after another.

"Sure," Nyx said. "If you're as good as you say, I can even get you a room."

✚

The sniper was tougher.

In a flat desert, the person with the greatest advantage would be the one with the sharpest shot. Nyx's aim had never been the best, and even years of training at Anneke's firing range hadn't improved her long-range shot.

The snipers and weapons techs who wandered in the next day in response to her new sign were all far outside Nyx's pay range, and a few were just ridiculous. One girl showed up in some expensive bit of chain-mail and the most impractical boots Nyx had ever seen. Her skin was so soft and unmarred that Nyx immediately pegged her as a First Family kid slumming.

"You ever held a gun?" Nyx asked her.

The girl puffed out her chest and declared that she had virtually killed over eight hundred opponents in something called a battlefield mimicry class. Run by rich people and their magicians, naturally.

Another girl came in like she was running headlong from her fifth-year graduation and into the wide world of bounty hunting. She was fleshy and bright-eyed and still had the use of all her limbs.

So when yet another little runt appeared at the door lugging a pack and ragged burnous that could have been nabbed off a corpse, Nyx didn't have high hopes. She was so small that Nyx immediately guessed she was Drucian before she pulled off her hood. Drucians weren't worth her time. They were notoriously frail little fuckers. She didn't need a frail fucker on this job.

She let Eshe screen her, and went back to her office. A few minutes later, Eshe ducked in and said, "You should probably talk to this one." He lowered his voice. "Especially if she can shoot with her tail!"

"Drucians don't have tails," Nyx said.

"Everybody knows they cut them off to fit in," Eshe said.

Nyx followed him.

The girl had pulled back her hood to reveal a sharp little Drucian face—tangle of black hair, gray eyes rimmed in yellow, petite features, sandy skin. On the whole, Drucians suffered a lot of asthma and sinus issues, in part, folks said, because of their tiny noses and crowded features. Whatever environment they had evolved to fit, it wasn't this one.

The top of the Drucian's head just reached Nyx's chest. From what Nyx could see of her limbs beneath the too-long trousers and tunic, she was stick-thin. Nyx sometimes suspected that Drucian limbs were shaped a bit like mantids beneath all the clothes, which would explain their funny walk. They were more modest than any Chenjan, though, and she had never seen one naked.

"We're not recruiting garbage collectors here," Nyx said to her. Better to let them down quickly.

The girl did not meet Nyx's eyes. She simply pulled the pack from her shoulder and began unloading it.

"I build my own guns," the Drucian said, to the floor. Her accent was terrible, but Nyx had spent a lot of time trying to make sense of the way Drucians mangled Nasheenian, so at least she could keep up.

She set a fine piece on the table. "This is a Z1070 scattergun. Originally fired only dead ammo. I adjusted that. It does blister bursts now. Lengthened the barrel. Better range. Adjusted the spin."

Nyx's specialty was munitions and mines, but living with gun-loving Anneke had given her a greater appreciation for guns, so she picked it up and examined it.

"You did all this welding work yourself?"

The girl nodded. Still didn't meet her eye. Another Drucian thing, and one of the most infuriating. They refused to look anyone in the face but lovers and close family. Worse than Chenjans.

"I've been interviewing all day and you're the first who brought her own gun. Can you shoot it?"

"Yes."

Nyx handed back the gun. "Let's prove it."

She brought the girl up onto the roof. Eshe followed them up. Ahmed the magician was still in the back, working on a bakkie she'd picked up. The space on the roof wasn't big, but it was private, tucked between two slightly taller buildings.

Nyx pointed out across the scrappy line of other hopefuls to the beggar squatting against the tile of the building opposite, the same one she saw her first day at the storefront. When the lines thinned, he should have gone off as well, but he hadn't. He was old, maybe fifty, skinny and sickly, with venom scars on his arms. Some hard-up war vet.

"I want you to kill that man. Can you do that?"

The girl's face remained expressionless. It was like trying to read a stone.

"Is that a problem?" Nyx asked. She watched the girl carefully. This was the toughest test of all. Would she kill on command? Could she?

The girl slid up to the lip of the rooftop. Knelt. Steadied her gun against her shoulder.

"Nyx—" Eshe said.

"Hush," Nyx said.

"You can't be serious, Nyx," Eshe said.

Nyx turned, and saw that Ahmed had joined them. He stood on the ladder leading up to the roof, only his head and shoulders visible.

"When am I not serious?" Nyx said.

She heard two shots in quick succession. Loud. Nyx pressed her hands to her ears, too late.

She went to the edge of the roof and looked down. The beggar was still. The Drucian had not shot him in the head, though. That injury would be too obvious. It was two to the chest. She must have hit some vital organ, because the man had simply bowed over, rather anticlimactically. No one outside seemed to be any wiser, though a few vets raised their gaze to the rooftop.

"Where you learn to shoot?" Nyx asked.

"Leaf bugs," the girl said. "We have a lot of leaf bugs." She began to pack up her gun, still expressionless.

Nyx had picked palm-sized leaf bugs out of her bed every night in Druce. "All right. What you want in exchange for service?"

"Room and board," the girl said.

Nyx raised her brows. "That it?"

"I just need to... get away."

They always needed to get away.

"What's your name?"

"Isao Kage."

"Kage, then," Nyx said. Second name first, with Drucians. "It's a deal." Certainly the best deal she ever made for a sniper, but then, Drucians didn't know how to deal properly. It put them at a disadvantage, one she was more than happy to exploit.

+

"You don't know he was a threat," Ahmed said.

Nyx stood with him at the window downstairs as the shadows lengthened in the street. "No? You see tomorrow. They'll be another beggar out there. Another addict, or worse. Somebody so hungry they don't care about the risk. Some dumb body. You wait," she said.

But the next morning, there was no new beggar.

Not until dark.

Nyx called Ahmed over. She watched as the young beggar pulled at the sleeves of his tattered slick to hide the venom scars on his arms.

"Satisfied?" Nyx asked.

Ahmed's eyes were half-lidded, his face—unreadable.

"You're the boss," he said.

"I am. Don't forget it."

She turned and went back into her office. Shut the door.

Nyx sat behind the desk and took a deep breath. Loyalty was a tricky thing. Aside from Eshe, her team was brand new, and she needed to win their loyalty. This was always the hardest part, being right all the time. Not fucking up. Killing stuff had always been easy for her, but getting a bunch of vets and outcasts to fuck around with her to the ends of Umayma—that was tough, and she didn't have a lot of time on her hands to make it all right.

Somebody was having her storefront scouted, somebody who thought they could follow her into the desert. If it was one of Fatima's bel dames, Nyx decided then and there that she would burn Blood Hill to the ground.

If it was somebody else… well, then she was already way behind in this race, and her chances of catching up were getting slimmer by the day. I'm being played, she thought, but I have no idea by who, or what the fuck for.

10.

The sky overhead was on fire.

Rhys stood just outside the circled carts and pitched tents of the caravan, smoking. It was the only way he could get warm. Above him, purple waves of mist billowed in the sky like a massive shroud. He had spent most nights out here at the edge of camp, watching the sky, since the lights started. The caravan was one of Payam's, led by a caravan leader named Araok who told him that's just what the sky did out here. During the day, the caravan was a sprawling, noisy affair—eighteen sand caterpillars, four sand cats, seven carts, and twenty-six people.

Rhys's appeal to Elahyiah had won him her company on the journey, but she had not spoken to him since they began. She spent her time in their cart with the children. When he spoke to her, she didn't look at him.

He believed all she needed was some new perspective. A fresh vista.

Rhys rode along with the caravan, sitting on the back of a caterpillar-pulled cart, while the heat soaked into his bones and water ruled his dreams.

At night, he sat with the other men at the fire and traded stories. When he bedded down with Elahyiah and the children, he began to take some joy in Rahim's constant squalling. The crying meant Rahim was alive, they were all alive, even after all the grit and horror the world had thrown at them.

Rhys put out his cigarette and tucked the remainder into his pocket.

He walked back to the ring of firelight where the men spoke in low tones. There were two other families on this trek, one of them relocating to a settlement called Tejal and the other paying their way to join family in another Chenjan settlement just a few more days north.

Beyond the ring of firelight, Rhys could see the darkness around them writhe. He shuddered. There were more insects out there, and… other things. Larger, more fearsome, and more terrifying than what ended up in the pot every night. They had encountered one of the *mauta kita* the day before, a monstrous creature fifteen feet long, banded in purple scales, that had devoured one of the fat, slow-moving caterpillars that pulled the carts.

Rhys trudged into the warmth of the fire's circle. He saw the men passing around a bottle. They drank a terrible concoction of fermented cats' milk called ashora that turned Rhys's stomach just to smell it.

"Would you like some ashora, Rhys?" one of them asked. He was a Tirhani man called Rafshan.

"He is Chenjan. He does not drink," said one of the Khairians, Abhinava.

"The *atishi baluka* may strike at any time," Rafshan said. "You should enjoy the time you're given."

Atishi baluka was one of the first foreign terms Rhys had learned when coming to the north. It referred to the flesh-eating sand, the sand that burrowed into wounds to devour the blood within, leaving behind a gutted, deflated corpse. Rhys had yet to see any of it out here, but he had witnessed a variant of it in action at a church in Tirhan a long time ago. He had no interest in encountering it here.

Rhys sat with the men in the sand. Somewhere nearby, a caterpillar snuffled.

"That boy of yours is quiet tonight," Abhinava said.

"God is good," Rhys said.

"Watch your family as we go further north. Be sure your girls do not wander of," Abhinava said. "It is easy to get lost here, and some of the nomads take slaves."

In the morning, after prayer, the caravan was moving again. A ceaseless routine of packing, sweating, eating, unpacking, smoking, sleeping. Rhys found it comforting. The suns were high and hot, but inside, the cart was hung with an organic drape that kept the interior bearable.

At dusk, three weeks into their journey, they came to Tejal where one of the families, Rafshan's, said goodbye to the caravan.

Rhys took the man by the elbow and wished him well.

"Luck to your family," Rafshan said. "And God go with you."

"And with you."

That night, Rhys slept well. He woke before dawn to pray with the other Chenjan and Tirhani men in the party and prepared for another day on the road. The heat was not terrible, so he traveled much of the way by foot, and rode for a time with Abhinava on his cart, trading stories about bacterial remedies and the most useful type of flesh beetle to treat burns.

At dusk, the caravan camped, and Rhys prepared to spend another night telling stories on the sand. He walked back to his family's cart. It was strange not to hear Rahim wailing this time of day.

He pulled back the organic sheet that protected his family from the worst of the heat… and froze.

The cart was empty. Not just empty of people, but empty. Their belongings were gone, everything but a single pack he had brought for himself. His heart thudded loudly. Some terrible sound filled his ears.

Rhys walked over to Abhinava's cart. The man's wife and Elahyiah had spoken often during their weeks of travel.

"Have you seen my wife?" he asked her.

Abhinava's wife shrugged. "I have not seen her."

Rhys moved into the opening of the cart. The woman shrank back. "I will ask again," Rhys said. "Have you seen my wife and children?"

"They got off at Tejal, after the caravan got underway," she said. "I'm sorry. It was her right."

"Her right?" Rhys said. "I am her husband."

"Among my people," the woman said, "it was her right."

Rhys's hands itched for his pistols. He backed slowly away from the woman. Tejal. Less than a day behind them. He would go there and find her. Bring her back. What madness was this? What was Elahyiah thinking, to betray him like that?

He walked to the popping fire to beg a caterpillar from the caravan leader. But as he approached the fire, he saw there was no one standing near it.

Three figures spoke in low tones several paces distant. He searched for the others.

"Rhys!" Abhinava called. "Arm yourself!"

"What?"

The attack was sudden, and fierce.

It took Rhys several breaths to realize what was happening. He heard three shots. Abhinava ran past him, shouting for his wife.

Rhys pulled his pistols and darted behind the nearest cart.

Whirling figures moved into camp in groups of two and three. They had covered their faces with long red scarves. As he watched, they cut the harnesses off the sand caterpillars, and called to them in a language he did not recognize.

More shots. The figure nearest him collapsed onto the sand, clutching at his chest. Blood welled. The attacker wadded up the length of his turban—Rhys realized the scarves were simply the longer ends of their turbans, pulled over their faces—and tried to quell the blood.

With the face revealed, Rhys realized the attacker was a woman. Or perhaps a very young boy. Tall, dark haired, with reddish skin and broad features, she did not look Khairian at all.

"Rhys!" he looked up. Abhinava shot the struggling woman in the sand, this time in the head. She went still.

"Come!" Abhinava said, and held out his arm. "We need your pistols."

Rhys ran after him.

More figures poured in from the desert. He had assumed the dozen were all they had, but a dozen more appeared every time their comrades were felled. Rhys took cover behind a cart with Abhinava and several other men. They had rounded up the others into just two carts.

"This is where we stand," Abhinava said, as another wave came in from the desert.

Rhys aimed to incapacitate the women, taking them each in the legs, with a preference for the knee, when he could manage it. He had not killed a man in a long time, and he preferred to keep it that way.

"What are they coming for?" Rhys asked. He saw more sand caterpillars reticulating out across the desert.

"They want the goods," Abhinava said, "and the caterpillars."

"Let them have them!"

"Are you mad?"

Rhys wondered why these people objected to the caravans so strongly. Wouldn't they appreciate trade and commerce in this blasted wasteland?

The smell of smoke pulled his attention from the raiders. He looked back and saw that the nearest cart was on fire.

Rhys broke away from the others, running across the sand. He saw more carts on fire, spewing smoke into the cool night air. He coughed and choked as he rolled down to the other side of camp. When he looked up, one of the desert women stood over him, serrated blade raised.

He fired.

She dropped.

Rhys scrambled to his feet. He saw a single sand caterpillar squirming at the edge of camp, its tawny, nearly hairless skin blending easily into sand. It was hitched to a small chariot used by the caravan leader.

He strode toward the abandoned chariot. His hands began to shake as he untangled the caterpillar's lead from its hitch. He leapt into the cart and pushed out into the desert, beyond the circle of the caravan. He kicked at the supplies in the chariot, and noted that he did not have much water. He needed to go back the way they had come and tell someone what had happened. He needed to get back to Tejal, to find Elahyiah and his children. But the wind had started up, smearing the caravan's tracks across the desert, blowing more smoke. He was bitterly cold. Above him, the sky was alive with purple fire.

He turned back once. The caravan was some ways distant. No one was following him. He heard screaming, then Khairian singing. The trembling got worse. He was tired of killing for lost causes. He closed his eyes, and tried to still his racing heart with the memory of why he had come to this Godforsaken place.

The night the bel dame assassins came for him and his family in Tirhan, they had taken his hands, nearly drowned his wife, and killed his daughters. They found Souri's body that night, but not his elder daughter, Laleh. He had searched for her body, and had the well dredged, and put in a report with the Tirhani order police. Elahyiah told him he was obsessed about a ghost, and after two years he let it rest. He had tried to rebuild his life, his family, even though he had failed to protect them that night, when the bel dames burned the world down around them.

So many failures. He no longer wondered what God would say to him at his death. He no longer anticipated paradise. He was a deserter and a coward. And a killer. What was one more body now that he had failed at everything else?

He was already damned. But he could not fail his family again.

Rhys huddled in his burnous against the chill and prayed for a warm dawn. A new day. A clean beginning.

But as the caravan burned behind him, he admitted to himself that there was no starting over.

Just running. Endless, mindless running across the desert, into a future much bleaker than the past.

11.

Inaya knelt at the foot of Saint Mhari, murmuring a prayer of safe-keeping she had intoned since her childhood, long before she understood the words. It was an hour after midnight mass, when only the most desperate and downtrodden still walked the dim passages and knelt in the narrow prayer niches of the church, seeking solace from lesser saints whose concerns, they hoped, were easier to bear than God's, and so could afford to pay them more attention. It was her mother who first took her here to these lesser spaces; the small, secret spaces.

"It is not the shouting that God cares for," her mother told her. "He rewards the obedient, the pious, the meek. What meek woman has the pride to speak directly to God? That is not our place. It is Mhari who will carry our prayers to Him. Mhari who protects us."

Inaya placed her fingers on the worn base of the idol, and peered into the inscrutable face. Her personal prayers were too private to say aloud, not here, not anywhere. But she knew Mhari would hear them. Knew they would find their way to God's ear, even if He didn't answer. He never answered.

Behind her, she heard Michel's familiar shuffling walk. She rose, but did not turn. He moved within a pace of her, then stopped.

"Mhari," he murmured. "Not the most inconspicuous place to meet."

"It's no fault of mine that you are not a woman."

"Mhari is the saint of martyrs and victims," he said. "That is not what we are."

"Mhari is the saint of women."

"As I said. Isn't it time we embrace our true power?"

Inaya watched the flickering light of the bugs in glass above them playing off Mhari's smooth, featureless face. Inaya wanted to see her weep blood, or morph into some base beetle. They were the sort of tangible miracles that could give her hope that some tiny portion of her time spent here was not time spent simply speaking to herself. The times she knew God, when she felt closest to Him, were when she shifted, when she gave in to her body's deep need to cut loose, cut free, slough off her skin and become something else, something more, everything. A piece of everything. Did God feel like that? she wondered. Was that why she felt so close to Him then? All the more reason they hate us, Inaya thought. We know more of God than his priests.

"Did you find her?" Inaya asked.

"Yes."

"And?"

"She went to Nasheen. I followed her across the border, and to the boy. She chose to stay with him."

Inaya's chest tightened. "In Nasheen?"

"Yes."

"You permitted her to do that?"

"I could not persuade her to return. I told you there was a danger in putting them together. Young love—"

Inaya's laugh was soft, rueful. She wanted to sink into the stones at his feet and slowly suffocate him in molten rock. Her body fairly vibrated with anticipation. She took a deep breath. It had been easier to control herself when she believed she had no choices, when life was something that simply happened to her. She had done all the correct things. Married sensible men, raised children, kept a good house. She was dutiful and obedient and pious. She was all of those things because she believed there was no other way to be. Knowing there was something different was a blessing and curse. And it hurt her now. It made her… less predictable.

She knew better than to use Isabet's name out loud, not here. "She was our best piece," Inaya said carefully.

"She was a diplomatic solution to a situation for which the time for diplomacy has expired."

"Your actions were unwise."

"It was her decision. Our people have lived as slaves for too long. I would not force her to do anything against her will. She wanted to stay with that boy. Let her stay. I'm sure they will be back in a week or two when they have… tired."

Inaya felt the heat in her face. She flexed her toes, an invisible gesture of frustration that she had perfected during her first marriage. When you had to smile and bow your head and stare at the ground every time someone disrespected you, you found ways to channel frustration. She hadn't even noticed she did it until she came back to Ras Tieg.

"That was irresponsible of you," she said.

"We should look ahead."

"To what? War?"

"A show of force. That is all." He moved a step closer—too close for decency. She felt the heat of him behind her. "We are powerful. And you are the most powerful of all, bound by no set form. If we show them our true power, they cannot help but take us seriously."

Inaya had watched God's Angels put black bags over the heads of her fellow shifters—old women and children, young men and teenaged girls—most of her life. It had only gotten worse now as the people they took away were her own operatives. She had made the same mistake with each of them, in the beginning, as she had made with Eshe—treating them like her own family, her own children. Every one of them had disappeared into some smoked-glass bakkie. No one saw them alive again.

"I believe they take us seriously enough already," Inaya said. "It is not *their* minds we must change. It is the people's minds. So long as they hate and fear us, we will not earn our place as human beings. And if we attack what they hold most dear, we simply affirm what our enemies say about us."

"It sounds cowardly to me."

"Let me tell you about cowards," Inaya said. "Let me tell you about the cowardice I saw among you when I first came to Ras Tieg."

That, at least, gave him pause. For a few moments they stood in silence, two renegade shape shifters in the last place any of God's Angels would think to look for them. What foolish animal crept into its enemy's house to hide?

"Tell me," Inaya said softly, "how many more have come over to our cause since I joined you?"

"Impossible to say."

"And who brought us the girl?"

"I still think—"

"I have not asked your opinion of my methods. Not in some time. Yet you still continue to offer up the same tired strategies. The same ones that nearly brought you to your knees before I joined you. I am done arguing with you on our path. It has been decided. Fly back to Nasheen tonight and bring her back."

"This is a foolish course."

"Do it, or don't bother coming back," Inaya said. She turned, and made to move past him, gaze lowered.

He grabbed her arm, jerked her toward him, made her look up. The space was narrow, and she did not have enough clearance to pull away.

She met his gaze. It was what he wanted, of course. Some acknowledgement of their intimacy. But there was no smile for him, no bowed head, no words to soothe his bruised ego. He was a grown man, and she would treat him like one.

"You were nothing before I found you," he said, biting. "How long would it have been before you and the boy took to whoring yourselves out? He was a thieving cur, and you his little bitch."

"How quickly your words curdle when you no longer have power," Inaya said. Her skin prickled, and she felt a subtle ripple slide across her skin; her body's desperate desire to be free. She was not a fool. She had been raised in Ras Tieg. When Michel followed Eshe back to the alley they shared in their first days in exile in Ras Tieg, she expected the worst. But he had remembered her from a diplomatic dinner in Tirhan, where he had posed as a servant in order to gain access. She thought him sly and moppish then—not trustworthy. Someone—her old contact, Elodie, perhaps—had told him she was a sympathizer. When he discovered who they were, when he understood exactly how they could be used, he invited them to join the resistance in Ras Tieg, the Fourré. She was under no illusions that he offered his hand in selfless friendship. They could eat and sleep there so long as they were useful. But one night, all of that changed, and in the morning, she was the leader, and he was second.

Until this moment, she had not realized that he believed that shift had been made in name only. He still thought she was the puppet, he the master.

Inaya let go.

It was a painful, delightful feeling, like giving in to the euphoric exhaustion at the end of a long labor. She took him by the shoulders—he was not a slim man—and let her arms melt across his torso, coating him in a shiny straightjacket of organic resin that roughly approximated the chitinous sludge of the bug secretions that made up the city's foundations.

Her body trembled, and sweat beaded her upper lip. She felt the stitch in the world open, ready to accept those pieces of her she did not use during the transformation. It took every ounce of self-control she possessed not to unmake her entire body into acidic mucus and devour him whole. She breathed deeply. Her sleeves hung, limp, against the narrow bands of resin where her arms had been, which now connected her to Michel. His face was pale, with the barest hint of a quiver. He had seen what she could do, certainly, but never had it directed at him.

"If you touch me again unasked," she murmured, "I will reach into your chest and stop your heart. Do you understand?"

He nodded.

Inaya pulled away from him as her body began to reknit itself. Organic sludge became human body, became tendons, sinew, tissue, skin. She dropped her pale arms so the sleeves covered them over before the stubs of her reformed fingers regenerated the nails. Her arms and fingers were sticky with mucus. The stitch in the world closed. And then the disappointment came over her. It happened each time she shifted back to human form, as if her body had half hoped she would never return to this soft shell.

"Come back with the girl," she said. "Or leave the movement. We have no need of you."

She moved past him, into the open ambulatory of the church. Three women sat in a pew at the front, weeping. Two priests with swords stood to either side of the massive altar, nearly fifty paces distant. The church was an organic monster, the largest thing in the city, built on the old bones of some dead ship and crafted skyward, with an open ceiling that protected them from the elements with nothing more than a custom filter. Expensive, considering Ras Tieg's lack of magicians, but most churches had them, so God could gaze down upon them. To remind them of where they came from. Of where, one day, God might return them.

Inaya spared a glance upward as she walked. Inside, the light of the lamps along the aisles was low, so above, the stars were visible. This far south, the sky was as crowded as it ever got, with bold pinpricks of light from far-off places. She wondered, sometimes, what would happen if she truly let go. Just how far and fast she could travel when she broke her body down to its smallest parts. What were all of them, really, but bits of something else? Bits of stars?

She wanted to build a better world. So why did so many others want to keep it just the same?

She stepped into the humid night air. A drizzling rain fell, and scattered clumps of rotten leaves clotted the drains along either side of the cobbled way. Two more priests with drawn swords stood outside. As she passed, both murmured, "Go with God."

"God bless," she said. She closed her long coat over her habit, tightly binding her body against the rain, and the stares from passersby, and stepped out onto the muddy street, alone.

12.

Nyx dreamed of bloody bel dames storming her seaside compound in Druce. She saw Anneke's children's faces mutilated, Anneke's twisted body broken in the courtyard, and a blood-spattered trail leading upstairs, to Nyx's bedroom. And there, at the top of the stairs, lay not the body of her lover, not the woman she had kept from Mercia and the bel dames, not the woman she was murdering blameless bodyguards to protect—the woman who loved the sea and tolerated Nyx and her monstrous history—but beautiful Rhys, his handless arms reaching out to her, the expression on his face a strange mix of horror and recognition.

"You can't hide from them. They'll come for everything you love," he said. "The way they came for me."

And she woke up.

The world was still dark. It was at least an hour from morning prayer. She was covered in a thin film of sweat, and every part of her body was taut, alert, flooded with adrenaline. There would be no more sleep for her.

You're a bloody fucking fool, she thought. The world will trash everything you care about. She had to let them go. The way she'd let everything else go. The way she'd let Rhys go.

Nyx rolled off the cot she kept in her office and walked into the back where Eshe had his pallet. He was still there, sleeping soundly, one arm thrown over his face. But the pallet opposite him—Ahmed's place—was empty.

Nyx found Ahmed in the kitchen, already awake, his com gear carefully laid out on a blanket on the floor. He was packing each item neatly into his pack.

"Thought you might be gone," she said.

"Where would I go?"

"Right," Nyx said.

"Is everything… all right?"

"Of course," Nyx said. The dream was fading, but the feeling it left her with was still there—a terrible premonition. She went to the sink and washed her face and hands.

"That new beggar is still there," Ahmed said.

"I expected he would be."

"How do you want to deal with it?"

"I don't," Nyx said. "Let them come."

It was the anticipation that nagged at her most. She didn't know how to solve anything unless she had the option of putting a bullet in it.

✚

Fatima's little spies showed up after dawn prayer.

Both women were young and scrappy, and there was something about the way they stood that made Nyx wonder if they were sisters or lovers. Whichever it was, they had known each other a long time.

The magician came in first, thrusting a scrap of paper at her that Nyx assumed was supposed to be a voucher from Fatima.

Nyx sized her up. She was a small woman, mid-twenties, with thick, dark hair tangled back with a frayed ribbon. Most of the flesh of her face seemed to have been packed into her cheeks, giving her a warmer, rounder appearance than her figure warranted. Her face was clean, but her clothes were grimy and tattered. She wore male garb—long khameez and trousers and somber colors—but her old burnous was a faded scarlet red.

The bel dame shadowed her. She was a head taller than her companion, wiry where the magician was skinny. She wore a sturdy pack and sensible boots. In the harsh light of dawn, the left side of her cheek and neck was a pocked ruin, as if flesh beetles had gnawed on the twisted face of some terrible demon. She turned her furrowed face to Nyx and said nothing. What was she, twenty-six? Twenty-seven? Hard to tell with a face like that.

The bel dame met her stare. She must have been used to people looking away, because when Nyx held her gaze, it was the bel dame who broke away first.

"This is my team," Nyx said. She introduced Ahmed, Kage, and Eshe.

The bel dame remained expressionless, but Nyx saw her staring off behind the three of them, as if searching for more bodies.

"That's it," Nyx said. "Six is already too many if it turns out we're headed north. What are your names?"

The magician jutted her little chin out. "Eskander Ilyas," she said proudly, as if the name should mean something.

"And you?" Nyx asked the bel dame.

"Khatijah," she said.

"Good enough," Nyx said. "Khat, let's go into my office and you can brief us."

"Khatijah," the bel dame insisted as she slid off her pack.

Nyx ignored her and escorted the team into her office.

The bel dame unrolled a portable slide and placed it on the desk. Inside the small office, the six of them were a little cramped, but Nyx liked it that way. She wanted to see how they all did together in close quarters. Things were going to get a hell of a lot closer.

"I was the bel dame heading up Hamza Habib's security," Khatijah said. She tapped open a schematic on the slide. A burst of lemony scent filled the room, and the schematic rose from within the slide, projecting a map of northern Nasheen and Khairi in the air above it, like a radio.

"Wait," Nyx said. "The bel dames were guarding Raine? Seriously?"

Khatijah pressed six points on the map. Nyx recognized them—waypoints for the caravans that went north. "When he went missing, we activated secure points across the country. We had sightings at these six."

"Sightings? And you didn't catch him?" Nyx said.

"I had no women in place here. Too many military personnel have been called back from the front, and now we've got bel dames in country policing all the military. That doesn't leave me much to work with."

"Who was he with?"

"That's a real good question. If I knew that, we wouldn't need you."

"And if you'd done your job, you wouldn't need me either," Nyx said.

Khatijah regarded her. Nyx grinned.

Eshe pointed to the furthest point on the map. "Why are there no more sightings after this? Is this where he is?"

"No," Khatijah said. "That's our furthest Nasheenian outpost. After that, there's nothing."

"So they just hauled him out into the desert? Why not kill him here?" Nyx said.

"Obviously they are not interested in killing him."

"So we start there," Nyx said. "And see what they can tell us about where he went."

Khatijah sighed and muttered, "Indeed."

Nyx leaned toward her over the table. Khatijah waved away the schematic and rolled up her slide.

"If we have a problem, Khat, we should hash it out before we leave."

Eskander patted the bel dame's arm and said. "No problem, right?"

"Councilwoman Kosan asked that I serve as your guide," Khatijah said.

"And what the bel dame council wants, it gets," Nyx said. "Don't think this was my idea either." She turned back to her team. "Ahmed, do one last sweep. Eshe, wait for me in the bakkie. Kage, go with Ahmed." And then, to Khatijah, "You and your sister can ride together in the second bakkie. We'll take the lead. Good?"

"If we're the guides, shouldn't we lead?" Khatijah said.

"You already showed me the map. I know where we're headed. That's a start. But after that, I hope one of you has some knowledge of what comes after Nasheenian-occupied Khairi."

"I've been there," Eskander said. "Out beyond the last outpost. I know where we're going."

"Obviously." Nyx regarded them both again—lean, guarded, an army of two. "I feel so much better running off to retrieve a man with the women who lost him."

"And I'm quite pleased to partner with a known traitor who slaughters bel dames and fucks Chenjans."

Eskander said, "I told you—"

"Oh it's fine, *Khat*," Nyx said. "It's all true. I murdered boys and babies, slaughtered my own brothers, blew up a hundred bel dames, and tried to fucking assassinate the Queen herself. All true. All but the fucking Chenjans part. That's just a bit much, isn't it?"

Nyx walked out. She heard Eskander speaking again, empty words about how much they needed to impress Fatima. Nyx had a lot more to chew on now. Fatima had been "guarding" Raine for some time, then. But why? And how the fuck did a bel dame lose somebody they were guarding? And why send this odd pair into the desert to find him with Nyx of all people? They weren't top operatives, for sure, though Khat certainly had potential. No, Fatima wanted them out of the way. Or wanted to punish them. Any bel dame could hand over a schematic and tell Nyx to go north. This was something else.

Nyx met the others outside. She sat with Eshe and smoked a cigarette for a few minutes until Khatijah and Eskander joined them. Khatijah's face was impassive again. Eskander was all smiles.

"Let's get underway!" Eskander said. "We are ready."

Nyx stepped into her own bakkie, one she had picked up for fifty notes from a hard-up former mullah with an addiction to military-grade sen. Eshe slid in beside her. Ahmed and Kage were in the back, separated by Kage's big gun.

"Am I right in thinking that didn't go well?" Ahmed said.

"Any time I step out of a room with another bel dame and my head's still intact, it went well," Nyx said.

Kage peered out the window, nose nearly touching the glass.

"Forget something, Kage?" Nyx asked.

"No," she said, but did not move her head.

"Great," Nyx said. "Let's see how far we get before the road runs out."

She put a lot of confidence in her voice, but she was still thinking about her dream, and the mangled, inscrutable faces of the women on her team. The job was simple. They always sounded so fucking simple. Find a kidnapped politician. Return him before the boys rose up against the Queen. Return him, alive, before the blood.

The sorry truth was, though—she couldn't remember the last bounty she brought in alive. And she feared this one would be no different. She was getting the feeling that that's why Fatima had hired her for the job, and that didn't sit well with her at all.

Eshe turned on the radio.

13.

The world was brighter than she remembered, and more intense. Some of the names had changed. Whole cities had disappeared, swallowed by the war during her imprisonment. But there was one place in the world that was just the same, and she walked there now, comforted by the shiny amber streets, the bright awnings above the tea houses, and the sounds of the soft, lilting accents of the Firsts.

Only a few individuals walked the streets this time of day. It was far too hot, and the suns too close, for any intelligent Family member to brave the street. The ones who did were concealed in slick organic burnouses and billowing organic trousers the color of spider's silk. They wore hijabs that wound around both head and face, with opaque, organic veils over their eyes to shield the sun. Her own blood-red burnous and uncovered head made her a subject of interest, but none stopped to question her. She had easily passed through the filter that led to the hill. Her blood was too old to be purged from that filter. To purge her code would have rejected one of every eighty Family members on the hill.

Her Family's estate was one of just forty-five that jutted from the dusty face of Mushtallah's second hill. Like the other hills of Mushtallah, the interior of the second hill was the shell of a discarded derelict. The face of her family's house was outside, molded to fit the landscape, but inside the Firsts still met and conspired deep within the old starship. The warm, organic heart of it still beat softly, powering much of the residences and the magicians' tunnels. Three thousand years was a long time for a ship to slumber, even one of the old colonial scouting ships, and she didn't expect this one would go on much longer. Like the Firsts themselves, it was a calcified old wreck, drunk on the memory of itself, its former power. She had once stood within a few meters of the heart, pressed her ear to the spongy walls, and listened to the ship muse about days long past. Most of it was madness, of course. After three thousand years, any organic thing would go mad. For her, it had taken much less time than that.

She paused outside her family's residence and tasted the filter there. It was a complex weave of scents, aloe and chamomile, beeswax and capsicum, and the peculiar nutty tang of crushed hornets. The mix of scents told her she was no longer coded for this filter. Unsurprising, given how long she had been captive. And for the reason behind it.

But the warp and weft of this weave were far looser than the filters of her memory, and it was an easy thing to unravel them. She called a swarm of red beetles, a cloud of mites, and a blue beetle. She extracted the chemicals she needed, and simply rewove the pattern of the filter. Some would have unstitched it completely, but in her time, too much tampering warned the conjurer on duty, and she wanted as little interference as possible, even if all the true conjurers were long dead.

She slipped through the benign section of the filter and onto the garden walk. Inside the filter, the air was moist, balmy, like a spring day in the Tirhani lowlands. Giant plants stretched above her, their weepy, massive leaves reducing the impact of the dangerous sunlight that trickled through the filter. Inside, there were no walls around the estate, just the greenery, which created a luxurious privacy screen.

From the height of a splayed, variegated leaf the size of a tea table, a pale green lizard regarded her. She never understood why her family insisted on keeping lizards. Unlike the bugs, they weren't good for anything but eating.

She pushed further into the lush little jungle. The path she took was laid with blue stones imported from Tirhan. Along the circuitous walk, she passed an open-air tent splashed with ornately decorated pillows. The space was dominated by a low tea table of real wood. The tent was different, but she remembered playing in a space much like it as a child. She had caught and killed lizards there, too, and cooked them over a smoky fire until the housekeeper found her and raised an alarm throughout the whole house, fearful not so much of a spreading fire but of the callous destruction of the garden's resources for something so banal as a real wood fire.

She rounded a bend in the path, and came upon the house. The primary residence was made from bug secretions, built up around an old deadtech foundation whose corrugated patches of rust and decay could still be seen floating within the secretions along the upper stories. The lower half of the house had been set with green and gold tiles. A single arched doorway led into the house—but of course, there was no physical door in that doorway. Just a filter. Only authorized Family members would get through it.

She stepped onto the tiled front patio and passed under the arch into the bright open courtyard. A fountain bubbled at the center of it, twisted into the form of a giant, undulating centipede, half again as tall as she was. A small child played in one of the massive garden planters lining the yard. Pink and crimson blooms towered over the child, each flower as large as the child's head.

The child peered up at her from the dirt. The child's face was at once familiar and foreign. It put her in mind of another child, one she had once seen in the mirror quite often.

For a moment, she thought the child might speak. But instead, the child leapt away and bolted into the house. That was just as well. It put off the inevitable.

She deftly, neatly, untangled this second filter to allow her entry, and stepped under the arch.

Inside, the house was cooler and drier than the yard. Natural light illuminated most of the smooth, rounded surfaces of the interior; the skylight it bled from was a smooth tunnel burrowed through solid secretions.

Two women lay in the recessed seating buried in the floor, settled just opposite a massive oven-stove that funneled most of the house's heat through the walls, effectively baking the inhabitants to the most optimal temperature, no matter the season. The women were engaged in an easy conversation as they wove an intricate pattern of mellow scents and mild, lemony red mist into what she guessed would soon become a locust tailored to play chess or screes or some other board game with them.

One of the women was hugely pregnant, which she found oddly

comforting. She had been traveling for nine days, and in all that time, had not seen one pregnant woman. Only the Families and a few undocumented refugees still birthed their children one at a time from the comfort of home instead of at the baby farms on the coast.

Beyond them, she could see out into the side yard where an older man wearing a long blue tunic and matching trousers tended the narrow rows of a burgeoning flower garden.

For a moment, none of them were familiar. But that was just a trick of the dim light.

"God the compassionate, the merciful..." the non-pregnant woman murmured, and stood. The organic matter they were weaving abruptly began to dissipate back into the world. The smell of it changed, too—burnt copper.

The woman was markedly older than her pregnant companion, but both bore the same slim build and petite frame. Her long dark hair was wound back from her skull in a knot. As she raised her hands to her mouth, the hennaed patterns that snaked from her hands and up into the drooping folds of her robe became visible. Her name was Sohrab sa Hadiyah so Ikram. She remembered the name because the city of Ikram had been swallowed by the war two hundred years before, and Sohrab would joke about it often at Family gatherings, telling lively tales about how one day she would rebuild it into a shining, ravenous traveling city mounted on the back of some monstrous scarab, a roving city exclusively for Firsts.

Family members were difficult to surprise, so she took some pride in the women's shocked faces. The pregnant woman even clutched at her massive belly, perhaps thinking she was there to remake her child in the womb.

"Who is this?" the pregnant woman asked, a note of true anxiousness in her voice.

But she was not here to catch up with her clutch mates. "Where's the rest of the Family?" she asked.

Sohrab's gaze flicked to the rear of the residence, past the interior courtyard, deeper, into the warm belly of the beast that sustained the Families.

"They are discussing what to do... with you," Sohrab said. "We did not... expect you."

"Oh, I'm sure you expected me. Just not so soon." She raised her hand.

The pregnant woman shrieked. Sohrab fell to her knees, clutching her hennaed hands. Neither of them were conjurers, and they knew better than to try and draw weapons on her. The man outside lifted his head from his gardening. She heard the soft sound of the child padding across the tiled floor, somewhere close.

She called the bugs from within the walls. Knit them from gut to wingtip from the old organic compounds that threaded throughout the house, binding the deadtech in place. She drew on the same stuff the shifters did to remake themselves, the ancient organic matter of the derelicts that had once been siphoned off to build the world. Now it was gelatinous, mutated stuff; unstable. But still useful.

Sohrab began to intone the Surah Al-Fatiha, her pronunciation of the ancient prayer language impeccable and haunting. It had been some time since she last heard those words recited with such beauty and passion.

Locusts appeared at the center of the room, sparking into existence as if from the air itself. The swarm coalesced, a massive darkness that steadily grew outward, like an expanding black hole. There were few places one could seemingly create something from nothing anymore, and she took a grim satisfaction in it, even as the pregnant woman screamed and screamed and the man rushed headlong inside, a machete in hand.

A few simple chemicals created a great hunger in the locusts. She pushed her hands out, compelling the air and the altered chemical compounds around her to direct the insects. They swarmed over the women and man. It took just ninety seconds for the hungry locusts to devour all three bodies to the bone.

When it was done, she clapped her hands, and the locusts and the flesh they had gorged on disintegrated into its base components and rejoined the organic compounds within the derelicts. A few tatters of flesh still clung to the bloody skeletons, like shredded wrapping on some festive package.

She walked across the inner courtyard. The fleshy doors leading deep into the derelict were partially open. For a moment, she suspected it may be some kind of deception. Then she remembered the child, the one she had passed on the stoop. She found it hiding just inside the door, huddled in one of the heaving, slimy crevices of the living ship.

The girl's eyes were squeezed shut, and she stank of urine.

She took the girl by the collar of her tunic and dragged her down the long corridor with her. The girl shrieked once, then squealed like a tortured puppy.

It meant they knew she was coming, and she did appreciate the aesthetics of a grand entrance, even after all this time.

They waited for her deep within the bowels of the ship, so deep she could feel the ship's heartbeat beneath her feet. Most of it had long since been reworked by conjurers far more powerful than she, centuries or millennia before, so their original purpose was unknown. The room they convened in was called Shahnaz, after some dead man. But older Family members called it the Heart of Umayma. It was here the Families met to decide how the world would be run. The Queen may have some power over everyday Nasheenian government, but she was just one pawn on a very great field.

As she had expected, it was not the full assembly today. Only her own Family, house Hadiyah. Thirty-nine members in all. Most were already standing when she arrived. Most already knew their fate. They were surrounded in the most potent weapon her people still possessed, but not one of them still had the power to shape it.

None but her.

Which was why they had condemned her.

She threw the squalling child at them. The child rolled across the floor. One of the men, Abdah, reached forward and scooped the child up. They all wore traditional clothes. Billowy white thobes for the men, and creamy khameezes for the women. They wore their hair long and covered—black turbans for men, and black hijabs for women. Within the pulsing dome of the ceiling ran several lines of silver prayer script that read, "God the Creator, the subduer, the provider, the forbearer, will return for you and light your path to the stars."

Inside the vast chamber, her stir of white-clad Family members were strangely frail, insignificant. She had spent a week outside among the mutant colonials, and she had been reminded of just how physically powerful those ravenous people had become outside the safety of the filtered residences and purified air enjoyed by the Firsts. Her Family and all those like it had stagnated here, desperately trying to maintain the conjurers' bloodlines and eradicate the mutations among them. But even isolation had failed, after so many millennia, and all the Families truly had left to leverage were the secrets encased in these living tombs, and the shaping power that only a few could still wield.

"Who's matriarch?" she asked.

When no one stepped forward, she simply cast her gaze across the sea of faces to suss her out. She knew much about being a matriarch. She had been one herself, for a short time. A very short time.

"I am," one of the older women said. She moved toward her from the back of the assembly.

She recognized her as Parvaneh Ibraheem sa Hadiyah so Mushtallah. The woman was slight at the wrists and ankles, with a delicate face so achingly beautiful that for a moment she feared she would cry. The walking corpses outside weren't half as pretty as the ugliest First Family outcast. After her exile among the colonials, this room of ravishing, large-eyed, soft-skinned beauties was like walking among aliens.

"We were just recently informed," Parvaneh said. A hundred years ago, Parvaneh had commissioned the building of the Orrizo, the great monument to unnamed dead men at the center of Mushtallah. She had lost three sons to the conflict—not an undue number for a woman who bore just four children in her lifetime. As a general rule, First Families did not serve. Protecting their blood from the same massive mutations that plagued the colonials required strict breeding practices, and they had long ago exempted themselves from service. But the boys had been willful, headstrong radicals, and got blown up into so many pieces that not even a well-trained scarab army could have put them back together.

"It appears you were informed too late," she said to Parvaneh. "As was I when they came for me. When they shut me up into that hole."

"It was for your protection," Parvaneh said.

"No. It was for yours." She peered at the small child again, caught up in the older man's arms. She knew him, too—Abdah sa Shukriya so Ifshira. Her great-grandfather's brother. It was funny how time passed so quickly when you were free, but dragged on into what felt like century upon century when your brain was clogged with poison and your identity stripped away. Sometimes she felt as if she had been gone millennia. She expected some of them to have died, or show marked aging. But no. They were the same. All of them just the same.

A pity she was not.

Parvaneh followed her gaze. "Let us leave here and discuss your place with us," Parvaneh said. "We are Family."

"Place?" she laughed. "I have no place with you." She pointed to the child. The child with her eyes, her chin, her *face*. "You already replaced me. Replaced a woman still living. Thought you could do better this time? Thought you could control *her*? You cannot control what you don't understand anymore. There are no more conjurers. Haven't been since me, and won't be again."

"Child—" Parvaneh stepped forward.

She felt the air condense. Unlike the Family members upstairs, some of these were still moderately skilled magicians, though not conjurers. True conjuring entailed far more than the rote trickery of a colonial magician. It was about more than simply directing or breeding or codifying existing flora and fauna. It was about creating something from nothing. Or, rather, creating something dynamic from an inert soup of primordial possibilities—chiefly from the organic composites of ancient wrecks like this one. That had been their purpose, after all, and it was that nostalgia for the safety and malleability of this ancient technology that kept the Families winnowing through this wreck, feeding off its brain-dead corpse.

"It's your turn now," she told them. She raised her arms.

"Hear us out, child!" Parvaneh said. "How can we aid you? Your mission? Surely you would not condemn a Family that could aid your mission. Your mission protects Family interests. They wouldn't have called you otherwise."

She smiled. The grin felt lovely on her face, but the faces that gazed back at her seemed to have no appreciation for it.

"Perhaps you can be useful in that, certainly," she said, because if she had suggested it, of course, if she had told them outright that it was information or death, these mantids would have gone deep into stony silence. She knew them well. It was what *she* would have done.

Abdah said, "You must befriend her enemies."

"And where can I find those?"

Parvaneh and Abdah exchanged a glance. Parvaneh said, "Go north, across the living seal, into the red desert. You still have the skill to open the Abd-al-Karim that far, do you not? They have been sent to the bones of Duha Dima. You remember it?"

"Not half as well as you do," she said, "but enough."

"You will know them when you find them," Abdah said softly. "They are just like you."

She half-thought to ask why it was anyone in the Families knew where to find a rogue colonial woman, but thought better of it. She wouldn't have been freed to bring the woman in if she was somebody her Family, too, did not find dangerous to the success of their political machinations. They had bent the world too far. It was too close to breaking. Now it had to stop.

"I hope you succeed," Abdah said. "There is a far more important task ahead. One only you can perform." He gazed skyward.

"Anything else you want to tell me?" she said.

Abdah said, "I wish it were not too late for you, child."

"Funny. I'm quite pleased that it's too late for all of you."

She raised her arms, and brought the whole fleshy cavern down upon them.

Only the little girl looked surprised.

14.

Things weren't particularly eventful until Kage shot Eskander.

Nyx wasn't even sure how it happened. They had stopped both bakkies at the side of the road for mid-afternoon prayer—at Khatijah and Ahmed's request.

Nyx was squatting just off the road's right shoulder, taking a piss, when she heard loud voices, a shrill cry, then a shot.

Eskander howled.

Nyx pulled on her trousers and leapt onto the road. Kage was standing over Eskander's prone body, the magician's gun in her hand. Kage's own custom gun was still slung over her back.

There was some babbling among the others, but Nyx didn't give a shit about that. She reached behind her for her scattergun, ready to put Kage down. When you took on a new team, you did it knowing that not everybody would work out. Oh, sure, you hoped it was all whiskey and fucking, but she had lived too long to expect it.

Eshe grabbed for her arm before the gun was half pulled. She started to swing at him, and he leapt back.

"It was Eskander!" he said. "She shot first."

"Why the fuck does it matter who shot first?" Nyx rounded on Kage. "Put that the fuck down."

Kage's face was smooth and unwavering as a water reservoir, like she was taking a stroll out in some Mushiran field trolling for grasshoppers. She neatly unloaded the magician's gun and placed it beside Eskander, who was clutching at her gut and shrieking.

"Cat bitch," Eskander said. She hissed and kicked at the dirt.

"I'll put a bullet in both of you if you don't shut the fuck up," Nyx said.

"They were bickering," Ahmed said, stepping up from the other side of the bakkie. "Eskander pulled a gun on her."

"Catshit," Khatijah said. "That little maggot made a threat. I'd have handled it different, but it's not a surprise she pulled a gun."

"First," Nyx said, "Why the fuck does a magician choose her own gun before calling a swarm? Second, I don't care who pulled what first. There's no gun-pulling on teammates. None." Nyx glanced over at Kage. Even though Eskander was small for a Nasheenian, Kage was shorter by at least a head and weighed a good twenty kilos less. Nyx half thought to gift them both boxing gloves and send them into a ring to sort it out.

"You do it again and we part ways," Nyx said. "Permanently. Understood?"

Kage nodded.

"She said something insulting, I think," Ahmed said.

"You think?"

"It was in Drucian."

"You're supposed to know Drucian."

"All I caught was something about hunting."

"Eskander?"

"She's crazy," Eskander said.

Nyx squatted beside the prone magician. She jabbed a finger at the bullet wound. Eskander screeched.

"What happened? I don't mind letting you bleed out."

Khatijah moved forward to protect her little magician.

Nyx pulled her scattergun and aimed it at Khatijah. "Hush now, kid. I'm in charge. I don't plan on killing anyone unless I'm provoked. Eskander?"

"It was nothing. A joke. Fucking maggots can't take a joke."

"You call her that?"

"I just said she was a baby-eater, that's all. I call all of them that."

"Well, stop," Nyx said.

Nyx glanced up at Kage. "And *you*—learn to deal with people slinging shit. I don't care if you pull a gun on somebody on your own time, but while you work for me, you only shoot people I tell you to. Understood?"

Kage nodded again.

Nyx stood, taking Eskander's empty gun with her.

"You can fix her?" Nyx asked Ahmed, nodding to Eskander's bloody torso.

"I… well, I'm not sure. I haven't before."

"Fuck you both," Eskander said. "It's deadtech. I need somebody to pull the fucking bullet before it festers."

"Just pull out the bullet, Ahmed," Nyx said. "She can make sure it doesn't fester on her own. Let's get this done and get back on the road."

Setting everyone into motion didn't take long. Like most folks, they just wanted somebody to make a decision, and if nothing else, Nyx was good at that. Whether they were always the best decisions was a matter of contention.

Ahmed and Khatijah pulled Eskander up and off the road.

Nyx went over to the other bakkie and checked the fuel gauge. They would need to juice it up in two hours. She sat next to the bakkie and pulled out a wad of sen.

Eshe came over, hood pulled up. "You figure them for lovers?" Eshe asked.

She followed his gaze to Khatijah, who stood watch just outside the group huddled around her partner in deception, Eskander.

"No. The hand gestures are the same. They use the same tired sayings, mannerisms, that sort of thing. Partners mimic, sure, but there's some stuff you just never pick up like you did when you were a kid."

"Sisters? They're too different."

"You never met my sister Kine," Nyx said. "There was stuff about us that was the same. Ways people stand, say things. It comes from growing up together."

"Inaya says I'm like you."

"Inaya doesn't know me. I'd say she's hardly in a place to judge how like me you are."

"Do you think people can be different? Different from the way they learned to be?"

Nyx peered at him. "Who are we talking about now? Those bloody-minded sisters, or you?"

Eshe shrugged.

"Listen," Nyx said. "Don't let that little honey pot tell you what you are. *You* make who you are. It's for nobody else to decide. Understand? If I learned any damn fucking thing in my life, it's that. Got it?"

"Sure," he said, but he was staring at the ground, not at her.

"Good. That's a bunch of catshit, letting people tell you who you are. Who do you want to be? Come on—who?"

"I… don't know."

"Then you better start knowing, and soon. Because until you know what you want to be, other people are just going to keep trying to make you into something useful for them."

"Nyx?" Ahmed said.

Nyx started. She hated it when they snuck up on her. Made her feel old. "What now?"

Ahmed wiped his bloody hands on his trousers. A swarm of red mites clustered on a brownish spot just above his knee.

"She's ready," he said.

"Can she walk?"

"Does she need to?"

"Teach me to agree on a magician like Eskander who can't hold her wormy little tongue." She stood, dusted her trousers.

Ahmed made a strangled sound. He turned away and coughed.

"God, don't you get fucked on me too," Nyx said.

He shook his head. "I'm fine."

"Then let's go have some more fun," Nyx said, and walked toward the forward bakkie.

"I had a trench commander tell me that once," Ahmed said, following her, "right before a burst blew her to pieces. Cleaned her guts out of my clothes for weeks."

"Charming," Nyx said. "You chat up a lot of women with that line?"

"I… What?"

"You'll get used to it," Eshe said.

Ahmed shook his head and hung back to speak to Kage.

Eshe walked with Nyx to the lead bakkie. "What did Suha used to say? You always did go soft as old cheese for the pretty ones?"

"I remember it was you always getting into trouble with pretty girls. How often did I drag you out of some mad woman's bed after too much to drink, huh? More kick than a cat in heat."

"Let's just go," Eshe said as his face began to flush.

Nyx banged on the bakkie's hood. "All right, folks. Let's go rescue some guy in distress."

✢

That night, they camped outside a bug juice station, huddled just outside the comforting lights of the parking area. Eshe had first watch. He counted two bakkies and a cat-pulled cart come in after dark. That was it.

When he hit his four-hour shift, Eshe turned back to camp to tell Ahmed it was his turn. Ahmed was still passed out, one arm around the scattergun Nyx had issued him. And Nyx was nowhere to be seen.

Eshe walked away from the edge of the parking lot and into camp. He supposed Nyx could have gone to take a piss, but it was strange he hadn't seen her.

He crossed to the other side of camp, the side facing the desert. He waited for his eyes to adjust. Nyx always told him trouble was more likely to come from the desert, but he had fixated on the parking area. That's where all the traffic was.

"Eshe."

He started so violently he nearly tripped over his own feet.

Nyx sidled up next to him, as if she'd simply congealed from desert shadow. How a woman that big could manage anything like stealth, he had no idea. Maybe I'm just out of sorts, he thought. He needed some sleep. Nearly twelve days with this crew was wearing on him.

"There's somebody following us," Nyx said.

Of course there was.

"You know who it is?"

"No. Single person, though. Tracks came in off the road, there—" she nodded in the direction she meant. Out past the camp, it was very dark. He couldn't tell exactly where the tracks had started. Pretty far away from the station, that was certain. Whoever it was had walked all the way past them, then doubled back through the desert.

"You know where she's hiding?"

"I want to try and flank her. You come with me?"

"Let me put Ahmed on watch first. In case she has friends."

"Good," Nyx said.

Eshe went back to camp and woke Ahmed. As soon as Eshe leaned over him, he jerked awake, clutching his scattergun.

"Your watch. I'm checking something out with Nyx. Be careful. There might be more than one."

Ahmed rose. Took up his gun. "Done," he said.

Eshe crept back to where Nyx waited behind the station.

Nyx motioned him beside her. She pointed toward a low rise behind the station. The moons were in recession, and wispy clouds streaked the sky, so it wasn't the best vantage.

"You sure it's not just some vagrant camping for the night, like us?"

"That spot gives her full view of our camp. Not the station. Not the road. Our camp. I don't believe in coincidences."

She motioned him to the right. She took the left.

He pulled his knife.

They crept across the desert. Eshe had learned how to walk softly back in his street days in Mushtallah. The secret was to step along the outside of your foot and roll it inward to take your weight. He had avoided some potentially nasty fights that way.

Nyx was heavier, and less patient. She got there first.

It was a dangerous thing to sneak up on somebody. Best case, you actually caught them by surprise, and killing and incapacitating them was fast and easy. At worst, they had already made you, and were waiting with gun drawn or blade ready.

Eshe always expected the latter.

He dove behind the rise a bare second behind Nyx, but she already had her arm around the woman's throat.

Eshe saw the woman's pistol on the ground. She had not been caught totally unaware, then. He needed to work on his stealth. Or not sneak around with Nyx.

Nyx shoved her gun to the woman's head. Not even so much a woman, really. She was petite, not too much larger than Kage, and swaddled in a large burnous and too-big trousers. But it was the pistol that gave her away.

"Wait! Nyx, let her go."

"What? Fuck?" Nyx said.

"Let her go. Please. Her pistol. It's Ras Tiegan."

"The fuck is that supposed to matter?"

"I know her, Nyx. Please."

Nyx let her go. Tore back the hood of the girl's burnous.

Isabet gasped.

"Who the fuck are you?" Nyx said.

"Isabet Softel. I'm..." She blustered a bit, seemingly trying to find the Nasheenian words for what she needed to say. Finally, in Ras Tiegan, she said, "Eshe, tell her who I am."

"I can tell her who you are, but not what you're doing here," he said, also in Ras Tiegan.

"None of that curry-mouthed catshit," Nyx said, waving her gun at them both now. "The fuck is going on?" She grabbed Isabet's discarded pistol and sneered at it.

"Inaya sent me after you," Isabet said, in Ras Tiegan.

"Give me a minute," Eshe said to Nyx as she popped open the chamber on the Ras Tiegan pistol. He switched languages again. "Catshit," Eshe said to Isabet. "What the hell are you doing here? Do you have any idea how much trouble you're in? How long have you been tracking me?"

"Since you left. Michel helped me across the border. He said that Inaya insisted that I bring you home. I thought it was a fool's errand, but—"

"For a very great fool," Eshe said. "Are you alone?"

"Yes, I told you—"

"How are you going to get back?"

"I told you. You're to come with me, and together—"

Eshe shook his head. He had to walk away from her, just a few paces, to try and clear his head. They were a long way from the Nasheenian border, an even longer way from the Ras Tiegan one. How she made it this far on her own baffled him. There was no way she'd make it all the way back alone. If Inaya had wanted him to return so badly, why send Isabet? Did she want to murder the girl? He closed his eyes, and thought of Corinne. Anything was possible with Inaya. Who knew what she was playing at?

Eshe said, in Nasheenian, "She says Inaya sent her after me. She says she can't go home unless I go with her."

"Tell her to wait in Nasheen then."

"I... Nyx, look at her. I can't send her back alone."

"She bring anyone else with her?"

"No."

Nyx regarded Isabet. In the dim light, he couldn't make out Nyx's exact expression, but whenever she went quiet it meant she was actually thinking something through, weighing her options. It was usually a good thing. Fewer people died.

"She do anything useful?"

"We worked together in the shifter rebellion. Inaya's Fourré. She comes from a rich family. Has a lot of connections."

"In Ras Tieg?"

"Yes."

"We're not going to Ras Tieg."

"No."

Nyx holstered her pistol and started to walk away. "Get rid of her."

"No, wait," Eshe said. "She's not going to give up, Nyx. She's going to keep following us."

"Let her follow."

"She'll die."

"Most of us probably will."

"Then why can't she die with us?"

"Because she's dead weight. I'm not feeding and watering somebody who's just going to end up a body later without giving anything back. You see how easy it was to jump her? We don't need any of that."

"Wait," Eshe said. He searched for something about Isabet that Nyx could understand. You couldn't appeal to morality. One body was very like another, to Nyx.

"She's trustworthy," Eshe said.

"What?"

"I trust her," Eshe said. "Isn't that exactly what we need right now? Somebody we can trust? Fatima's people are just spies, and that Ahmed guy, and the Drucian. We don't know them well. Listen, this girl is smart. She may not seem like much, but she has… she has tact. And she can handle herself when things get bad." He remembered pulling the sack off her head after he killed the priest and seeing the shock on her face when she saw the priest's body. But she hadn't gone to pieces.

Nyx chewed on that awhile. Shook her head.

Fuck, he thought.

Nyx said, "She comes with us, blood's on you. And so's her loyalty. That honey pot turns on us and I'll have you kill her. You understand me?" She reached out, took his chin, the way she had when he was a kid stealing bullets from the hub. She made him look at her. Hard black eyes.

"I understand you," he said.

Nyx walked back to camp.

Eshe went to Isabet. She was packing up her things. Some food, a copy of the Ras Tiegan Good Book stuffed with documents of some sort, and a small camping stove. He thought the documents were a little odd, but didn't say anything.

He crouched beside her. "I have a deal for you," he said. "If you come with us, you need to do everything Nyx says. Everything. Maybe you've heard some stories about her. Maybe you know not everything we do is going to be good. But you do exactly as she says. Do that and when this is all over, I come back to Ras Tieg with you. Deal?"

"Where are you going?"

"We've got to bring in a politician who was kidnapped."

"Sounds easy enough."

"Yeah, well… you've never tried bringing in a bounty with Nyx."

"Bounty?"

"It's not like she's doing it for free."

Isabet sighed and squinted at the eastern horizon, toward Ras Tieg. "What does she want me to do? I have some experience in—"

"Just… do as she says. Trust me on this, Isabet."

"Trust you? Well, I won't go that far. I'm just here to bring you back, as Inaya told me."

"She promise you a raise or something? Better quarters?"

"Michel said I need to prove myself," she said. "It's a test."

It was the stupidest thing he'd ever heard. "You think you're ready for that?"

"Of course," she said, nose turned up, tone haughty.

He picked up her gun. Pointed it at her. Pulled the trigger.

Isabet jumped like a startled lizard.

He handed the gun back to her. "First tip. Get a new gun. As soon as a Ras Tiegan gun gets sand in it, it's useless. They don't work out here."

Isabet's hand was trembling as she took the gun back. "You seemed very certain of that."

"Nyx unloaded it while we were arguing," he said. "If you want to keep up, you'll need to start paying attention."

15.

At the edge of the white desert, a tangled forest of massive insect-tailored mounds littered the undulating landscape for as far as Rhys could see. He paused the thirsty caterpillar in the sand and tried to sense some life or movement from the mounds, but to his senses they were just dead things—relics of some vast termite-like colony that had once thrived here, the woody substances that had once sustained them long lost to dust.

As he led the caterpillar into the shadows of the mounds, he found that the mounds were so tall that they blotted out the sky. He kept the caterpillar headed north, pausing every few minutes to gauge the angle of the sun. In this desert, traveling at night was best, but he had pushed himself to go another hour in the early morning light so he could reach the cairn before he camped. Cairns marked the caravan route, Abhinava had told him, so if he kept moving south from the location of each, he should find water within five or six days from the one before. Abhinava had also shown him the secret to uncovering the wealth of water beneath.

And Rhys had repaid his kindness by running away.

Amid the mounds, Rhys searched for a particular hand-shaped protuberance. He expected it would be something made of the same bug-cemented sand as the rest of the mounds—but no, the hand-shaped figure he found was made of dusty gray stone, seemingly carved from a solid piece. It was twice as tall as Rhys, and half the height of the nearest mound. It stuck up from the now reddish-brown sand as if it had simply been grown there. When he reached out to touch it, expecting the cool, gritty texture of stone, he found instead that it had a subtle give to it, like a live thing—a fungus or lichen.

The cairn was half-buried in the sand to the left of the obelisk, just a tumbledown of rotten stone bound with bug secretions. He climbed off the chariot and knelt at the edge of the cairn. He began removing stones to reach the guardian below. A waft of cool air met his face. It was the most delicious thing he'd felt in days. The sun was already high and hot, and even with the hood of his burnous up, the heat was oppressive. In the darkness beneath the cairn, he sensed the guardian—a wormlike insect as big around as his head, quietly resting in the cool dim. It took a few minutes to find the right combination of pheromones to affect it. When he finally felt it respond and go inert, he carefully reached his water bulb inside. He filled four more and then began replacing the stones.

He raised his head.

Women emerged from the world around him.

They seemed to come up from the sand itself, like Nasheenian women did in his dreams—half a dozen of them, wearing calf-length dhotis, breast-bindings, and heavy turbans the color of fresh blood, that wound about their heads and faces. The ends trailed out behind them like tattered flags. The clothing was the same color of the sand in this part of the desert, as if it had been dipped in blood and left to age in the sun.

The women were nearly the same color, reddish-brown, darker at the knees and elbows. But it was their height that impressed him. They were tall as giants—the tallest rose above him by a full head and shoulders.

Rhys froze. His bullets were deadtech—difficult to replace out here—and he was down to his last four. Two short of what he needed.

"What happens now?" Rhys asked, in Khairian.

The women said nothing.

He began searching for a swarm. He felt something stir beneath his feet. Something large. Not at all the type of thing he wanted to wake up and try to control. But it was there, waiting. A few others clung to the edges of his awareness—fire ants, scarabs, and wilder things, bugs he had no names for but the impressions and scents they used to differentiate themselves from one another.

"I'm employed by a man named Hanife," Rhys said. He knew they had not come for that. Knew they did not care for that. But he had to say it anyway, to everyone he encountered. If the man was as Payam said he was, he would be loved or despised in equal measure. Best to play a bet on finding the man's allies. "He lives north of here. I was separated from my caravan during… a sandstorm."

But the women were unmoved. They stayed still for so long that Rhys wondered if they were truly live things, or a hallucination. He passed his hand in front of his eyes, but the women remained rooted to the spot. Watching.

"I've done nothing wrong," he said. "I just needed water."

The woman nearest him said, in Khairian, "We have come to collect blood debt for Circle Bavaja."

"I'm sorry," Rhys said. "I have no idea what you mean."

"You have defiled one of ours," the woman nearest him said. She was fleshy in the face, soft compared to her taut, lanky body. "You have fed a body to the sand that was not yours to take. We have come to claim vengeance."

Rhys took a deep breath. He flexed his hands, preparing to draw his pistols.

"There has been a mistake," Rhys said. "It was an accident."

"It is not an accident to spill blood. Vengeance must be taken. We are the avengers of the blood."

They moved toward him like a desert wind over hard stone—fast and fierce.

He drew his pistols. He was a fast draw, and a good shot. But he got off only one round. In the next breath, one of the women had his wrist twisted behind him. His pistol was on the ground, and pain screamed up his arm. He fell to his knees and lost his grip on the other pistol. She released him. He let out his breath and shook the pain from his twisted arm.

The women made a circle around him. The fleshy one said, "Your blood debt will be paid, stranger."

"I have nothing to give you," he said.

"You lie about that," she said. "There is always your blood."

"The bodies of our kin lie ten days back at the Rovanish water cairn where you slew them as we came to reclaim that which is ours. Now we have come to collect blood debt for your crime."

"Who are you?" he asked.

"Avengers," the woman said. "We have come to avenge the lives you took."

"There has been some mistake." My God, Rhys thought, I am a thousand miles from Nasheen and they have bloody *bel dames* out here? Would he never be free of them?

"We don't pass judgment. We merely collect," the woman said. "Your fate will be decided by Circle Bavaja."

"And if I don't agree to come with you?"

"You will come with us."

He glanced from one set of dusty desert eyes to another. Their expressions were all shrouded, indecipherable.

He tensed. Then he turned. Tried to break away from their circle.

He wasn't sure where he was going, what he would do. He just needed to get away. Far away. Back to Elahyiah. His family. He meant to put it all right.

Something heavy thudded into his back before he got three paces. He stumbled. Fell. Pain radiated deeply across his lower back. It was like someone had skewered him with a flaming brand.

He tried to claw forward, but the women were already there, one at each elbow. Black pain bit at his consciousness.

"Elahyiah," he said, and that was all.

16.

When Kage dreamed, it was of cool, dark spaces. Soft voices. Walls that hemmed her in, close enough for her to reach out and touch. Comforting. Her perfect world was a smooth crevice at the back of a cave. She knew her way around the dark. For her, the nightmare was the desert. Wide-open, unobstructed views. Big, bold sky.

As the road turned to gravel, then hard-packed sand, it was still dark outside, and comforting. But as the sun rose and the way smoothed out she realized they were headed toward a vast expanse of absolute nothingness. It was like being devoured by some great-mouthed monster with an unfathomable appetite. The desert scrub grass and rocky protrusions quickly became hard-baked brown playa. Flat. Limitless. The vast lavender sky met the brown desert in every direction, as far as she could see. It was terrifying and unsettling. She gripped her gun close. After a time, she found that the most comforting thing she could think to do was stare hard at the seat in front of her.

The first time Kage slept under the open air, she was thirteen and still raw and sore from her blooding the day before. It all started happening at once, for girls, after the blooding.

She slept under the vast sky that night with a handful of other women, all of them older than her, if only by a few years. She felt completely exposed, vulnerable, for the first time in her life. Yes, certainly, she was small, even for someone of her people, but she was fast and limber. She knew where to hide in a fight. Knew exactly where to hit to land the most amount of damage with the least amount of effort. Her mother had taught her that—tricks she picked up from the Nasheenians she watched in the factories.

"When you're old enough," her mother told her, "you will do your time in the factories. Learn Nasheenian. Make enough money to earn the right to a spouse. Perhaps a pair of them."

It was a rite of passage, of sorts, to go out into the factories and return with the goods and currency her people needed to survive. Everyone left, but not everyone came back. It was those who did not come back that made her most nervous. Where did they go? Did the sky eat them? Did they fall into it, explode like stars? Or was it the Nasheenians that ate them?

Now she traveled across a landscape so alien that waking to it each morning gave her vertigo. When Nyx asked her if she was all right as they rode along in the spitting organic contraption they called a bakkie, she half thought to claw open Nyx's face and scream about how the sky was going to eat them. The feeling came over her most at dawn. It was a breathy, oppressive thing. Like holding on to a great flying beast that you knew you could not hold.

"You all right?" Ahmed asked. He sat beside her at the wheel of the bakkie, as unconcerned as the others about the limitless space as the suns came up over the desert.

She nodded, once, and gripped her gun a little tighter.

The bakkie ground to a halt the next day. Sunk deep in the sand. Nyx had them work an hour or so to try and free it. When that didn't work, she told them to unload all they had and start walking. To where, exactly, Kage was not certain. All she cared about was that it was very far from her country, Dei Keiko, the country the Nasheenians called Druce.

Kage raised her head and stared at the unending landscape. She had not anticipated this. What she expected, she wasn't sure. Maybe riding in a bakkie or caravan the whole way. Perhaps taking a series of trains. Or trekking up and about mountains—solid, massive hulks of stone to hide on and within. She had not expected this insecure place.

"Won't we be exposed out here?" she asked softly as she pulled on her pack.

"Caravans are few and far between," Nyx said. "So hitching a ride isn't much of an option, but we might run into one. Bakkie isn't much good anyway. Easier to spot than a group of people in dusty burnouses."

But Kage knew that Nyx was wrong about that. Groups of people were very easy to spot at a distance. What she must have meant was that they no longer presented just two targets. Now they were six—seven counting the Ras Tiegan girl. On foot, it was less likely they would all be taken out at once. The others would serve as decoys, letting Nyx and her boy escape. Kage sometimes wondered if this strange woman knew she was so transparent in her self-preservation.

Ahmed asked Kage to help clean out the bakkie's cistern of bugs. They collected them into jars and packed them away for seasoning up meals later on. It was easy enough work, and she enjoyed crooning to the insects as they worked.

Their newest member, the arrogant little Ras Tiegan girl, was standing behind the second bakkie, hopping from foot to foot on the hot sand. She had not brought proper shoes. She and Eshe were arguing. They had been arguing all week, ever since Nyx pushed the girl into camp and announced she was coming with them. Kage still didn't understand why, and each day they traveled with her, her unease grew. Ras Tiegans were not trustworthy people. She hadn't slept properly since the girl joined them. All her dreams were murky with blood and the ominous purring of Ras Tiegan-talk.

"We're three days out from clan Shafiori territory," the tatty little magician, Eskander, said. Kage had already learned to despise the sound of her voice. "They're a typical Khairian border clan. A little more settled than most, and they take bugs in exchange for water, mostly."

"Mostly?" Nyx said.

"Well..." Eskander said, fiddling with the ornate hilt of her useless pistol. Kage couldn't understand why Eskander's assassin companion let her carry it around as if it were a real weapon. "They take blood and slaves too. But who doesn't really?"

Kage stiffened at the mention of slaves. "What kind of slaves?" she asked.

Eskander seemed to notice her for the first time in days. Her eyes narrowed. "Oh. Not Drucians. Your kind don't last long up here. They mostly prefer Nasheenians and Chenjans, when they can get them. Chenjans get fewer cancers."

"Let's hope we have enough bug power to be persuasive," Nyx said.

“Kage, I might have you hang back when we get close. Just in case we need a quick exit.”

“Oh, they aren’t violent or anything,” Eskander said hurriedly. “They won’t give you any trouble.”

“I’ve known a lot of black market slave dealers,” Nyx said. “They search for weakness. When they find it, they take advantage. I expect these won’t be much different. So we need to have straight spines. That includes you, magician.”

“Of course, of course. Straight as an arrow.”

“When did you last see an arrow?” Ahmed asked.

“We trained with them.” Eskander made a pointing motion with her right hand. “It taught us proper trajectory. Helps with the bug stuff. But surely you went through that training?”

Ahmed shook his head. “I wasn’t that sort of magician.”

“I would not have expected that. Surely you—”

“I’m talked out,” Ahmed said, and started walking.

Kage followed after him. She wasn’t particularly fond of nattering magicians either.

The sun was too high and hot for traveling, but Nyx had them walk in it anyway. Kage kept her hood up and nursed at her water. The Nasheenians hardly drank anything at all, and that worried her. Was she going to be a liability out here, soaking up too much water? She put her water bulb away and resolved not to drink again until they camped.

She put one foot in front of the other, plodding across the sand for hours. Head down. She listened to the others as they chattered for the first few kilometers. The stupid Ras Tiegan girl finally shut up an hour into the walk, out of breath. But Eskander kept talking, always boasting about nothing. To Kage, it was all dull air, but Eshe seemed to be listening to every word both women spit out, even if nobody else had much to say. Khatijah took up the rear of their party, lingering behind often to ensure they weren’t followed.

Ahmed, at least, was steady and quiet, so Kage began to keep pace with him, though he was much taller, with a longer stride.

When Nyx said, “Hold up there. Kage, Ahmed, hold up!” she didn’t know how long they’d been walking. But as she raised her head, she saw that the suns were low in the sky, and a brilliant sunset was melting across the fathomless horizon.

For some reason, though, her feet kept moving, as if of their own volition. It took a great deal of effort to slow, then stop. The world wavered.

"Kage, sight that out for me," Nyx said. She was pointing off to the left of the sunset.

Kage tried to bring her gun out of its holster. It should have been a simple move. Just untie and pull. But her arms felt strange. Like some kind of jelly. Now that she was standing still, she noticed a buzzing in her head, like a low cicada's whine. She managed to close her fingers around the stock of her gun, and worked it out.

But as the gun tugged free, the weight of it pulled her down. She stumbled. The gun was tumbling into the sand. Her stomach clenched. Sand in the gun. It would need cleaning. It would misfire. She went down in the sand with the gun. Clutched it against her. Tried to keep it away from the sand. Her vision blurred, and her tongue felt large in her throat.

"Kage?" Ahmed's face appeared above her. Black spots juddered across her vision.

She moved her mouth, but no sound came out.

"Water!" Ahmed said. It sounded like water.

But the world was going blissfully black now. Black as her warm little cave at home. It was strange how you didn't realize how much you loved a place until you had lost it so completely. Everyone believed the world outside was better. But it wasn't. It never was. If things had gone differently, she would be home now. Curled up in the dark, wrapped close with her loved ones, with her children. It was near the Festival of the Ancestors now. She would be walking down into the bowels of the world with her family, carrying bug lights and singing old songs about death, rebirth, and new worlds. They would tread softly down into the murk, and through the doors of the re-spun wreck of their star carrier. They would light lamps at the base of their ancestors' rotting metal coffins, their bones long since turned to dust by the strange bacteria of this world. What was left of their people was what the few survivors could patch and piece together from the still-living tissue of those who had died in the descent. Shot out of the sky, abandoned by their own ancestors, denied the world they were promised, this was their purgatory. They had subsisted on thin hope, these many centuries, the same thin hope that sustained her now. As the world went dark, she felt her mind float up and away. It was lovely. She hoped this was death, that she was finally ascending to the world they were promised each year in the guts of the dead starship—the world that lay on the other side of the eternal blackness of Umayma's western sky. The world they had been forever denied.

She woke to a splash of cool water, and a dusky blue sunset.

Eshe and Eskander leaned over her, their faces blotting out the bruised sky.

"She's awake," Eskander said.

Kage averted her gaze from their faces, and looked past them, into the dusk.

"Keep drinking," Eshe said, and pressed a water bulb to her mouth.

She drank. It tasted good… but not as good as the darkness.

After a time, she was able to sit up. She saw Ahmed sitting just behind Eshe, and a flickering fire-beetle blaze popping a few paces away.

Eskander yelled at Nyx, "She's fine, little maggot. Just dehydrated."

Kage reached about for her gun, and felt a rising panic when she could not find it. "Where is it?" she asked.

Eshe and Ahmed exchanged a glance.

"It's here," Ahmed said. He reached behind him and handed her gun back to her. "Nyx needed to get the position on some movement southwest of here. She needed to use your scope."

Kage pulled the gun close. It would need to be cleaned.

Eshe brought over a thin gruel of mealworms and gravy that made her gag, but she choked it all down. The world was jumping back into focus. The fear began to set in. She had been unconscious, totally vulnerable, with these people. She stood and walked farther away from the fire, though the air was cool, almost cold.

"Where are you going?" Ahmed asked.

"I need to clean my gun." She dragged her gun and her pack as far away from the camp as possible, deep into the black. She found an outcrop of stone a dozen paces distant. She crouched behind it. Removed all her clothes. Rubbed herself with sand until her skin burned. Shivering, her skin tingling, she dressed herself once again and then sat down to clean her gun.

How long this all took, she wasn't certain, but as she was beginning to put the gun back together, she heard heavy footsteps approach. She turned to see Nyx coming up behind her. She froze in the middle of locking her scope to the barrel, fingers still.

Nyx paused a few steps behind her. She was chewing sen. Kage could smell it. The old mercenary just stood there for several minutes. Chewing.

Kage did not move. Did not speak. It was easy, to wait out Nasheenians.

"You need water, you ask for it," Nyx said.

Kage firmed her mouth. Saying anything at all risked exposing weakness.

"You heard me?" Nyx asked.

Kage nodded, once. Then realized the Nasheenian would not be able to see her, in the dark. Not like one of her people.

"I understand you," Kage said.

"I have too much at risk here. If you can't take care of yourself, then I'll stake you out on the sand and leave you. You understand that, too?"

"Yes, master."

"I'm not your fucking master."

Kage gritted her teeth. The words bubbled up, something fearless, from the darkness. "You say you are not my master, but you threaten me with violence for not complying to your will. What else is that, but the act of a master over a slave?"

Nyx was quiet a long moment, chewing. Then, "You could shoot me here. Any of you could. Hardly slavery when I arm you, is it?"

"Then why threaten me?"

"So you know I'm serious."

"I don't understand."

"Listen, kid. I'm here to bring in a man alive, and if we do this right, we save a lot of people from dying. I have to sacrifice a few people to save a lot, I can do that. That's what I am. I don't like it. I don't want to kill anybody I don't have to. But when I say I need your scope, I need your vision, I need your talent, you have to deliver. Pretending you're invincible doesn't help me. Being fucked up is fine so long as you compensate for it. You have to carry extra water, that's fine. But don't lie to me. Don't pretend to be something you aren't."

Kage flexed her fingers. Took a deep breath. "I will carry more water," she said.

"Good." Nyx threw her a water bulb. "Start with that."

She heard Nyx turn away and start back into camp. Kage looked back at her. "Was there a danger? Did you see anyone through the scope?"

"We have some folks on our tail," Nyx said. "Don't seem like bel dames to me. Mercenaries of some sort. Ahmed's eyes are good, but not as good as yours. They melted back into the desert when they saw the gun—yours is kinda hard to miss with a scope that reflects light like that—but they weren't just traders. Not enough gear for that. Not dressed like Khairians, either."

"What were they dressed like?"

Nyx spit on the sand. "Drucians," she said, and started walking away.

Kage turned back to her gun. Ran her fingers across the smooth metal of the stock. Did she know? Or just suspect? And if the time came, would she cut up Kage and leave her out on the sand for them after all, despite her good sight? *I have to stay useful*, Kage thought. If she failed again, her chances of surviving to the other side of this wretched place—and her freedom—were slim.

She took the water bulb and packed it away with the others. If she wanted to stop the men who hunted her, she would need to turn around and hunt them herself, or hope she and Nyx could lose them at the next settlement. Whatever she decided, it would be a risk—Nyx or the *fukushu-sha*.

The *fukushu-sha* she knew, would kill her now, but it was Nyx she feared in the long run. She was only as valuable to Nyx as she was useful, and she feared her use would run out once they freed their quarry.

Staying with Nyx kept her alive a few days longer. Turning back meant death within the day.

She hoped only that she would not regret choosing to live.

17.

"They've asked for a letter."

"A letter? Why?"

Inaya stood over the table slide in the communications room, sending data to her eight cell leaders. It had taken her three years to switch from a regular com console to a slide. She still preferred the more refined manipulation of the com console, but Michel had insisted that though a slide was less secure, more of their operatives were familiar with the slide technology. Receiving and storing data sent by the bacteria on her slide to their portable ones also took longer, and it gave a permanent record of communications that made her nervous. It was why she kept a regular com console in the next room, for more sensitive information.

Michel stood now in the doorway to the communications room. It was early, far too early for him to be up. Only the cook was awake at this hour. Inaya could smell grilled meat.

"I am uncertain," Michel said. "They have become skittish since the death of the last priest, and I fear they no longer trust me. I am hopeful that a few words in your hand will calm them."

"Perhaps I should call them," Inaya said. She had been the first to get the Savoie family's financial backing for the Fourré, despite Michel's many attempts. To be fair, it was only when she made the trip with Isabet at her side that she finally won them over. It was not a good time to lose them.

"Their former pattern has been purchased by a protein farm in Clairie.

I fear I do not have their new pattern," Michel said.

"I will need some time. I have other things to attend to, but I will have a letter for you tonight. Are you delivering it personally?"

"Of course."

"Fine, then." She turned away, dismissing him, but he lingered a moment longer in the door. Just as his gaze began to discomfit her, he retreated into the hall. His behavior was becoming increasingly disturbing of late, but she was uncertain what to do about it. To cut him loose risked making a grave enemy. The best she had been able to manage was to give him less critical duties, and cut him out of key decisions. But Michel was a prideful man, and not a stupid one. It would not be long before he confronted her more forcefully about his place in the Fourré. She needed to be ready.

Inaya spent the remainder of the morning debriefing with the primary contact for the six cells in Ras Tieg's capital, Montmare. She saw him only four times a year, and even those visits were risky. Just eight individuals were ultimately responsible for the organization's work. Any of the eight could identify her if she did not wear a glamour. She trusted these men and women as if they were family, but like family, there were rifts—disagreements.

Hynri sat with her in the shuttered office of the abandoned textile mill that rested above the organization's central operations. He was a slim young man, just twenty-five, but he held himself like a man much older, cynical of the world.

"They call us terrorists," he said.

"Of course they do. It's why we must stay away from civilian targets. We are already feared and hated. People must see the good we do," Inaya said.

"We have tried that for generations," he said. "People see what shifters have to contribute. They choose to murder and enslave us all for it. You asked us to act out violently and now you want to rein us in? I don't understand."

"You will. We have gained their attention. Now we must hold it. Twist it. We must rewrite our story from one of fear to one of celebration. When you discovered you were a shifter, what did you do?"

"I wanted to kill myself, to be honest."

"And you never told anyone what you were."

He shook his head. "I joined the Fourré just a few months later. My family never found out."

Inaya leaned toward him. "We have a narrative in this country that shifters are in the minority. That we are some statistical anomaly. But my mother and I, we lived for many years without anyone knowing what we were. If we all admitted to what we are, how many shifters do you think would be revealed? I don't believe men and women want to kill their children. I believe we want what is best for them. When the priests come for children, and not just those who are not careful, I think we will see a change."

"You propose to turn over the nation's children to the priests?"

"No. There is something more than violence that Nasheenians taught me, and that is the awful brutality of speaking absolute truth. I propose that we begin to unmask ourselves. We speak the truth of ourselves. We tell them just how many of us there are."

"They will see us as an even bigger threat."

"Will they? Or will they simply see that they are condemning their own sons and daughters, mothers and fathers? We can show them another future."

"What future? Us? *Our* lives? Our lives are not glamorous, Madame."

"Aren't they? I know many shifters, not just those in the movement. They have families. Husbands and wives. Sons and daughters. They live respectably."

"And covertly."

"It is our obligation to convince them to live otherwise."

"They'll be killed. I have seen it happen, Madame."

"Some may die," Inaya conceded. "But many are dying already."

"Blood will run through the streets. I see genocide, Madame. I see it as plainly as I see you."

Inaya placed her hand on his. His hand was cool. She saw the terror in his face. These were men and women who had killed for her, and for themselves. They risked death and dismemberment each day in the fulfillment of their duties for the Fourré. Yet here they were, in shocked terror at the idea of doing the one thing that may set them free: speak the truth of what they were.

"There will be a great many of us. The priests can stop a rill, but they cannot stop a river. We must show them our true numbers. Our true strength," she said.

His eyes filled with tears. He pulled his hand away and he wept openly in front of her, like a child or a priest. He was so young—nearly the same age she had been when she fled Ras Tieg, terrified and newly pregnant, running toward an uncertain future that, she believed, held nothing but death and dishonor.

"You tell us to be brave," he said. "You tell us not to be violent, but I heard about the murdered priests."

"It was a rogue act. The boy is no longer part of the organization. It will not happen again. We will not tolerate further violence."

"I don't want things to go back to what they were. We lived in so much fear before you came to us, Madame. So much terror. You showed us we have power. Now you want to take it away."

"No. I want to give you real power. Lasting power. Violence is a not a true tenet of our faith."

"The priests would say otherwise."

"I am not a priest."

He grinned through his tears, and wiped his face with his sleeve. "No, you are not."

"Come, now. You had faith and trust in me five years ago. We have come far since then. Now it is time for our final act. It is time to take our place in Ras Tiegan society as true equals. You must have faith, Hynri."

He touched his breast, the space between his ribs where she guessed a saint's pendant hung. "I will trust it, Madame. But the others… I don't know how successful I'll be."

"In three weeks' time, we will be holding an event."

She saw his eyes widen. "Event" was the euphemism they used for some violent act—a bombing or kidnapping or raid.

"I will be asking all of our cells to reveal themselves. And all of their shifter allies. We will walk onto our streets, and we will shift. Together. We must show them how many we truly are."

"They will murder us, Madame."

"They may. They may murder a good many of us. But we cannot go on as we are."

If they went on as they were, it would all end in blood. She could see a bloody civil war, a revolution, on the horizon, and she had seen enough bloody revolutions.

They spoke for a few minutes more, and she ensured that he was calm and composed when he left her office. This evening, she would speak to three more cell leaders like this one. Softly, carefully, she would share this same message. And each time she said it, she had to believe in it just a little bit more. Because if her own faith wavered they would know it. And it would all come undone.

Inaya rose from her seat and stretched.

"Madame?" A knock at the door.

"Yes?"

Adeliz cracked the door and peered in, revealing only her face, as if seeking to present a smaller target. "I have a missive for you, Madame. Michel has asked to meet you."

"Where?"

Adeliz held out her hand.

Inaya pressed her palm to Adeliz's. When she pulled it away, she could see a faint line of characters, encoded in her and Michel's ciphered script. It read:

Meeting urgent. Cannot return without being compromised. I have found the girl. Saint Affia.

"Thank you," Inaya said to Adeliz, and quickly excused herself to her room to dress.

As a rule, she did not like to leave the sanctuary of their quarters often, but Isabet's identity was of such extreme importance that she trusted none but Michel and her secondary general in the capital, Gabrielle, with the information.

She slipped out into the cool night, grateful for air that did not stink of wet dog and roasted meat. The sweet air lasted only until she cleared the warehousing district, and then the powerful stench of curry mixed with open sewer became nauseating. Some day she would retire to the country, with enough wealth to fund a filter that kept out the worst of the wild contaminants. She had visited a farm once belonging to an uncle, and reveled in the vast greenery, the open spaces. Clear water and knee-high grass spoke to her of some childhood she never had.

The statue of Saint Affia lay on the other side of the city square. This time of the evening, a few families were still out, some making prayers and pledges to the four-dozen saints given niches in and around the city center. Affia was a little-loved saint, known for just four miracles and reviled by some revisionists as a fraud. Every decade, some group of priests petitioned to have her sainthood revoked. Yet here she stood, defiant in her niche.

As Inaya approached, she saw that no one had lit candles at the saint's feet, and the restaurant opposite was already closed and dark. She hesitated in the alley, watching the shadows for movement. Seeing no one, she approached the saint and knelt. Sometimes Michel left notes beneath the feet of the saint, though she felt that Isabet's whereabouts would be too sensitive to leave to writing. Meeting in person made more sense. She closed her eyes and left a prayer with Affia, saint of travelers and wayward souls. She prayed for Isabet's safety. And Eshe's. She was not so callous that she did not think of him.

She heard the sound of a vehicle approaching, and started. The streets here were narrow, generally only traveled by sleds. But the sound she heard was distinctively that of a popping and hissing bakkie rolling across the cobbles.

Inaya stood. Turned.

Six men were leaping from a still-rolling bakkie. They wore black cowls.

Fear knotted her stomach. She turned and ran in the opposite direction, up the street and past the restaurant.

She turned down the first alley she saw. But another bakkie was barreling toward her, seeking to cut her off. She doubled back. The alley didn't go through to the other side of the street.

The six men behind her were gaining. She saw more leap out of the second bakkie.

Inaya looked up. Her skin rippled. She prepared to unmake herself.

Something pounded into her gut. She flew backward, landed hard on her seat, and knocked her head against the paving. Her vision swam. She clutched at her gut, thinking she'd been shot. But no, she was still whole. Instead, her hands came away coated in some sticky substance that smelled distinctly of saffron.

Oh, God.

Inaya clawed her way up. Her head spun. She heard their boots on the cobbles. She released her hold on her body's form, set it free.

Her skin prickled. She shivered. But she remained in her form. Imprisoned.

The stink of the saffron filled her senses. Saffron prevented shifters from making the change. She had known that, but never experienced it herself. It was terrifying. She scrambled forward, searching for a way out.

Another bakkie popped toward her, this time coming from the road ahead. The forward lights blinded her. She covered her eyes.

The men put their hands on her. She screamed. Screamed and screamed.

She carried no weapons. Why would she? She was a shifter, a mutant shifter, with the ability to be and become whatever she wanted. Unless someone knew what she was—unless they brought saffron with them, and incapacitated her with it before she could shift—she was untouchable.

But now—she was nothing. Just this. Just another woman. Another thing.

They slipped the bag over her head.

She could not stop screaming.

18.

The desert was so hot it ate the spit from stones. Nyx figured they had a day or two on the mercenaries—or whatever they were—maybe more if she could get Kage to push harder. Eshe and Ahmed had a mind to stay behind and simply shoot them, but Nyx didn't know enough about who had hired them to take the risk. Best guess was it was the Families funding them, and mercenaries—especially Drucian ones—who dealt with the Families were a whole other sort entirely. Families didn't muddy their business with bel dames, and no order keeper would agree to do work out here at the ass-end of nowhere. So that left mercenaries and bounty hunters, and not the kind who worked out of the Cage back in Punjai. Drucians were notoriously good at stalking people at night, and like Kage, most had great eyesight. If these two knew how to shoot like she did, though, Nyx expected they'd all be dead.

Nyx spent most of the long, dusky nights and mid-morning marches gnawing over her new team like a cat at a bone, watching what they ate, how they slept, where their eyes roamed. It was Ahmed she hoped to catch by watching his eyes, but he stared only ahead, always ahead, scanning the horizon for… what? Well, she knew, didn't she? Bursts, enemy soldiers, sand vehicles, giant bugs, and maybe something worse, something more personal. The way Ahmed watched the horizon and slept with his back turned away from the fire each night made her wonder just what it was he expected to find there. Most boys she knew who got shoved home without proper decompression time blew right the fuck up. They jumped off bridges or walked naked into deserts or picked off people in the market with some patched-together weapon. He made her uneasy.

By the time they made camp, it was full dark already, and cold, but they were running low on fire beetles. It wasn't cold enough to waste what was left.

"Three more days?" Ahmed asked as he took his rations from Nyx. As usual, he didn't meet her eye. It was getting old. His averted gaze made him seem like some kind of house boy, or—worse—Kage.

"How far out are we from the next post?" Nyx asked Eskander.

Eskander was gazing back the way they had come, her face perplexed, as if she had dropped something along the way. "Maybe longer than three days," she said.

Nyx followed her stare, squinted. Whatever she saw there, Nyx wasn't privy to it. "That's the wrong way," Nyx said.

Eskander turned, frowned. "Yes, I know. It's just… I thought I saw a light out there."

"Lot of strange things in the desert," Ahmed said.

"Eshe," Nyx said, "you see anything out there? Our mercenaries show up again?"

Eshe stood and peered into the darkness. Khatijah joined him. The sky was only getting darker the farther north they went, and the moons were tracking lower in the sky.

"Might be something," Eshe said. "Specs?"

She dug a pair out of her pack and tossed them over. Eshe donned the specs. If he still couldn't see anything, she'd call Kage over.

"Looks like two… three people. Hard to say who they are. Just burnouses. Pretty standard."

"How are they walking?" Drucians had a peculiar gait.

She saw him chew at his lip. A new thing, that. She didn't like it—appeared too much like indecision.

"There are a good number of nomads up here," Eskander said. "If I had to bet, I'd say it was some of their scouts. We must have lost those mercenaries by now."

"Eshe?" Nyx said.

"They're heading northwest now. If we just lie low, we should miss them."

"Then let's do that. Huddle up. Eshe, keep an eye on them. I want you to take first watch tonight. I'll do second."

"I can do second," Ahmed said.

"I didn't ask your opinion," Nyx said. He had been volunteering for quite a few watches, as of late.

Nyx bedded down with the others. They kept their circle pretty tight. She didn't want anyone wandering off or conspiring after dark. The circle let her keep an eye on all of them at once.

Most nights, Nyx didn't think she was going to sleep, not until her head hit the sand and the world bled away like some bad dream.

When she finally put her head down, she was out.

Sleep was like water, which was a good thing, because Nyx couldn't seem to find enough of it. Nyx dreamt often of water—vast pools of water so cold and clear that she could see the ruins of old cities there. They always seemed close enough to touch, even though she knew they must have been thousands and thousands of strokes away.

Dreams were her only escape out here, so when she started awake some time later, she resented the intrusion. She glanced around to see what woke her, but the camp was quiet. She counted every bed, and all were accounted for but Eshe's. When she turned, she saw him standing three paces away on top of the sandy ruin of some kind of massive container, peering into the night.

"Eshe?" she said. "You see something?"

"I'm… not sure. Did you hear something?"

"Fuck, kid, am I on watch or are you?"

She slipped out of her bedroll and joined him on the rise. What she saw not a hundred paces distant was something she couldn't quite wrap her head around.

She had heard things about wild beasts in the north—something besides bugs and cats and shape-shifting dogs, parrots, ravens, and even the elusive foxes. What kid hadn't? But when you got old, got out into the world, you generally came to realize that all those stories were just junk your mothers told you to keep you from wandering around in the desert after dark. She had been a farmer's kid. Encouraging children to stay within the confines of the irrigated land and brushy thorn fences and windbreaks meant keeping them alive another season. Plenty of kids got hauled off to war or indentured servitude on the interior back then. Those stories were scarier than animals, so wild animals made the best children's stories. She heard a lot about vicious desert beasts with massive talons and tails and thorny ridges and poison mucus.

But you never really expected to *see* any. Not really.

"What the fuck *is* that?" Nyx said.

"I have no idea," Eshe said, "but there are at least six or eight of them… and they're coming this way."

"Up!" Nyx yelled back at the camp as she drew her sword. "We've got incoming!"

The whole team—all but Eshe's Ras Tiegan—were up and armed in less than sixty seconds. Nyx had about three seconds more to appreciate that fact before the first of the things hurled itself into camp.

It was some kind of animal. That's about all she could say about it with any certainty. If it was a dog, it wasn't like any dog she had ever seen. Matted dreadlocks covered the face and hooked snout, and fell in a long, jagged frill along its spine. The paws were big as a cat's, and clawed, visibly clawed—

The tail swept out behind it, thick as a table leg, knobbed at the end with a spiky protrusion that looked like something on a thorn beetle. It must have been about the size of a sand cat, which meant the head was as wide as Nyx's chest.

What the fuck did a thing like that eat?

You, Nyx thought as it came at her.

She swept her blade low and pivoted right.

Three more of the things barreled past her, snarling and grunting like a pack of mutant cats. Maybe that's really all they are, she thought, but that thought was short lived as the one snarling at her lashed out a forked tongue that slapped the back of her hand, leaving a long trail of stinging mucus.

Fantastic.

She tossed her blade into her other hand and jabbed at its head. But the more she jabbed in the dark, the more she realized the regular vulnerable spots just weren't effective. It was like her sword hit some kind of cured leather or bony scale every time. In frustration, she swung at the thing's legs. It howled and fell. The joints at the knees were weaker than the rest.

"Go for the legs!" Nyx yelled. Beside her, Ahmed and Kage were emptying rounds into one of the beasts, already broken, as it tried to crawl toward them on its good front legs.

Someone was screaming.

Nyx turned.

Isabet, the bloody fucking Ras Tiegan, had an arm down the throat of one of the things. It had clamped down hard, and now her arm was buried to the elbow. She shrieked and gouged at its eyes with her other hand.

Eshe leapt forward, trying to find some purchase with his knife, but these weren't the sort of animals you wanted to use knives on.

Nyx pulled her scattergun. She walked right up to the thing's face, and pulled the trigger.

Isabet screamed again. As the animal flopped back, she went with it, arm still locked in its mouth.

But someone was still screaming.

Nyx made a full turn, trying to find out where it was coming from.

"There!" Ahmed said. He bolted past her, drawn by something she couldn't make out in all the darkness. She followed after him.

They converged on a snarling mass of flesh. Two of the animals were locked in a struggle with Khatijah. Her left hand was already a mangled wreck, and she was missing a vital chunk of her left leg. Nyx watched her bleeding out on the sand while Eskander wailed from her perch on a narrow wedge of rock sticking out from the sand, just large enough for one person to evade the snarling animals.

Nyx and Ahmed unloaded more bullets into the things. The beasts turned their rage just in time for Kage to finish them off from ten paces away. The monstrous bang of her big gun was the best sound Nyx had heard all night.

Khatijah succumbed then, crumpling.

Eskander slithered down from the rock, screaming, still screaming. Sweet fuck, why was she fucking screaming so goddamn much?

"Don't let her die!" Eskander cried. "Please, please!" She turned a tear-streaked face to Ahmed, and in that moment she appeared much younger than Nyx had first guessed. What was she? Nineteen? Twenty? "Please."

"She's bleeding out," Nyx said. "Call a swarm or something."

Eskander's shoulders shook. She grabbed Khatijah and hugged her limp body to her—blood, sand, sweat, and all.

Nyx saw Khatijah's eyes going glassy. Cool, black fog. She knew that feeling. She had been there before. Something inside Nyx clenched hard. Her gut roiled.

"I'm not that kind of magician," Ahmed said softly.

"Oh, for fuck's sake, is anybody going to *try*?" Nyx said.

Isabet ran up to them. She had what remained of her mangled arm tucked up against her body. She pulled the scarf from her neck with her good hand. With Ahmed's help, she knotted it around Khatijah's upper thigh, though Nyx knew it was far too late for that.

Nyx weighed her next words. Khatijah's body was limp, but her blood had stopped pumping out. Nyx thought that was odd. Lot of blood, when you clipped that artery in the leg. Then she realized the bug in Khatijah's head—the one that sustained every bel dame for a few hours after technical death—must have kicked in.

Eskander was sobbing so hard she was choking now. Nyx found it a little embarrassing.

Isabet told Ahmed something in Ras Tiegan.

Eshe yelled something at Isabet. She yelled back.

"What the fuck is going on?" Nyx said.

Ahmed said, "Isabet wants me to pass her blood into Khatijah."

"We don't have the bugs for that, do we?"

"No, but Khatijah has a bug in her head, like any bel dame. Her body just shut itself down. She'll be in stasis for, what? A couple days?" Ahmed said.

"You ever brought a bel dame back before?" Nyx said. She wasn't so sure she wanted to bring the bel dame back, even if he could.

Ahmed shook his head. "I'm a torturer, not a healer."

Nyx appreciated the honesty. She watched Eskander holding the mangled body of her sister. It was like seeing something happen from a great height—something that happened to some alien thing outside herself. If she thought about it too hard, she would remember her own sister's body, cold and lifeless in a tub full of blood.

"She can't die!" Eskander said. "Please save my sister. She's a bel dame. Bel dames don't die. I know you can bring her back."

"Then you fix her," Nyx said.

"I told her," Eskander wailed. "I told her to bring a real magician. I'm just a com tech. But she wanted to bring me. She said she needed someone she could trust. Now look where we are!"

Nyx holstered her scattergun. Yelled back at Kage, "You and Eshe do a perimeter sweep. Make sure there aren't more of those fuckers out there."

Kage nodded and darted off.

Eshe said something to Isabet. She ignored him.

"Can you do it or not?" Nyx asked. Eskander cradled her sister's head. Nyx's chest hurt. She fucking hated feeling things. What the fuck did she care for one more dead bel dame?

"The Ras Tiegan says she knows how to do it," Ahmed said.

"She a magician?"

"No," Eshe said, finally, in Nasheenian. "She says she worked for someone with a bug, once, like a bel dame. She says she brought her back."

"That makes no sense," Nyx said.

"I've heard of it," Eshe said. "Ras Tieg's living saints use them."

Nyx wondered just how much Eshe didn't know about his little Ras Tiegan friend. But she had weighed her options, and made up her mind. "Do what you need to do, then. I'm running a sweep with Kage. Eshe, you too. Let them do what they can."

Eshe yanked his knife back out and went after Kage to make sure there were no more beasts prowling in the dark.

Nyx watched as Ahmed called a swarm of flesh beetles. Khatijah's body spasmed. Nyx had to turn away then. She considered saying something grimly optimistic, but then her gaze fell on Isabet's ravaged arm, and she decided against it.

"When you're done, see what you can do for that stupid white girl," Nyx said. "I don't mind if she loses the arm. If she's got experience running around with minor Ras Tiegan gods, she might prove useful later."

✚

When the blue dawn came, Eshe was positioned on a squat pillar overlooking the camp, watching Isabet get her arm hacked off. Ahmed had the sense to drug her first, which Eshe appreciated, because he didn't want to hold her down. She was screaming when they put her down, though. She knew what was coming. He tried not to care.

He didn't do a good job of it.

Eshe got up when they were through and squatted beside her. She was laid out on a burnous, her left arm taken off at the elbow. A swarm of flesh beetles busied themselves beneath the bandages on her stump. He wanted to tell Isabet to turn back now, and keep walking, alone. But now that Nyx saw something useful in her, changing his mind about Isabet would be a harder sell without telling Nyx a lot more about his business in Ras Tieg than he wanted.

Eskander and Ahmed argued a few paces away over Khatijah's body. She had a pulse now, but not much else. Eshe half hoped she wouldn't wake up either. Some part of him expected it would just be him and Nyx at the end.

It was about to get hot. He could already feel his flesh warming, recovering from the deep evening chill

"Are you angry with me?" Isabet said.

He glanced down at her. Her eyes were gummy with sand and mucus. Her hair was tangled. He looked away and stared off into the distance, watching the second sun break over the horizon, turn the world bloody violet.

"You worked for Genevieve Leichner, didn't you? The living saint in Inoublie," he said.

"Yes," she said. "It's a little more complicated than that, but… yes."

"You were one of the virgins tasked with keeping her alive. She lives on your blood, right?"

"She does live on blood, and… replacement organs. But I wasn't exactly one of her servants."

"We've saved a fair number of women from Genevieve. You know she wants to die, right? It's the priests who keep sacrificing you all to her."

"I know. I'm sorry I didn't tell you sooner, but Inaya didn't want me to tell anyone who I was."

"Why does it matter? Some organic fodder for one of the saints. There's plenty more where that came from."

"I'm… I'm a bit more than that, I'm afraid."

"I'm sure this is good."

"I'm her daughter. She's paralyzed now, you know. She speaks directly to God, but since the stroke she speaks through me. She advises a good many people, Eshe. Priests, magistrates…. Even the Patron himself once came for advice."

"If all that's true, Inaya wouldn't have sent you here. She'd have kept you under a rock in Ras Tieg."

"I... It's just all very complicated, Eshe." She half-reached for her left arm with her right, then hesitated. Rested her fingers on her belly. Gazed long at them.

"Let me tell you about something complicated," Eshe said. He had seen enough mangled people. Why should he have any sympathy for her? "My first partner was a woman named Corinne. She wasn't a shifter, but her sister was. So she joined up with us. Thing was, she was pretty enough to catch a priest's eye. One of the ones who worked for your mother. They took Corinne one day, at the market. I wasn't even there. Heard about it later. I tracked her down. Killed a lot of people to do it. When I told Inaya where she was, Inaya sat on that information for three weeks. Why? Because she was with Genevieve Leichner, the living fucking saint. Your fucking mother." Eshe snorted. "I can't believe Inaya put me with you."

"It's not my fault that—"

"I'm not finished. Inaya never mounted any kind of raid. Never bothered to try and help her. The living saint was too important to piss off, she said. She said we needed her on our side."

"My mother could be a powerful ally for the movement. I won't pretend—"

"Can you shut up for five seconds?"

"Sorry."

"Corinne is dead," Eshe said.

"I don't understand."

"See, you Ras Tiegans have this thing about being a virgin. Especially women. And especially those serving a living saint."

Isabet seemed uncomfortable, finally, with more than the passing haze of the drugs. "Eshe—"

"Corinne wasn't a virgin. So they didn't need her. And they killed her. I never saw the body, but I know."

"Eshe, you have to understand—"

"I understand everything I need to," Eshe said. "You thought it would be fun, running off into the desert, because you're so bloody fucking special where you come from. Well, I have news for you, Isabet. Out here, you're nobody special."

"I know," Isabet said, and now she raised the stump of her arm. Her breath caught, and she choked on a sob. Squeezed her eyes shut.

"You'll live," Eshe said. "Just like your bloody-minded mother."

"You're one to talk about bloody-minded mothers."

Eshe stood. He saw Eskander slipping under Khatijah's burnous, wrapping her arms around her sister, and felt some lingering moment of loss, or maybe regret. Was he broken the way Nyx was? Would he ever be able to trust anyone the way Eskander did?

"Eshe?"

He sighed. "What?"

"I'm sorry I disappointed you."

"It's just the way things are," Eshe said, and went off to scour the blood from his hands.

19.

Rhys woke to terrible heat. His throat was dusty, and his tongue felt swollen—three sizes too big. He tried to open his eyes, but the lids were caked in sand and mucus. Unfamiliar voices babbled around him. And there was some other sound droning on in the background—like the sigh of a ceaseless wind.

He tried to lift his hands to his face, and found that they were unbound for the first time in many days. He wiped the grit from his eyes and sat up in a pool of gray sand ringed in stone. He gazed beyond the ring and into a blinding, bustling desert city.

But it wasn't a living city. Not one where humans lived, anyway. The rough and tumble ruins of the city were swarming with bugs. Bugs eating, nesting, excreting; rebuilding the city in their own image, for their own ends. Reclaiming it.

Octagonal towers of azure sand and rubble, thirty meters high, rose from the ruins and glittered like the backs of jeweled beetles. Any sane man would have guessed the towers were human made, but Rhys knew better. The flawless geometry of the towers had come from the insects. What kind of insect they were, he had no idea. They were massive, winged things, large as his head, with giant mandibles as long as his fingers. They swarmed the ruins like a pack of industrious dogs, occasionally hopping from the height of the towers and gliding to the ground on their broad, glossy wings.

His captors stood a few paces distant, at the edge of the gray stone circle. The women kept their heads and faces covered, more for protection for their lungs than modesty—he had seen more of their bodies during their trek across the blasted wasteland than he believed any but a Nasheenian would freely offer to a stranger's eyes.

Now they spoke in low tones to a small caravan. The man at the front was young, the same color as the women, and tall as they were, with the same weathered skin and eroded features. It was as if the wind had worn away their very faces. Generally, these desert people had wide, flat noses like Ras Tiegans, and flat foreheads, teardrop-shaped mouths, and very narrow, almond-shaped eyes that reminded him of an alien he had seen once from New Kinaan. In his many days—weeks?—traveling with these women, he had also discovered that they prayed almost constantly. When they camped each night, the first on watch would take up the prayer, so there was always someone in the group muttering the litany. Most of it made little sense to him. He recognized traces of the prayer language. If he closed his eyes, he could pretend it was the true language of prayer—perhaps the way it first sounded in his youth, before he understood it—something he felt he should know intimately but couldn't quite make out.

The man they spoke to wore a long red dhoti and leather baldric bristling with weapons. Behind him were two chariots that appeared to be harnessed to a dozen massive green beetles, their jeweled carapaces sparkling in the sun. The beetles' humped backs were waist high, their mandibles tall as Rhys's knee—the perfect height for cutting off a man's leg. The chariots were manned by soldiers in expensive black organic slicks and frilled turbans that gave them another hand of height. These men were paler than the others, but only just. He supposed they could easily have been the richer strata of this society, kept paler and smooth behind filters, like the First Families of Nasheen, but he doubted it. They didn't seem native to the desert.

The chariots flanked a more… unconventional craft. It was a little like an open-air bakkie hung with prayer wheels, only instead of tires, the frame was buoyed by what must have been several million ants, each as large as Rhys's thumb. They had to have a nest within the vehicle's primary cistern. Perhaps it bred its own replacements? Ants and bees were especially easy to tailor for conducting specific tasks. They lived and died according to the instructions they received from complex chemical compounds. Rhys supposed it wasn't much of a stretch to replace a bakkie's expensive semi-organic tire structure with a more durable, cheaper alternative that wouldn't get buried in the sand. Still, the sheer skill it must have taken a magician to create these kinds of insects—strong and pliable enough to reliably carry a vehicle and its inhabitants across shifting sand—was extraordinary. He wanted to meet the magician who'd done it.

There were two men in the vehicle—the driver and the man who was obviously in charge. He was a pale man like the charioteers, and at that awkward age where the muscular build of his youth had begun to thicken as he entered his middling years. A wiry beard hid much of his expression.

Behind the caravan, another ten men in dhotis and baldrics stood stiffly in the sweltering heat. Rhys wondered why they hadn't passed out yet. And why in the world his captors wanted anything to do with these people.

The man in the vehicle gestured at Rhys's captors, motioning for them to come forward.

One of the women closest to Rhys bent over and took hold of the front of Rhys's robe. Apparently it wasn't the women the man wanted a closer look at. It was him.

Rhys did not have the strength to struggle. He had been thirsty so long he forgot what it was to live without dreaming of water. The rations the women kept him on were barely enough to sustain a colony of dragonfly nymphs.

The woman hauled him up to the side of the vehicle. This close, Rhys could sense the pheromones that directed the ants, and some underlying stink that told him the vehicle was even more fully organic than he suspected. Was it made entirely of bug secretions? Molded by what type of insect? It was a massive, specialized job that would have taken years back in Nasheen.

The large man leaned toward him, and sniffed a little. He was younger than Rhys suspected—not even thirty. The lines at the corners of his eyes were deceiving. It must have been the desert. Did they have filters out here? He had yet to see one, but he couldn't imagine that any society that could build this vehicle didn't have effective filters.

The man said something to him. Like the strange prayers the women had made, it felt as if he should understand it.

Rhys shook his head, and said in Khairian, "I apologize deeply. I do not understand you." The literal translation of "apology" in Khairian was "I will share my water with you when we meet next," implying that there would be no water shared today, and that was regretful.

The man guffawed, as if it were the funniest thing he'd ever heard.

"You do not speak Yazdani?" the man asked, in terrible Khairian.

Rhys shook his head. He had never heard of anything called Yazdani. "Is that one of the Khairian dialects?" But he knew it wasn't. To his ear, it was too different from Khairian.

The man turned away. He waved at the woman and shook his head. He said something again in the first language—Yazdani. Rhys noted that some of the words were the same as the first time, and guessed they likely had to do with understanding the language.

Rhys decided to take a risk.

Another few weeks in the desert with these women, and he would be dead—hauled off to some unknown fate in some unknown place. If they meant to pawn him off on this man and his caravan, there was some hope of getting out of the desert. Their technology was obviously more advanced, and though the stir of men in dhotis and baldrics acting as muscle there at the rear of the caravan was a little stoic, they did not seem abused or starving. There were worse places to end up.

"I have a talent with languages. Give me a few weeks and I can become conversant in Yazdani," Rhys said.

The man raised his brows, so thick and dark that they gave Rhys the impression that he had two caterpillars sitting above his eyes. "Is that what you think I need?"

"That's certainly a large part of it."

A smile touched the man's face. He leaned back into his seat and made a circling gesture with his finger. "What else do you think I need?"

Rhys gazed at the men again.

"An army, I'd guess," Rhys said.

"A cheat, surely. Have these old hags told you of me?"

"I confess, I do not know who you are."

"I think you do. I have been searching for you, ever since Payam's caravan was ransacked by these hags' sisters."

"You're Hanife?"

The man pressed his hand to his heart. "I am. Hanife of the Yazdani. The ocean people. That's what they call us, though where we come from, the ocean is only liquid three months a year." He jabbed a finger at Rhys's captors. "They are always looking for ways to call us soft, but in our language ocean people has a rather agreeable sound. I suppose you will learn that soon enough."

Hanife motioned one of the women forward. Rhys expected to see a transaction completed in bugs or blood, but instead the man reached into the back of his vehicle and pulled out what appeared to be a rune or relic made of obsidian. It was smooth and flat on one side, and on the other bore lines of text in a language Rhys did not recognize.

The woman took it reverently, as if embracing a lost child.

"Come now, this desert will surely kill you in another few hours," Hanife said. "Get in the back. Efsham, give him some water, will you?"

The driver handed Rhys some kind of seed pod. Rhys shook it. Something watery sloshed inside.

"I'm indebted to you," Rhys said.

"Nonsense. Payam is indebted to me. His caravan should have been better protected."

"The caravan was… overrun?"

"Of course. Surely you were there? All dead, just north of Tejal. All but you. The gods were kind to spare you. I have taken on the blood debt you owed for whatever hoo-hoo you killed out there in the desert. I understand. These things happen. But as long as I own the blood debt, I'd suggest you not run off anywhere. It'll take you four years to work it off. That's not so bad a time, then?"

"What?"

"Your blood debt was worth far more than five thousand notes. Twenty thousand, at least."

"Twenty thousand?" Rhys could not imagine such a sum. "You're indenturing me, then?"

"Indenture, yes. I had forgotten that clever word. It's the southern ones who use it, mostly. Here it is simply called working off your blood debt. Which begins now. It's another few weeks until we get back to the hold, so I suggest you begin learning Yazdani now. My staff is at your disposal. I will caution you though. If it turns out you have lied to me… If you are not as clever as you pretend, well… Many men die in the desert. You understand."

"I understand," Rhys said. "But what about—"

Hanife shook his head, and started talking to him in Yazdani.

Rhys crawled into the back of the vehicle, and drank his water. When he was done, they gave him two more, as if water were not the most precious resource in the world. Compared to traveling with the austere desert women, his new companions were chatty and gregarious, especially Hanife.

Among Rhys's many concerns was Hanife's epithet. He had said something about... gods. Rich men could be good allies, but rich men without a shared morality—infidels—were dangerous. He needed to tread even more carefully here. The desert women he could understand. They reminded him of bel dames, of Nasheenians, and he knew how to regard them. But these people, these Yazdanis, were something else entirely. Something unknown. He was reminded of a story about a beggar accepting water from a beautiful woman at a well, and how after offering water, she had offered her charms. The devout man in the story had refused her, but they were both eaten by djinn. She for harlotry, and he for accepting soiled water from a known harlot.

But as the driver passed him yet another water pod and the world began to feel cooler, and not so disjointed, he remembered that it was actually a Ras Tiegan story.

What was the Chenjan one? Why could he not remember? Or were they so much the same that he confused them?

He drank.

20.

Eskander had them turned around again.

Eshe watched her kick about in the loam like a lost dog. From a distance, the land here had looked like an oasis, but up close the tangled fingers of the structures that towered over them were spiny, lichen-covered ridges made of some bone or mineral. Bits of detritus had gotten caught up in the tops of them. He saw sage, desert grasses, and even the mangled body of some parrot or raven that must have died on impact. The air smelled of death here, though Eshe saw no other dead creature. It took him some time to realize the smell came from the loamy soil surrounding the lichen-trees.

Eskander wandered about the maze of lichen-trees in slow circles, raising and lowering her hands.

"Poor excuse for a magician," Ahmed muttered beside him. "I can feel her tapping into swarms like she's asking directions, but most of it's just jumbled and confused."

Kage walked up to join them. She, too, gazed at the magician.

"Are we lost?" she asked.

"It appears so," Ahmed said.

"Fatima put her in charge," Eshe said. "What did you expect? Shortest path?"

Isabet chimed in, in Ras Tiegan. "This is a waste of time. You should shift and scout."

Eshe sighed and moved past her, toward Eskander. "You don't want to see how much food I'd have to eat to come back after a shift out here," he said.

"You did it in Ras Tieg all the time."

"There were a lot of things I did in Ras Tieg," he said. "Not all of them are a good idea here. Or did you not get that yet?"

He glanced behind them. Khatijah was the problem. They had spent far too long waiting for her to recover, and her walk was much slower now. Painful. Ahmed said he did what he could for the pain, and Eshe knew that whatever drugs the bug in her head pumped out helped, but she and Nyx were supposed to be their strongest members. Now, with the missing hunk in her leg, and persistent limp, she wandered around like a shambling corpse. And then there was Isabet, of course, and her stump of an arm.

"What are you looking for?" Ahmed called down at Eskander.

She jerked her head up. "Eh?"

"What bug are you trying to call?"

"Oh, it's a tricky one. Tricky, tricky," she muttered. "A kind of sand worm. The larva sometimes has memory of its parent. Should be able to tell us where to go."

Kage said, "That does not sound—"

Ahmed cursed softly. "She's madder than a Tirhani martyr."

Eshe shook his head. Since Khatijah nearly got devoured by wild animals, Eskander had only gotten madder. He wasn't even sure why Nyx pretended the "magician" knew where they were going. He slid down the dune and met Nyx as she was pulling up her trousers. Khatijah had already finished, and stood at the height of the rise, favoring her bad leg, watching them all like a disapproving squad commander.

"She has no idea what she's doing," Eshe said.

Nyx said, "That makes seven of us." She moved past him.

"I say bleed her out. Kage can eat her," Eshe said. Khatijah was just out of ear shot.

"We can ask somebody at the next settlement," Nyx said. "There were nomads earlier. One of them will know the way."

Eshe snorted. "The way? The way to where?" He stepped forward, and—dropped.

He felt the rush of grainy soil, darkness—

Eshe landed with a painful thump on spongy ground. He heard voices coming from above him.

"Fuck!" Nyx said.

Then Ahmed: "Wait. I'm lighter. We have a rope?"

Eshe shook his head, and tried to push himself up. The floor was sticky. Blood? God, he hoped he wasn't bleeding. The darkness was absolute. His fingers touched something, the edge of some textile, non-organic. He yanked his hand away.

"Go!" Nyx said—the voice sounded muffled, but still intelligible. "Khat, help me hold him!"

Eshe reached into his pocket and pulled out a fire beetle carapace. He tore the frayed end of his burnous free, and lit it with the beetle.

A flare of light hurt his eyes. He heard a sputtering above him, and a shower of soil.

Just above him, twice as high as he was tall, he saw Ahmed's torso burst through the grainy ceiling. Ahmed windmilled for a moment, his torso hanging suspended in the air.

"Eshe? Are you hurt?"

Eshe saw large, spiky protrusions all around him. Like teeth. It was a blessing he hadn't hit one. He was becoming aware of a pain in his leg, though, the one he'd landed on. He moved the light toward the textile he had brushed in the dim, and caught his breath.

"There's something down here," Eshe said.

"Yeah. *You're* down there. Stand up. I need to know how much rope we need. It looks like there was a glamour or organic skein or something over this pit."

"Where's Nyx?"

"Who do you think is holding me up?"

"Tell them there's a body down here." Eshe waved his fiery rag over the wizened leg beside him, tangled with a very new-looking sandal. The body had begun to mummify, but Eshe still recognized the features, and the shiny token hanging from the corpse's throat.

"What does it matter?" Ahmed said. "Get up here."

"I know her," Eshe said.

✚

It wasn't the only body in the cavern.

When Nyx crawled down into the abyss with Ahmed to see what Eshe was nattering about, she counted four bodies, all of them young Ras Tiegan women dressed in red Khairian burnouses.

"Why didn't the bugs eat them?" Nyx asked.

Ahmed shrugged. "The smell alone should have drawn them. Maybe the floor eats the bugs?"

The air down here still reeked of dead flesh, rot, though these bodies were mostly desiccated.

"How did they die?" Nyx asked.

"No sign of injury," Ahmed said. "They could have just died of dehydration."

Eshe was standing next to a slim, dark-haired body, favoring his left leg. Nyx hoped she wasn't going to have to hack it off. She had already reached her fill of amputations.

"Who is she?" Nyx asked.

"Her name was Corinne," Eshe said. "I knew her in Ras Tieg. She was one of the living saint's handmaidens."

"Living saint?" Nyx said.

"What are Ras Tiegans doing out here?" Ahmed said.

"It's a sort of holy person," Eshe said.

Nyx held a portable glow globe aloft, giving them a full view of the cavern. It was a spherical room lined in thorny, calcified spikes. The floor was strangely pliant, like walking across a tongue.

"Anybody else get the impression we're in the gut of some beast?" Nyx said. The smell was stronger down here, but shouldn't have been. The bodies were too dry for it.

Eshe gazed up at the strange ceiling, and the knotted rope. "We should go," he said.

"You're the one who asked me down here," Nyx said. "Give me a minute."

She inspected each of the bodies. They were not bound, and carried no weapons. She did find several water bulbs stacked near the feet of one of them.

"Nyx," Eshe said, and pointed.

She turned, raised her light. There was something scoured deeply in the cavern wall. It looked like writing. "Is that in Ras Tiegan?" she said. "It say anything useful?"

When no one said anything, she glanced back. Eshe's face was slack.

Ahmed answered. "It says, 'we were betrayed.'"

+

There were ways to get under just about anybody's skin, Ahmed knew. Eshe was an easy mark. Young, outwardly cocky, but unsure. Isabet was his female counterpart, only far less capable in a fight. It was easy enough to get an edge in under their insecurity. Khatijah had her pride. Eskander was… well, Eskander was many kinds of unstable. A poor wind would unsit her. Kage, he had already seen snap. But needling Nyx was like poking a hibernating cat. He was just never sure when she was going to turn around and claw his face off.

"And she knows nothing about this?" Nyx said again, more loudly, as if that would get her another answer.

Ahmed sighed. He looked over at Isabet, who was sitting in the soil, trembling, the stump of her arm pulled against her body. Eshe stood a few paces distant with Khatijah. Kage and Eskander were a more tactful distance away, breaking for midday prayer and a meal. He resented not praying. Even during interrogations at the front, they never required him to miss a prayer.

"I can hack off some more limbs if you want," Ahmed said, "but she says she doesn't know anything about it. Inaya, this rebel leader, sent her after Eshe. She hasn't heard from her mother, the saint, in over a year."

"And you believe that?"

"No," Ahmed said. He was good at what he did, but out here in the blasted desert wasn't the place for it. "I think she had some other reason to come out here that she's not telling me or even Eshe. But unless you want to beat it out of her, I'd leave it."

"Why the bloody fuck are Ras Tiegans out *here*?" Nyx muttered.

"The Queen has always been friendly with Ras Tieg," Eshe said.

"So what's the Queen doing with Ras Tiegans out here?" Nyx said. And then, to Khatijah, "I thought you said it was First Families that took Raine."

"We aren't sure who took him," Khatijah said. "That was a best guess. No one ever thought the Ras Tiegans would be interested."

"I feel like we're all knotted up in one big game," Nyx said, "and I don't like playing games without knowing the rules."

"Why?" Eshe said. "It's not like you'd follow them."

"Yeah, but everybody else would," Nyx said. She made an impatient gesture at Ahmed. "Fine. Let's keep moving. We can work this out while we go."

"After prayer," Ahmed said.

"I stutter?"

"After prayer," Ahmed insisted, again, because he knew if he didn't push now, he was going to keep getting rolled over.

"He's right," Eshe said.

"You too?" Nyx said. "Fuck and fire we have more important things to worry about." She stomped back toward camp, yelling, "Eskander! Stop fucking around and head north. North. No, the other way. Sun rises in the *east*, so what way is north? The fuck, woman, you act like you never prayed before."

Ahmed closed his eyes and thought of his farm. There was a real life at the end of all this. A better one. If he could outrun the war. When he opened his eyes, he saw the bristling lichen-tree forest ahead of him, a blasted wasteland where nothing of substance thrived. I should not have come, he thought. There would have been better paying positions. But all of those would have been in the city, and he couldn't afford to be in the city right now among the bel dames and their red notes for criminals. There was little forgiveness for men like him, even after the end of war.

He had left behind a lot of things in Nasheen, but not as much as he'd left at the front. He thought of the call he'd made in Amtullah. The familiar voice. At least not all of the men he cared for were burned up in Chenja.

"Ahmed?" Eshe said.

"Yeah?"

"We'd best pray now, before she leaves us behind."

Nyx stood in the campsite as Kage and Eskander packed up. "Hate to break your fine meditation there," Nyx called, "but we've still got those fucking Drucian mercenaries behind us. Unless they get caught in that kill hole, they're coming for us next."

"This shit will be over soon," Eshe said, and unrolled his prayer rug.

Ahmed thought he meant it to be comforting, but it came out ominous. It was what he told every prisoner the night before they were gutted and burned by the cleanup crew. He remembered thinking it was a kindness, then, to promise and deliver release. But most were so far gone by then that he wasn't sure how many understood what he was talking about.

Ahmed knelt beside Eshe, and began the prayer.

21.

When Nyx went hunting, she needed to know a few things about her target. It was always good to know who they were, what they liked, sure. You wanted to know favorite hangouts and who they owed money to and who they'd done favors for. But more than that, you wanted to learn what was most important to them. For most people she hunted in all her years as a bel dame and a bounty hunter, the answer to that question was generally a person, or people.

So whenever she caught sight of the Drucian mercenaries, trailing them just at the edge of the horizon, ever-present, seldom visible, she sat down and thought about what it was they thought was most important in life. What was worth coming out here to the edge of the known world for? Money just wasn't enough. She still didn't understand as much about Drucian culture as she probably should have after her years in exile. She hadn't exactly had a lot of Drucian friends.

She sat now on some tumbled fragment of stone among a heap of loose rubble and scrub brush. She chewed absently on a smaller stone she kept in her mouth to ward off thirst, and gazed into the dim horizon. Sometimes the Drucians were easiest to see in the violet dusk.

Someone came up behind her. From the length of the stride, she guessed it was Ahmed. She turned.

Ahmed hesitated, just an arm's length away. He followed her former gaze, out at the horizon. "You thinking it's time to take them out?"

"Rather figure out what they want, first."

"I assume they want to kill us."

"Can't go around thinking the whole world's out for you. It's a big place. Lots of people in it."

He, too, was sucking on a small stone. Eskander kept promising them that they were near a settlement, and kept them running along on a thin stream of drivel. Nyx wasn't sure how much longer she could put up with it.

Ahmed folded his arms. "We used to have Chenjan scouts follow us like that. They were usually doing it to make sure we ran right into some ambush."

"They aren't Chenjans."

"What does that have to do with anything?"

"It means not all of us think alike." Nyx turned back to camp. They weren't bedding down this time, they were just getting up. Being out in the desert this exposed meant it was time to start traveling exclusively at night, with a short break during the deepest part of it. Traveling at night meant they needed less water, but it didn't mean they thought about it any less. She saw Kage sitting at the edge of camp. She, too, was staring out toward the eastern horizon. Nyx had caught her at it a few nights now. She suspected that putting Kage on watch for them would save her a lot of time. The girl was far more vigilant.

"Ask Kage to come over here," Nyx said.

Ahmed looked puzzled, but obeyed.

A few moments later, Kage stood next to her, massive gun in hands, gaze on her feet.

Nyx nodded to the figures on the horizon. "You know those folks?"

"Not all Drucians know one another."

"You seem to take a special interest in these ones."

"I do not trust strangers."

Nyx wished she had some sen. She'd spit it on the girl's sandaled toe. "Then maybe you can give me some insight. What you think folks like those are doing still trailing us after all this time?"

Kage said nothing.

"I remember I once got a visit from some Drucians," Nyx said. She decided not to mention that she had still been in Druce at the time. "They were dour types. Dressed in formal robes, black. Funny hats and topknots. Strange guys. They told me they were searching for a criminal.

If you exile all of your criminals, why would anybody go to the trouble of finding one?"

"Criminals must be... tried. They must be formally removed from their households. If they leave without undergoing this ritual, they are never dead."

"What's wrong with never being dead?"

"They are ghosts."

"So?"

"After they die, they can come back and haunt you."

Nyx sighed. It wasn't any worse than believing in djinns or demons or a God that sent men to war, she supposed.

"So it stands to reason that these guys are either criminals who took a tough job or they're hunting criminals themselves?"

Kage hesitated.

"What did you do, Kage?" Nyx asked. "You fuck somebody you shouldn't? Cut off somebody's tail?"

Kage's grip on the gun tensed.

"All right, let's have this out now. We can take them out, Kage, but I need to know what they are. Drucian bounty hunters? I'm not going to turn you in. Whatever you did is done. You start with me, you start fresh."

Nyx waited. She was terrible at waiting, but she did it anyway while the wind purled across the desert and Kage drew soft breaths through her nose.

Finally, Nyx stood. God, she hated waiting.

"They will never stop hunting me," Kage said.

Nyx grabbed her by the collar and drew her up. The girl couldn't have been more than forty-five kilos. Her feet left the ground. She hung suspended, eyes still averted.

"I said, who the fuck is after you? Or do I just kill you myself and leave you to them? Your choice."

Nyx released her.

Kage dropped lightly to her feet, as if it had been her idea to get picked up all along. She hopped back a few steps.

"I'm done with this," Nyx said. "Give me your gun and get out of here."

Kage shook her head.

Nyx held out her hand. "Give me the gun. I bought it when I bought you, didn't I? I own it."

Again, she shook her head. Nyx wanted to twist her head off. She reached for her own scattergun.

Kage moved like water—sudden, smooth, deliberate. She slid her gun free and fired, point blank.

Nyx had the sense to flinch, though she knew what was coming. The gun didn't fire. Simply clicked, then gave a small gasp.

"I'm not completely stupid," Nyx said, yanking the gun from Kage's hands by the barrel. "Though you all sure keep treating me like it."

When she spotted their tags again the night before, she had Ahmed stifle the barrel with a particularly gummy insect that secreted a mucus that disabled firing, knowing Kage cleaned her gun at night, not in the morning. Kage might sleep with her gun, but an insect could get past her. Nyx wasn't going to risk a confrontation with an armed teammate.

"Kage," Ahmed said softly. Nyx started. He had snuck up on them from camp. God, how many times did she need to tell him not to interfere? "Let us know who's following you. We can help. You don't need to shoot all of us."

Nyx begged to differ about just how much she was willing to help, but Ahmed was the one with the slick tongue. She settled for putting Kage's weapon aside and remaining taut and ready to draw her own loaded gun if necessary. She wasn't so sure how she felt about Kage pulling the trigger yet. A lot depended on how good her story was. It always did.

Kage breathed deeply through her nose. She seemed to settle herself back into her skin. The more relaxed stance made Nyx want to stop worrying about her gun. She decided that was the whole point of it, so didn't give her the satisfaction.

"They are *fukushu-sha*," Kage said. "Hunters. Blood avengers."

"How far are they willing to go to get you? How—"

"Kage," Ahmed said. Soft voice, again. Measured. "Do you know how we can defeat them? Can we pay them off, distract them?"

Kage shook her head. "I am a criminal."

"Aren't we all?" Nyx said. "That doesn't tell me—"

"How can we stop them, Kage?" Ahmed said.

"You can deliver me to them. That is all. But I won't go. You must kill me first."

"What's waiting for you back there if you go with them?" Ahmed said.

"Do they mean to kill you?"

"No. It's… It's our business." She shook her head. "Why would you help me? You don't know me."

"I need your eyes. And your aim," Nyx said. "Things aren't going to get much better out here. I eliminate your hunters, you owe me a favor."

"That's all?"

"That's all."

Even to Nyx, it didn't sound like much, not with thirst bearing down on her like a fucking freight train. That, paired with Eskander's mad babbling, Eshe and Isabet's bickering, Khatijah's dour stares, and Ahmed's disapproving frown, meant she was in dire need of a little more than simple goodwill. She had no idea where the fuck she had been or where the fuck she was going. Bring back Raine from the end of the world? Sweet fuck, why? But this was what she had, and she needed to get the best from it. God help her.

"All right," Kage said.

"How do they hunt? In pairs?"

Kage nodded. "There will just be one pair. Just two."

"Good," Nyx said. "And if they're anything like you… they'll have a lot of water with them, won't they?"

Kage nodded again.

Also good. Stealing from these shadowy hunters could give them four more days of water, or more, if she could keep Kage upright on a little less. Staking out teammates to die in the desert this early on was bad for morale.

"And? What else? What can I use against them?" Nyx asked.

Kage raised her head, just a fraction, but it was enough for Nyx to see her eyes directly for the first time. Kage's gaze met hers for a moment, so quickly Nyx half thought she imagined it.

"They want me alive," Kage said.

It was the best thing Nyx had heard all day.

+

There was very little high ground in this place, just one more reason Kage found to hate it. She had volunteered to scout out the position of the *fukushu-sha*, but Nyx had Eshe do it. For once, the mewling magician made herself useful putting together bugged transceivers for them. Kage held the mealy little wire-threaded worm in her hand, dubious, as the others stuck the things in their ears like it was a perfectly reasonable thing to do.

"Let me help," the Ras Tiegan girl said in mangled Nasheenian. She was standing just behind Eshe, like a lost dog.

Kage glowered at her.

"I can be very good at scouting," she said. Trying so hard to be useful.

"You aren't welcome," Kage said.

"What if assassins wander into camp? Kill me and Eskander?" Isabet said.

"Can't say I'd cry over it," Nyx said. She passed something to Eshe. "We've got exactly one pair of thermal specs. Don't lose them."

The girl spouted off, then, in Ras Tiegan. Kage knew a few words of it, but not enough to make sense of what she was saying. Instead, the syrupy sounds of the language just put her in mind of another night, another band of Ras Tiegans. She very nearly jammed the butt of her gun into the girl's face. She took a deep breath instead, and focused on the toes of her sandals until Nyx gave the order to move.

Kage brought the worm up to her ear, then palmed it into the pocket of her trousers. She could speak to them just as well with the worm set on the end of her gun once she was in position.

Kage broke away from the group and made her way southeast toward what they hoped, from a distance, was a decent perch. Nyx and Ahmed gave Eshe a head start, and he went northeast, to come at the *fukushu-sha* from the opposite direction.

In truth, none of them were certain where the *fukushu-sha* were now. It would be a long night.

Kage trotted across the rocky terrain, gun and water bulbs strapped to her back. She was used to traveling alone, and though the desert was large and intimidating, there was some comfort in setting her own pace again.

The rise came slowly into view as the moons rose, blood-red, over the desert. She crouched a little lower, already far closer to the ground than any Nasheenian could get. She once heard a Nasheenian call her people spiders, because of the way they moved across the ground, crouched low, arms splayed, as if fearful they would fall off the flat plain of the world.

It was not a sand dune or a rock, but some bit of wreckage. An abandoned vehicle of some sort? It was covered in several feet of sand at the base, but the top was just a little dusty. She climbed atop it and dug in on the roof of the contraption. She lay on her belly and set up her gun's simple bipod. Affixed the scope. She peered through the scope and made a long pan of the desert to the north. Experience told her that Nasheenians did not see well in the dark, but for her, the world on the other side of the scope was as bright as a blue dawn. But it was going to be just as easy for the *fukushu-sha* to see Nyx and her crew as it was for Kage.

She sighted what appeared to be Eshe from her vantage. He had gone down on his belly in the sand, his body obscured by his burnous, which trailed around him, dusted in sand and bits of desert scrub. He held the specs to his eyes, but Kage did not put much faith in them. She expected to wait here until morning. No *fukushu-sha* slept exposed.

Kage pulled the bug from her pocket and set it next to her. "I need a position," she said softly. Her voice triggered something in the bug. It spasmed. The filament surrounding it gave off a soft blue light. She quickly shoved her hand over it to cover the light. Hoped she had been quick enough.

When the light faded, she removed her hand. A tinny voice said, "Eshe is still scouting. We've got nothing. No holes, no caverns. Nothing like that. Got any other ideas?"

"If they have no physical shelter, they will sleep under the sand."

Kage would have. The only reason she cocooned herself in a sleeping roll instead of beneath a comforting layer of sand was because she feared that Eskander's ridicule would become so enraging that she would do something regrettable.

The line was silent for a time.

Then, Nyx said, "Eshe. Hold up on your position. I know how we do this. Remember how I taught you to flush a field for mines?"

Kage peered through her scope. She saw Nyx crawling up behind Eshe. She did another sweep, searching for Ahmed. He was at least a hundred paces further north, given away by the soft blue glow of his transceiver. By all the gods, she should have told them not to use those. Why hadn't they said they glowed?

Kage loaded her gun and trained her eye back on Eshe and Nyx. They had positioned themselves two arm's lengths apart, and now they crawled slowly across the rocky sand.

They would need to find an area that had been recently dug up, but with their poor sight, they wouldn't be able to make it out unless it was right under them.

Kage searched for it from the relative safety of her position.

"Nyx. You need to come further south. About… eight paces. Then go up another fifty paces. You'll miss them if you keep on that route."

Nyx and Eshe adjusted. They came up in a crouch now, to cover the distance more quickly. Kage knew Eshe was quiet, but Nyx looked like a lumbering animal out there. She was likely making enough noise to raise a swarm of palm bugs.

Kage covered their approach.

They got within twenty paces of the disturbed ground when it began to stir.

Kage moved her finger to the trigger.

But what leapt out of the sand wasn't human at all.

Kage let off a staccato of rounds.

"Fuck is that?" Nyx's voice from the transceiver.

"They're over here!" Ahmed's voice. "Not there! Fuck!"

Kage's response was immediate, fluid. She left Nyx and Eshe to battle the thing and repositioned herself with a clear view of Ahmed's blue transceiver.

He was too far to see anything clearly. Just black shadows. Blur. She took control of her breath. Long breath in. Long breath out. Darkness moved across the soft blue light. Estimating the distance was the most difficult part. Gravity would pull at the bullet the moment it left the gun. One small mistake here could mean missing her target by four or five paces.

She fired—right at where the light would have been.

Her reward was seeing the light blink back to life. But whether she had truly hit the assassin assaulting Ahmed or merely shot him in the back, she was uncertain.

The light was moving again.

Good sign.

Another blink. Another shadow.

She fired.

The light disappeared.

This time, she held her breath. Waiting. No light. Had he run, or had she shot him?

Nyx and Eshe were still yelling, their voices audible through the transceiver. But she didn't check their progress. She wanted the *fukushu-sha*, not some giant bug or beast. She quickly packed her bipod and reloaded her gun. She sprinted across the sand, desperate to make the distance to where Ahmed's light had gone out.

She pointed the gun ahead of her, watching for any hint of movement. She stumbled on a loose pile of rock, twisted her ankle, but didn't go down. Coming up gun first, she pushed forward, ignoring the knife of pain driving up her leg.

The voices had stopped. She realized, just a hundred steps from her goal, that she had left her transceiver behind.

She saw a crumple of figures ahead. She raised her gun to her shoulder. Her arms burned.

Kage heard the sound of a gun being cocked. She dove for the ground. Rock bit at her elbows and knees.

"Nyx?" It was Ahmed's voice.

"It's Kage! Where are they?"

"One of them's here. The other one got clipped and ran off."

Kage shoved herself to her feet and limped the rest of the way to where Ahmed lay, tangled with a slender figure dressed all in deep umber brown. She hissed in a breath, expecting the worst, but the figure moved as she approached. Not dead.

Ahmed clutched at his arm. Kage saw blood beading between his fingers. The assassin wasn't the only one she had clipped.

Kage dragged herself to the assassin. She pushed him over with the butt of her gun. This close, she wasn't worried as much about weapons. They didn't want to kill her. No Drucian wanted to kill another, no matter how bad things got.

The man was breathing heavily, but she saw no injury on him. His gaze found her, but, as was polite, he did not meet her eyes. Still, she recognized him.

"I did not think they would send you, Aya Haruto."

"I should have expected you to act this way," Haruto said, in Drucian.

"I did not aim to kill."

He snorted. Blood bubbled from his nose. He was a young man, not even twenty. Where was his injury?

"We have a magician. She can help you."

"Too late for that, I think."

"That is fool talk. If you're injured, you have to go home. You have to send someone else. Who was with you?"

Haruto showed his teeth. Bloody teeth. He was clutching at his chest now.

Kage knelt next to him without loosening her grip on her gun. "Where are you hurt?"

"You shot me in the back. One cannot expect anything better, from a baby-killer."

She wanted to put the gun in his face this time, the way she had seen Nyx do it, but she still had some pride left, some sense of morality, even after all that had happened. Sadness and fear filled her. Sadness for this needless death, and fear that it was just one of many. She would never repay her debt at this rate. She could not stay long with these people.

"He will go home now," Haruto said. "Just as you hoped. But it is me you killed. And it is I who will haunt you. I and those children you murdered."

It cut at her every time they said it, even now, a year after the last body was burned.

"He will go home," Haruto repeated softly. His eyes started to lose some light. "Go home, brother. I will haunt her. I will avenge…"

That's when Kage felt the damp at her knee. She gazed down and saw a black pool of blood beneath Haruto's body.

She wanted to wail.

Ahmed stood over her now. She hadn't noticed him get up.

"So they won't come for you again?" he said… in Drucian.

She started. By the gods, he'd understood every word. She shook her head. "The other will go home. But they will send more. More and more, until I am caught and caged again. It won't ever end. All we can do is delay it a little while."

"I know the feeling," he said. "But don't tell Nyx that." He offered his hand. "We better move now."

22.

The swill they served in the bars and taverns now smelled even worse than she remembered. There were many things about what the war had done to Nasheen that turned her piss to vinegar, but the acceptance of the sulfur-tasting beverages that passed for liquor was among the ones she most despised. She ordered tea at an old haunt near the Orrizo. She did not mind much if she was recognized here, though few of the Firsts even came down to nicer colonial neighborhoods like this one. She sat near a window so she could get a good view of the street. The call to evening prayer wailed over the city. She watched the hubbub on the street subside as women pulled out prayer rugs or made their way to mosques. In her day, every woman and man went to prayer. It was practically a prerequisite for citizenship. But since the end of the Caliphate, secular law had become more accepted in Nasheen. Only in the state schools was prayer still compulsory. It depressed her and excited her all at once. She enjoyed watching the changes wrought by time, even if she mourned some of the old ways. Faith was malleable, she knew. Each age had to interpret the words and tenets differently. If things remained unchanged from the time of the Caliphate, she would worry about the health of the world.

As she listened to the opening prayer, she heard someone come up behind her, and casually turned, brandishing her cup in one hand, prepared to break it on the counter and use it to slice open the sneaking cat.

She was only moderately surprised to see that it was the woman who had come to her in her confinement and given her the job. In the open air, among the colonials, she stood out—taller than many of the others by a head. She had knotted her hair back into a twist of braids, and rimmed her eyes in kohl, an affectation she had not seen outside a fighting ring in many years. She wore a long, billowing blue robe stitched in organic material at the hem and cuffs to absorb filth.

The woman approached the counter, within an arm's length of her, but did not sit.

"I am surprised to see you still in Mushtallah," the woman said.

"I had unfinished business."

"I thought we had an understanding of the job that needed to be done."

"We do. I have my own methods. You did not say how, or when. I am biding my time."

"You know your target is no longer in Mushtallah."

"The ones I need are no longer in Nasheen at all," she said.

The woman appeared to be perplexed, but not yet fearful. She must be a more powerful magician than she had pretended when they first met. Now that her mind was not so muddled, she could sense the way the air responded to this woman. It was a trick magicians and conjurers had, the ability to sense their own, but sensing a talent in no way told one just how much talent a person had. That you only knew if you pushed them.

"We are not pleased with your actions since your release," the woman said.

"I expect my family is not, either."

"This is a delicate time. It will be known, soon, who it was who entombed your family. We cannot keep it secret with you provoking them."

"You will give me the time I need," she said. "You would not have woken me unless things were very dire. I think you will do what is necessary to help me achieve my goal."

"I must issue you an ultimatum. You must be gone from Mushtallah by morning, or we will be forced to reinstate you in your former quarters."

She snorted and pointed out the window, to the glaring light in the southern sky, just visible now in the dusk. She had spotted it the first night of her release, and had seen enough of them in her time to recognize it immediately. She knew, now, why they had really called her from slumber. "Why not just have me deal with the real reason I'm here? Why run me around in circles after this woman?"

Her handler followed her gesture, and stood a long time staring at the light. "She *is* the real reason you're here. If you don't eliminate her, we can't eliminate that threat there. She's working against us, in her way. I know what you can do, but you need access to the tools to do it. I can't get you access until your target is dead. If you fail at this..."

"I never fail. Who are the aliens on that ship? More mealy-mouthed djinns, like the Dei Keiko?"

"The Drucians? God, no. They were the last of their kind. These are... something else entirely."

"You're afraid those aliens will send more ships if we destroy this one?"

"I know they will send more. But they will do so regardless. This shows our teeth, and buys us time. It's many years to their planet and back. The Queen tried diplomacy for far too long. We simply did not have the resources to take out this threat. Now, with the boys home and our country united... perhaps we do. Perhaps we stand some chance of remaining autonomous. But it will require all of us working together, and that is something we have not done in a long, long time."

"How long before another ship comes?"

"Eight years before they know the ship was destroyed. Some time for them to mobilize, then eight years to come back. We could have twenty years to sort out our differences before facing an interstellar war."

"What do they want? To colonize us?"

"No. To conquer and strip us bare. There are very few habitable worlds left. It was only a matter of time before they extinguished theirs."

"Twenty years of peace."

"Yes. Have you ever been asked to deliver such a thing?"

"The war has been on and off only three hundred years. We had over two thousand years of peace before that. It was a very dull time."

"Only because it did not need monsters."

"Monsters like me?"

"As I said."

Foolish child, she thought. It was monsters like me who ensured the peace. You all forget that now. She sighed.

"I will complete your little mission for you," she said. "But you must promise me the ship is mine."

"I can promise you nothing. It is not my decision to make. As yet, this is the only mission I have for you. If you fail, Umayma falls to outsiders for the first time in three thousand years." She hesitated. "So don't fail."

"You pretend I care a great deal for Nasheen."

"I know you care little for Nasheen. But you do value your freedom. If those aliens come here, you will be the first of our… old weapons… to be turned over to them. Why do you think I chose you for this mission?"

"You would rather I die spectacularly than get turned over to the enemy?"

"I would rather see this all go another way," she said.

The prayer ended. Around them, women began rolling up their prayer rugs. People returned to the streets.

"Get out of Mushtallah," the woman said.

She watched the woman step abruptly backward into the wall of the tavern, but instead of smacking hard into the wall, the woman simply passed through it, through the veil of some glamour that likely led below, into one of the magicians' tunnels—the Abd-al-Karim—that linked key cities from the old world.

"I will leave Mushtallah in my own time," she murmured into her tea, and turned her gaze once more to the sky.

The Families, too, had their own shortcuts to the other side of the world. She had only to choose her moment.

Above, the alien ship hung still and silent in the night.

23.

It did not take Rhys a week to become conversant in Yazdani. It took two.

By then, he had learned that Hanife was one of three brothers come down from Yazdani, a country far beyond the desert wall. Rhys had never heard of it—had never heard of anything beyond Khairi—not the desert wall, and not Yazdan.

"Of course not," Hanife said. "Until we crossed the Wall and made peace… well, stopped making war with these damned unbelievers, we thought all their stories about a world beyond the Wall on our side was a myth. Ships never make it out of harbor up there. And going overland, well, that requires coming to this godsfucked place. You can understand."

"How far are we from there?" Rhys asked one night as they camped under a black, cloudless sky. The only stars he saw were far to the south, ringing the horizon behind him. The further north they went, the blacker the sky. He wondered if he would see anything at all but the moons and the billowing purple curtains of light if they went any further.

Hanife was feeding some kind of dust into the fire. It popped and crackled, burning high and hot for hours. He and the driver and the charioteers slept near the fire, but the desert men slept beyond them, in the cool darkness. They drew a circle around themselves, and clustered at the center of it. One man remained on watch all night. It was a different man each night, but never in shifts—though it seemed the nights themselves had grown longer.

"From where, Yazdan? Oh, we aren't even past the Wall yet. Don't you know where that is? Ever seen it?"

Rhys shook his head. He had heard there was a wall, but he had seen many walls in his time.

"How many people go beyond the wall?"

"Not enough," Hanife said. "Or maybe too many."

"Is there a market for slaves there?"

"Slaves?" Hanife looked appalled. "That word. The gods frown on that type of thing. The Yazdani don't take slaves."

"Don't you enslave the nomads?"

"Well, some, maybe. They are a godsless people. Worshipping sand and wind and all manner of nonsense."

Rhys had certainly met nomads further south who worshipped gods of wind and sand, but his captors had not been among them. There were many who still followed the one God, even out here in all this blackness.

He thought of Elahyiah, and the children. Did she still live? Did she think of him, or was she so relieved to get away that she did not spare him a thought? He closed his eyes, and remembered the happy years of their marriage, before the bel dames came. Everything had been destroyed after that. It was foolish to think he could put anything back together. Wasn't it? Who was he now, without Elahyiah? Without Mehry and Nasrin and Rahim? Was he a man at all?

✚

After so many weeks of travel, one became used to shifting vistas, hard-packed beds, and picking mites and midges from the bedding.

When the bugs became especially virulent, Hanife shared his repellent, and Rhys slathered himself in it every night, but in the morning—inevitable as the blue dawn—cysts had formed in the warm, dry flesh between his toes. He spent many of his waking hours coaxing them out and stowing them in a pouch so he could burn them each night. The scents released when they burned tended to act as an additional repellent. Hanife thought him mad to cut them out, but Rhys knew it always hurt worse if you let the little ticks and midges grow and split open on their own in a rush of blood and pus.

He got so used to traveling that it was not until the third day after

Hanife told him they were nearing the end of the desert that he finally noted the thin black line on the horizon.

Rhys peered out past the group of desert men scouting ahead of them and said, "My God, what *is* that?"

"The end of the world," Hanife said.

"My God," Rhys said.

"Indeed," Hanife said. "Now you are stuck with me, my friend. Now we are true partners."

24.

E she threw three bandoliers of water bulbs onto the ground at the center of camp. He was wheezing. Blood oozed from three long slashes across his chest. Whatever thing they had battled out there while Kage shot at Ahmed and the assassins had lashed out with six sharp claws and then retreated into the darkness, yowling. He still trembled with the memory of that scream. It had sounded human.

Kage carried a second bandolier. She put it down next to his. He saw there were six or seven individual canisters missing from the bandolier, and wondered where she'd hid them. How many others had she smuggled away before he got over there to her and the assassins?

"So how many days is that?" he asked.

Nyx knelt next to Ahmed, digging Kage's bullet out of his arm. At least Kage had used deadtech bullets. Nyx regarded the pile of water bulbs, blood streaming over her fingers.

"Depends," she said. She glanced back at the hemorrhaging wound. "How many days to the next settlement, Eskander?"

"A few days, a few days," Eskander said. But she wasn't looking at any of them. Her tattered burnous was filthy, and she stank, like she had been messing herself in her clothes for days.

Khatijah stood next to Eskander, out of breath. The bel dame hadn't taken the running and shooting well. He knew they had to keep at least one of them alive until the next settlement. They knew more about what waited up there than anyone else. After they met their contact there, though… well, he figured Nyx was already cooking up new and interesting ways that she could lose them after that.

Isabet sat on the other side of the banked fire, hugging her knees to her chest with her good arm. She stared at the pile of water like a starving dog presented with a corpse. It was time to call this bluff. He had seen Nyx do a lot of stupid things that ended up well, but more often than not, it meant a whole lot of people died to get to the end.

"I think there's another question maybe we should ask," Eshe said.

"There!" Nyx said. She popped out the bloody deadtech bullet from Ahmed's arm. It was a black mass. Ahmed cursed at her.

"Nyx," Eshe said, but the closer he got to saying it, the more nervous he got. "Nyx, what if… If we turned around now, would we have enough to get back?"

All heads turned. Even Eskander. Khatijah even laughed.

Nyx knotted a loop of gauze around Ahmed's arm, using one hand to hold the bandage flush and tying it taut with the other end in her teeth. When she was done, she spit out the bandage and said, "How long it take us to get this far, Eshe?"

"I don't know. Four, five weeks."

"How much water is there, Eshe?"

"I don't know."

"There are seven of us," Nyx said. "On a regular day, we'd all drink about four times what we've got. I can stretch it two days, maybe three, because of Kage. So with this? Five bandoliers, eight on each. Maybe another five, six days, at best."

"No going back, then?" Eshe said.

"No going back," Nyx said. She stood, smearing Ahmed's blood on her trousers. Ahmed retched.

"Our best bet is heading north and hoping we run into some nomads or this mythical settlement. There are people who live out here. We just need to hang on long enough to find them."

"Then what?" Ahmed said. He covered over the vomit with sand, using his good arm.

"Then we go north. That's what you all signed on for, right?"

Eskander giggled.

Eshe glanced over at Isabet. She shook her head.

"Let's get moving," Nyx said.

"What direction?" Ahmed said.

"You miss me the first time?" Nyx pointed north.

Eskander babbled something.

"This is a foolish course," Isabet said, in Ras Tiegan.

Eshe handed her a bandolier. "You heard Nyx. You can't keep up, you can turn right around."

"I can't go without you."

"So you keep saying." He wondered just how thirsty and crazy she would have to get to turn back. He thought the loss of her arm would affect her more, thought Ahmed's interrogation would intimidate her, but after some water and rest, she was as steely-eyed and determined as ever. He couldn't help but admire her a little. For a rich girl, she had guts. And I haven't exactly been nice to her, he thought, and cringed. If he acted like Nyx all the time, he really was going to end up just like her. He watched Isabet for a time, and his resolve softened. Don't be a fool, he thought, remembering the words carved into the loamy cavern. There is something rotten going on out here, and she could very well be a part of it. Couldn't she?

Nyx took the lead, and eventually, they all followed. An hour before dawn, Eshe was so tired he kept expecting someone would just run off into the desert with the water and take their own chances. If he thought Nyx would still speak to him if he ran off, he might do it himself. But out here in all this nothing, Nyx's stubborn determination was comforting, like a stone pillar in a sandstorm.

Beside him, Isabet struggled to keep up. She had the long, dead-eyed expression of somebody about to pass out. The only person slower than them was Kage, who trailed after him and Isabet in a strange sort of half-crouch, arms splayed out like a spider. It was eerie, sometimes, to watch her move.

He reached for Isabet, and made her drink some of his water. She shook her head at first, and said some nonsense words, something like, "Kittens need cool coats," and then she lapped the water from her lips and drank.

Eshe put his arm around her. She was so out of it she didn't even push him away. He set his gaze on Ahmed's back, and focused. Dug deep. If he had learned nothing else from Nyx, it was that he could always go on a lot longer than he thought he could.

At dawn, Nyx had them bed down in the long curve of a small crater. Eshe had seen a few others a long way back, much bigger than this one, and suggested that they stay in one, but it was always at the wrong time. Nyx wanted to get just a little bit further before they stopped.

The blue dawn had already warmed the sky, and the orange demon was blazing a new morning across the desert.

Eshe helped Isabet into the crater, then straightened and stared at the sunrise. For one awesome moment, he let himself just see that sunrise, really see it—a fiery crimson-gold hemorrhage across a deep purple sky, like a bloody wound at the center of a massive bruise. The flat of the desert was different now—ahead of them lay rolling amber dunes, or maybe foothills, and something else. Chalky white protrusions, like massive rock chimneys, grew from the distant desert, prickling across the dunes like the spines of a fish.

He decided to muse on what that meant for the next leg of the trip later, and slid into the crater with the others. The cold desert was beginning to warm. When he settled down in the crater, Isabet crawled next to him like a child and gripped him close with her remaining hand.

His whole body tensed. She murmured something he could not make out. He wasn't entirely sure what to do with his own hands. This close, even after long, filthy days in the desert, the scent of her beneath the cloying stink of sweat was strangely alluring. It was her hair, he decided, that smelled so good. Even here.

He closed his eyes, and tried to relax.

"I'm sorry I came," she said, in Ras Tiegan. For her, he knew, it was like their own private language. But Ahmed spoke it, and the way Kage sometimes watched them, he thought she might understand some of it, too. So he was careful about what he said.

"I still think Inaya was mad to send you."

"She worried about you."

"She worries about a lot of people. That doesn't mean she sends other people after them, especially not daughters to saints."

"I'm… sorry. She's in charge."

He watched Nyx get up on the edge of the crater to take first watch. She dug into a small packet of dried meal worms. "I know what that can be like," he said.

Isabet's shoulders shook. After a time, he realized she was crying, only without any tears. She was too thirsty to cry properly. He gazed up at the bright lavender sky. He needed to sleep.

Isabet shuddered against him, squeezing him so hard it hurt. He wasn't sure what to do. Should he tell her it would be all right? He couldn't guarantee that.

"Here, drink," he said, and passed her the last half of his water bulb.

She took it in her dirty fingers. Drank.

"I lied to you," she said, and her face contorted again.

"Not the first time I've been lied to."

"Inaya didn't send me. Michel did."

"That makes even less sense than Inaya sending you," he said. "Why the fuck did Michel send you to Nasheen?"

"I'm pregnant," she said.

✚

Ahmed was on watch three days later when Eskander crawled out of her bedroll, stripped herself naked, and started doing a slow dance on the sand. She was remarkably flat-chested, and wore no breast binding. He expected her to at least keep on her dhoti, but that went too, and then she was just a whirling, stomping mad woman in the dark.

Ahmed woke Nyx. "I think Eskander finally lost it," he said.

Nyx got up and they stood together at the edge of camp, watching Eskander flail.

Nyx's expression was impossible to read. She looked at everything the same way now, like she was attending a particularly distasteful funeral.

"Let it go," Nyx said.

"Are you sure?"

"It saves me a bullet."

"You're all so generous," Khatijah said. She limped up behind them. The pain in her face was obvious. Ahmed wondered how much longer she was going to be able to push through it. "I'll talk her down."

"Listen," Nyx said, "I need at least one of you at the settlement. I can't—"

"If you can't wait, go on without us," Khatijah said. "I'd do the same if it was your sister." She pushed past them and started out after Eskander, dragging her bad leg behind her.

Ahmed went with Nyx to Eskander's sleeping place. They found six notes, a dead locust in a traveling box, her gun, knife, and a copy of the Kitab with some pressed flowers inside.

Ahmed opened the Kitab. Flipped to his favorite passage. He could once recite the ninety-nine names of God, but when he tried it now, he could only get to fourteen.

"Are we going to die out here?" he asked.

"Not all at once," Nyx said. "Wake everybody up. Give them an extra water bulb this morning. Then we get moving."

He watched her face as she said it. He had followed a lot of women in his time. Strong, confident women who made decisions of life and death with the sort of expression he saw on her face now. He would be lying if he said he hadn't gone to bed with some of them just to try and shake up that calm surety. He had a pretty face, and women appreciated that as much as men did. But what he found when he got close to them was that it wasn't as easy as they made it out to be. He often wondered if Nyx would be the same, if he could put his hands on her and open her up and find some soft, vulnerable human being inside. It had become a challenge, later in his career, to sleep with all of his commanding officers. It wasn't that he found them all that attractive. Most of the people he cared for in his life were the men he fought and sacrificed beside, not the women pulling the strings. But he did what he had to to survive.

Something told him that getting under this woman's skin would require more skill than he possessed.

"What you standing there gawking for?" Nyx said. "We have a long way to go."

Khatijah and Eskander followed at a long distance, Eskander still naked and babbling. When they settled down at dawn to camp and sleep out the heat, the sisters finally caught up with them. Both were much worse, but Eskander may as well have been a corpse. She was like something that had clawed up from a bug-ridden grave, covered in oozing sores that looked like they had harbored some kind of flesh-nesting insect, but seemingly uncaring.

Ahmed looked to Nyx for some kind of guidance. Eskander simply babbled along, nonsense words.

"Thanks for your vote of confidence," Khatijah said to Nyx as she threw her pack down next to the fire.

"You'd do the same."

Khatijah shook her head. "We're not all like you. Not even us bel dames."

Nyx just shrugged. "That's what you say now. But we're not at the end of the line yet. Tomorrow, though. Tomorrow we'll see what everybody's really made of."

+

Nyx stumbled. The sun was up already, but she had forced them to carry on because this was the end of the road. They might make it another night, maybe less. She held the last bit of excess water they had in addition to their personal bulbs: a quarter-full bladder. As they finished the bandoliers of bulbs, she had them keep hold of them, promising to fill them at the next oasis.

It was just something to say, telling them to hang onto the bandoliers. Something grimly hopeful. If she started telling them to throw away the empty bulbs, they'd know she had given up.

Nyx clutched the bladder to her chest. Three times, she had nearly tossed away her scattergun. It was so heavy. Everything was so fucking heavy. She knew heat sickness. She had been dehydrated and sick many, many times. But recognizing a thing and doing something about it were entirely different problems.

"Nyx! Nyx!"

She kept walking. She was afraid that if she stopped, she wasn't going to go on.

"Nyx!"

She glanced back.

Eshe knelt next to Isabet. She had crumpled on the sand. That surprised Nyx. She had expected Kage to be the first to go. But Kage was still trudging after them, maybe a dozen paces distant, plodding on.

Nyx turned and slogged back toward Eshe and Isabet. Walking across the crusted sand here was like walking through snow, something she had done only once and never wanted to do again.

"We need to stop and rest," Eshe said. He had the girl pulled into his lap now. She was so dehydrated she wasn't even sweating anymore.

Nyx shook her head. "Come on. We have to get up."

"I'm not leaving her," Eshe said.

Woman down. Never leave a woman down. God, there were some things she wished she hadn't taught him. She gazed out at Kage, still struggling in the caked sand far behind them. When it came to the desert, Nyx wasn't a total fool. She knew when to push on, and when to play her last hand. She was pissing a lot less these days, and the stone trick wasn't keeping her mouth wet. Now Isabet had moved on to severe dehydration, which meant Kage and Eskander were next. Ahmed and Khatijah still struggled on ahead. Ever since she'd slogged her way back into camp, Khatijah had been pushing hard. She was a woman with something to prove. Nyx had to admire that.

Nyx pulled the strap of the bladder over her head, and pushed it at Eshe.

"I want you to drink deep."

"No, not until Isabet—"

"Drink, then shift. I want you to shift and go north. Find an oasis. A settlement. Anything. Bring water. Or come back and point us in the right direction."

"Once I shift, I can't shift back unless we have enough food. If I try and shift back…"

"You'll starve in a few hours. I know. Why you think I waited so long to ask?" She pushed the bladder at him again. "Drink. Let's hope you find somebody."

He gazed down at Isabet's dry, reddened face. "Promise you won't leave her."

"I won't leave her."

He met her gaze. "Promise, Nyx."

"You need to go now."

Eshe shoved the bladder back at her. She was surprised he still had that kind of strength left. It made her decision easier. Aside from Isabet, he was the youngest of them. In raven form, he could fly faster and see farther.

"*Promise*," he said.

Her insides twisted, and not from hunger or the peculiar mix of shit they'd been eating the last week.

"I promise," she said.

He nodded.

How strange, she thought, that my word still means something to anyone, even after all this time. It's because you're such a fucking bad liar, she thought.

He took the bladder and drank.

"Slow," she said. "Slow at first."

He drank until he was sated, then gave a good deal of what was left to Isabet. She came around just long enough for him to tell her something in Ras Tiegan. Then he handed the water back to Nyx and walked away from the group.

"North?" he said.

"North," Nyx said.

He shifted. It was not a pretty thing. Never was, watching a man shake loose from his bones. His body trembled violently, then began to lose mass, twisting in on itself. It looked the way her hunger felt—some dark, feral thing eating itself from the inside. In a few minutes he was free of his clothing, stark naked, growing smaller, sprouting prickly black feathers, his features narrowing, elongating.

Nyx finally turned away.

She portioned out the last of the water with Ahmed, Khatijah, Eskander, and Kage who had just caught up to them.

Kage drank deep. She didn't seem much better than Isabet.

Eshe squawked at them from the air.

"Come on," Nyx said. "We keep going north until we find some shelter. Need a good place to hole up."

"There's nothing out here, Nyx," Ahmed said.

"There's always something," Nyx said. She crouched next to Isabet and pulled her up over her shoulders. Nyx grunted with the effort. Fuck, she should have been able to carry this girl like she was nothing. She wasn't any bigger than one of Anneke's kids.

Nyx plodded forward.

Eshe squawked one more time, then he was off and away, north. Ever fucking north. To the land of missing politicians and, possibly, nutty Ras Tiegans.

Nyx fixed her gaze just a few feet ahead of her. Dangerous thing, to narrow your vision, but so was falling down in the desert. They needed to find shelter. Two days back, they had passed through a voluminous field of giant calcified tubes three times Nyx's height. She wished for some of those now, but the crunchy dunes ahead of her just went on and on. She could never see past the one ahead of her, and they seemed to get taller and taller.

Beside her, Ahmed trudged along. He was carrying Kage's gun now, which meant Kage was either half mad or Ahmed had softened her up a great deal the last couple weeks. Nyx had caught them speaking in Drucian a few times—and look what it got him. A heavier load.

And what did it get *you*? Nyx thought grimly, acutely aware of Isabet's soft bulk. Look what load you're willing to carry.

They walked.

Nyx started to see things scuttling along the sand. Tattered blurs of light. Black tendrils licking at the corners of her vision. Easy enough to dismiss, for a time, though she knew what it portended. Her breathing was coming a little more rapidly now, and her heart beat a little faster.

I have done this before, she thought fiercely. One foot. Another foot.

Three hours later, Ahmed said he saw something. She raised her head. There were four or five figures moving along the dunes, about three hundred paces distant. They were dressed in the dusty crimson of the Khairian nomads, leading two caterpillars and a sand cat with them.

"Hey!" Ahmed called. "Hey!" He raised his arms, waved at them.

Nyx squinted. The group noticed them, but did not stop.

Ahmed moved toward them.

One of the Khairians opened her mouth, and began to sing.

There was a shushing sound in the sand between Ahmed and the nomads. He leapt back as the sand began to roil with foot-long desert worms. The air filled with sand flies.

"Come away!" Nyx said. She pulled him back.

"Fuck!" he said, and covered his head. "What the fuck was that?"

"Not sure I want to find out," Nyx said. "But you should shoot one of those worms for dinner."

They did, and then coughed and spat up sand flies for the next hour.

The body Nyx carried was getting heavier. Her dead sister Kine was getting heavier. Kine started saying things to her, which was funny, because Kine was dead on the other side of the world.

"You are safer on your own," Kine said. "You are always better off alone."

"I ain't never been alone in my life," Nyx said. But it sure did feel that way.

Getting burned up, coming back from the dead… they were all things you did on your own, but coming back from them meant relying on a whole host of others to bring you back.

She set her gaze on the sky, watching for Eshe the raven.

But the sky was still mercilessly clear, brilliant lavender, and if they didn't find shelter soon she was going to have to just burn Kine and be done with her. But burning her with what? She couldn't bury her. She didn't want her to come back as one of those massive rotting corpse beetles.

Nyx realized she wasn't sweating anymore. A bad sign. She was in that bad place that you knew was bad, but were so fucking out of it you just didn't care. It was a cozy place to be in, like having all your senses muffled with honey soaked cotton.

You can die now... the thought tugged at the edge of the shroud. The bug in her head was all used up. She'd die just as easily as anybody else in Nasheen. And fuck knew plenty of them died in the desert. What did she care for another dead politician? Truth was, she didn't. But she wanted to know the real reason they risked summoning her from exile, and she'd only know that if she had Raine. Until she knew, she couldn't be safe. Nobody in her life would be safe.

Somebody was wailing. She stopped. Let Isabet down off her shoulders. Tried to catch her breath. Turned.

Eskander had fallen in the sand. Far behind her prone body, Kage was still moving, but Eskander, the Nasheenian, the one who should have been able to take this desert best, was already down.

Nyx waded past Ahmed and Khatijah and crouched next to Eskander. The woman's eyes were sunken. When she took Eskander's wrist, the skin was dry and loose. She was mouthing some words, but no sound came out.

They had not given Eskander a pack, or weapons, just a burnous to cover her ruined body and a single water bulb. Nyx's movements were slow, uncoordinated, as she reached behind her for a dagger. She concentrated very hard at each little thing. It was like being drunk. She took Eskander's water bulb and pocketed it, then removed four empty water bulbs from her bandolier.

She heard Ahmed stumble up behind her, asking, "What are you doing?"

Nyx pushed Eskander's head back with one hand and jabbed open her throat with the dagger. Blood spurted over her hand and started pumping out rapidly, in time with Eskander's heartbeat. Nyx shoved the water bulb against the wound to collect the blood.

"The fuck you doing?" Ahmed said.

"Can't piss," Nyx said. "Blood's got more salt than urine. Still, might keep us going another couple kilometers."

"You're fucking mad as she is."

"Was," Nyx said. She finished filling the bulbs and attached them to the bandolier again, all but one. The last, she offered to Ahmed. White static juddered across her vision, and she blinked rapidly.

On the sand in front of her, Eskander shuddered.

"What are you doing?" Khatijah stumbled, fell, just short of Nyx's arm. Nyx shrugged her away.

"What the fuck are you doing? What the fuck!" Khatijah howled.

Ahmed shook his head.

"We're just about fucked," Nyx said.

"I'd rather be fucked," he said.

"Bloody traitor!" Khatijah said. "Monster! Oath-breaker!"

Nyx brought the warm blood to her mouth, and drank two swallows of salty, coppery blood. It was enough to wet her mouth and throat and trick her body into anticipating—for the barest of moments—that water was coming. With any luck, it would make her urinate, and that, at least, could gain her another day.

She capped off the rest of the blood and snapped it to the bandolier.

"Fucking mad," Ahmed said.

Khatijah started keening.

Nyx didn't bother pulling the burnous from Eskander's body. It was a cheap one, not organic, and wouldn't be saving any of them.

Kage came down the dune, then. When she saw Eskander's body and Khatijah's trembling shoulders, she came to a halt. Swayed a little.

Nyx took Eskander's full bulb from her pocket and tossed it to Kage. Kage didn't catch it, just let it fall to the sand at her feet. Kage stared at her, unmoving.

"That's yours," Nyx said. "Don't worry. By the time you fall over, we'll be too far gone for blood."

Nyx turned away, easily slapping off Khatijah's weak grab, and went back to Isabet's body. She didn't watch to see if Kage drank, or if Ahmed and Khatijah fought over it. Never knew how people would react, about this time. Whatever you did about now could be forgiven.

Nyx heaved Isabet up onto her back again, the coppery aftertaste of the blood still thick in her mouth.

Two down, she thought. Wonder how many more to go?

She slogged. Time passed.

"Can't see," Ahmed murmured. His voice sounded distant.

She turned, saw him rubbing at his eyes, blinking, squinting out ahead. She was surprised to see him still walking. She couldn't see anyone behind him.

"Just desert blindness," she said. "It'll pass. Just follow after me. You can hear me, right?"

"I can't see, Nyx."

"Just follow after me, Ahmed. Just follow."

Time stretched. She must have blanked out for a while, because when Nyx glanced up next, she was walking alone, dragging Isabet behind her with her hands looped up under the girl's armpits.

She paused, swung her head up. Khatijah knelt in the sand not a dozen paces distant, swaying softly. Ahmed's body made a muddy S-shape in the desert behind her, just an arm's length away. There was a low wind blowing, and it piled up sand along the edges of their bodies. It wouldn't take long for the desert to conceal them. Far behind Ahmed, she noted a suggestive black clump at the top of a dune—Kage, long since given up the fight.

Nyx squeezed her eyes shut. Survival, up to a point, was just a mind game. Your body could do more than you thought it could. But when you reached your body's breaking point, well, it was just that—the end. If she dropped Isabet she might make it another kilometer. It was possible. She could see a break in the dunes now, and just a stroll away the crunchy sand became hard playa again, and she could see the soft, comforting breasts of mountains in the distance. Logic told her she would never make the mountains. Thirst and delirium said otherwise.

Her head hurt. The sun was blinding. She was thirsty enough to consider carving Isabet up and drinking up all the coppery liquid that spilled from her fragile little body, the way she had with Eskander. Had that really happened? She wasn't even so sure.

She dropped Isabet. Shed a great burden.

She yanked one of the bloody bulbs from her bandolier, uncapped it.

Brought it to her lips. The blood had congealed. Her stomach roiled. She dry heaved, and the bulb fell onto the sand, oozing

Why am I carrying her? Nyx thought. She gazed off toward the mountains again. She could make it. Surely. Alone, she was much stronger. Alone, she could make the mountains, and the promise of water. She could achieve so much more, alone.

She would never have come here if she'd been smart, and lived out her exile alone. It all came apart once you starting caring for something outside yourself.

She stumbled forward, half the distance to the playa, before she fell headfirst into the sand.

She grappled back up. Dragged herself forward.

The sun was moving off into afternoon. She heard the hiss and scuffle of some insect, and a giant amber beetle reared up at her in a gush of sand.

Her foot caught at the edge of the seam of the playa. She fell again, this time on the hard, cracked red surface. Her head thumped against the dirt. Her legs went numb. She tried to move her arms, to claw forward. They didn't respond. The beetle pounced. She yelled and smacked it with her head; it scuttled off.

Dying always felt so peaceful.

She came to in the dim blue light of dusk. The ground was still warm, but the air had turned terribly cold. A sharp wind blew sand granules into her face. She coughed, and realized with a surge of hope that she had a terrible urge to urinate.

Nyx yanked her collapsible stew pot out of her pack and pissed in it. She brought the pot to her lips without hesitation. It wasn't the first time she had to drink her own urine.

After, she lay on her side, chewing on her last strip of sunbaked worm until the final sun went down.

Then she was up again. How, she wasn't so sure. One minute she was on the ground, and when she came to next, she was walking again, plodding forward like some half-dead, cancerous wanderer.

Then she raised her head and saw a black form winging its way across the night, just there at the edge of the surge of blackness in the northern sky, visible only because as it moved south the stars carpeted the sky behind it.

It was a raven. It alighted on her shoulder.

She blinked, and the bird was off again. For a moment, she wondered if she'd just made it up. Some blotchy darkness that her mind had turned into a bird.

"Bring water, you fuck!" she wheezed.

But it kept cawing, kept circling.

"Fuck you! I had to drop her! Wouldn't have made it… made it this far." She was out of breath. Wheezing. Her heart pounded in her chest.

She caught herself drifting, swimming through a cool waterfall in Druce with Radeyah.

She fell again. Fell hard. The breath left her body this time, and she gasped for air, rolled onto her back, faced the star-studded sky.

Dying wasn't so bad, so why did she keep trying so hard to live?

She stayed down.

Closed her eyes.

She was back at the waterfall again, laughing with Radeyah like some drunk school kid. She had never laughed so much as she had in Druce. How was that possible? It was a contaminated little slice of exile, with oozing bugs and rot that ate Anneke's first three gardens and secretive little people who all pretended they couldn't speak Nasheenian. But there was also a whole lot of quiet there—outside Anneke's shooting range, at any rate.

When she opened her eyes, her whole body was moving. She was covered in bulbous armored bugs, big as her fist. They were chewing at her bloody chest.

Nyx let out a yell, pushed back. A few of the bugs lumbered off her, slow as some fat inlander. They were chewing at her bandolier. They'd broken open the containers of blood, and were lapping it up with thorny proboscides that needled at her skin beneath her tunic.

She tried to push them off, but her hands weren't responding again. One of them crawled up the length of her: dainty little feet across her neck, her cheek. She gritted her teeth. It perched there on her face, waving its antennae. It came up on its hind legs, waved its front legs like a charging beast.

Nyx snapped at it with her teeth. It was like crushing a grape, or a balloon. The thing just burst, and warm, wet fluid spattered her face, wet her mouth. She choked on bits of the thing, spit it out.

Her fingers twitched. Responded. She grabbed one of the ones on her chest. Mashed it with her hand. It popped, spilling warm, clear liquid across her hand. Nyx slowly brought her hand up to her face, sniffed at the liquid and shattered carapace. It was odorless. She licked it. It was clean and clear, like… water.

Or tasteless poison.

But for a woman who had slurped down another woman's blood and her own urine just a few hours back, that possibility wasn't enough to put her off.

Nyx grabbed another of the bugs making a meal of Eskander's blood, and twisted open the end of it, like pinching off the end of a woody fruit. She sucked out the liquid inside.

It might not have been water, but it was close enough. She grabbed another one, and another, until the sluggish little fuckers began to catch on. As they started to pile off her and go lumbering off toward some rounded mounds in the sand, she scrabbled to her feet, still dizzy, and shed her burnous. She looped the end of it into a sack, and started collecting the bugs and tossing them in. When it was full, she tied it off and collapsed again.

Water, after a very long time in the desert. The feeling was better than any fuck, better than good whiskey, better than dying.

The raven was watching her from the top of another of the mounds, head cocked.

"Eshe?" she said.

No answer. Just the quizzical stare.

She peered, again, at the mound the raven perched on. There were at least a dozen or more mounds beyond it, all about the same size and shape. More ruins? More desert garbage?

She slumped onto the ground again, lost some time.

When she woke, the raven was pecking at the top of her head. She growled and snarled, tried to bat it away. The bird jumped back three hops, cocked its head.

It was still dark. She thought of something Yah Tayyib once told her. It was the secret to winning any contest, he said, in life or in the boxing ring—you just had to get up more often than you fell down.

There was a rising wind, then a clattering racket, like a thousand voices raised in the market, or some mess hall.

Nyx raised her head. Above her, the sky was full of ravens.

Some primal fear filled her, something far more terrifying than dying. She scrabbled to her feet and stumbled toward the mound the raven was sitting on. She hoped to dig into it and find some shelter.

She got within arm's reach—and fell again.

She put out her hands, expecting to meet resistance.

Instead, she fell right *through* the mound—and into cool darkness.

25.

They left her for six days.

It was a blessing, though Inaya did not realize it until the third day, as she sat against the roughhewn wall, staring at the narrow shaft of light that brought in cool air during the day and buzzing insects at night. She had large, swollen bumps on her arms, legs, and face. Late summer heat soaked the humid air; there was no temperature control at all. She sweated during the day and shivered at night. There was a single refuse pail in one corner, caked in some specious gunk that made her gag. The pail had yet to be emptied, and her slop spilled over the lip of the bucket now and pooled in one corner. Her clothes were filthy. She, like her cell, stank.

During the day, Inaya listened for voices, conversation, to try and glean some hint of where she was. The type of holding cell was important. This one had a filter instead of a door, which was expensive. It was where an important prisoner would go—one suspected of being a shifter. If she was in some central city cell, they likely had an idea of who she was. But if she was still in Inoublie, there was hope that she could play at being falsely accused. Of what she was accused, of course, she still had no idea. Repeated attempts to talk to those who deactivated the filter long enough to pass her food and water—all of it infused with saffron—met with failure. The guards were all men—older, experienced men with sour, grimacing faces that told her exactly what they thought of her and her kind. She begged and pleaded with them like an innocent woman. In her situation, shedding tears wasn't difficult.

But not one man spoke to her.

It made it easier, in the end, to sort out her story before they came for her. She knew what an interrogation looked like. Her second husband, Khos, had been a mercenary—a very good one—and he had worked for one of Nasheen's best bounty hunters. God's Angels, however, were not as... blunt as Nasheen's bounty hunters. They would only use force against a woman if they had to... or if they could prove she was a shifter. If they knew she was a shifter—without a doubt—she would no longer be human in their eyes. And from the cheerless faces of the men who brought her food, her humanity—if not in question—was already suspect just for being here. She had to convince them otherwise.

On the fourth day, they threw another prisoner in with her. Inaya did not know her, and her first fear was that it was some trick—put two shifters together and hope they incriminate themselves.

But the girl was young, only fourteen or fifteen, and not a shifter at all. Not unless she was playing the same game Inaya was.

"I don't know why I'm here. There were riots. Did they take you in the riots?" the girl asked.

"What riots?"

"They say it's the misborn"—Inaya could not help but grimace at the use of the derogatory term for shifters—"and a bomb went off at the Angels' headquarters in the capital. There have been retaliations. It's horrible. Really horrible."

Inaya felt a wave of fear, but kept her tone neutral. "How terrible."

"They're going door to door. That's why they took me. But it wasn't me. I had nothing to do with anything. It's all just a terrible mistake." She wrung her hands.

Inaya stopped asking questions. She was afraid what the girl would reveal.

The filter was released on the sixth day. A woman entered. She wore a long black habit and blue wimple. Inaya paid special attention to the woman's feet, because they were closest to her from where she sat on the bug-ridden floor. Some ant nest had spawned its queens overnight, and they tumbled into her cell from the narrow skylight. Their abandoned wings littered the floor, and made shimmering patterns across her own soiled habit. She had lost one of her shoes in the tussle with God's Angels. What most interested her was not the woman's sturdy, square-toed shoes, but the fact that she was not wearing any type of stocking. From far away, that fact may have been easy to miss, but from where Inaya sat, it was a glaring inconsistency in a Ras Tiegan woman whose hygiene and decorum had to be immaculate in order to gain a place as one of God's Angels. It told her immediately that there was a chance she was still in Inoublie with lesser Angels. No woman in a major city would dress without stockings.

The woman wrinkled her nose, presumably at the stench of the cell, and said, "I'm to get you cleaned up. You'll be meeting with one of the Arch Angels."

Inaya's eyes filled with tears. "Please, will someone tell me why I'm here? I went out to pray and these… men… I'm so frightened."

"It's not for me to say. The Arch Angel will see you. Stand up. Stand up or I will have you dragged out."

Inaya stood. She let the tears continue. Her hands shook. She was suddenly self-conscious next to this clean, primly dressed matron. It took all the self-control she possessed to calm her nerves, and bite back her fear, shame, humiliation… This was a game. She must play her part consistently, or it would be her body getting cut up in some magician's laboratory, dissected on a slab—possibly while she was still alive. And then the Fourré would break. Michel and Gabrielle could not tolerate each other at the best of times. Without Inaya as a go-between, it was quite possible the whole movement could become fragmented. In her mind's eye, she saw all of her first-tier cadres devolve into violence and murder. She saw them give her away by demanding her release. What if they had already done it? What if that's what the rioting was about? What if Michel had used her abduction as an excuse for going back to the tactics she explicitly wanted to move away from? She did not doubt for a moment that her abduction was a calculated one, but she did not yet know how or who. Michel, Adeliz, even Isabet could be suspect. And then there was Gabrielle. And the top tier of cadres. All eight of them had reason to doubt her new direction. To hate her for it.

The woman stripped Inaya bare and threw her under a cold sluice of water in a tiny room plastered in broken gray tile. The corners of the damp, slippery floor were teeming with cockroaches.

The water was cold. The woman threw a palm-sized washing cloth at Inaya and said, "Wash yourself."

Inaya did what she could with the clean rag and no soap. When she stepped out of the water, hugging herself, shivering, the woman tossed a towel at her. It hit her in the face and fell onto the wet floor.

"Dry yourself."

"I have a family," Inaya said. "There has been some mistake."

"Do not speak out of turn again. Follow instructions, and this will all go easier."

Inaya picked up the damp towel.

She dressed in a shapeless gray habit and matching wimple. The woman carefully examined her head and face to ensure that not the barest hint of hair had escaped the severe, stiff wimple.

"You are acceptable," the woman said.

Inaya wanted to ask why it was she had been detained again, but decided to wait to ask someone in authority. She knew better than to guess that this woman would be her interrogator. Anyone with any authority in Ras Tieg tended to be a man, generally a priest or a man with strong ties to the church. This woman may have influence, but she was not the one to plead her case.

She followed the woman through a low-pitched hallway. She heard muffled sounds from behind spongy doors that crawled with scarabs. The bugs kept the exact conversations muted, but the tone carried: pleading, sometimes frantic. She let herself wonder just how many people they kept here, and if all of them were shifters.

She noticed the woman glancing back at her as they walked. Watching for signs of distress? Discomfort? She was tired and hungry and slightly nauseous from all the saffron they were stuffing her with. She wanted to pretend she felt perfectly at ease, but would an innocent, non-shifter woman act that way? Or would she be trembling, terrified? Inaya had already picked her part. She needed to play it. So, though it pained her, she lowered her eyes and wrung her hands and began preparing herself for more weeping. One of her aunts had been a professional mourner, and she had always envied the way the woman could call up a sob on command. It got her what she wanted, and more. Men did not like to see women weep. It reminded them of their own failings.

The woman paused at one of the doors. This one was without scarabs. Inaya heard nothing on the other side of it. The woman knocked and entered.

Inaya was not certain what she expected. She had never been incarcerated before. She understood interrogation, but in her mind, interrogation meant fear, pain, torture. And those types of interrogations generally only happened if one was certain they had a person with information, didn't they?

The room was without any kind of furniture. The floor was soft, spongy—some organic thing that ate whatever bodily fluids had been spilled here. It had the feel of any other type of cell, only cleaner because of the organics. The room's only light came from glow worms set beneath a translucent band at the center of the ceiling. The worms inside were dying, so the light was orange instead of pale yellow. There was nothing else in the room.

"Go on," the woman said.

Inaya walked into the room.

The woman shut the door. Inaya heard the soft chitter of the scarabs as they descended outside the door to muffle all sound. But the sound of what?

Inaya leaned against the door and pressed her ear to the soft interior surface. The walls were coated in the same organic matting as the floor. Her face came away sticky.

She moved away from the door, into the light. Was she to rot here, then? Brought into one cell after another? What was happening?

Inaya paced for a time, then finally settled into one of the corners furthest from the door to wait.

And wait.

It was many hours before they came for her. She had to squat in one of the empty corners to relieve herself. She expected a man, an interrogator, but it was another woman. This one said only, "Come," and refused any and all questions.

They moved her four more times, to four identical rooms. After a while, she started to wonder if they were simply taking her around in a circle and plunking her down into the same exact room time after time. During one of the many moves, they fed her. Some curried meat and rice slathered in saffron. She had eaten so much saffron the last week, the smell of it made her gag. But hunger and boredom overcame her queasy stomach, and she kept it down.

Every time she thought she might sleep in one of the rooms, they moved her again. It was then that she realized they must be watching her, and purposely disrupting her sleep. The rooms were all windowless, and the lights were always on.

When the door opened for the fifth time, she was so tired and disoriented that she almost didn't recognize the woman at the door as the one who had come for her the first time. As the woman moved into the room, a second figure came in behind her. The fear came, then, the fear she had been tamping down for days.

The man was dressed in the red robes and black cowl of a God's Angel. He was young, younger than she expected, a few years her junior. He had a neatly trimmed beard and dark eyes set in a lean face with a sallow complexion. He carried nothing. His hands were folded neatly in front of him, hidden in the long sleeves of his crimson robe. His gaze met hers, and at once she felt filthy again, and somehow inadequate.

"Inaya il Parait?" He stopped a few paces from her, but she could see that he was a head and shoulders taller than her, nearly as tall as a Nasheenian.

It was startling to hear that name aloud, after all this time. But she still had the sense to shake her head. "No, that isn't my name. Please, I think you have me confused with someone else. I just want to go home."

The man nodded to the woman, and she shut the door.

"What time is it?" Inaya asked.

"That has little relevance here," he said. "You say you are not Inaya il Parait. I have witnesses who say otherwise."

"Then they too are mistaken. I'm sorry, I don't know who that is. I just want to go home."

"And where is home?"

"Tirhan. My family is there."

"Is that so? You openly admit to marrying a Tirhani?"

"What? No. My husband is Mhorian."

She had assumed they brought her in in connection with the Fourré. It had never occurred to her that they might think she was a Tirhani spy. Oh, God, she had not prepared to talk her way out of that.

"And what is his name?"

Inaya hesitated. Knew he saw her hesitate. It was that, his knowledge of her deception, that made her finally burst into tears. "Please," she said. "Please, I just want to go home."

"I have a list of names for you," the man said. "Tell me which are familiar to you, and you may go home. It is quite simple."

"Please, I don't know why I'm here."

"Because you are Inaya il Parait, a well-known shifter sympathizer. And much more, aren't you? Shall I tell you what I know, or will you allow me to dispense with this pretense and get straight to the matter? Just a few confirmations of known associates, and I will send you straight home to your husband and children."

"I don't know the il Parait family," she said. "My husband is Khos Khadija. I am Inaya Khadija, and before that I was Inaya il Tierre. Ask anyone. I don't know this woman you're talking about."

"Let me tell you about your life, Inaya il Parait," he said. The Angel still did not approach her. His voice was deceptively warm, and his gaze, very soft, as if he felt he were speaking to a particularly adorable child. "Your father was a shopkeeper in Nanci, selling mostly tea and spices. He was not a wealthy man, and married just once. A woman from a family of known terrorists. Your mother was a shifter, well-known for it in your neighborhood, and often caught fornicating with dogs in the street. She bore two children before the state sterilized her. You, and your brother Taite. Should I go on?"

"I do not understand why I'm here. I have never heard of this family."

The Angel gestured to the woman. She opened the door and stepped outside. For a moment, Inaya was tempted by the open doorway. Could she find her way out? What was security like? All she had seen of this place were the hallways and the cells.

A moment later, the woman returned, ushering a young man ahead of her.

Inaya recognized Hynri almost immediately. Hynri, the leader of cell number seven. He had been scrubbed clean and dressed in a gray habit like hers. A snarl of fear gripped her. Oh, God, how much had Hynri told them?

"Do you know this man?" the Angel asked Inaya.

The words were easy. But she could not look at Hynri. "I'm sorry, no," Inaya said. "Perhaps I have seen him around the city, but it's difficult to say. Should I know him?"

"I told you," Hynri said. When Inaya glanced up, she saw Hynri, triumphant.

"You are certain?" the Angel said.

"Of course," Inaya said.

"Because if you cannot vouch for him, I'm afraid he has been sentenced to beheading."

"For what crime?"

"Conspiring to overthrow the government."

"This child?" Inaya watched Hynri's face. His expression was coolly blank, but his eyes were glassy.

Hynri said nothing.

The Angel watched them both.

Finally, the Angel raised his hand, and the woman escorted Hynri out.

Inaya stared at her hands. She expected God to strike her dead.

The Angel moved toward her. She stiffened. He leaned into her. She felt his warm breath on her neck. "I don't have to touch you. I don't have to torture you. You have already given yourself away."

And then he left her.

Inaya cried.

The woman came back for her and escorted her away, back through the winding hallways to the drab, dirty holding cell where she had originally been housed. But the woman who had been with her was gone.

Inaya curled up on the floor and sobbed. She was exhausted and hungry, and the world was completely out of her control. The logical part of her knew it was all a trick, just a trick, but fear and hunger crowded out that small, still, voice. It took a great deal of sobbing before she found peace again.

Later, one of the guards came by and pushed in a tin of food. Inaya shouted after him. "The girl. The girl who was here earlier? What's happened to her?"

"She's hung herself," the guard said. "Two days ago."

Inaya let her head sink. "Oh," she said. "Oh."

The guard bent over, peered at her from a safe distance. "You see how it is here, animal? We don't have to do anything at all to you. You all do in yourselves. Wonder how long it'll be before I cut *you* down?"

Inaya stared at the filter. He put his hand to the plate outside the entrance and the filter went opaque. He had not explained what the girl could have possibly hung herself with. Certainly not anything she had in the cell with her… not unless they gave it to her.

Inaya knelt, clasped her hands, and began to pray. "Martyr Mhari, full of grace…."

It was another eight days before the door opened again.

An unfamiliar guard stood there, outfitted all in crimson.

"Your husband is here to see you," he said.

26.

Nyx stumbled into a soft valley on the other side of the first few humps of the hills that bordered the playa and into town without knowing it was a town, only that there seemed to be people walking about on the humped ground. She was babbling like crazy Eskander, talking to dead people. Above the settlement, the stir of ravens coalesced, some murderous cloud. She was covered from head to foot in terrible gouges, savage bits of her taken out by the marauding ravens. Her chest was slathered in Eskander's dried blood from the burst water bulbs.

She lurched toward the first person she saw and yelled, "THEY ARE WAITING!" in Nasheenian.

The tall, dark-skinned stranger watched her with funny amber eyes and backed away slowly. The woman was immensely tall, her breasts about the height of Nyx's head, and she carried a basket of bulbous little bugs, the same ones that had tried to eat Nyx in the desert. Nyx wasn't sure where the woman was going with it—she saw no tents, no shelter, but in that moment, she wasn't exactly running on logic.

Nyx grabbed at the woman's long blue robes. Her clothing was slick, organic. Expensive. So soft.

The woman yanked the fabric away and babbled at her in some foreign language. It didn't sound like anything Nyx had ever heard. Not even Khairian.

All the babbling drew others. They came out of the ground like insects. One minute—humped, chalky soil, and the next... people. In a few minutes Nyx found herself surrounded by the tallest, darkest people she'd ever encountered. Ringing her the way they did, they cast her in cool shadow.

Nyx clawed at them like a trapped cat and pushed her way out of the circle. She stumbled and caught herself before she fell. Her body was done. But she wasn't.

"Nyx?"

She raised her head.

Eshe was running toward her. Where had he come from? Did they live in the air? He was dressed like the others, in bright, expensive robes. He was clean—even his hair had been washed. Extravagance, Nyx thought. Fucking waste of fucking water. Water.

He ran up and took her by the shoulders.

Her mutilated skin protested.

"Nyx, are you all right? Where's Isabet?"

Nyx surged toward him. She threw a hard left at the center of his face. His nose cracked, popped, sprayed blood like a burst balloon. He stumbled back, but didn't fall over.

"Good thing I'm a corpse, you fuck," she said, "or I would fucking kill you."

She keeled over then, hoping to pass out. She didn't.

Eshe leaned over her, bleeding on her, and then he was dragging her away from the crowd, down into the soil, into darkness.

✣

Ahmed's first sight upon waking was Nyx's sallow, bloodied face. "Need you to translate," she said.

No pleasantries. No soothing words. Not even a smile.

There was a tall woman standing behind her, wearing a flowing turquoise robe and matching turban with a loose end that trailed to her ankles. His vision was still fuzzy, and in the dim, he thought it was someone he knew.

"Who have you brought here?" he said. He squinted. Was it one of them? Had they found him? "Fuck, Nyx, who is that? Get her away from me!" He tried to move, but he was sore, and thirsty. Wherever they were was cool and dim. The walls gave off a greenish light, a pale bioluminescence that reminded him of something in a magician's gym.

"Hush now, hey," Nyx said, and took him by the shoulders.

Ahmed tried to rub at his eyes, but his arms felt weak.

"She's just a local, Ahmed. Nobody you know."

Ahmed relaxed, and she pressed him back onto the floor.

"I need you to translate, all right?" Nyx said.

He nodded.

"Do you speak Khairian?" he asked the woman.

"I do," she said. The accent was remarkable. It almost sounded Nasheenian. "At least one of you is half-civilized."

"Ask her about where we need to go. How far is the next water cache? Where can we find other Nasheenians? Big fat man calls himself Hamza Habib. Ask her that," Nyx said.

"Nyx, she has no idea what that is."

"Ask her."

Ahmed swallowed, tried to wet his mouth. "Could I have some water?"

Nyx pushed some kind of fist-sized bug toward him. He flinched. It had a bulbous back end that had been gouged open.

"Go on," she said.

Ahmed raised his head and sniffed at the ass-end of the mutilated insect. The tantalizing promise of water overwhelmed his initial repulsion, and he drank. The carapace of the insect was soft and papery, but the water was cool, familiar, and unexpectedly tasteless.

"You must go. You are not far from the Wall."

Ahmed translated.

"The wall? What's the wall?" Nyx asked.

The woman told him. Ahmed translated, "The end of the world."

"Well, that's fitting," Nyx said.

"It does sound promising," Ahmed said. He tried to get himself up on one elbow. He squinted in the dim light. It felt like they were in a cave. Eshe stood behind the foreign woman, dressed in strange clothing. His nose was newly broken; the blood and bruising was still fairly fresh. Ahmed saw other bodies around him. He realized they were what remained of Nyx's team—Kage, Isabet, Khatijah.

Ahmed asked the woman, "Where are we?"

"These are our prayer niches. Your companion stumbled into one, drawn by the call of the ravens that nest here. You should go. If we tend to you, you must pay us in blood or bugs. You have neither. You must go, or you will indebt yourself to us. The boy already paid in blood."

"What she say?" Nyx asked.

"We thank you for the hospitality," Ahmed said. He tried to remember the Khairian social mores regarding hospitality, but his mind was still muddy. Indebted to them? What did that mean, exactly? It had the weight of something far more menacing than some social nicety. He was reminded of the strange two-faced language of Tirhani false politeness, and realized there may be something similar happening here that he didn't understand.

"Do not use that word. We have given you nothing. You must go."

"We'll die in the desert," Ahmed said.

"What is she *saying*?" Nyx repeated.

"You are only a few days from the Wall," the woman said. "I do not know your destination, but there is little past that. You can purchase or sell all you like at the Wall. But not here. You must leave."

"How many days?"

"The way you travel?" Her gaze moved across his body. She shook her head. "Three days."

"She thinks it's pretty important that we leave." He regarded the others. "How are they?"

Nyx shook her head. "Khatijah woke up a while back. I hydrated everybody best I could before I went out again."

"You… went out again?"

"Eskander kept saying the settlement was only a few days away. I held her to that. I left you here and kept looking."

Ahmed watched the other woman. She was, outwardly, composed, but there was something about the way she gazed at him that made him uneasy. He felt the first stirrings of fear.

When he worked in intelligence, he found out quickly that there was no actual way to determine if someone was lying to you—not any that was better than a roll of the dice, anyway. Instead, what you watched for were indicators of stress. If you figured you had the guy who planted an acid-frag mine, you first asked him about other things—blades, guns, bursts, and looked for indications of stress. If there were none, you'd ask about mines, and then the actual specific weapon itself. More often than not, you'd see a growing number of stress indicators the closer you got to talking about the actual incident. That sort of thing worked on typical grunts, but spies and special operatives were another matter. They were smart enough not to talk to you about anything. Your only leverage was in learning something personal that you could use against them.

He knew nothing about how this society worked. Khairians often had multiple husbands who raised children and—in some cases—were even able to nurse them. Umayma was a wild place, with incredible mutations. He wasn't going to make any assumptions.

"You must be gone by dawn," the woman said. "Tell your people to be gone by then. We cannot be responsible for what happens. The boy has paid us in blood. He can attend your sickness. But you must go."

"We have until dawn," Ahmed said.

"I can't fucking move our people at dawn," Nyx said.

Ahmed sighed and told the woman, "You can see that we are not well. We can't be gone at dawn."

"Then you will die here," the woman said, and turned. She walked directly through the wall behind her.

Ahmed closed and opened his eyes, thinking he had imagined it. Eshe and Nyx were still there, staring at him.

"Did I just…? That wall…?"

"It's an opaque filter," Nyx said. "There are a couple dozen of them out here, all covered in sand. Fell into it myself."

"And you… you dragged us all back here?"

"It was that or leave your sorry asses to bake. I considered it."

He must have had a strange expression on his face, because Nyx reached out a hand, gripped his shoulder, leaned in. "I'm a lot of things," Nyx said. "I do a lot of shit you might not like. But I'm not fucking stupid."

"What happened to you?" Ahmed asked Eshe.

"I found the settlement. But I don't know any Khairian, and when I got here I was pretty sick and starving for protein. They fed me, but wouldn't let me leave. They took my blood. I bled out a pint of it for the food and clothes."

"Do you know why they don't want us here?"

He shrugged. "These are some kind of… I don't know… mosques or something to them. We're not supposed to be here."

Nyx sat with her hands on her knees, watching Kage. "Ahmed, you get the impression there's more going on than that?"

"Yes. I don't know what, though."

"They're mutants," Khatijah said.

Ahmed turned. The bel dame was sitting up, drinking from one of the bugs Nyx had offered Ahmed. She must have been awake long enough to see him drink from one.

"Mutants?" Nyx said.

Khatijah stared into the ass-end of the bug for a long minute. "Yes," she said. "There are ravens outside, right? This is the last settlement. The last place we got any record of Raine. We employ one of their little ravens as an informer."

"How are they mutants?" Eshe said.

"Haven't you seen them? Those aren't individual ravens out there. And these aren't bugs. It doesn't matter. My contact is here. She can help us."

"What about all the yelling at us to leave?" Nyx said.

"She's right about that. We do need to leave, or we'll get eaten up into one of these places so they can use all our organic bits to create new shit." Khatijah worked off her pack. Eshe moved to help her, but she waved him away. She pulled out her slide and tapped out some code.

Ahmed smelled peppery lavender. She was trying to send a message.

"Do you need—" Ahmed began.

She nodded. When she spoke, her voice was a little hoarse. "I need you to call a bug to carry it. Eskander would have done that."

Ahmed glanced over at Nyx, but her expression was perfectly neutral. He called a small swarm of red beetles. They ate the message Khatijah had coded, then buzzed out through the opaque walls of the shelter.

"She couldn't tell you where Raine was headed before now?" Eshe said.

"That's not a secure way of sending information. In case you haven't figured it out yet, we're not the only people looking for him. The only way she'd talk is if we came here. Somebody scared her bad." She gazed up at the ceiling. "We need to get out of here. Can we set up our own camp? This is a bad place to recover."

"You're welcome," Nyx said, but she stood, and began packing up.

✚

The ravens still circled the sky above the settlement. Nyx walked across the hills with Khatijah to meet the messenger. They had camped several hundred paces from the settlement, but Khatijah worried it wasn't enough.

"You know I can't move anybody," Nyx said. "We had to drag Isabet and Kage. I don't even know if they'll wake up."

"Perhaps you can leave them, then. Or is your decision to leave people to die in the desert more personal than you pretend?"

Nyx walked a good arm's length from Khatijah, wary of her reach. Weak she may have been, but Nyx wasn't feeling ready to go three rounds in a ring with a bel dame, either.

"Eskander was falling apart. She wasn't going to make it much longer."

"It's as I expected. Fatima sent us out here to die."

"You're still pretty close-mouthed about the whole thing for a woman who was sent off to die."

"You don't understand Fatima."

"I'm afraid I do. She sent me to prison. Tortured me. She's no friend of mine, Khat."

"*Khatijah*," she insisted.

Nyx stopped at the top of the hill. Below, a soft, scrubby valley spread before them. After so long in blinding desert, it was delightfully inviting. "If we're going to keep on, I've got to know why Fatima was having Raine tailed. Since when do bel dames put security on a politician? Bel dames go after terrorists and deserters. We're not order keepers."

Khatijah sighed. She, too, paused at the top of the hill. "Now that you've used up the bug, I'm going to die out here, right? So what's the difference?" She grimaced. "He was marked as a terrorist. We had a note all written up for his head, but the Queen stayed our hand. She felt it was more dangerous to kill him. We didn't know what the boys would do. So she put us on watch, just to make sure nobody else decided to kill him."

"Like who?"

"Anyone. Chenjans. First Families. Rogue bel dames. The boys are a perfect munitions shell, primed to burst. All they need is a catalyst. His death would be it."

"Then why'd they kidnap him? Why not kill him and set it off?"

"I don't know. I wouldn't have come out here if I knew that. All I know is, I got sent off on a fool's errand with the most hated bel dame in the fucking country. You killed a lot of friends of mine in Tirhan."

"Not so friendly, I think, if you weren't there with them," Nyx said. She folded her arms. "What the fuck is Fatima playing at?"

"There," Khatijah said, and pointed to a small figure making its way into the valley from the opposite side.

Nyx and Khatijah walked down to meet it.

As Nyx got closer, she realized that the black robe the figure wore was actually made of ravens' feathers. The figure appeared to be a woman; small, dark, with a pinched little face that appeared almost Drucian and hands knotted up like claws, as if she suffered from some terrible arthritis.

Khatijah nodded when she met her; the closest a Nasheenian ever got to bowing.

"I'm Khatijah Basima, sent by councilwoman Fatima Kosan of Nasheen."

The woman held out her fingers, and Nyx realized she had some kind of insect affixed to the ends of her ring and index fingers. Their mouths covered the tips of her fingers completely. Stingers protruded from their ass-ends.

"I must taste you to verify," the woman said.

Khatijah held out her hand. The woman pricked her with the insect stingers, then drew back. She pulled her hands into her robe, no, not a robe, some kind of cape or burnous, and began humming. She closed her eyes.

Above, the murder of crows over the settlement let off a cacophony of cawing that hurt Nyx's ears.

"Good, good," the woman said. She opened her eyes and smiled. Her teeth were rotten. Nyx didn't see many rotten teeth in Nasheen unless somebody was using sen or had their teeth blown out in some accident. The water was treated to prevent it.

"Thank you for speaking with us," Khatijah said.

"I am always thankful to speak with my ancestors," the woman said.

Mad as a fucking magician, Nyx thought.

"You told us you saw Hamza Habib brought through here several months ago. Do you know where they were taking him?"

"And *who* was taking him?" Nyx asked.

"They are going beyond the Wall," the woman said, and pointed her clawed hand north.

"How far is that?" Nyx said.

Khatijah glared at her. "I've got it, Nyx. Thanks,"

"A few more days," the woman said.

"But where over the wall?" Khatijah asked.

"Bomani," the woman said.

"What is that, exactly?" Nyx said.

"One of the old purifiers. They are going to remake him."

"Into... what?" Nyx said.

Khatijah held up a hand to Nyx. "Can you give me a moment, please?"

"Can you hurry the fuck up, then?"

Khatijah said, "Who is going to remake him? And why? Is it the Chenjans? Bel dames like me?"

"Oh, it's much worse than that," the woman said.

"Who, then?"

"The First ones have taken him. They have a mind to retake Nasheen."

"Wait," Nyx said. "Retake Nasheen? Nasheen is already taken. They already run Nasheen."

"Not *your* first ones," the woman said. "Go beyond the Wall. To Bomani. You will find them. I spoke to them before they left. They drained our cairns dry, and remade many people before we stopped them."

"Remaking into what?" Nyx asked.

The woman cocked her head at her. "Back to the beginning. Into the stuff that makes the world. The shape shifters know of it. It is the place we go, the place we put our bodies when we are in form. They wish to put us all back there. Start over. Jealous gods."

"This make any sense to you?" Nyx asked Khatijah.

She shook her head.

The woman bowed her head. "Is there any other way I can assist?"

"No, thank you," Khatijah said. "Unless you can convince the other people here to let us stay a few more days?"

"Oh, you don't want to do that." The woman stared at the cloud of ravens. "No, you don't want to do that. Keep going north. It is much safer there than here."

"Something tells me that's not as comforting as it sounds," Nyx said.

Khatijah reached into her burnous. She pulled something out and placed it into the woman's outstretched hand.

"Thank you," Khatijah said.

The woman nodded and turned away. She started back the way she had come.

"What did you give her?" Nyx asked.

"Nothing," Khatijah said. "It's an empty gesture. It's just... what's done out here."

“You gave her nothing for that information?”

“You heard her. She has her own reasons for helping us.”

“This trip just went from fucked up to totally fucking crazy shit,” Nyx said.

“I expect it’s all about to get much worse,” Khatijah said, gazing north.

“What are we dealing with here?”

“I don’t know. Only Eskander’s been out any further than this.” She glanced back at Nyx. “But that doesn’t do us any good now, does it? You figured I was the real guide, didn’t you? That I was the only one you needed.”

“I figured your sister was insane. You were a safer bet.”

“You were wrong,” Khatijah said.

27.

Nyx had always wondered what lay at the end of the desert. Now she knew.

At the end of the desert was a wall.

She had never seen anything like it, not in half a hundred cities. The Wall was a black shadow. The sand pooled against it like weevils caught up in honey, the living crawling across the dying to the source of the desert's darkness.

They entered the wall's shadow somctime in the early afternoon, after two days' walking from the as-yet-unnamed settlement. They had traded for what little food there was, and drank freely from the settlement's water, but that was all.

Now they walked toward a massive red line that took up the horizon. They soon found that they could travel longer, though, because the suns tipped below the massive wall much sooner, and they could spend much of the afternoon plodding through artificial dusk.

Khatijah pulled out a glow globe an hour before the first sun set. "Looks like a fucking toilet hole out here," she said.

And when the first sun set, it really did look like a hole. Sound was magnified. Every step across the sand sounded like walking over glass. The echoes got eerie. Nyx heard things beyond the circle of light. Bugs, beasts—not cats or dogs or ravens, parrots, no—but something more primitive; something made of the desert, as old as the world itself.

"Are we going to stop here tonight?" Eshe asked tentatively.

"Could be interesting," Nyx said.

Ahmed snorted. Isabet said something mushy in Ras Tiegan and pulled closer to Eshe. Nyx rolled her eyes.

"The light might keep through the night," Khatijah said.

"Light doesn't always keep the dark things away," Nyx said.

"It helps," Khatijah said.

Nyx couldn't argue that.

"They said there was a city near that Wall," Ahmed said. "Maybe we just can't see it yet. Further east, maybe?"

Nyx wasn't so sure of that. She figured they would have seen or heard it by now. She wanted to camp at the base of the Wall, but when the moons came up, they were still a long haul from it.

"We'll get some sleep now," Nyx said. "I got first watch."

"I can go a little longer," Eshe said.

"It'll be just as bad another kilometer ahead. I can't see any lights. We need to sleep."

"God knows we are not waiting on the light," Khatijah muttered.

As they bedded down, Ahmed began drawing a circle in the sand around them. It was something the woman in the settlement had told them to do, if they insisted on going further north. Nyx had a good idea of what the sand would do out here without a circle. She had seen what it did back in Tirhan, when it was unleashed on a bunch of bel dames. She wasn't looking for a repeat.

Nyx took first watch. The night had fallen some time before, and she could hear the chittering and moaning of some foreign thing bawling across the desert. Out here, the desert was a chunky ruin of scattered stone croppings, some twice as tall as her, others just large enough to trip over. Kage had knocked one of the protuberances over, and it had vomited a sea of green chittering bugs with triangular heads and soft, luminescent bodies.

Ahmed joined Nyx on an overturned outcrop, some broken thing long ago sheared off and gone dormant.

"You have any sen?" she asked.

"Not for a long time," he said.

They sat in silence for a while. Something hissed, far off. Nyx peered off in that direction, but the sound didn't come again.

"We'll lose everything to the bugs eventually," Ahmed said.

“I’d rather we gave them a run for it,” Nyx said. She glanced at him sidelong, considering. He was pretty, she’d give him that. And tough, for all his prettiness. It’d been a long time since she could say a pretty man was tough.

Ahmed caught her looking. “I’m not that man.”

“What man?”

“The one you’re always thinking about when you look at me.”

Ahmed hugged his knees to his chest. The night was cool, but despite the necessity, the gesture was surprisingly boyish. In the dim light, he reminded her of her eldest brother, Amir.

He peered at her. “What?”

“You remind me of my brother. Dead a long time now, with all the rest.”

“You must have seen a good number of dead men.”

“As have you.”

“And a good many women who put them there.”

“Wars don’t keep on unless everybody’s behind them. Men just as much as women. Turn a dead eye to it, profit from it, roll over and accept it… if you’re not actively resisting it, you support it.”

“I’m not going to debate politics with you. Not now. Not out here.”

“I’ll accept that,” Nyx said. “If you answer a question for me.”

“What?”

“At the settlement, when that woman came in, you thought she was somebody else. Who did you think she was?”

Ahmed shrugged. “I was disoriented. I don’t know. You know how it is, after you come back. Every night’s a fucking war.”

The sound started out low, isolated. It came from just north of them, from the open desert.

Nyx thought at first that it might be some stray cicadas, maybe a small mutant swarm. But the sound, like all the others, simply flared and faded, like some gasping giant gone back to slumber.

“You have second watch,” Nyx said. “You should get some sleep.”

Ahmed stood. Gazed back into camp. “I’m worried about the girl.”

“Which one?”

“The Ras Tiegan. She blistered badly. And her arm isn’t pretty. I’m concerned about infection”

“Well, not everybody stays pretty forever. She’ll be fine. Gives her character.”

"She's Ras Tiegan, not Nasheenian."

"I like our way better."

"Do you?" He sounded genuinely surprised.

The sound came again, the sighing chitter of some unknown mass. Nyx waved him off. "Go on."

Ahmed gazed toward the sound, pensive. "I know you're used to leading folks off to their deaths. So I'd like some of that false reassurance now. The kind I'm sure you're good at."

"It'll be fine," Nyx said. "It'll all be fine."

"That's all you've got?"

"Sure you don't have any sen? Some whiskey?"

He shook his head.

"Then that's all I've got," she said, and resumed her watch.

28.

"Sure is a wall," Eshe said.

"Sure is," Nyx said.

They had followed the red line of the Wall east for half a day along a track at the base of it. The Wall itself was so massive that, this close, it seemed to touch the sky.

Nyx told Eshe to take point. He was in the best shape. Kage had recovered more quickly than any of them expected, but Nyx put her at the back, with Isabet, whose blistered face and hands were still so painful that she wept at night.

Some part of Eshe felt Isabet's pain was his fault. He knew it wasn't true, but when she wept, it physically hurt him. He knew he was a fool. Felt like he was being played. When he flew into the settlement he hadn't been in the best shape either, and he'd been worse after they sucked him nearly dry of blood. What they used all the blood for, he didn't know. They stuck giant bugs on his arms and let them eat their fill until he passed out. Only then was he given water, and clothing, and enough food to bring him back from the edge of death after shifting.

Whoever those people were, he wanted nothing to do with them ever again. He'd been too weak to go after Isabet and the others, and he hated himself for it. Hated himself for no good reason. She was everything he hated about Ras Tieg. So why did he care so much about what happened to her? Why couldn't he just turn it all off the way Nyx did?

The cat scat along the way got fresher, the path more solid, and by evening Eshe caught sight of their first fellow traveler, a tall, dark man wearing a purple turban and shiny robe whose surface seemed to move as he walked. Eshe assumed it was organic until he got up close, and saw that the bugs weren't the usual tiny nits, bound together so small as to seem like one living skein, but thumbnail-sized roaches linked jaw-to-belly. The man led a small sand cat on a leash. The cat wasn't more than knee high, but it hissed back at them as they approached.

Ahmed asked the man, in Khairian, how far the settlement was. The man glanced back once. He shouted something in some other language, then quickened his pace.

But it meant they were likely going the right way. By evening, there were others on the road, and Eshe began to hang back with Nyx and the team, less worried about desert creatures. Soon, he saw the first indications of the city. A dusty pall hung over the horizon, and as the suns set blue, green, and amber lights became visible.

Beside him, Isabet began to cry.

Eshe took her hand.

"I thought we would die out here," she said.

He didn't tell her he had thought the same.

As they walked, Eshe saw a mass of light and movement all along the Wall ahead of them. He saw the people climbing up and down it. There were residences up there, and intricately carved balconies. The Wall itself was made of red stone, he thought, but when they finally got close enough to touch it, he found that it more closely resembled bug secretions. When he stood at the base and stared up, he could see dozens of people milling about along carved outdoor walkways, leaning over balconies. One man, nearly the same color as the Wall, wrung out some garment, and a rain of green beetles cascaded over the side. Eshe shook out his hair and stepped away from the edge of the Wall.

"Food, a place to sleep," Nyx said. "Let's see if they'll take Nasheenian currency."

"They'll take bugs," Ahmed said. He, too, was looking up at the people milling within the Wall.

"Find out what goes for a good price, and see what you can wrangle up."

"There are tents ahead," Khatijah said. "I think we should stick to what we know. The Wall… not sure we're permitted there."

"I'll look too," Nyx said. "We need to find something better for carrying the water we'll need on the other side of it. We need another guide, too. Let's avoid doing what we just did again."

"Can we find something for Isabet?" Eshe asked. He didn't mention his own busted nose. If he was unremarkable before, a bent nose wasn't going to do him any favors. Nyx owed him.

"We'll get there," Nyx said.

"When?" Eshe said.

Nyx stopped. Turned. Her expression was hard. "I didn't ask her to come after us, Eshe. That was her choice. We get to her when we get to her."

"Nyx—"

"That's all," she said.

+

Morning was painful, but at least it wasn't on the sand. Ahmed woke in a cool room plastered in red sand. Kage sat in the round doorway, gazing at the teeming street below. The windows were set with the glassy, semi-transparent wings of some giant dragonfly. Eshe and Isabet were still asleep, their bodies almost touching. Isabet's blistered skin was slathered in a sticky unguent that had soothed her enough to keep her quiet for the night—for the first time since they stumbled away from the strange settlement on the edge of the desert. Nyx was gone, presumably already off to start haggling. The woman who rented them the room had taken Nasheenian currency, but far too much of it for Ahmed's taste. He wasn't sure how much Nyx had left, but at the prices being charged out here, it wouldn't last long. He needed to call up some bugs to trade.

Kage glanced back at him. She had not blistered like Isabet had—she'd been better protected from the suns—but her face was still pinched and hollowed. None of them were eating well.

Ahmed wasn't sure how long Kage was going to stick with them. He figured she would bleed off into the city once they reached it. She wasn't built to come out here in the first place, and things were only getting worse. He wouldn't blame her for telling Nyx to fuck off. He'd thought about it himself. Many times. He told himself he stayed because of what he had done back in Nasheen. But in truth, this was the perfect place to get lost.

Kage called back down onto the street. "He's awake!"

"Tell him to get down here!" Nyx's voice.

"She wants you to help her," Kage said.

Ahmed drank from one of his water bulbs, then moved past Kage and into the corridor set into the Wall. The room was three stories up, dug into the Wall with a score of others. He heard half a dozen languages he had no name for, men and women calling to one another, children playing, and a small group of people far down the Wall, singing.

He took a deep breath and swung over the side, gripping the handrails set alongside the deep grooves in the Wall.

Nyx waited for him below, arms crossed, impatient. As with any other weakness, she had shown no sympathy for his fear of heights.

"I found a place," she said.

He didn't ask for what. Asking her questions just made her more impatient these days.

He watched Nyx lurch ahead of him, and regarded her confident, big-hipped walk, and the way she kept tabs on the movement around them. He knew that there was something else driving him north now besides fear of capture. He had served under a great many women like her—literally and figuratively—but some part of him felt that all of them were striving to be exactly who Nyx was—and Nyx had achieved what they were pining for without any effort whatsoever. All dozen of them insisted they were tough women with big appetites and no regrets, but at the end of the day, they wept over their dead and fought over their lovers, like real people. They couldn't deny their humanity the way this woman had. They couldn't truly become monsters.

It was the monster in her that fascinated and repulsed him. He wanted to know how she could live that long without giving a shit about anything but herself. When was the last time she had a lover? Did she call anyone friend? Or were they just all business partners, the way Eshe seemed to be? That relationship alone was bizarre enough. The way Eshe looked at Nyx reminded him of the way he gazed forlornly at his own mothers, desperate for love, acceptance. But no matter how hard he worked or what he accomplished, they never regarded him with any sense of pride. To them, he was like a beast already scheduled for slaughter. Why get attached to something that served only one purpose?

Nyx led him through a maze of tents and rocky protrusions that had been repurposed into food and drink stalls. She entered a great orange tent. It was held in place along the bottom by toothy worms, their pointy teeth affixed to the end of the tent, the rest of their bodies driven into the ground.

Inside, he expected to find a smattering of purely practical commodities, but the tent was packed from floor to big top with a dizzying array of goods, many of which he had no name or use for. The spills of round, spiky fruits and red, fleshy vegetables were unfamiliar, as were the hooked instruments hanging from a pole at the far side of the tent. There were piles of textiles, all of them smooth, supple, organic swatches fine emough for a First Family to wear. He saw massive beetle heads, as large as his own, and piles of jagged insect legs and incisors stiff enough to serve as weapons.

Nyx passed him a flat bladder, something that must have come from a long, serpentine creature.

"This is what I was talking about," she said. "See, you carry it like the bandolier and bulbs, but it holds twice as much. Distributes it better, too."

"Are you heading further north?" a man said in Khairian.

Ahmed had not noticed him amid the stir of goods. He was a slight man, no larger than Kage, with a knot of dark hair wound about his skull like a crown. Ahmed might have guessed he was Ras Tiegan, if not for his brown skin and bold nose.

Ahmed had found a few who spoke words of Nasheenian and Chenjan, but there were far more languages in the air, only a handful of them related to Khairian. It was strange, to find a world on the other side of the one you knew, something you never knew existed.

"We may be," Ahmed said.

"You have a sponsor then, to get you over the Wall? Well, you must be careful. It's cicada season."

"I'm not sure what that means," Ahmed said.

The trader must have thought he meant the cicadas, not the sponsor, because he rattled on. "Have you seen the cicadas out here?"

Of all the writhing, gliding, squirming, clacking, chittering things Ahmed had seen out here, cicadas weren't one of them. "No. They mutants?"

Nyx set three of the water bladders in front of the trader. "Ask him if he has sen," she said.

Ahmed shook his head.

"They come out every twenty years or so," the trader said. "This is the season. I saw them when I was a kid. Big fuckers. Eat a caravan whole. Big teeth."

"Cicadas don't have teeth," Ahmed said.

"Sen," Nyx said.

"Do you have any sen?" Ahmed asked.

The trader shook his head. "Not sure what that is."

"How much for this, then?" Ahmed asked. And then, to Nyx, "Is this all? There's no sen."

The trader preferred bugs, but they didn't have any, so Ahmed served as middleman while they haggled in Nasheenian currency.

Once they were agreed, Ahmed loaded up their goods.

"What was he saying?" Nyx asked as they walked out.

He told her.

"Why'd you argue?"

Ahmed snorted. "I wasn't arguing. I was educating."

"Let me tell you. Best way to get yourself staked out on the sand and left for dead is to ignore the locals. You don't know this place."

"Teeth!" the trader called after them, making claws with his hands.

"Peace be," Ahmed muttered.

"Let's get breakfast and find a guide," Nyx said. "I heard there's a tea house where folks hire themselves out to caravans seeking to cross the Wall."

"Can we afford a guide?"

"Of course not. But we can afford to feed and clothe somebody, now that the magician is dead. Here, the tea house is this way."

Ahmed followed her through the riotous mass of colorful people. He wondered where all the people had come from. Weeks and weeks across this desert, and they hadn't seen more than a handful of figures, most of them moving away from them.

"You don't speak Khairian. How did you find out so much around here?"

"You don't have to speak a language to pick up on things. People talk without speaking all the time. You should know that. You worked intel."

"Did you pick up on why there are so many people out here?"

"It's a trade city, intelligence boy."

"Did you see a lot of people out there?"

"Not any people who wanted to be found," Nyx said. "You forget we're in somebody else's country. They've got their ways of avoiding outsiders, don't they?"

He thought of the raven-filled settlement, and the strange prayer niches. They could have come within three hundred paces of that settlement and not seen it. It took stumbling right into it to find it.

"Hurry up," Nyx said. "It's just here."

Among the stir of semi-permanent tents and rocky structures was a globular, red-and-purple-streaked monolith. To Ahmed's eyes, it was as if something had been shat out of a giant roach as tall as the sky-high Wall whose shadow protected the inhabitants of the city. Like the Wall itself, the monolith had been carved by many hands until its interior was mostly hollow. Nyx led him to the lip of the monolith and started inside the cool corridors. Bioluminescent insects pulsed across the arched ceiling and ran in neat horizontal lines where the floor and walls met. Ahmed paused to examine them, and saw that they were set behind a transparent skein that protected them from the foot traffic—something a lot like the lacquered dragonfly wings that made up the windows.

He ran to catch up with Nyx. She was stepping into a steamy doorway. As he rounded into the doorway, he collided with a tall, reddish woman with a sea of dark hair that nearly touched her ankles. She was arguing with Nyx, and acknowledged him only long enough to push him away.

Ahmed stumbled against the far wall. He reached for a gun, then hesitated. The argument had drawn a crowd in the already packed tea house. The woman herself bore no weapon. She spat at Nyx in surprisingly good Nasheenian.

"She says you own her," the red woman said. "If you own her, you answer for her crimes."

"In my country, fucking's not a crime," Nyx said.

"What's going on?" Ahmed said, pushing his way back to them.

Nyx met his look. "It seems our little Drucian has a more active life than we thought. She apparently fucked this woman's girlfriend."

"I have been insulted," the woman said, "I challenge you to a circle."

"Sorry, I don't accept."

"That is not done."

"Well, I'm doing it. You speak Nasheenian, you should know that we don't have the same rules you do."

The woman drew a weapon—a serrated insect leg like the ones Ahmed had seen in the trader's shop. She was over a head taller than Nyx, thinner and fitter, and at least two decades her junior. But Nyx didn't blink.

"You're in my place. You obey my rules," the woman said.

"They aren't strictly your rules, though, are they?" said another woman, in Nasheenian. Ahmed recognized her accent immediately. It was Chenjan. She sat at the nearest window, by the door. As she spoke, she stood and walked next to Nyx. She was a small woman, compared to all the rest. Her hair was bound in a turquoise turban, and she wore an amber robe made of the same jawed insects that many of the others in the tea house wore. Her complexion was as Chenjan as her accent. He had never seen a Chenjan woman without a burqua before.

"We're all visitors here, aren't we?" the Chenjan said. "Beyond the Wall, your people have rules. In Nasheen, they have theirs. But here in Kiranmay there are different rules, aren't there? Shall I call an enforcer and see what he has to say?"

The woman with the weapon frowned. She pointed the insect leg at Nyx. "Don't think I'll forget. When we meet next, we settle this."

"Sounds bloody fucking wonderful," Nyx said.

The woman sheathed her weapon and slid out the door. The crowd that had gathered around them began to dissipate.

Nyx raised her brows at Ahmed. "You're even better at making friends than I am."

"Your woman dishonored her," the Chenjan woman said.

"And who are you?" Nyx asked.

"Afareen."

"Just Afareen?"

"Out here? Yes. I belong to no one but myself out here."

"Let me buy you some tea," Nyx said.

Ahmed said, "Is that necessary?"

Nyx grinned. "You'll excuse him. He's just returned from the front."

Afareen said, "I lost all my men to the front. Husband, brothers, sons and all. So perhaps I am not as threatening as you hoped."

"That wasn't what I meant," Ahmed said.

"Wasn't it?" Nyx said, and gestured for the Chenjan to join them at a table.

Tea with a Chenjan. What was next? Ahmed thought. Dinner with bel dames?

+

"If your intent is to get beyond the Wall, you best turn back now," Afareen said.

"Not an option," Nyx said.

The three of them sat at Nyx's table at the back, propped up on low cushions. Nyx had listened to the tea shop owner smoothly transition between a dozen different languages in the quarter hour they'd been seated. She had never had much of a head for languages, and the idea of packing that many into her brain made her dizzy.

"Passing over the Wall requires a sponsor. One of those women must speak for you."

"Like the one who threatened Nyx?" Ahmed said.

"The one you insulted, yes."

"I can't believe it was Kage," Nyx said. "Maybe there's some other Drucian running around."

"Not out here," Afareen said.

"Why one of these women?" Ahmed asked.

"They are the Aadhya. They rule the world beyond the Wall."

"You ever been there? Beyond the Wall?" Nyx asked.

"No. I have been here some years. It was my intent to reach the other side of the continent, to discover what lay beyond the Wall. But the Aadhya are, as you saw, a prickly people. Unless you have something of great value to offer them, they will not permit you entry."

"Hasn't anyone just climbed the Wall?" Nyx asked.

"It's two kilometers high, and the other side is sheer. The dangers are… many. Those who live stay on the caravan route. To stray means death."

"So people do get across," Nyx said.

"Of course. Traders are welcome. Some of the Aadhya even serve as guides. You may have a more positive experience with others." She finished her tea and stood. "Now I must apologize for my own rudeness, but I am expected elsewhere. If you are seeking employment here while you wait to cross the Wall, I may have something for you. I live in the western quarter. Ask for Afareen of the red tent. Someone will direct you."

Ahmed watched the Chenjan go. She walked past the bar, which he only now realized was made of the undulating carapace of a massive arthropod. He shivered.

"Well, that's something," Nyx said.

"Sounds like a dead end," Ahmed said.

"Why, because she's Chenjan?"

"I wouldn't trust an open hand from a Chenjan."

"Because you'd never offer one to a Chenjan yourself?"

"It's just suspicious, that's all. Why's she here? What kind of Chenjan woman hangs out at the end of the world?"

"We have our reasons for being here, and she has hers. We could use the work, especially if we're stuck here for a while."

"I already have a job, Nyx. I'm working for you. If we're stuck, I don't want to go on. I'd bet a lot of the others are done, too. You think Kage's going to stick around after what we just went through? It sounds like she was already looking for a way out. And Eshe and Isabet, well, it's just a matter of time before he fucks off with her. Then what?"

Nyx shrugged. "I recruit a new team. Plenty of people here looking for work."

Ahmed sat back on his heels, anxious to call her bluff. "That's catshit."

"If you want to go, go. I'm not keeping you here."

"You promised payment."

"I promised food and a roof over your head. You've had that. And any payment I might have implied was for the end of the job. Not just getting to the job."

"We'll see how the others feel, then," Ahmed said.

"Indeed we will."

They walked together from the tea house, but in a few strides, Nyx was leading again, striding confidently back to their rented room as if he had not threatened to disband her entire team. He thought her supremely arrogant.

Eshe was at the ladder leading up to their residence with Kage. They were speaking to a woman who turned as they approached.

Her appearance caught Ahmed up short. He stopped breathing.

The woman raised a gun and pointed it at Ahmed. "So good of you to finally make it, Ahmed al Kaidan," she said.

Ahmed heard the shot.

29.

Inaya expected Michel to come for her. Or even one of their minor operatives working out of Inoublie. She did not actually expect her estranged husband. She had left Khos Khadija nearly seven years before in Tirhan, and had not spoken to him since. He raised their children with his second wife while Inaya led a revolution. She had regretted that decision many times. But what mother consigns her children to live in a world that hates them, when she could transform it into something different?

Her captors brought her into a tiny windowless room divided by an organic filter so tight that it made her skin crawl the moment she walked in. The closer she got to it, the more her skin itched. She began to wring her hands as she waited. Stopped. Then paced. Three steps right. Turn. Three steps left. The light was haunted; a ghastly, dying orange light produced by worms in glass. When the door began to open on the other side of the filter, she was hopeful. She and her operatives could speak in code, at least. They may even be able to slip her something on another occasion to neutralize the saffron. If she could shift and avoid the filters, she could escape. Fourré operatives knew what she needed. She had organized escapes from prisons before. None this secure, it was true, but the basics were the same.

The door on the other side of the filter opened. A large man filled the doorway. She knew him instantly.

It really was her husband, Khos Khadija.

She was suddenly unsteady on her feet, yet buoyant with emotion. The fear, longing, hurt, and sense of betrayal that swamped her was overwhelming.

He entered the room, and someone shut the door behind him. They were alone, but Inaya knew better than to believe they were unwatched.

Khos approached the filter. The expression on his face nearly took the breath from her. She had not seen a man look at her with so much love in a long time. He had grown out his hair again, and it hung in long yellow dreadlocks, knotted at the nape of his neck with an amber cord. He was thick in the shoulders and chest, and tall; her head barely reached his shoulder. The blue tattoos that crisscrossed his body were mostly covered. He wore long dark trousers, boots, and a pale coat that fell to mid-thigh. Compared to Tirhan, Ras Tieg could be a chilly country, and the clothing appeared new.

They stood a long moment on either side of the filter, neither saying a word, for some time.

"When did they send for you?" she asked, finally.

"Nine, ten days ago. It was the soonest I could get here."

"And what did they tell you?"

"They said I'm to sign for you, and bring you home."

"Home?"

"Tirhan," he said.

"Exile, then?"

"It's better than losing your head, isn't it?"

"Don't be dramatic. They don't put women to death here. They would send me to a work camp."

"To die."

"Eventually, yes."

She watched him, trying to decide if there was anything else he was trying to tell her. Their marriage had not been a close one, or a happy one. None of that was his fault. She could not help what she was. But it meant she was not as close to him as she needed to be in this moment, to understand if he had come to her with some kind of salvation, a plan, or if this was all there was.

"There must be a price for exile instead of the work camp," she said. "What do they think I can give them?"

He frowned. Yes, there it was. The furrowed brow. The unwillingness to meet her eyes. "They need to know the names of the people you work with. That's all. Then you'll be free."

"Free to go home with you."

"Is that worse than prison? Worse than a work camp? To come home with your husband? Go home to your children?" Even after all this time, she heard the strain in his voice, the hurt.

"How are the children?" she asked softly.

"They still ask about you."

"And what do you tell them?"

His eyes filled. She caught it just as he lowered his gaze. "Come home, Inaya. You have done all you could here."

"Have I?" She wanted to touch him, but not because she longed for him. No, it was because she wanted to comfort him. He had come all this way, after all this time, and she still could not bring herself to love him the way she should.

He raised his head. His eyes were clear again. Crying among Mhorian men was considered proper, he once told her. It showed that you cared for something greater than yourself. But her Ras Tiegan upbringing always saw it as weakness, and he had started hiding his tears a few years into their marriage. "I can't go back without you. I can't leave you here, Inaya. The things they'll do to you…"

"Did they tell you what they would do?"

He nodded.

"It's no worse than anything you saw in Nasheen, then."

"I loved nothing of what I did, or saw, in Nasheen. We left that place to have a better life. I thought I had given it to you. But you chose… this."

"You know why."

"Do I? Looking at you here, I'm not so sure." He lowered his voice, moved within a breath of the filter. "Inaya, they will kill you. They will get what they want from you one way or another. I have seen what people do when they want information. I've been the one who did those things. It isn't romantic or honorable. And it always ends in death. Yours and whoever you're working with. Please. Just tell them what they want and let me take you home. You know they won't offer again. They never do."

She shook her head. Stepped back from the filter. "I've done nothing wrong," she said. "They should let me go on that account."

"You know that isn't how this will go," he said.

Inaya turned away.

"Did I ever tell you how I got these tattoos?" he said.

Inaya faced him again. She had asked once, the night they arrived in Tirhan, the first time he asked her to marry him. He said he would tell her if she told him why she had fled Ras Tieg the way she had, alone, in the dead of night. She had refused, of course. They had eventually built their marriage around this mutual silence.

"It was before the *brit malah*," he said, "When I turned twelve. Mhorian kids die as often as they do in Ras Tieg. No inoculations, unless you're rich. Not like the Nasheenians and Chenjans. That's why they wait so long for the *brit malah*, and give us proper names."

"But yours isn't a proper Mhorian name," Inaya said.

"No, it's a Nasheenian one. Because I left before I had a name. I refused the *brit malah*. They give you that choice."

"Why would you do that?"

"We reach the age of majority at thirteen. You can decide to exile yourself from the community, or to join it. If you refuse, it means giving up everything. Your fathers. Your friends. The hope of having children with a Mhorian woman. Your whole life. I gave that up because I could not love a woman who belonged to everyone else. Couldn't see my children raised communally. I was a selfish man then, and a selfish one now. I know that. But it doesn't make me want you any less." He began to unbutton his coat.

"Khos—"

"Let me finish," he said, and began to speak to her in Nasheenian instead of Tirhani. "They gave me the tattoos before I left. They are the record of my family, from the time we fell until the time I left them. Inaya—" He opened his coat and revealed a tunic with a long, scooped neck that bared most of his torso. She saw the familiar tattoos there, spidery lines that she had come to learn were Mhorian text. "*Look to what you devour*. Soon it will give you the power to transform all this. And when it does, all that my family is or has ever been will be at your disposal. We'll wait for you."

It was such an unexpected thing to say that she found herself speechless. Khos buttoned back up his coat. He walked to the door, knocked. Looked back.

For a long minute, they gazed at one another. His face was hard now, completely unreadable, the love and compassion neatly erased.

Had he come straight here after being summoned? Or had he met with her people first? Would he have been smart enough to do that? Or was this a message regarding some plan he had cooked up on his own?

"Goodbye, Inaya," he said, in Nasheenian. It was the first language they ever spoke to one another. And the tone this time was not the forlorn, lovesick one he had used when speaking of bringing her home, but the resigned, hard-edged one he had used the day she told him she was leaving him.

"Goodbye, Khos," she said.

The woman in the hall escorted him out.

They came for Inaya sometime later, and returned her to her cell. She sat down at the center of the ghastly space and wept.

The door opened. It was her unpleasant female jailer again. She carried something with her.

"Hush now," the woman said, strangely compassionate after all this time. She passed Inaya two slips of regular paper and a long stylus. "At your husband's request, you've been permitted to write letters home to your children. I advise you to make them quite eloquent. It may be the last your children hear from you."

Inaya took the paper with trembling fingers. She wished she could think of some way out. Some opening they or Khos had given her that she could use to her advantage. But all Khos had to offer was what she already knew—"Look to what you devour"—yes, the food was toxic to her. It kept her from shifting. Was that all he really had for her? Why he had come all this way?

She cried as she wrote the letters. Just the act of writing such private correspondence to her children when she knew her captors would comb over them felt obscene. But Khos had been her last chance out. There would be no more offers. No more bargains.

Inaya completed the letters and folded them neatly. She held them in her lap until dinner came, and with it, her female jailer. The woman took away her letters.

Inaya stared at the plate of curried saffron rice and flat bread. Hunger gnawed at her. What did it matter now what she ate? If she tried to starve herself, they would see. Everything in these cells was watched and recorded.

She gave in and scooped up a bit of rice and curry with the flat bread. The smell of saffron was usually so overpowering that it made her nauseous. But this time, the food went down more easily. Perhaps she was getting used to it.

She stared at her empty plate. *Look to what you devour*, Khos had said. She turned over the plate. It was a simple platter, made of fired clay. Unmarked. She set it back down. Drank her water. Examined the cup. Nothing.

That night, as she lay awake staring at the filtered light of the moons coming through the skylight, thinking about her children, she remembered Khos baring his tattoos, and wondered if he had added her name there, and the children's. Was that all she was, now, a footnote in someone else's story? There was a time when that would have been enough. Wanting something more still felt sinful. She was prepared now to meet God as a terrible wife and mother, but to have given up so much and gain nothing for it would destroy her.

In the morning, she was stiff and sore. She had lost weight, and when she sat up now, there was no proper cushioning between her vertebrae and the hard floor.

She was surprised when, several hours later, the woman jailer came for her again. She was shepherded back into the twisting corridors and installed in one of the organic, windowless cells. This one had a large round table at the center. She walked around it, wondering if it was some new trick. Garish light swam beneath the skein of the ceiling.

The Angel entered. It was the same one who questioned her before.

"Will you release me now?" Inaya said. "Surely you realize I've done nothing wrong."

The Angel carried a slim portfolio. From it he pulled a single sheet of creased paper. He set it on the table before her. She peered at it. It was one of the letters she had written to her daughter, Isfahan.

"I don't understand," she said.

He pulled out a second sheet of paper. It was a different color; soft green, organic. The edges were browned, as if it had begun to rot before being saved from its fate by some skilled magician. He set it next to her daughter's letter.

She had signed her daughter's letter "Maman." The letter beside it, in the same neat, controlled hand she had learned in school, was signed

"Madame de Fourré."

It was the letter Michel had asked her to write to the Savoie family to help ease their fears and loosen their purse strings. The handwriting on both letters, of course, was identical.

Inaya went numb. She was aware of herself as if from some great height.

"We have you out, Madame de Fourré," the Angel said. "Is there anything more you wish to say before we separate your head from your body and end this petty insurgency once and for all?"

30.

Nyx tagged the woman as a bel dame almost immediately. It meant Nyx already had her scattergun half-drawn when the bel dame went for hers. Young women always liked to shoot off quips before their guns.

Older women knew better.

Nyx's gun went off a breath before the bel dame's. She stepped into the woman's space as she shot, batting away her gun with one hand while continuing to shoot with the other. Four shots to the chest put her down.

It was one of the quickest fights Nyx had ever been in.

Nyx let off her last shot into the woman's hand, ensuring it was too mangled to work the gun that had fallen just out of her reach.

She pressed a knee onto the bel dame's stomach to hold her still and leaned over her. The woman was coughing blood. She couldn't have been much more than twenty.

"Who sent you?" Nyx said. She pressed the gun to the woman's face. Not that it mattered much. She was out of rounds, and the woman was dead anyway.

Just coughing. More blood. And fear. It was strange to see fear in a bel dame's face, but death was different at twenty than forty. She watched the bel dame bleed out, right up until her eyes went dead and the bleeding stopped as the bug in her head kicked in.

Nyx glanced up at the others. Kage had pulled out her gun and circled back around Ahmed, looking for more shooters. Ahmed still stood exactly where he had when the bel dame pulled her gun, a dumb expression on his face.

"You want to cut off her head?" Nyx said. "She was after you, not me."

Ahmed shook his head.

"Well, I'd recommend you do it, or somebody's going to bring her back," Nyx said. "Then you and I need to talk."

✚

The room was surprisingly cool, a blessing after so many days in the desert. Eshe sat in the doorway watching Isabet sleeping in the far corner of the room. Kage was below, washing up at the communal well. They all needed it, but the water was costly. Kage had traded something of hers for it, but Eshe wasn't sure what. Nyx was off with Ahmed speaking to the local authorities about shooting the bel dame, and Khatijah had gone with them. He was content to be alone with Isabet for the first time in many days.

Her tangled, dirty hair was knotted back from her blemished face. The salve had soothed much of her inflamed skin overnight, but she had gone too long without it. She wouldn't have the lovely complexion of her rich parents anymore.

He knew what he needed to do back when they came to in the organic pods and he had seen her lying beside him, skin enflamed, face slack. He imagined she was dead, and the fear and loss that cut through him was so painful he thought his chest might burst. He was angry at himself for it, but it didn't change how he felt.

Isabet opened her eyes.

"I'd like to take you back to Ras Tieg," he said.

"I can't," she said. Her eyes welled with tears again, but she did not shed them.

"We'll get on with a caravan. A proper one. It won't take nearly as long to get back if we're with someone who knows where they're going. Let me take you home. I can't watch you die out here."

Isabet sat up, wincing. "I told you I can't go back."

"Because you're pregnant? What does that matter? Inaya won't care about that, or anybody else. It's not like Inaya's kids were all born with fathers around. We can… we can say it's mine."

He had been thinking and praying a lot about it, and what it meant to offer her a way to return to Ras Tieg with some semblance of honor intact. It meant marrying her, he knew, or at least telling people they were married.

"You think that's better?"

"Better than going back to Ras Tieg a whore, and getting stoned for it? Yes."

"You don't understand."

"Tell me what I don't understand. You just ran off here because you fucked some guy? I don't understand why you all don't have hexes on you like Nasheenians. I couldn't get a woman pregnant without a lot of effort."

"Nasheenians tamper too much with God's will."

"So it was God who got you pregnant, now?"

Isabet touched the unguent on her face, absently. "The voices were supposed to go away," she said. "That's why I did it. I wasn't coerced or anything. You're not supposed to get pregnant the first time. Everyone knows that."

Eshe threw up his hands. God save him from ignorant Ras Tiegans. "That worked out well, didn't it?"

"I wasn't supposed to be able to channel God through my mother if I wasn't a virgin. But… I still hear Him."

"And what does He say?"

"I don't know. Nothing you could understand."

"Because I'm a half-breed heretic?"

"It was my choice to come here."

"Just as it was your choice to fuck Michel, I'm sure." Eshe stood.

"I never said it was Michel!"

"Why else would you have come?" Eshe said. "Why would he have sent you here? It wasn't Inaya, was it? It was Michel." He was done. He wanted to leave her here, so she could understand what it would really be like, to make it on her own. But if he did that, how would he be any better than Michel?

"You're a bastard," Isabet said.

"Every Nasheenian is a bastard," Eshe said. "That insult means nothing to us." He stepped out into the corridor. "I'm going down to wash up. Would you like to do the same, or lob more insults?"

He could see Kage making her way back up the ladder, mostly clean, lugging her massive gun with her.

For a moment, he thought Isabet would refuse. He almost hoped she would. Then she said, "All right." And the hope fluttered up again, the hope that maybe he could build some kind of life after this. That maybe they weren't all going to die for Nasheen.

Kage met him on the balcony.

"You leave any water for the rest of us?" he asked.

Kage moved past him without a word. How did people like Inaya get others to like them? Even love them? He seemed to fail at it, even when he said all the right things. Kage hadn't spoken two words to him in more than a week.

"So what kind of work has Nyx found for us?" he asked Kage, hoping something that wasn't rhetorical would get more of a response.

"We won't need to hire ourselves out," Kage said. "I found us a guide."

+

"She's a First Family," Nyx said. "Is this supposed to make up for you fucking that giant?"

Kage sat with her on a cracked slab behind a string of temporary tents selling smoked cat meat and fried sand crawlers.

"I don't know what that is," Kage said.

"Families or fucking?"

"My business is my own. All you need know is that woman helped me find this one."

"You're all a slippery bag of trouble," Nyx said.

The woman walking toward them was one of the most elegant Nasheenians Nyx had ever seen. Being pretty wasn't an asset in Nasheen, but this woman wore it like it was one. She was strikingly beautiful, the sort of insidious beauty that knocked you flat in the street when you saw it. Her complexion was smooth as a child's, brown as burnt butter. She had a face like a proud cat—large eyes, plump cheeks, generous mouth. She wore a pale yellow shalwar khameez stitched in red and orange geometric designs. Her hijab was purple, wound loosely around her head so her cascade of dark, wavy hair hung free to her waist.

"Is this your employer, then?" the woman asked as she approached.

"Yes," Kage said. "Nyx, this is Safiyah."

Nyx said, "Sorry. Been a misunderstanding. I don't run with rogue First Family. Too much trouble. Too much paperwork."

Safiyah laughed, a surprisingly ugly sound considering her pleasant exterior. She sounded like a rabid dog hacking up a bit of foam. "Oh, they won't pay anything for me back home if you try and turn me in. So don't bother working out how much I'll go for."

"Come on, Kage," Nyx said, and started to move past Safiyah.

"You have another way over the Wall, then?" Safiyah said.

"We have plenty of other offers, thanks."

"Oh do you? I admit I am surprised. Only one of those red djinns can get you over."

"So I've heard."

"Of course, *I* could get you over."

"Is that so? And how would you do that? Dig?"

"Fly." Safiyah turned to Kage. "And your little friend here can help with that. It's why I approached her in the first place."

"I think we'll make our own way," Nyx said.

"What, with the Chenjan? Oh, please. Ask her what work she has for you. Ask her what she traffics in. There's a thriving market in human flesh here. There will be money made for your bodies, no doubt, but you will not be collecting it."

"You seem to know a lot about what we're up to."

"I have a single-minded interest in arriving on the other side of this wall. To achieve that, I need a Drucian. It so happens one works for you. I propose a simple partnership until we reach the other side. Is that so remarkable?"

"Fuck, you even talk like a First Family," Nyx said.

"I've found it's easier to be who you are instead of pretending at something else. Fewer things to remember."

Nyx regarded her once more. She was slight in stature, a head shorter than Nyx, and it made the size of her generous breasts and hips altogether more distracting. But Nyx was not so besotted that she failed to notice the fine scarring on the inside of the woman's wrists as she spoke, the peculiar worm-wheels of a venom addict.

"Let me talk to my team," Nyx said. "We have a few choices. They'll want some say in it."

Safiyah smiled, like a cat with a roach. "That is a fine line, honey sweet, but I suspect there is only one woman making all the decisions."

"I'll be in touch," Nyx said.

"I'm sure," Safiyah said.

✚

"Remember what happened the last time we took on an addict," Eshe said.

Nyx knew very well what happened the last time she took on an addict. Eshe wasn't present to torture and kill her, but Nyx was. She resented him just a little for bringing it up.

"Thanks for that, Eshe," she said.

"Listen, even if she is an enemy… you always said known enemies were better than unknown ones. So why not keep her close?" Eshe said.

"You put up a filter to deter bugs. You don't invite them in to sleep with you on the off chance you can swat them later."

"She's a magician who knows the territory. And Nasheenian," Ahmed said. "I trust a Nasheenian magician—even a First Family—far more than any Chenjan."

"But she could use that against us," Nyx said.

"She could just as easily use it against us if we don't take her along," Ahmed said.

"Kage, you have anything to say about this?" Nyx asked.

Kage had her gun resting across her thighs. She seemed to be contemplating the floor. She raised her head. "I did not think this was for voting."

"It's not," Nyx said. "But I want your opinion."

"If we do not go over soon, we will run out of money. And food. We will die here. Or die working here. It's just logic. We must take the magician's offer."

"And it doesn't concern you at all that she picked you out as some key piece of whatever plan she has for getting us over."

"No. It means you need me to get over the Wall, too."

That was a motive Nyx could understand. "All right. We ditch the Chenjan and take the magician's offer. But if it all goes to fuck, I'm blaming Kage."

Kage stiffened.

"It's a joke," Nyx said.

"Not sure it's the best time for jokes," Ahmed said. He stood. "I'm getting a drink. Anyone coming?"

Nyx was, for the first time in a long time, tired of drinking. She just wanted to sleep. "I'm staying in. We'll have shit to do tomorrow."

"I'll go," Eshe said.

Nyx figured Eshe was due for a drink.

"Anybody else?" Ahmed said.

Isabet turned her back to them and curled up in her burnous. Khatijah shook her head.

Kage uncurled from her seat. "Can I go tell the magician we will accept her offer?" Kage asked.

"Sure," Nyx said.

"Let's go," Ahmed said to Eshe. "I'd like one more drunk night before some magician turns me into a cicada."

✚

Eshe and Ahmed asked around and found what the locals called a shebeen, just a knotted hunk of stone piled against the side of the Wall where a man sold bitter liquor from the carapace of a monstrous insect head the size of a small incendiary burst.

The liquor hit Eshe hard, harder than he expected, and two rounds later, the desert was a soft, gauzy sea of delight. He hadn't felt this pleasant in a good long while. It made him want to buy more of whatever the liquor was to take with them over the Wall.

Ahmed didn't seem to be faring much better. Eshe bought another round and finally asked him.

"So who was that woman tried to kill you? You tell Nyx yet?"

"It doesn't matter. She's dead. Did you see how fast Nyx was with that shot?" He held up his hands as if he were sighting down the barrel of a gun. "She moves faster that you'd expect, a woman her size. If I could move that fast I wouldn't have been in intelligence." He sighed into his drink. "It took the best people."

"What, and left people like you and Nyx?" Eshe said.

Ahmed snorted. "Yeah. Bad guys."

"I never wanted to be a bad guy," Eshe said.

Ahmed raised his glass. "Sorry, kid. You are." He drank. "I never wanted to be a hero. I wanted to be a farmer."

"You ever worked a farm? I have. Forced into it by my house mothers. It's shit work."

"I did the same. I liked my house mothers a good deal more than you, though. They had a farm. It was a good life. Predictable."

"Dull," Eshe said.

"How'd you get out of it?"

Eshe shrugged. "Same as any boy. Dressed up like a girl and ran away."

Ahmed ordered them another round.

Eshe shook his head. "I think that's enough for me."

"One more," Ahmed said. He leaned toward him. "What are you going to do, at the end of this? Run off with your girl?"

"Who? Isabet? She's not mine. Or anybody's. Stay the fuck away from her. She's trouble."

"It's not her I'm interested in."

A veiled woman came over and refilled their drinks from a burnished brown vessel. Eshe could practically see the fumes coming off the stuff.

"Why'd you run away?" Ahmed said.

"You know why," Eshe said. "You know what they do to boys."

"My childhood wasn't yours. I stayed with the same family my whole life. Sounds like you didn't."

"It was just like anybody else's shit. You know, hired out to other people. Like a dog. Like a slave. It was a long time ago."

Ahmed reached out, put his hand over Eshe's. "Tell me. I was a house boy, too."

Eshe didn't pull away. Leaned toward him instead. His head felt lovely, relaxed, as if it were bobbing in a warm sea. He thought of Isabet, and what life would be like with a wife and child. It wasn't a family he wanted so much as a sense of belonging. He wanted to matter to someone.

"Who cares what they did to us? It's what we do with it that matters. That's what Nyx says." He polished off his glass. As he went to set it down, he nearly missed the table. Best to pace myself, he thought, but it was a faraway notion, like listening to someone else calling to him from across a wide gully.

"I think Nyx is going to grind us all up out here," Ahmed said. "The same way our house mothers did."

"It's not like that. Nyx isn't like that."

"What's the difference?"

"Nyx doesn't fuck me and whore me out. How's that?"

Ahmed pulled his hand away. Eshe grimaced.

"Sorry," Ahmed said.

"Everybody's always sorry. But it doesn't change anything, does it?" Eshe said. The look on Ahmed's face made him feel bad, so he reached out, took Ahmed's elbow. "You really don't get it. You think she's some kind of fucking monster. But Nyx I get. As long as you're useful to her, you're safe. And she'll protect you. What woman in your life ever protected you?"

"Women said I had a pretty face," Ahmed said. "Fucking some squad commanders protected me at the front."

"Nyx isn't like that."

"You just have to die for her, then?"

"You don't get it." Eshe released him. He tried to stand, but the table moved from under him. He sat back down, hard. "Everybody betrays you. It's just a matter of when."

Ahmed leaned toward him, so close Eshe could smell the liquor on his breath. Ahmed patted his cheek with his warm hand. The touch lingered. He stroked Eshe's brow. "I'm sorry. You're a good kid. I'm just worried that you're with her. I don't think anything good will come of it."

Ahmed kissed him softly on the mouth.

Eshe pulled away, disoriented. "We should go. I have to take a piss."

"I could have been a powerful magician," Ahmed said. "Could have trained for it. I had the talent. But I didn't want to be a weapon. Instead, I hacked off men's arms and poured blood worms into women's eyes." He snorted; it sounded something like a laugh.

"We do what we have to do to stay alive," Eshe said.

"How much longer do we have, I wonder?" Ahmed said.

"Let's go."

They stumbled away from the shebeen and followed the shadow of the Wall. Eshe stumbled behind a stir of dark tents and took a piss. When he finished, he went to where Ahmed stood a few paces away, his back to him. Eshe grabbed his hand.

Ahmed turned, and leaned into him. Kissed him on the mouth again.

"I'm pretty fucked up," Eshe said.

"It's a good thing I'm perfect, then."

+

It wasn't until he was entirely nude that Nyx thought to slow down, and only because his beauty stirred something both passionate and remorseful within her. After six weeks in the desert, lingering at the edge of death, staring into the black abyss of nothing every day, every hour, his beauty was nothing short of shocking, and the intensity of her own desire overwhelmed her.

Nyx came awake with a start, to the sound of someone vomiting. The dream lingered, hot and tangled. God, she wanted a good fuck now. Who had she been fucking?

The room was dark. She heard someone on the balcony outside, and went to go check it out.

Kage and Ahmed were there, flanking Eshe as he crouched at the edge of the balcony, heaving. Ahmed held a water bulb. When Eshe finished heaving, he washed his face with it.

"Get some fucking sleep," Nyx said. "Kage's little friend has us going over the Wall tomorrow."

Eshe heaved again. Just a thin stream of mucus now.

"When did they get back, Kage?" Nyx asked.

"Not long," Kage said.

It was only a few hours until morning prayer. They still called it out here, though Nyx wasn't so sure it was Nasheen or Chenja's God everyone was praying to.

When Eshe raised his head this time, Nyx could see him clearly in the blue glow of the balcony lights. He seemed very young, and lost, and so totally alone that for a moment he reminded her of her youngest brother Ghazi when he first learned he was going to the front, and that turned something in her gut.

"Get cleaned up and get to bed," Nyx said.

Ahmed's expression was fierce, and unexpected.

"We'll be there in a minute," he said, and Nyx felt that something had shifted, some subtle loyalty on her team that she should have paid better attention to.

"See that you are," she said, and went back inside.

31.

"They'll be moving you soon," said the girl who delivered Inaya's saffron-laced curry.

Inaya pressed herself to the floor and tried to see the girl's face before the filter went opaque again. But all she saw before it snapped back on was the heavy, dusty hem of the girl's muslin habit.

"Where?" Inaya whispered, but the girl was already moving down the hall.

She sighed and pressed her cheek to the cool, gritty floor.

The tally of days on the far wall had gotten muddled. Inaya suspected someone came in and wiped away her old marks whenever they took her out for interrogations. Or perhaps they put her in a new cell each time? Did all the cells look alike, or had she simply gone so mad that she'd lost the ability to think critically about anything at all, even her own surroundings?

She spent much of her time gazing through the vent that brought her air and light, contemplating the filter that masked it. Even if she could shift, the filter posed a problem. The grounds would be wrapped in filters, all of them coded for different individuals. This one would be coded for no one. If she got herself up there and tried to reach through, no doubt it would devour her arm. She needed a way out that did not rely on her suppressed skills.

For a time, she tried to get to know the guards, but they would not speak to her. The girl's words were the closest thing to a friendly voice she had heard in many weeks.

Look to what you devour... When she closed her eyes, she sometimes thought of Khos, baring his marked skin to her. She tried to remember what was written there, but the words were all in Mhorian, weren't they? Had she missed some vital clue?

They would move her now, to some work camp, and kill her there. Her only hope was to try and find a way to break free when they moved her. Or perhaps from the camp itself? How secure could it be, if they labored in the open air? Or would they put her underground in some mine? She'd never see the open air again.

Inaya lay on the floor contemplating her fate. It was the uncertainty that hurt her most. The cold, the deprivation, all of that was fine. She didn't mind being on her own. She didn't even mind the boredom. It gave her time alone with her thoughts. But the not knowing...

Over the next few days, she heard more movement outside. More heated words. She once heard three Angels walk down the corridor, talking about "riots" and "madness" but she couldn't make sense of it. She heard women yelling at their jailers for news before their filters were activated.

Then her filter went transparent, sometime in the early evening as the blue dusk bathed her cell. She sat up. Her bones ached, and she was getting sores on her hips from lying still for so long.

Two male jailers dressed in deep brown robes escorted in a tall, thick woman at least twice Inaya's size.

Inaya found herself backing up further into her cell to make room.

"Sorry, cat gut," one of the jailers said. "We're full up in here and you gotta make room."

They stepped out, and the filter went opaque again, but not before Inaya saw another woman being escorted down the hall. She was not screaming but screeching, one arm half as long as the other, still webbed and covered in black feathers. Someone had stuffed her into a plain gray habit; it was damp and twisted with mucus and dried blood.

Inaya turned to her new cell companion. "What's happening out there?"

"Revolution," the woman said, grimly. Her face was puffy and badly bruised. She was at least two decades older than Inaya, with the beefy body of some cook or well-fed shop laborer. They had not bothered to clean her up yet. She still wore the clothes she had been picked up in, reeking of sticky saffron.

"You're a shifter?" Inaya asked.

"Me? No. My husband was, though."

"Was?"

The woman shook her head. "God only knows what bloody things are happening out there. He revealed himself. Now we're lost."

"What is happening? Please, I've been here for many weeks."

"You don't know? No, I don't expect they'd tell you, in here. Someone released a burst in Montmare. The Patron's cousins were killed, and hundreds of others. The Patron took issue with his kin, and the people mourned the civilians, and then… you know the rest. You know what they do to people like my husband."

"What are they doing? Please, exactly what are they doing?"

"Smoking them all out," the woman said. "It's the end days. The final purge of every shifter. There's war in the streets. Everything's burning."

"And the Fourré? Who's leading the Fourré?"

The woman looked confused. "What do you mean? The same as always. The Madame de Fourré is leading them. Who else would go on such a bloody rampage?"

Inaya leaned against the wall, slid to the floor. "This is very bad," she said.

"Worse than that," the woman said. "My sons have no parents now. I told these goddamned heretics that, but they don't care. They just want to lock us all up and burn us. They won't kill women though, will they? There's still a chance for a trial? Tell me there's a chance?"

"Of course," Inaya said softly. "There is always a chance." Inaya had known for some time that she'd been betrayed, but until now, she didn't realize how badly. Michel must have turned the whole movement—Gabrielle, and the eight cell leaders—even Hynri!—all of them, in lock step with some bloody scheme to topple the government itself. But what would the people think of shifters now? They had become everything the people feared they were. Whatever the priests and Patron wanted to do to them now, they would have free rein to do so, without any repercussions. If her people were not bottled up in jars already, they soon would be.

"How long have you been here?"

But Inaya was staring up at the filtered blue light coming in from above, watching it slowly darken and fade all together, blanketing them in blackness.

32.

"It's a lot of fucking rope," Nyx said, eying the bundle knotted securely to Kage's back.

Kage was used to carrying her gun; the weight of the rope was nothing. She endured their chatter only because in the many weeks she had traveled with these people, she realized very little would shut them up.

"It's a lot of fucking wall," Safiyah said.

They finally stopped in the shadow of the Wall. Kage, Nyx, and Safiyah led. The others were still far behind, bickering over rations.

"That," said Safiyah, pointing to the seemingly sheer face of the Wall, "is why I need a Drucian."

Kage watched Nyx try to figure it out. This section of the Wall was different from the rest, and Kage could see why immediately. Three hundred strides up the face of it, there was a crack, a crevice.

Kage faced the bare rock wall while Safiyah and Nyx spoke. The Wall was a lovely thing, she supposed, as much as anything outside could be. She scouted the climb as they bickered. Once she saw the best way to the top, she simply stepped onto the rock face and began to climb. The mutters of those behind her faded quickly. It was easy enough to let their words become nonsensical. Making any sense out of Nasheenian was difficult on a regular day. Doing so while scaling a wall was nearly impossible.

They nattered on, though, until one of them finally noticed that she was climbing. Then, cool silence. If it meant keeping them quiet, she would climb for days.

Though the Wall appeared to be sheer from far away, it was not. There were irregularities here, caused by some malformation in this part of the Wall. It was her size and dexterity the magician had needed, that was all. What concerned her was only that the magician had known enough about Drucians in general to bet that Kage could scale the Wall. Fat-fingered Nasheenians and their flat-footed magicians would be useless on surfaces like this one. But Kage had grown up climbing walls. None quite so tall as this, perhaps, but the mechanics were the same.

And if she fell off and died, well—at least then Nyx or the *fukushu-sha* couldn't kill her.

The magician had taken them far from the city, an hour before first light. But from this height, Kage could already see the city plainly in the distance, a dusty smudge in the shadow of the Wall. As she climbed, the wind picked up, and she had to stay focused. She paused on occasion to remap her route to the crevice. Her arms began to tire, and she had to rest more often. The wind became insistent.

Breathe.

Her mothers would have told her to breathe. To connect with the face of the Wall itself, to imagine she was part of it. A permanent, substantial thing. Not frail. Not fallible. Strong. Immovable.

She breathed, and took her next hold.

Below her was a stir of mad people who did not care whether she lived or died. Behind them, far to the south, her own family no longer saw her. Here, on this blighted mountain of a wall, she was alone. Totally and completely alone.

She caught her breath. Clung to the Wall. Suddenly rigid.

Breathe.

Live alone. Die alone. If she let go, would it matter? Nyx would not accomplish her mission. Perhaps the team would disband. No one would burn her body, or return it to the darkness of her family's vessel. No one would sing over her. No one would care.

"It is the worst fate," her mother Sokai had once told her, "to die alone, in silence, among strangers. Promise you will always come home."

But she could not go home to a place that no longer saw her.

She glanced up. The gaping maw of the crevice was still far from her reach. She pressed her forehead against the gritty wall. She needed silence, but for the first time in many weeks, now that she had it, her mind wanted to clutter it up, use it to till up old sorrow.

Reach. Climb.

She moved up the Wall again. The sun was coming up, and at this height, it beat down on her exposed neck and shoulders, heavy as a winter coat.

She exhaled, and reached for the next hold.

Her fingers slipped.

The world broke then. Some carefully muted thing inside of her howled, and her children were screaming again.

The sun was blinding.

Her children were dying.

Kage regained her hold, and pressed herself against the Wall. The muscles in her legs and forearms were trembling violently.

The raiders were Ras Tiegans. They stormed through the settlement and smoked them out of the caves; picked them off one by one with pistols, and when the pistols jammed up, they used swords. Ras Tiegans had a longer reach, and better weapons, than any Drucian. The Nasheenians helped ensure that.

They were young people, always, and they laughed as they did it, as if it were some game, some adolescent rite of passage, to murder Drucians in their homes.

But Kage had seen them coming. She had climbed the sheer face of her family's cave, her newborn twins strapped to her back, and hidden there as her people were smoked out and killed.

The Ras Tiegans drove X-shaped markers into the ground in front of every cleared cave, and tied purple banners to them.

Kage watched as two of them chased her cousin up the side of the hill just opposite her. One grabbed her cousin by the ankle and yanked her down.

"Can Drucians fly?" he yelled, and tossed her back down the rise to the sharp stones below.

His companion leapt on Kage's cousin, stabbing again and again with his sword until her blood ran freely.

It was then that Kage's children began to cry.

Let go. Fly.

Show them Drucians can fly.

Kage's grip loosened.

If she had let go then, would things have been different?

"Hush, hush," she had told her babies, but they had cried, and cried, and she wrapped them tightly and pulled them to her breast as the Ras Tiegans routed her people.

It was not until long after, when the valley was filled with corpses and the smoke began to dissipate, that she realized her babies had stopped moving.

Let go.

Kage opened her eyes. The sunlight hurt her eyes, and that was fine. Everything hurt. It meant she was alive. It was what she told herself when her kin discovered her dead babies, and she fled everything she ever knew to evade the formal ceremony that would have stripped her of everything she was.

She released her right hand from the Wall. Wondered what it was like to fly.

Then she gripped the next hold, and pulled herself up.

Three more moves, and she had both hands on the lip of the crevice.

She pulled herself up into the cool darkness and rolled onto her back. Beneath her, the interior of the Wall was warm and spongy. She stared at the moist ceiling. As she watched, it seemed to rise and fall with the pace of her breath. She sat up. Pressed her hand to the Wall. Recoiled. It was like putting her hand onto warm, still-living meat.

The Wall was... *alive.*

✚

"Fuck me," Nyx breathed. "Did she really get up there?"

"They're a remarkable people," Safiyah said, "for infidels."

"Eshe, you ready to shift?" Nyx asked.

"Not until Isabet is pulled up safely," he said.

"You make it sound like you don't trust me with her," Nyx said.

Eshe frowned. Nyx wasn't quite sure when she started losing him. About the time Isabet started bedding next to him at night, she supposed. It was a dangerous time to play this game, when they were so close to the end.

The rope came down. Three hundred paces of it, braided into a ladder so flimsy that it turned Nyx's stomach to see it. She wasn't so sure she was going to get up it, let alone anybody else. Her plan with Isabet was just to tie her to the end of it, and pull her up last.

Ahmed went first, then Khatijah, then Safiyah. Nyx figured that put it at three against one in case Safiyah went turncoat.

Nyx stayed back to have them haul up the gear first, then she mounted the ladder. She was not a fan of heights. And not twenty anymore. It took well over an hour to make the long, bloody fucking climb.

She arrived at the top trembling and sweating. She lay back in the crevice and chugged a water bulb. For a minute, she thought her senses were fucked up, but no… the ceiling above her seemed to be… moving. Like it was breathing. "Fuck me," she muttered.

Ahmed came over and leaned over her. "Not what you signed up for?"

"There better be a fucking better way back over," she said.

Safiyah smiled, but it wasn't a pleasant smile, more like the way a cat who's just left a dead roach on your pillow looks right before you head to bed. Nyx stared past her where Kage was reloading her gun onto her back. Of all of them, Kage seemed the most composed. How that kid took everything in stride was baffling. Nyx had been with novice bel dames who cracked under less pressure.

Once Eshe had secured Isabet, Ahmed and Nyx pulled her up. Eshe was last, squawking into the narrow space just as Isabet's fingers met the lip of the crevice.

Ahmed untangled Isabet from the ladder. They left it in the crevice. Nyx paused, waiting for Eshe to fly past her or catch a ride on her shoulder, but instead, he landed neatly on Ahmed's shoulder. Ahmed glanced over at him, looking surprised. Eshe took flight again, heading for the other end of the crevice.

Nyx started walking through the dim corridor after him. It was just a matter of time, she suspected, before Eshe's allegiances started shifting—Isabet and Ahmed were the best picks, she figured. Isabet for being pretty and Ahmed for being pretty and cunning. What, did she think he'd be a kid forever? No, she'd just hoped she taught him better. Taught him not to give his heart to just any pretty fool who crossed his path. You started caring about somebody, you did stupid things. Like murder a diplomat's bodyguards. And haul a bunch of outlaws across a desert.

Never ended well.

Safiyah, Khatijah, and Kage had already reached the end of the long corridor. They stood framed in the light, blocking her view.

"What? Don't tell me there's not a way down like you said?"

Nyx pushed past them, just squeezing by in the narrow space. She came up short at the edge of the opening, and grabbed the warm wall to steady herself. She gazed onto an alien vista. The sight of it twisted something in her belly. It tasted like fear.

A boiling mass of black-violet clouds swathed the sky. Below them was a crimson sea of sand so bloody red that Nyx had a moment of dissonance. Some raging, nameless feeling of dread overcame her, and she thought, My God, this is what hell looks like. I've been sent to hell. Had she been dead all this time, just locked in some death-dream?

Towering, funnel-shaped structures swelled from the bloody desert, mountainous features so high that their bulbous tops pierced the oppressive cloud cover. Far below, at the base of them, the wind whipped up eddies of red sand, obscuring whatever lived or grew or preyed on the ground. She wondered if the seven gates of hell were down there, or if this was just one of the seven in the Wall. It wasn't impossible, was it?

Safiyah grinned. "Looking for the angels? Guardians of hellfire? Oh, I assure you they are there. Perhaps not as dangerous as they once were, but potent enough. The Aadhya rule this hell. We are just travelers."

At Nyx's feet, a long tier of stairs dug into the face of the Wall terraced gently downwards, into the spitting sand.

"Before we go, I advise you all to cover any wounds you may have," Safiyah said. "The sand here feeds on blood."

"All of it?" Eshe said.

"All of it," Safiyah said. She opened her arms to the sky. "You will learn to love it. Or it will destroy you. Neither is unpleasant. Are you coming, or shall we gawk at the gate all day?"

She started down the steps.

"Safiyah?" Nyx called after her. "Why is this cave up here? What for?"

Safiyah laughed her hack-hack-snort laugh that made Nyx cringe. "The Aadhya of course. How do you think they escaped from this hell in the first place?"

"Why were those people walled up here?" Khatijah asked.

"Truthfully? They walled themselves in with this contagion, millennia ago." Safiyah regarded the bloody, swirling landscape and shrugged. "I suppose it worked. The world could have been much worse, you see. It could have *all* been like this."

"How did they… do this?" Eshe asked.

"There have been bursts that ensure that nothing bred in a place will ever come out straight again," Safiyah said. "Chemicals that twist blood codes out of shape. You don't see them much anymore, but they exist. I wouldn't have put it past the early magicians to cook up something like that, something that mutated far beyond their control." Her stare got distant then, like she wanted to sit there at the table with those same magicians and see what they were cooking up. Nyx had seen the same expression on bel dames thinking about some boy they hadn't killed yet.

Ahmed turned to Nyx. "Why would anyone take a political prisoner out here?"

Nyx gazed into the abyss. "Because they could do anything they wanted to him here. Question is, what the fuck was it?"

33.

The noise outside Inaya's cell got louder. The voices, more frantic. There was more screaming. Not just during the day, but at night as well. People were being dragged through the halls.

"I can't stand this," Inaya's cellmate, whose name was Mettie, said. She chattered on the first few days, but, like Inaya, eventually fell into a deep depression.

They spent the time playing word games and exchanging stories. Inaya's were always general, guarded. She shared some of her family life in Tirhan, but little else. It still felt too dangerous, even now.

Mostly, Inaya listened. Not just to Mettie, but to everything happening in the hall. Things were not cooling outside the walls, but getting worse. She desperately yearned to take back control of it all. Every time she heard a cry, her body tried to shift, to break free.

"I'm going to kill them when they come for me," Mettie said.

"It's not worth trying," Inaya said.

"No, no," Mettie said, and her gaze got a faraway look, as if she were back with her husband and sons, watching her whole world get torched. "No, when they come for me, I will fight. Not like you. I won't sit here and rot like you."

But it was not Mettie they came for first. It was Inaya.

A new female jailer, one Inaya had never seen before, hauled her through the filter. Mettie tried to run, but the jailer cried out, and two more men came from the other side of the hall. They tackled Mettie. She made a good show of it. Inaya admired her attempt. Why haven't I tried to run? she thought.

The female jailer led Inaya away as Mettie still fought. Mettie cried after Inaya, "Break out the first chance you get, girl! They will eat us here!"

Inaya found herself back in one of the organic rooms with the glow worms in the ceiling. She found it to be a nice change of scenery. She wondered if she could ask for a change of clothes. A shower, perhaps. Then she started to cry, because it was insulting, to realize how deferential she had become in just a few weeks. Months? They had not even touched her, really. They had not cut off a limb or suspended her over fire. They had not even starved her. Yet here she was, cowed and broken.

The Angel entered. Not a new one, but the same one who had caught her out with the letters. She found it oddly comforting to see him again, and hated herself for that, too. For his part, he did not seem as confident this time. There was worry on his face, and something more. Inaya recognized it immediately, because it was something she had felt every moment of every day now for some time. It was fear.

He had brought the letters. He pulled them from his ledger again, and threw them onto the floor in front of her.

"Those are yours," he said.

She said nothing, as she had done last time.

"Those are *yours*!" he said again. "You are the Madame de Fourré. And we have you. So who is leading in your stead? I need names."

Inaya simply stared at the letters.

"We hoped it would break apart without you," he said. "And we certainly aren't going to make a martyr of you. I have every intention of letting you live here the rest of your life."

"No one likes a martyr," Inaya said softly.

"Exactly," he said, and there was excitement in his voice. She realized she had given him what he wanted, again—speaking meant he was getting somewhere.

She sighed. What did it all matter now?

"But without those names, you are useless to us. If you are not the Madame de Fourré, you are nothing. Just another of the misborn. If that's so, I send you to a work camp and take off your head. And the heads of your children."

"My children are in Tirhan."

"That is where you are wrong," he said. "Your husband and children are still here. And we will take them apart piece by piece until we have those names."

Inaya laughed. She saw him start at that, and it made her laugh more. "You don't have my husband," Inaya said, "but that is a very pretty bluff."

"Do you have any idea what we can do—"

"You've done all you can do to me," Inaya said. She met his gaze for the first time. She looked at him, really looked, and she realized how young he was, how fearful. Yes, he had power over her, but little else. If they really thought they had the Madame de Fourré, she realized, she would have been moved from here already and given over to some other Angel, someone older, more experienced. He still wasn't sure. My God, she thought, why didn't I understand that sooner?

Her silence had made him unsure, and it was his uncertainty that was the only thing keeping her from being cut up and put into jars.

"I assure you we can do much more," he said. He crossed the room to her.

A part of her—the part that had been here for so many weeks or months—wanted to cringe away from him. But instead, she stood her ground. He was only a head taller than her, and slender. He smelled of cinnamon and perfumed pomade.

"Do you have children?" she asked. "A wife?"

"I need names," he said.

"What is your wife's name? Surely they prefer God's Angels to have wives. I suspect they think it gives you focus."

He took her by the arm, twisted it behind her.

Pain radiated up her arm, and she bit back a cry of pain. It was the first time he had resorted to physical violence. She felt as if she had won something.

"I need to know who your cell leaders are," he said. "Tonight. Or I will start unmaking you from toe to tit."

Inaya knew, then. "You're a shifter," she said.

He released her. Inaya danced away, out of arm's reach. "My God," she said. "Not just any shifter, though, are you? Not a raven, a parrot, a dog… not even a fox. No, you're… you unmake things, you said. I have… heard… all about unmaking."

"Then you know what I can do to you."

"How can you work against your own kind?"

"My kind? My *kind*? You rabid animals are nothing like me. You're locked in one form. One guise. Just some beast. God's Angels are all things. We can become anything. Everything. We're the very hand of God Himself."

Inaya had believed herself many things, but never the hand of God. She steeled herself. She wanted to shout and clap. Her skin rippled with the renewed desire to shift, to giveaway what she was. I am like you! She wanted to tell him, but of course, that wasn't true. She wasn't like him at all.

"What was it like, when you first shifted? When you gave in and became something else?" Inaya said. "Did you feel you had sinned?"

"Names," he said. But she saw his disquiet now. He had given himself away. He pressed his hands together. She saw the skin ripple. Saw the slight twitch of his eye. He was a mutant like her. He could become any organic thing he wished. He could reach inside of her and stop her heart.

"You're the same as all the people you murder," Inaya said. "How lovely that must be, to murder yourself every day."

"You know nothing," he said. "You're an animal. Just like the rest of them."

"And you're a god, is that it?" She laughed again. "I wonder what God has to say about that."

"You can ask Him when you see Him," the Angel said. He retrieved the papers from the floor.

He left her. The female jailer returned, and escorted her back to her cell.

Inaya waited in front of the filter. It went transparent. Her jailer pushed her inside—into a pool of blood.

Inaya slipped on the floor, and fell to her hands and knees. Mettie's large body was laid out on the stones. She was very still. Blood pooled from a gash in her head. Inaya crawled forward and found that Mettie was still breathing.

"Wait!" she called after the jailer. "She's been hurt! Please. She needs a magician!"

"That's what happens when dogs like her argue with God's Angels," the jailer said, and the filter went opaque.

"Mettie? Mettie?" Inaya cried.

She tried to staunch the flow of blood, but as the hours passed, Mettie's breath got shallower. Inaya's cries for help went unanswered.

In the morning, Mettie was dead.

And the prison was terribly, terribly quiet.

Breakfast did not come.

Nor did dinner.

Inaya sat at the edge of the filter and screamed for someone to come for Mettie's body. Then she screamed for food and water. She could hear other prisoners yelling, their voices muffled by the filters. But no guards. No prisoners being transferred. It was as if life in the prison had stopped.

Mettie's body was beginning to stiffen, and Inaya was terribly thirsty. She began to test the filter. She tore off the end of her habit and pushed it through the filter. The habit sizzled and disintegrated. She tried a few strands of her hair. The filter ate them, leaving nothing behind.

Mettie's blood caked the bottoms of her shoes, and that gave her an idea. She wiped her shoe with Mettie's blood and stuck it through the filter, quickly.

When she pulled the shoe back in, the blood was gone, and some of the cloth had frayed, but it hadn't disintegrated.

Inaya regarded Mettie's thick body. Nasheenian filters were much worse than most. They'd take off limbs, eat entire people. But here they wanted to keep prisoners alive, and that meant keeping filters dangerous, but not deadly. She would not be eaten going through this filter, not all at once, but she would be badly injured unless she protected herself with something the filter would find equally as appealing.

She listened to the world outside the filter. A few prisoners had taken up pounding on the walls with their plates or refuse buckets, but that didn't last long. Everything was made of clay, and eventually broke into shards. Inaya knew that because she had once tried doing the same.

Eventually, she would excrete enough saffron that she could shift, but even then, escape wasn't certain. The walls were made of solid pieces of stone, and the filters would eat her in any organic form, no matter which she took. She was no magician; she couldn't change the direction of the nits in the weave.

That meant the only reliable way out… was through.

Inaya took a deep breath.

She went to her overflowing refuse bucket and poured it out into one corner. She gagged as she banged the bucket on the floor until it broke.

Then she took the largest shard and knelt in front of Mettie's body. Her blood would coagulate soon. Then what chance did she have?

Inaya gritted her teeth. She plunged the shard into Mettie's chest and sawed her open from neck to navel. There wasn't much blood there, though. She had to heave the body over onto its side, to get at her back where the blood had pooled. The blood was partially congealed already, like gelatin. Inaya coated her legs and arms in the stuff, but knew it wouldn't be enough. If she could shift, she could repair herself on the other side of that filter. But the saffron had not worn off yet. If she arrived on the other side incapacitated, she'd be no better off than she was in here.

The more she thought about what she needed to do, the less likely she was going to be free. For the first time in many, many years, she asked herself what Nyxnissa so Dasheem would do.

She disrobed. The blood was already cool. She covered her shoes and habit in blood as well, then put her soiled clothing back on. Shivering now, she finished gutting Mettie's body. A heap of entrails lay beside her. She stopped twice to vomit. Then she dragged the body to the edge of the filter.

Inaya knew she was going to have to push through very quickly. The soles of her shoes were slick against the bloody cell floor. She had hollowed out Mettie's body as best she could with her crude tools, but she knew it wasn't going to be enough unless she could push the body out ahead of her very quickly.

The filter popped and crackled. The sounds of her fellow prisoners had grown fainter. But it was the promise of water that decided her.

Inaya took a few gulps of air, then pushed her head and shoulders as deep into Mettie's body as she could.

She grabbed the corpse at the rope belt that tied the habit, and heaved herself and the body forward.

They rolled through the filter together.

Inaya's skin burned. It was instantaneous.

She yanked herself free of the corpse and threw herself clear.

The body's skin was scorched. She smelled burnt flesh. Gray ash covered her own skin. Her habit from the chest down had disintegrated. She slapped at her bare skin, wiping away the ash to reveal rosy skin beneath, as if she'd spent far too long in the sun. But it was not a burn. The blood, her habit, her shoes, and the top layer of her skin had been completely eaten. She put a hand to her face. Blood and offal still covered her face and hair and shoulders.

Inaya stared at the filter. The corpse's feet had not made it clear—from the shin down, it was still caught in the cell.

She looked left, then right down the empty corridor. Her raw skin was starting to tingle. She stood on tender feet and began limping forward. When her jailer took her to the organic cells they usually went left. So she went right.

She passed cell after cell, each of them protected by opaque filters. There was no way to turn them off unless she had the proper organic code. They would be tailored to specific individuals. Until she had the ability to shift and recode her blood to match those codes, she could not help them.

Inaya stumbled to the end of the hall. There was a solid door here, no filter. She stood on her toes and peered into the next hall. It was empty. Just a large reception room.

She yanked on the handle. It was locked.

"God be merciful," she muttered. She saw there was a faceplate beside the door. Like the others, it would require someone with the correct blood code to get through.

She swore and turned back the way she had come. There had to be water somewhere. She minced back the other way, toward the interrogation rooms. Her heart beat a little faster.

There's no one here, she reminded herself, but without knowing what had become of everyone, she couldn't say when they would return. What if it was just some emergency that required their assistance? Or the facility was in lockdown? What if they were due back any moment?

The scarabs that previously covered the doors of occupied cells were gone. Every cell door was open. She peered into each of them, looking for a discarded glass or bulb of water. Found nothing. They were all empty.

All but the last cell.

In the last cell, she found a man.

He was sprawled on the floor. If there was any blood, the organics would have eaten it all. She recognized the crimson robe and black cowl of God's Angels. There was a table at the center of the room, like the room she had stood in when they presented the letters.

On the table was a clear water pitcher, nearly empty, and one half-empty glass.

She paused in the doorway. It occurred to her that this may all just be some elaborately concocted scheme to get her to further incriminate herself. Or maybe the water was poisoned, and that's what killed the man? She had not run an underground organization for nearly five years by being stupid.

But the insanity of that—of staging a riot, and a prison lockdown, all to get her to definitively declare who they already knew she was seemed a little mad even to her. Her thirst won out over caution.

Inaya ran to the table, circling as far away from the man as possible. She drank straight from the pitcher. The water was lukewarm at best, and tasted as if it had been sitting a good long while.

She watched the man on the floor. He still hadn't moved. Her skin prickled, and she realized she had a way out. As soon as she could shift, she could copy this man's blood code, free the others in the cells, and open the door on the other end of the hall.

But she had to wait. And this water had to last… for as long as it took. She peered back outside. The corridor running away from the regular cells kept going. She glanced back at the body again.

There was, of course, another option.

She pulled the tattered bits of what remained of her habit from her shoulders and wiped her face and arms with it. Then she began disrobing the corpse. Did they have female God's Angels?

She was about to find out.

34.

"It's just the wind and sand. No figures," Kage said. The spitting sand severely limited their visibility. Nyx had hoped Kage would have better luck with her good eyes and a scope.

"We'll camp here," Nyx said. It was less than an hour until dark. Getting down the Wall had taken nearly as long as getting up. The footing was treacherous, and the wind got worse as they descended. In any other landscape, Nyx would have preferred to keep going through the darkness, but the way Safiyah talked, that was a bad idea.

Nyx glanced back at the magician. She had drawn her hijab across her face, and like Kage, wore goggles. Nyx wondered why she hadn't thought to bring her own fucking goggles. The sand stung her eyes, and sand fleas bit her shins. At least, she hoped they were sand fleas, and not something toxic. What the fuck had she gotten herself into? When she found Raine, she was going to pummel him herself.

"If you're camping, you'll want to draw a circle!" Safiyah called over the howl of the wind.

"No circle will stay drawn in this weather!" Ahmed yelled back.

"I'd do it anyway," Safiyah said.

Nyx pointed Kage to the nearest rock formation. It would offer some protection from the scathing sand. Nyx's skin was raw with it.

"The nomads sometimes camp here," Safiyah said. She pointed to carved rings in the rock face. "We can attach the tent there."

"What tent?" Nyx asked.

Safiyah shrugged off her pack and unrolled a billowing canvas sheet. "You really should have come to this desert more prepared," she said.

They made camp against the hard face of the formation. Ahmed and Khatijah roped the top of the canvas to the carved rings and staked out the other end in the sand.

"Does this ever let up?" Eshe yelled over the howling wind.

"Not this close to the Wall," Safiyah said.

Behind the rudimentary tent, life was more bearable. Ahmed laid out their burnouses on the floor, and staked the open sides of the canvas down once everyone was inside.

"Who wants first watch?" Nyx said.

Silence. Blank stares.

"All right," Nyx said. "Not like we can see shit out there anyway." She took up a position near the staked entry, and listened to the wind yowl while Eshe broke out the rations. She kept her heat specs close. She emptied out her sandals, grateful for a lifetime of callouses so thick she barely registered blisters or bruises anymore.

The others bedded down after eating. As soon as the sun dropped, the desert got cold. Bitterly cold. Eshe started a fire with a handful of fire beetles. They didn't have much to feed the bugs, so he used far too many to get a steady heat, even in the small space.

Nyx pressed her back against the rock, which still held some of the suns' heat, and peered out between the flaps of the canvas. Eshe and Isabet argued about something in Ras Tiegan. Ahmed lay on the other side of the tent with his back to all of them. Kage and Khatijah methodically cleaned their weapons. Safiyah sat nearest the fire, talking to herself. On the one hand, Safiyah made Nyx increasingly wary. On the other, the realities of this place meant that relying on her knowledge of the area might be the only thing that kept them alive on this side of the Wall.

Nyx nodded off. When she woke, Safiyah was sitting across from her. Staring at her with big, dark eyes.

Nyx started.

Safiyah grinned. The cat's-got-a-lizard grin that creeped her out.

"Do they teach anything of the heavenly bodies in the schools for grunts?" Safiyah asked. "I assumed that's where you were schooled."

Nyx glanced back into the tent. The others were mostly asleep, or trying to be. The fire beetle carapaces popped.

"Why?" Nyx said.

"Surely someone in your life taught you something of the stars?"

"No one in my life gave a shit about the sky," Nyx said, but that was a lie. She thought of her mother. "I needed to know how to point and shoot. And not up there."

"Ah, yes. So you learned to count bullets and calculate the trajectory of bursts. So quaint."

"You'd have thought it was mighty useful when you were hip deep in a trench about to be overrun and trying to remember how much ammo you had left. Not that any of your people would get that."

"Still, it's a pity," Safiyah said. "There are gravitational points between high-density planets called Damira's points. It's when the pull of one planet is no longer stronger than the pull over another body. At that point in the sky, debris becomes forever caught in these areas. So debris wanders through, becomes caught in the tide, and then is pulled back into the vortex in an endless rotation. Forever trapped between two great heavenly bodies in space."

"What the fuck does this have to do with anything?" Nyx said. Outside, the wind had subsided. She donned the heat specs and surveyed the landscape. In the cold night, people would stand out like flares.

"Your team is like that, I think," Safiyah said. "Just bits of debris. Rubble. Space junk. Right now they are circling you, but this desert, these people, they are a powerful force in their own right, and they have much to offer. Now your people will be caught between the two. But this impasse will not last forever. Eventually, one body is disabled, atrophies, is set off kilter. And when that happens, well… Everything falls apart after that, doesn't it?"

"Know what I think?" Nyx said, lowering her voice. She looked over the top of the specs at Safiyah.

"I have not the faintest."

"I think you should keep your fucking head out of the sky and back in the desert. If you did, you'd have seen there's a fucking scout watching us from the next outcrop."

Safiyah hissed and flattened herself on the ground. "God be merciful, woman, why didn't you say anything?"

"I know how much you love to listen to yourself talk."

"Menace."

"You'll learn to love it," Nyx said, and slipped her scattergun from its holster. In the specs, the green, human-shaped outline merely held its ground. She expected others, so she waited with gun out.

"Just the one?" Safiyah whispered.

"She's not doing anything."

Then the figure moved. Not toward the camp, but away, back down or behind something so Nyx lost sight of it.

Nyx shook her head. "Gone now."

The magician was shaking her head. "Not gone," she said. "Going back to consult with her circle leaders to decide what to do with us."

"That doesn't sound good."

"It's not. We should start moving again soon."

✚

They didn't wait for dawn.

Nyx kept Safiyah with her up front, and Khatijah and Kage made up the rear guard. The sun took a lot longer to come up here, and when it finally did, the roiling clouds kept the whole world bathed in lilac for the first two hours of sunrise. The light made the journey incredibly unreal, like pounding through some spectacular dream. The landscape here had a strange hush about it, expectant, like the creamy red sand was just lying in wait for things to happen. For blood to be spilled.

They walked through a forest of white structures twice as tall as Nyx, all of them twisted into a grotesque semblance of trees, or, in some cases—human figures. The structures oozed some kind of clear, snotty mucus. Nyx hated them.

"Have you heard of Bomani?" Nyx asked Safiyah as they walked.

"Ah, yes. It's one of the major congregations here. Something like a city."

"You can get us as far as Bomani?"

"Am I being employed as guide now? I don't believe we've negotiated for that additional service."

Nyx sighed. "Never mind. You just seem to know your way around."

"Indeed. Only not as keenly as perhaps you would hope."

"Nyx?" said Khatijah.

Nyx turned. The wind wasn't as strong today, but still persistent. The sand stung her eyes. She squinted.

"What?" she said.

"There's movement back this way."

"Eshe, see what she's talking about," Nyx said. He was closer than Kage, and to be honest, Nyx was too exhausted to haul herself all the way to the back of the line again.

Eshe sighed. "You're welcome," he said. He pulled out his specs and walked over to join Khatijah.

Khatijah pointed.

Eshe lit up like a burning bush.

Nyx didn't even hear a shot or an explosion. One moment she was looking back the way they'd come, following Khatijah's arm, and the next—a pillar of fire shot out of the ground where Eshe stood.

Nyx threw herself behind the nearest twisted white structure. She could feel the heat through her cover. She squeezed her eyes shut. Eshe's keening cry was cut short.

Then someone else was screaming.

Isabet.

"Get to cover!" Nyx yelled.

Nyx let out a breath and looked for Ahmed. He might be able to call a swarm out here to shield them from view. From her position, she saw no one. They had scattered when the flame appeared.

Not one had knuckled forward to help Eshe. Not even her.

Her own fault. She had not hired heroes.

Nyx dove to the next mound. Ducked around a corner, searching for her fucking magician. Sand stuck to her where the mucus had adhered to her body.

"Ahmed!" she yelled.

She heard three shots.

Somebody squealed. Hers or theirs, she wasn't certain.

"Ahmed!"

She ran for the next cover.

Halfway there, the sand around her erupted. She threw her arms up and leapt back, expecting shrapnel. Her whole body went taut as adrenaline rushed through her. Every instinct told her it was a mine.

But she was still whole, and there was a dusty woman swinging a sword at her from the newly blown crater.

Nyx backpedaled to her former cover, yanking at her own blade as she retreated. She was nearly out of bullets, and at close range, she was more comfortable with a blade.

Someone shouted behind her. The woman ahead of her stopped swinging. Nyx stabbed at her. The woman danced back.

"You are mine! I challenge you!"

Nyx turned. The oddly accented Nasheenian was familiar, though she could not place it.

Another woman strode toward her through the formations. Like the other, she was tall and red-brown, with a mane of dark hair. Nyx remembered her. The woman from the tea shop. The one insulted by Kage's casual fuck.

Well, shit.

Nyx raised her blade.

The woman held up her serrated insect leg, but did not advance.

"I, Shani of Jithra's Circle, challenge you."

"And I don't fucking accept."

"You're on Circle Jithra land now," Shani said. "You accept or I kill you the way I did your boy."

Nyx regarded the scorched sand where Eshe's blackened husk lay smoldering. There were more women nearby. She saw a few glimpses among the formations.

"Where's my team? You fry anyone else?"

"Not if you circle with me. Put away your blade. You'll call the sand with blood out here."

"But burning up a boy is fine, is it?" Nyx said. She could smell the burnt flesh. Her memory roiled, and then everything just tumbled apart. She swung.

The woman had the sense to look startled. The blade came down on her shoulder, drew blood before she could dance away.

"Hold your blade!" the woman yelled at her. "You'll call the sand! You fool!" And then she was nattering off something in her language.

Nyx leapt forward. She felt a dart of flame shoot up behind her, right where she'd been the moment before. She swung again as the woman danced behind more cover. Nyx's blade cracked against the white structure. It trembled. The tip of her blade whacked the desert woman again, this time in the face. It opened another wound. Blood spilled.

Nyx kept on, relentless, moving among the formations in time with the desert woman. She was aware, distantly, of something hissing around her. And voices. The Aadhya were calling to one another.

A gout of crimson sand burst from the ground ahead of her. Nyx stumbled back. Shani screamed. A twisted, spitting tornado of sand erupted from the ground around Shani. Nyx watched it tunnel into Shani's open wounds and fill her skin to bursting. Shani's body became a bloated sack. Her eyes bulged. Then her skin burst, and the sand spilled out, darker than the stuff that went in. The bloodless shell crumpled to the ground. The bloody sand joined the rest of the stuff at Nyx's feet. She felt it ripple beneath her. This was not like the sand she encountered before in Nasheen. It was the wild variety, eating blood alone, leaving baggy skin and bone corpses behind.

Nyx turned away before she could retch, and ran back through the maze of structures. She found Eshe by following the smell of burnt flesh. When she reached him, she threw down her blade and pulled him into her arms. His skin was blackened; his face, unrecognizable. The clothes were burnt away or seared to the skin. His eyes had melted. In death, there was nothing that marked him as being any different than any other Nasheenian boy, burned up and left to die at the front.

"Eshe?" she said. But he was dead, of course. The same way her whole squad had died, melted up by some mine she had triggered instead of clearing.

She saw Ahmed a few steps away, and Kage just behind him. Ahmed didn't hold a gun, but a long length of garroting wire. Isabet was crouched near Kage, behind one of the formations. Three dead Aadhya lay on the ground, with no visible open wounds. One's head was cocked at an unnatural angle, and the other two looked like they had been garroted.

Surrounding them all were over a dozen living Aadhya. They said nothing. Did not move. Simply watched.

"Is this what you wanted, you bloody cats?" Nyx said.

She released Eshe's body and drew her sword. She hadn't seen Safiyah or Khatijah, which meant they were either dead or in hiding. She brought her sword to her own throat.

"Get the fuck out of here. I'll call the sand myself, and my team will shoot each of you in turn. It'll eat us all together. That's a fine thing, isn't it? All of us dead because Shani got jealous about who was fucking who?

That what you want?"

It wasn't until the silence stretched that she realized Shani may have been the only one among them who could speak Nasheenian.

The women stood in silence for some time. Nyx looked them all in the eye, but reading them was impossible. She didn't know what lines had been crossed. Didn't know what they respected, what they revered, only that this rogue woman had been insulted enough to want to fight her, and murder Eshe as an afterthought.

Sweat ran into Nyx's eyes. The grit between her toes itched, and she wondered if she had bleeding blisters down there, wondered if the sand would slowly suck her dry—toes first.

Then the women began to turn away. First one, then another. They covered their faces with the ends of their turbans as they went. The women were so long-legged that they were lost among the formations within just a few strides.

It wasn't until the last was clear that Nyx let her arm relax. The blade slipped from her fingers. She made herself look at Eshe.

Ahmed and Kage approached. She stared at Eshe's melted eye sockets. Wondered if he'd ever convinced his white bitch to love him.

And that thought, oddly, was the one that cut her deepest.

She rounded on Kage. Took her by the collar. Smashed her up against one of the structures. It spurted a fresh gush of mucus.

"And you. *You*, you fucking maggoty cat in heat, you worthless fucking Drucian rag. This is your fucking fault. What the fuck were you doing fucking red women in the desert? This is what comes of it. *This*. This is your fucking doing," Nyx spat.

Kage turned her cheek away. "It is private."

"Private?" Nyx hauled her up again. She took Kage by the back of the neck and thrust her face down against Eshe's charred body. "Private like death? Like my fucking kid's death?"

"You don't understand."

"No, *you* don't understand," Nyx said. She pulled her scattergun.

Ahmed stepped forward, "Nyx—"

She swung the gun at him. "Can you fix him?"

Ahmed held up his hands. "He's not a bel dame, Nyx."

"Then shut the fuck up."

"She wanted children," Kage said. "I had to purge my debt. The debt for the lives I took. And the ones I've taken for you. There are just two ways to do that. Bearing children or saving a life. She asked for children."

"What? You're a woman, Kage. How the fuck did you give her children?"

Kage sucked in a long breath. "I am a woman, yes, but I can also give children. It's… private."

"Fucking *what*? Fucking *Drucians*." Nyx shot off a round above Kage's head. Kage flinched, at least. "I am so tired of your fucking secretive catshit. You're barely fucking human."

"We prefer to give life, not take it. Is that not human?"

"Fuck you," Nyx said. "I need a minute." She walked away a few paces. Isabet began to wail again. Nyx heard the Ras Tiegan run up behind her, to the body.

Nyx stumbled against one of the structures, far enough away that the smell of burnt flesh wasn't as strong. Then she retched everything she'd eaten that morning, and dry heaved awhile longer after that, until tears came.

"You all right?"

Nyx raised her head. It was Khatijah. She must have run off in this direction, gotten clear of the women first thing.

"Yeah, cheery," Nyx said.

Khatijah crouched next to her. She handed Nyx a water bulb. Nyx drank, not bothering to rinse the bile from her mouth. She valued the water too much.

"He was your kid?"

Nyx shook her head. "Took him on when he was eight. Street kid. Did a lot of work for me. Sent him off to Ras Tieg. It was safer. He bloody fucking hated me for it."

"Shit happens."

"I know that better than anybody." She handed back the water.

Khatijah took it. "I'm a bel dame, Nyx. I may not have seen as much as you, but I had to give stuff up, too."

Nyx wanted to shout at her, wanted to tell her nobody had given up more than she had. That was a lie, but it felt so true in that moment that keeping herself from screaming it at this young, stupid bel dame was physically painful.

"If Fatima is playing us with this, I'm going to fucking kill her," Nyx said.

"Get in line," Khatijah said. She stood and held out her hand to Nyx. "Ready?"

Nyx took Khatijah's outstretched hand and stood. "Who was your first note?" Nyx asked.

"My brother," Khatijah said.

"Ah," Nyx said.

"Yeah."

"Sorry, Khatijah."

"Khat," she said.

"Khat."

"Yours?"

"Woman, actually. Sixteen-year-old signed on for two years of service. Deserted after a month. I was twenty."

"How'd you get her?"

"Didn't. Never brought her in."

Khatijah looked genuinely shocked. "You brought in all your notes, though. All the bel dames talk about it. The woman too stupid to give up a note."

"I gave up that one."

"What happened?"

"She was infected. Some shit from the Chenjans. Forty people died, mostly her kin."

"Oh."

"That's why I always brought in my notes, after."

"They don't teach anybody that."

"The note was never registered to me. I had some people change it."

"You ran black work from the beginning, didn't you?"

"I never pretended to be a good woman, Khat."

Together, they walked back to Eshe's body. Isabet was kneeling over him, weeping.

Nyx took Isabet by her good arm and yanked her up. She didn't mean it to be kind. Isabet cried out in pain.

"You listen here, kitten," Nyx said. "I don't have patience for weakness. You cry over him tonight. I need you focused for whatever the fuck this desert flings at us next, including more of your Ras Tiegan handmaidens. Understand?"

Isabet shook her head. No, of course she didn't understand. Nearly eight weeks in camp and her Nasheenian was still fucked.

"Tell her, Ahmed."

He did.

"How do you want to handle the body?" Ahmed asked.

"Need to cut off the head," Nyx said. She had nothing to burn him with out here, and if they left the head intact, he was at risk for coming back as some lumbering beetle.

"You want me to do it?" Ahmed asked.

She gazed off toward the horizon. "I'd prefer that, yes," she said. Because I have become a weak old woman, she thought, but she could feel something coming loose inside her. She was losing some vital piece of herself. It was all about to unravel, and she feared that prepping Eshe's body would be the catalyst.

"Won't that call that… sand?" Kage said.

"Fuck," Nyx said.

Safiyah appeared, quite suddenly, from the structures ahead of them.

Nyx had her scattergun out and her finger on the trigger before she realized who it was.

"Took your time," Nyx said.

Safiyah raised up something she held behind her. It was a woman's head. "Found their pyromancing magician," she said. "That's a conjuring trick I haven't seen in a very long time."

"Magician?" Nyx said. "A magician can do that?"

"Not just any magician," Safiyah said. She tossed the head into the forest of white. Nyx realized the head was bloodless. "That's a woman with some very old skill, something you don't even see in Nasheen anymore."

"And they can just blow people up like that?"

"They can do more than just control bugs," Safiyah said. "They can combine… let's say, small particles, elements, to create new elements. It's quite a trick."

"This is getting worse and worse," Ahmed said.

"How far to Bomani?" Nyx said.

"Funny you ask," Safiyah said. "It's just on the other side of this forest. One problem, of course. We never did consider how it was we were going to get in."

35.

Hanife paid him often, and well, in Tirhani currency, all of which Rhys paid him back at the end of each week, to pay back the blood debt.

Rhys thought it funny. He had no use for Tirhani currency out here beyond the Wall anyhow. No one took it. So instead he gladly gave it back at the end of each week, and tried to figure out how he would escape from Hanife's stranglehold.

The world beyond the Wall was worse than he anticipated. Hanife needed a translator for all sorts of business, most of it sordid. Interrogations, treaties, remediations. He had no idea there was this much politicking going on in the far north of the world. He thought the world ended at Khairi. He had been very wrong.

Rhys spent most evenings with some of the Aadhyan men, watching them sing to insects the way Khairians did. He tried to understand what they did beyond the song to call the insects.

"How's it done?" he asked as one man called a small arthropod to him from across the courtyard.

The man laughed. "It's not something you teach. It's something you do."

"I have some talent with bugs, though," Rhys said, and with some effort, called a small swarm of beetles.

The men regarded one another. One of them nodded.

"Come," they said. "We'll teach you to sing, but only if you teach us Yazdani."

That was how Rhys came to learn why it was he only saw Aadhyan women in the desert, but only men out here.

"Hanife has asked us to join his army," one man, Jahrin said. "We're outcasts, mostly. That's the Khairian word. Ours is… far worse than that. Women rule the sand, because it rarely eats them."

"If they bleed with the moons, it won't attack an entire party," another man, Tarik, said. "That's why only women can become Circle leaders. They become fighters. If we spill blood on the sand, we're sure to be eaten."

"I don't understand," Rhys said. "If you'll die spilling blood out there, how is it any different than spilling it as part of Hanife's army?"

Jahrin said, "You can't come here for a few weeks and expect to understand everything. Think less of politics and more about singing. Foreign fools. Always thinking they'll know a thing after a few questions. You won't know the Aadhya."

Tarik laughed. "Come. You have a terrible voice."

Rhys spent most of his days trapped inside cold, moist rooms, longing for a window. Hanife had two brothers, and they enjoyed piling translation work onto Rhys's desk. Once they found out he had a fine hand, he began learning the written version of Yazdani as well.

It was several weeks before Hanife finally asked him to come downstairs to do some "interrogation work."

Rhys didn't particularly like the sound of it. When he went down into the cells, he liked it even less.

A man was strung out on a stone slab. He seemed to be Ras Tiegan, or perhaps a mix of Ras Tiegan and Heidian.

"Tell him I want to know who else attacked my caravan," Hanife said.

Rhys translated.

The man pressed his lips firmly together.

Hanife waved another man over. A man wielding some very sharp knives.

Rhys found himself staring at the ground while the man screamed. It was a very long day.

After, Rhys went down to sit with Jahrin and Tarik for supper.

"You look like you have seen a bloody djinn," Tarik said.

"I think I have," Rhys said.

Jahrin sighed. He reached out and squeezed Rhys's hand. "This is what happens when you run away, as we did. You try to find a free life, but instead you find you are just a weapon in someone else's war."

Tarik grumbled into his fried meal worms.

But Jahrin's words touched something in Rhys that had lain dormant for some time. How often had he run from a bad situation into something even more terrible because he could not face the consequences of his actions? Because he was too scared to fix what was broken?

Rhys thought most often of escape when he counted out the money Hanife paid him. It all meant nothing out here. Just sorting bits of useless paper. But in his mind, every note was a way to ease Elahyiah's burdens, and school his children, and build some future from the ashes of the present. Somehow. If he ever found them. If she ever forgave him. Was there forgiveness to be had, after all he'd done?

Three weeks after he arrived at Hanife's hold, Hanife called him down again to the interrogation room. Rhys expected more horror, but instead, there were three Ras Tiegan men there, standing free and easy.

"Tell them I appreciate our friendship," Hanife said, "and I will do all I can to ensure their man's safety."

Rhys translated.

"We are pleased to do business with such an honorable man. We look forward to sharing our discoveries with him as they progress," said one of the Ras Tiegans.

Rhys relayed the information. Hanife looked pleased. "That is well. Very well! Tell them they are invited to have supper with me. They can marvel at this army I have carved out of the desert. Let me tell them of this hold and the four others I have conquered."

Rhys watched the four men start back up into the main hold, leaving him and the jailer in the room. Rhys couldn't help but glance into the only occupied cell in the block.

The light was dim. He squinted.

Recognition hit him like a fist to the kidney. He stumbled away from the door. Bit back an oath.

He knew that man.

36.

Nyx had figured Bomani would just be some kind of rock and mud-brick construction. Maybe a collection of hovels arranged inside a stone circle. It's not like she expected anything like civilization this far north, not behind a bloody-minded desert wall in the middle of some flesh-eating sea of sand. This place was nobody's friend, least of all any collection of people.

As they came to the edge of the forest of formations and gazed out to the rising dawn, she went still. There was a massive black conurbation blotting out a portion of the horizon. She peered at it. It was no derelict. This was… something else. Something constructed here? Not fallen… placed or grown. Nyx tried not to stare at it. It made her skin crawl.

"That's the place," Safiyah said.

"What is it?"

"It is Bomani," Safiyah said.

"No, really," Nyx said. "What the fuck is that? All right, what *was* that thing? That was nothing made by humans. Is it some bug house or something?"

Khatijah shrugged. "The Aadhya would know better than me."

But Nyx hadn't battled giant beasts, fought off mercenaries, run from pyromancing magicians, or hauled bodies across the desert just to walk back up to the nomads who'd slaughtered Eshe and ask them about a bunch of stories.

Safiyah smirked. "It's not so strange. Just something your droll little mind could never conceive of," she said.

"You've seen one before?" Nyx asked Safiyah. She should have thought to ask Safiyah—the fount of useless knowledge.

"There's still some record of the early days of the world that is taught. I've seen illustrations, of course. A few tatty drawings re-created from old bug captures. The magicians who made the world habitable didn't live in Nasheen, not the first magicians—the true conjurers. They lived up here in the beginning, long before the moons were even properly inhabited. For a thousand years they tended these great conflagrations. These organic machines powered all of their conjurings, even helped filter the atmosphere. There were six or eight, as I recall. The nomads continue to put them to use."

"That's far too big to be a machine," Ahmed said from behind them. "Something with that many moving parts would have to be partially deadtech, like a bakkie. It would require constant maintenance."

"What do you know about it?" Safiyah said. "Our people were greater than any alien, once. It was the catastrophe on the moons that sent us down here too early. Only a portion survived. Imagine how different things would be, if the world had been fully formed when we colonized it, and our people here in full strength? It would be us out there in the stars spreading our knowledge to those aliens. Not the other way around."

"Sounds like an excuse to me," Nyx said.

Safiyah narrowed her eyes. "What's that?"

"Sounds like a pretty story lazy rich people tell themselves to justify not doing a goddamn thing to change the world."

"And what exactly are you doing to change the world, little fly?" Safiyah said.

"I just cut off heads. Never pretended to be anything else."

"Come," Khatijah said. "Before they send out the dogs."

"The dogs?" Ahmed said.

"I don't get the impression the people here are going to be any more welcoming than their friends back there."

"Blood and fucking," Nyx said.

"I generally prefer it the other way round," Safiyah said lightly.

Nyx watched the structure. It pulsed slowly, as if it were breathing. "Can you cut us into that thing?" she asked Safiyah.

"Certainly. But there's bound to be a guard. We'll need a distraction."

Nyx glanced behind them, where they had left the intact bodies of the Aadhya… and Eshe.

"I can give them a fucking distraction," she said.

+

Despite Ahmed's protest, they went back to where they left the bodies and buried them. If Nyx couldn't cut off their heads for fear of drawing the sand, she'd rather something else took care of them.

"You can control them?" she asked Safiyah. "When they come back up?"

"I cannot see all futures."

"Can you or fucking can't you?"

"It's likely," she said. "But you'll need me to cut open Bomani to get inside. As soon as I do that, I'll lose control of them. After that, Kage will need to bring them down, or they could turn on you."

"Then let's finish this shit," Nyx said.

Once the bodies were buried, they walked back to the edge of the forest, and began the long hike toward Bomani. Nyx pointed them to a jagged rise overlooking the hold; a good vantage for a sniper.

As they got nearer, Nyx was able to make out more of it. The stronghold was like something out of a lurid historical radio show. A bulbous, burgeoning conflagration that pulsed like a living organ in the low light. There were several towerlike structures protruding from its compass points, like minarets. The outside appeared to be ringed in the wind-effaced heads of some kind of twisted creatures for which Nyx had no name. They reminded her a bit of the beasts that attacked them early on. Monstrous, ravenous things with impenetrable skins.

Nyx noted that there didn't seem to be much activity outside. No one was coming in or going out. She didn't even see a door. It was just one long shimmering green skein, all the way around.

"Who runs this place?" Nyx asked. "The Aadhya?"

"They're ruled by three brothers," Khatijah said.

Nyx raised her brows. "And how is it you know this?"

"You think I was just sitting around in Kiranmay doing nothing?"

"It crossed my mind…"

“The men come from the other side of the Wall, many more weeks from here. It’s called Yazdan, and there’s some ocean over there, so they call them ocean people. The brothers buy and sell people out here, and a whole host of other things.”

“For what, labor?”

“Sex, I think.”

“I’m sorry,” Nyx said. “What?”

“People want to control things they’re afraid of,” Kage said. Nyx couldn’t argue with that. Still, most of the folks she kept around were good for more than just sex. Sex was a bonus, naturally, but not the main event. And people who were only useful for sex were a drain on resources. Wherever Yazdan was, it must be a rich sort of place.

“Maybe some of us could pass for them.” Khatijah peered over at Kage. “She could pass, maybe. And Isabet.”

“I’m not a fan of hiding out among loose skirts unless there’s no other way,” Nyx said. “Once we’re in, what’s our cover?”

“There is an easier way,” Safiyah said.

Nyx waited.

“I’m a magician,” Safiyah said. She sniffed. “And a far more skilled one than your torturer.”

“Yeah, but once we’re in, we need to find Raine. How’s that happen if we just suddenly appear?”

Khatijah sighed. “The people-selling angle is looking better.”

“Oh, *everyone* does that,” Safiyah said. She clapped her hands. “How about a glamour? I haven’t done a good glamour in… *such* a long time.”

Nyx said, “How many people can you realistically hold a glamour on?”

“You, the bel dame, and perhaps the Drucian. It will be very dark in there, after all, and they are better in tight spaces. We don’t need the curry eater or the torturer.”

“Kage needs to stay on the high ground and shoot the bugs. She’s not going with us.”

“You’re going to seriously leave me out here with the girl?” Ahmed said.

Safiyah shrugged. “I am being practical. But, of course, the final decision rests with Damira here.”

“Very funny,” Nyx said. She looked at what remained of her team. Her heart hurt at not finding Eshe there, knife at the ready. His sly walk, fast hands, and keen eyes were made for this part of the run. Instead, he'd be helping out as… something else. She grimaced. There was no way out of this hell for her.

You don't go in with the team you dream about, Raine once told her, you go in with the team you've got.

Fuck you, Raine, she thought, but said aloud, "All right. Let's camp out and wait for the bugs." She pointed to a low ridge overlooking the hold. "No fires. Keep a low profile. We'll scout it out once the bugs are up. Once we're in, if we're not back in two days, you head home."

Ahmed snorted.

She held up a hand. "Come on. Let's pretend we're not all going to die out here, all right? I'm not living like a corpse. I don't expect you to think like one. Got it?"

"Sure," Ahmed said.

"Any other ideas?" Nyx said. "Because after the sun goes down, we're going in."

✚

Ahmed had seen what men became when they were not beheaded or burned or shipped off to the containment centers for decontamination and deprocessing. He waited on the rise with a pair of specs, staring out into the white forest, waiting for the bodies to come back.

What Nyx proposed was dangerously *haram*—forbidden. It turned his stomach. He would have rather hacked them all apart and risked the wrath of that blood-sucking sand than see those people devoured from the inside and come back as lumbering, hulking wrecks.

Those people. One of whom was Eshe.

He gritted his teeth.

Nyx came up beside him, folded her arms. "Anything?"

"No," he said.

"You're not happy about it," she said.

"It's forbidden. It's obscene."

"I've done worse."

"Not to your own kid."

"Care that much, do you?"

"He was a good kid."

"How good?"

Ahmed pulled the specs away, and glanced up at her. She kept her gaze on the long sweep of the forest.

"What's that supposed to mean?"

"Seems to me that all the fucking on this team has gotten us all into trouble."

"That was Kage, not me."

"Was it?"

He grunted. Fuck her. Fuck all the officers like her.

"You don't have any respect for anything," he said.

"What you did with Eshe was *haram*, too," she said. "If you're following the Kitab by rote."

"Fuck you, Nyx."

"I called it," Khatijah said, walking up behind the two of them and holding out her hand to Nyx. "They totally fucked. You owe me a note. I won the bet."

"Goddammit," Nyx said, and pulled a note from her burnous.

"Is this all some kind of a fucking game to you?" Ahmed said. "What the fuck is wrong with you? Both of you? Bloody fucking bel dames. You make up all the fucking rules and then you break them like they're nothing. Like it's all so much catshit. Is life just catshit to you? Do you feel anything at all?"

Khatijah pointed toward the forest. "Check that movement. It's them."

Ahmed raised the specs to his eyes. Three dark shapes lumbered at the edge of the forest. He saw a fourth just beyond them, small and willowy. He had to look away.

"Safiyah," Nyx said. "Your turn."

✚

Nyx thought she'd prefer approaching Bomani in the dark.

She was wrong.

There were wispy green lights in the towers, speckled along what might have passed for a parapet of some kind that ringed the hold. But for the most part, the world was a wash of darkness, and Bomani was an inky blob of black against the night.

She and Khatijah waited until the lumbering bodies made contact with the far end of the hold. More lights flickered up top. She heard voices.

Then Nyx ran in the opposite direction, hoping to make it into the shadow of the building before anyone noticed.

Khatijah trailed her.

Nyx didn't think about the bodies. Or the lights. Didn't think about anything until she made it to the wall. She pushed herself against the wall, and her hands came away wet and sticky. She grimaced as she put her back to it and crouched low.

Khatijah caught up to her, and did the same.

They waited in the darkness, breathing heavily. Nyx listened to the spatter of voices above her. She couldn't make out a damned word. Someone was shouting. At least the giant, flesh-sloughing beetles were making an impression.

Nyx glanced back to the front of the structure, where the beetle-bodies were clicking and slavering at the organic matting of the hold. She appreciated that they looked like beasts, in the dark. Just beasts. Shambling things.

Safiyah finally made her way toward them from the top of the rise. The hail of voices had gotten louder. Nyx heard shots. She wondered if dead beetles would draw the blood-thirsty sand. Probably. Probably time to go.

A fine skein of translucent mayflies surrounded Safiyah's head. Her look was stern. "I must release them now," she said. "Be ready to slip into the skin once it's open."

She flicked her hand, and the mayflies dispersed. Then she put her hands onto the squelchy wall and murmured something that sounded to Nyx a lot like a prayer. Not a good sign.

Nyx heard the chittering scuffle of the giant beetle-bodies. Shots rang out from above them. With Safiyah's attention on getting them in, the beetles were free to shamble where they liked. The flesh-ragged beetles huffed closer, moving down the edge of the hold toward them.

Nyx drew her scattergun.

Safiyah let out a breath. There was a sucking sound. "In! In!" she whispered.

Khatijah pushed herself into the spongy rent in the wall.

Nyx kept her weapon out. Only two of the beetle-things were still alive. The other corpses thrashed at the base of the wall. She heard the hissing call of the hungry sand.

The lead beetle was hunched over, cloaked in a burnous and torn trousers. The face was split in two, revealing the shiny black beetle carapace beneath. The bugs grew faster out here, and bigger. She saw Eshe's belt. Eshe's dagger. What remained of Eshe's dark hair, tangled with coagulated blood and sticky bug secretions that must have hidden the scent from the sand.

Nyx put her finger on the trigger. Above her, more voices were shouting. More shots.

"Sorry," Nyx said.

She pulled the trigger.

The beetle's craggy visage exploded. Wet bug guts and the remains of Eshe's mangled face spattered her tunic.

A whirlwind of sand spat up at her feet.

Nyx vomited.

Someone grabbed her from behind.

She grunted.

They pulled her into Bomani, into darkness.

+

Bomani was a living, rotting thing. It was as if it were constantly sloughing off its old skin and regenerating new and more intricate parts all the time. Nyx stared up into the guts of the thing. It was, she decided, like some gigantic bakkie that had been left to grow out of control for millennia.

They had walked across sucking, pulsing tissue and into a long, low, empty hall that made Nyx suddenly claustrophobic. The walls were practically dripping. The only light came from a line of blue bioluminescent fungi that crept along the walls.

"Where is everyone?" Nyx asked, low.

Safiyah closed the new gap behind them. Every wall was easily breachable, with her in the lead. "This is an outer ward. Most activity will be further in. I told you there was no need for weapons yet."

Nyx kept her scattergun out. She was down to a handful of shells. The pistol ammo wasn't faring much better.

"Does anyone even know how to run this thing?" Khatijah asked.

"There are some conjurers who shape it," Safiyah said. "They simply apply the whims of whatever party rules the holdfast, though. Inside and out, these places grow and change depending on the vision of the one who rules them."

"Do they do anything anymore? Think they could get fixed or something?" Khatijah asked.

"Fixed? I don't understand."

"If they helped make the world, can't they still do it? Help… I don't know… make it better or something?"

Safiyah shrugged. "They have been rebuilt and repurposed and renewed so many times… What all these parts and pieces originally did, no one is certain. Even more important, it's quite possible that none of the organic circuitry here is original. It's all been changed many times. And unless someone has a record of what it was supposed to be like… well, we can all breathe well enough."

Nyx stared up at the great guts of the beast.

"Come now," Safiyah said. "Let's build a proper glamour." She raised her hands, and Nyx felt a wave of nausea. Next to her, she saw Khatijah's image waver, then bleed into the long, leggy form of one of the Aadhya. Her features, coloring, clothing—it was all different, and so much like Shani that Nyx had to resist the urge to draw her blade again. She likely looked the same. When Nyx looked back at Safiyah, the magician, too, had taken on the guise of an Aadhya. She was, admittedly, more conservatively dressed than either of them, in a short red tunic and burnous in addition to her turban.

Safiyah smiled. "Must be a new thing for you two, running off into the desert to save men instead of kill him."

"We have to find him first," Nyx said. "Khat? Ideas?"

"I guess we go deeper into the hold, and find out how many people we're dealing with here."

"And hopefully who," Nyx said. She glanced back at Safiyah. "You can really hold this glamour the whole time?"

"As long as you like."

Khatijah led, and Nyx took the rear, protecting Safiyah's back in case someone broke her calm. Though honestly, the way things were going Nyx was beginning to think that few things would do that.

Nyx heard voices ahead, and fought the urge to pull a weapon. She needed to walk carefully, here. Smoothly. Like she belonged.

Khatijah rounded a corner. The three of them passed into a massive room. It appeared to be an eating or gathering hall. There were over a hundred men there, eating and talking in loud voices.

Khatijah glanced back at Nyx. Nyx urged her on, gesturing to what looked like another door on the far side of the hall. The men here were all tall and lanky desert men, with the same reddish skin and dark hair as Shani and her sisters. As long as no one tried to have an extended conversation with them, they should be able to pass through.

Nyx was four steps into the hall before she realized there had been no men among the people Shani brought with her. She stopped cold.

Three men at the end of a table nearest to Khatijah yelled something at her. They stood. A few more heads turned. The men began gesturing at Khatijah angrily.

"Safiyah," Nyx said. "Do men and women generally hang out a lot among the Aadhya?"

"Yes," Safiyah said. "The women generally do all the fighting, though, and they own the men. So I'm not sure why these are here."

The men were getting angrier.

Khatijah tried to bluff her way forward. Kept walking. Nyx held her head a little higher. Her hands itched for a blade.

One of the men grabbed Khatijah's wrist.

She broke it neatly.

That was enough to incite the others.

Twenty or thirty men swamped them at once. Nyx pulled her blade. Safiyah squawked and jumped back the way they had come. Nyx lost sight of her. Nyx cut down the first man who got within reach of her blade and sliced back another one.

Two more came up from behind. She kicked back. Broke someone's knee. She pulled a dagger. Sliced two more men open. Her hands were slick with blood. She heard Khatijah curse. The men kept coming. A swarm of them, fodder for an endless war…

Like her brothers. Like her squad. Like Eshe.

Like her.

She was so bloody fucking tired. There was no retirement for bel dames, not really. There was no soft, gentle end. No fading away. Just this, always this. Cutting down wave after wave of men. Burying boys in the desert. Death in some black place, alone… like Eshe's body—a crackling husk in some godfucked desert.

Eshe. She didn't know whether she wanted to vomit or weep. Neither would do much good. Neither changed anything.

Another man swung a club at her. Nyx countered. Batted it away. Came in with a palm to his nose. The weapon came around again. Nyx pivoted left, not away from the blow but into it. The weapon came crashing down on her skull. Blackness flashed before her vision. Crashing light.

Then, blessed darkness.

37.

Inaya walked further down the hall, dressed in the crimson robe and black cowl of one of God's Angels. She passed more interrogation rooms, and… other rooms. The Angel who interrogated her told her he didn't have to torture her. But from the look of the mangled bodies in these rooms, there were many others they saw fit to torture.

She kept moving, searching for a way out. Surely there was more than one way out?

Finally, she came to the end of the hall, and an arched entry. She hesitated. Beyond the doorway was a wide reception room. She stepped through. Turned the corner.

Three figures, dressed as God's Angels, stood huddled around a fourth person. From the look of the clothing, it was another Angel.

Beyond them, Inaya could see yet another door, half-open—and beyond that—daylight.

She took in the measure of the chamber. It was a stark white room with a large domed ceiling. Lockers ran along the full length of it. She wondered if this was the entrance for the Angels.

She closed her eyes and tested her ability to shift. Her skin rippled. She tried to let go, to bleed into the floor, but once again, she hit some kind of barrier. A—nothingness. Held her head high. How had she seen them walk? She gripped her hands together in front of her, so her long sleeves hid her arms, and began to walk purposefully across the room.

As she neared, she could make out the voices.

"You deserve to die here for what you've done," one of them said. "If you had broken her we would not be in this mess."

"We should have had her case transferred a month ago," another said.

"The letters should have made her crumble, with the right delivery and persuasion. Are you so unskilled that you cannot release a confession from a weak-minded woman?"

Inaya glimpsed the group from the corner of her eyes. The Angel on the floor was unmistakably the one who had interrogated her these many long weeks. No, months, from what they were saying. Months. An entire season, perhaps?

"You do not understand," her interrogator said. "I could not condemn an innocent woman. How many times—"

"Fool! None of them are innocent. No one brought to this place is innocent. Don't argue innocence. Not here before God's fist."

"I humbly request—"

"Leave him incarcerated here with his charges. He made this mess. He can soak in it."

"No, please. I am still useful. You must understand!"

Two of the Angels picked up her interrogator and hauled him back the way she had come.

Inaya quickened her pace until she was on the other side of the room. Her fingers met the door. She turned the handle. It opened.

A burst of cool, humid air met her face. She gasped. In her hurry, she nearly stumbled over her robe. She walked out into the rainy afternoon, and was struck by how... *normal* everything looked. There were a few outbuildings here, but for the most part, they were surrounded by jungle. She would need to wait to shift before she traveled, or hijack one of the bakkies. If they were indeed very far from a major city, there would be no proper transit station.

Inaya heard the door open behind her, and scurried forward to a nearby bakkie barn. She crouched behind a parked bakkie.

"The entire facility is a loss," one of the Angels said. "I want it shut down until the emergency is over."

"What about the girl?"

"We need to bring her to a senior Arch Angel. We'll have her transferred. The records are a mess. I'd have to go through every cell to find her. Then we'd have to transport her ourselves. I'm not doing that without the proper help. Let's come back with a relocation team."

"And what of Pieter?"

"Let him die here. I care nothing for weak-willed men. Those drugs will last for three days. He'll be dead by then."

Inaya heard them get into a bakkie. Heard it cough and sputter away.

She pressed her back against the outbuilding. Pieter. Her interrogator. He had a name. Of course he had a name. But in those long, terrible sessions she did not see him as a person. Just as he did not see her as one.

It would be hours more before she could shift. She settled down and waited. Sometimes waiting was the most difficult thing. She had waited many months. Already she was tired from all the walking, and desperately hungry. Surely there was more food inside?

Inaya crept back to the door. Her hand hesitated again at the handle.

Don't be a fool, she thought. She pulled her hand away. She would wait until she could shift.

While she waited, she tried to doze, but she could not rid her mind of Pieter, the Angel. He was going to starve in there, the way he had left her to starve.

Goddammit, she thought.

She prayed.

✚

Dusk. She woke to thirst… and something more.

Inaya's body felt suddenly lighter, her mind, clearer, as if a curtain had been pulled away from her mind. She struggled to her feet.

And let go.

She surrendered to the delightful freedom of changing forms. She burst into a soft, wispy cloud, then yanked herself back and rebuilt her form into that of a large sand cat, then a tremendous black beetle. And finally, a wispy green mist—the fastest way to get back in.

She descended back to the compound, and slid under the door. She raced to the cells where the other shifters were kept. She coded her blood to match that of the dead Angel whose clothing she had stolen, and released them all.

In the last cell, as it went from opaque to transparent, she recognized Pieter.

He stood as the filter changed, and stared out at her—or, the misty wraith she had become.

"I knew it," he said.

Would he murder all the shifters she had just released? Would she endanger them by releasing him?

He came to the edge of the filter. For a long time, they regarded one another.

Inaya made her decision.

38.

Nyx came to lying on her side. Went from blissful black nothingness to painful muzzy-headedness in the space of a breath. Tiny insects crawled across her face. She jerked upright. Her wrists were bound, so she wiped the bugs away on her shoulder. Turned out they were ants. Some kind of biting ants, and they bit hard. She put her face between her knees and scrubbed it clean.

Sometime during the rubbing, she heard a low babble of voices. Then a grunt. It rose to a ragged scream. Then nothing. The sound was coming from beyond the door. She slid back down onto her side, and tried to peer underneath the door. She saw some kind of holding room. There were other doors across the dusty floor. More prisoners? But the air smelled funny for a cell, and a closer inspection of the patterns on the walls told her this had been a cellar long before it was a cell. A cellar meant she was underneath Bomani. Not a great place to be, for her. But a great place to muffle screams. She wondered if Ahmed would have approved of the space.

There were a few pairs of sandaled feet surrounding the table, but from the crack beneath the door, she couldn't see who or what was on it. One of the desert women?

She heard the same scream again, high-pitched, biting. Like somebody taking a knife in the gut. There was some talking again, this time in some muddy language she didn't understand. There was a brief moment of silence. Then a soft, strangely familiar voice said, in Nasheenian, "All they seek is the location of your sisters. We know there are more of you outside. How many?"

Silence.

Nyx kicked herself closer to the door. She shoved her face right into the spongy floor, mashed her nose against the door. That was a voice she knew. A voice she had not expected to hear again. And sure as hell not out here.

The feet moved around a bit. Nyx heard a scraping and chittering sound. Sharp intake of breath. Then full-throated screaming. Not just once this time, but over and over again, like water running over stones.

Nyx pushed against the door to gain some leverage. Stood on shaky feet. Her ribs were sore, and her face felt like it'd been mashed with a shovel. She wondered how long they'd beaten her before throwing her in this cell. She tried to find some kind of key hole or window, but there was nothing.

The screaming stopped.

The muttering started again. She heard someone moving closer to her cell door.

Nyx stepped deeper into the cell. There were at least four of them out there, plus the translator, and they would be armed. But there was nothing she could use as a weapon in here—not a rock or stick or bug—just dirt. They had stripped her down well for non-Nasheenians, and even her sandals were missing. About the only thing she had left were the needles in her hair. But with her hands tied behind her, they were impossible to reach.

The door opened.

A pale man wearing a bloody apron beckoned her forward with two fingers, as if she were a dog.

Nyx bared her teeth.

He sighed, and called in the others. But Nyx wasn't looking at them. She was staring behind them, to the translator. The familiar voice.

The men took her by the arms and hauled her out. She finally got a clear look at the translator, and grinned. Then laughed. The laugh seemed to shake the men. They halted. She realized she was laughing over the bloody, mutilated corpse of Khatijah, staked out on the table like some magician's specimen.

The translator finally met her gaze, but his face betrayed nothing. In that moment, when he saw her and knew her and said nothing, when not a muscle in his face twitched, when the only hint of recognition she noted was the way he squeezed his right hand into a fist—in that moment she knew this was very, very serious. She knew this was not just another routine interrogation where she would walk out with most of her limbs intact. Because if he pretended not to know her, it meant he feared these men and their power more than he feared her. And that was a scary fucking thing.

The pale men blathered on about something.

Rhys translated. "These men would like to know if you would join your friend or if you will cooperate and spare yourself her fate."

"Tell them she's not my friend," Nyx said.

"Indeed. I told them that already, but you can see they remain unconvinced."

She shrugged. "You do what you have to do, then."

He cleared his throat. Gestured to the men, and said something in their language. She half wished it was Ahmed who was caught along with her so he could translate what Rhys was actually saying. But if it'd been Ahmed, it would be him dead on the slab now, and nothing would be any different.

One of the men took a giant hook from the table and chunked it into Khatijah's torso. He hauled the corpse off the slab. It thumped to the floor. Just so much meat now. She had to admit the fact that Khatijah had held tight to the end, even on this botched job. Khat had been a proper bel dame. The way they were supposed to be. And then you threw the fight, Nyx thought. And you got her killed. You got all of them killed. This is your doing.

Another man shoved Nyx toward the slab.

"What, they don't buy me dinner first?" Nyx said.

"I'm afraid not," Rhys said. "This isn't Nasheen."

"In Nasheen, I'd fuck you first," Nyx said. And this time, she meant it.

"Promises," Rhys said. He boldly met her gaze. It was the first time she could remember him looking her in the face when she brought up anything to do with fucking.

Despite the circumstances, and the blood, and the body, and the mumbling men, she realized she had missed him. Missed him more than she had any right to miss him. He's lived this long without me around, she thought. Now that I'm here, how much longer does he have? She glanced over at Khatijah's corpse. The bodies were piling up. She had to get away from him.

One of the men shoved her again. She rounded on him, teeth bared. There was more than one way to claw your way out of a hole.

The man smashed her in the face with the butt of his gun. She was fast enough to turn away as he did it, and avoided a broken nose. The butt struck her jaw. Black, hot pain seared her vision. She tasted blood.

They nattered on. She watched the one nearest Rhys drag Khatijah's mutilated body away and pile it up near the door with a wet, fleshy sound.

"They're asking one last time if you want to share the location of your desert friends. They know you didn't come alone. They want to know what you're here to do," Rhys said. "You can understand their… concern."

"I understand that they're already illegally squatting here," Nyx said. "They've got no more claim on it than I do."

"What are you here for, Nyx?"

"They really going to let me go if I say?"

"Probably not."

"Then what's the point?"

"They would have me tell you that you might live."

"We both know otherwise though, don't we?"

He nodded.

She shrugged. "Then let them do their worst."

Rhys sighed, and spoke to the men in their language. She was hoping it was about what she said, but he rambled on for a good long time—long enough to start making her nervous.

The men argued. They weren't happy with whatever he was saying. But Rhys kept talking in that soft, calming way he did. Eventually, they relented.

Rhys said, "They've agreed to give you a few hours with the body of your friend. To… think things over. I told them it would be very effective, since Nasheenians have an aversion to blood."

"You said that, did you?"

"They're from very far away," he said. He gestured to the men.

One of them grabbed the hook and chunked it into Khatijah's body. Hauled it back into the cell. The others escorted Nyx inside with it.

They shut the door.

Nyx let out her breath.

The men talked for a time. She stayed wedged up against the door. It was slightly spongy, like the floor. Was everything made of some organic shit? She found she could not look at Khatijah's ruined body. Her bug was spent. There was no chance of bringing her back, even if Rhys was ten times better at being a magician than he actually was, or if he'd even help her. What the fuck was he doing here?

She gingerly touched her jaw where she'd been hit. It could have been worse.

Nyx looked around for a way out. The whole room was dark. A line of the blue bioluminescent lighting ran along the upper edge of the cell, but that was all. No windows. No openings. Where did the air come from? When she pressed her cheek to the wall and felt it breathe beneath her, she remembered. It was a living thing. Like being trapped inside some porous lung.

The voices outside finally ceased. She heard the squelch of boots across the floor. The sucking sound of a door closing. Silence.

Nyx hated prison.

She made herself look at Khatijah's body. Maybe dying really was the only way out. She brought them to this. It was time to let go. It was time to throw the fight again—hers, this time. It wouldn't take too long to convince them to kill her. She always managed to find the perfect way to piss people off.

When she decided to die, it was almost a relief. Water in the desert.

She heard something outside again. Footsteps.

"Nyx?" Rhys's voice.

Nyx stood.

The door opened.

She let out her breath. Rhys reached forward and cut her bound hands.

She tried to think of something grimly optimistic to say.

Rhys embraced her.

It was sudden, and wholly unexpected. Nyx found herself gripping him tightly. He was thinner than she remembered, less muscular. The last time she'd held him this way they were both mostly naked, hiding atop a desk in a ruined Ras Tiegan church, trying not to get eaten by mutant red sand. It had been a long time since she thought about that day, clinging to him amid all that death. If she thought about it all, it was painful, just like every other fucking thing from her bloody fucking past.

He released her.

"So you came for me after all," Rhys said.

She shook her head. "Sorry. Not me. I had no idea what happened to you. You made me swear not to look for you, remember?"

Something dark passed over his face, like disappointment. "Yes. You're right. I did. You took a blood oath. But then… Why are you here? You and…I'm sorry about her."

"We're here to bring Raine back to Nasheen."

"Raine." He hesitated. Then, "Yes. I'd thought he was dead."

"People don't stay dead in Nasheen."

"Why would you come all the way out here for him? This place would kill him as well as anybody."

"I didn't come here to kill him." She grimaced. "I sort of came here to save him."

Rhys raised his brows. "You came here… to save Raine?"

"Sorry."

"It's just odd how that happens, Nyx. Like last time. When you burned away my life." The congeniality was gone. Why? Because she came here for somebody else?

"Doesn't look like there's much left to burn this time."

"And whose fault is that?"

"You tell me. I don't blame anybody else for my life. When I left Tirhan, you had a wife and a job. If you don't anymore, that's none of my doing."

"That's catshit, Nyx."

"Your mouth used to be a lot cleaner, too."

"Let's not start this again."

"I didn't start it. You were the one acting like a fucking ass. As always. Without a change. Not a fucking change in what, six, seven years?"

"Seven years," he said. He regarded her. "The years haven't been kind."

"Not to either of us," she said, because though Rhys would never be an ugly man, he had gone from pretty to handsome in the ensuing years. His hair was a little longer, his face more drawn, tired. He was so thin that the lines in his face were more prominent.

"Can we fuck about it later?" Nyx said. "These people creep me the fuck out."

Rhys shook his head. "You never change. Do you have people outside who can help you?"

She thought of her little team. Ahmed, Kage, Safiyah, and Isabet. She couldn't trust them any farther than she could throw them. She already lost the one she trusted most. "I have a team. But they're cobbled together."

"Where are they?"

Nyx felt a moment of hesitation. He saw it.

"I'm not here as an interrogator, Nyx."

Could she really trust that? "They're out there," she said. "That's all you need to know."

"I can't help you if I don't know."

"And I can't… Rhys, I can't trust you."

"What?"

"Would you trust me?"

Rhys looked at the floor.

"Yeah," she said. "All right. Fuck."

"Let me see what I can do," he said.

"He's not going by his old name. They call him Hamza Habib now."

Rhys said, "Yes, I know. Shit."

"Fuck, your mouth has gotten bad. You drink now, too?"

"Nyx, why are you always turning up looking for the most dangerous people I know?"

"Why are you always fucking around with dangerous people? Blame God, not me."

"I have no interest in talking about God with you." He stepped back into the interrogation room. "I'll return." He closed the door.

"Rhys," she said.

"What?"

She tried to puzzle out what to say. It all felt confused. "Don't fuck me over. I know I deserve it. For what happened. I'm sorry."

She heard him on the other side. When he spoke, it sounded like he had pressed himself against the door.

"I know how you died. You were coming to the house to warn me. You were just…" And his voice caught.

"I was too late," she said. She saw Eshe burning.

"I have to go," he said.

He went.

Nyx slid to the floor. Put her head in her hands. Her fingers touched the end of her poisoned needles.

Poison.

She raised her head, and gazed across Khatijah's body to the far wall.

Nyx pulled a needle from her hair and jabbed it into the pulsing wall. Then she took the second and third and jabbed them into the section as well, making a perfect triangle in the spongy tissue.

She wasn't even sure it would work, but the idea of sitting around waiting for Rhys to figure something out scared the shit out of her.

Nyx waited. After a time, black tendrils of rot began to appear, like cracks, from the wounds around the needles.

It took a good two hours to peel away the dead tissue. She worried the infection wasn't going to do the right kind of damage. Finally, she got a hole big enough that she thought she could wiggle through. On the other side was another nondescript corridor. She wondered how anyone navigated in this fucking place.

She pulled herself into the narrow hole. Her shoulders didn't quite fit. For the first time, she wished she was a lean, scrappy type like Anneke, or even Kage. She rested her elbows just inside the hole, squeezing as best she could into the tiny space. She got her head through and gazed down either side of the corridor. She imagined the wall repairing itself, growing smaller and smaller until it cut her head off.

It would be fitting.

Nyx expelled the air from her lungs and twisted her torso sharply to the right. She got her left arm free. Stretched it out into the open air. Her head was out next. She braced herself against the outside wall with her free arm—and pushed.

Her body moved a hand's length further through the hole—and her right shoulder jammed up against the inside wall. She tried to suck in a breath. She was stuck so tight her chest hurt. One more shallow breath—then she exhaled hard a second time and kicked her way free.

Nyx scrambled into the corridor, pressing herself hard against the wall. She had no idea what to do next. She had no weapons. No sense of where she was.

She took a deep breath and padded down the hall, listening for voices. After a time, she heard a strange buzzing sound coming from the floor. She paused. That's when she realized that she had still not run into any doors. Where did all of these halls lead?

Nyx started to run. She needed to get out of this fucking pit.

She heard a sucking sound to her left.

Something reached out from the wall.

She shrieked. Stupidly.

And tumbled through the other side, into Safiyah's arms.

"There you are," Ahmed said, beside her. There was a swarm of insects at his feet, palm-sized cicadas with giant mandibles. "Big teeth," he said, "but also a fine sense of smell."

"Get me the fuck out of here," Nyx said.

"Gladly," Safiyah said.

+

Back at the camp overlooking Bomani, Nyx wiped the organic sludge from her skin with sand. Ahmed sat next to her, eating the last of their dried worm meat.

"Are we calling that it?" he said.

"I don't know," Nyx said. "If Fatima really just wanted to kill all of us on some fool's errand, she's succeeding pretty well."

"Why did you take this job if you knew it'd kill you?" Ahmed said.

"Why did you?"

Ahmed gazed off toward Bomani. Behind them, Kage sat cleaning her gun, Isabet slept, and Safiyah was muttering to Ahmed's little army of cicadas. About what, Nyx didn't care to know.

"That bel dame came looking for me because I killed my commanding officer," Ahmed said.

Nyx sighed. "Of course you did." It was her own fault. She should have had each of them checked out on the bel dame boards before she signed them. Why hadn't she done it? Because they were discharged, of course. She had assumed that every boy discharged from the front was being let go as part of the ceasefire. She wouldn't think to sit around and weed out the ones who deserted for crimes committed. But this was a fine time to come out of the trenches if you were a deserter, wasn't it? It was a lot harder to track a boy among a sea of boys than a young, pretty face surrounded by women and a scattering of old men.

"I had my reasons," he said.

"Didn't we all."

"You've killed bel dames before."

"I've also killed a lot of boys before," she said, pointedly. "Don't get me started on which is easier."

"I'm sorry, Nyx."

"Fuck," she said. "Fuck." And then everything started to unravel. His calm way with each member of her team, slowly and carefully building alliances for the inevitable showdown. The way he showed just enough interest in everyone to say he was your friend, but not enough to show any one person they were a favorite.

"You should have told me this up front."

"You wouldn't have signed me. I honestly thought they would stop at the Khairian border. I'm not all that important."

"Aren't you? What was her name? Who was she?"

"Just… I don't know. She was just…"

"Don't fuck with me, Ahmed. I'm not in the mood. Tell me who she was."

"Just another officer. They were all the same to me."

"Did you kill all of them?"

"No."

"Did you fuck all of them?"

Ahmed turned away.

Nyx half thought to drive a knife through his skull herself. Why not? Why not just leave another long line of bodies out behind her in the desert? She had a powerful magician in Safiyah. But Safiyah worked for herself. Nyx expected to wake one morning and find out she'd fucked off into the desert somewhere, or just ridden some giant arthropod out. No, she needed desperate people. Desperate people could be counted on to act consistently. Bel dames or no, Ahmed needed her. In fact, with bel dames after him, he needed her more.

"For what it's worth, I'm sorry I didn't tell you sooner."

Nyx sighed. She was so goddamn tired. She hadn't been this goddamn tired in a long time. She missed Radeyah. Suddenly. Powerfully. But there were no nice girls for people like Nyx. Nobody sitting up waiting for them. She knew that when she left. Knew she was giving it all up. But what choice did she have? Nyx just wished that she could figure out solutions that had lower body counts.

"Nyx?"

She had zoned out. A dangerous thing. She started, and saw Ahmed pointing down toward Bomani. There was a dark figure there, walking in the crimson moonlight.

Nyx motioned for them all to flatten themselves on the ground. The figure gazed up, straight at where Nyx lay. She knew him.

"It's Rhys," Nyx said.

✚

"I'm here to bring you back," Rhys said. He wore a deep violet burnous, organic.

"Good luck with that," Ahmed said, and leveled a gun at him.

Nyx raised her brows.

Rhys took the measure of him with one glance. "I'm a faster draw. And she isn't worth it."

"Hold on," Nyx said.

Ahmed's expression was dark. "He's Chenjan. What does it matter?"

"I said hold."

Ahmed didn't lower the gun.

"What are you doing here?" Nyx asked Rhys.

"I told you. I'm bringing you back. I may be a poor magician, but I have some experience tracking you with hornets. Go if you want. But I'll find you."

"The red desert, Rhys. Why are you here?"

He looked at Ahmed and the gun again. "It's a shame about your magician."

"What?"

The expression on Rhys's face then was something Nyx recognized. Some dark thing from many dark nights in back alleys, tracking bounties. Rhys was a fast draw. He had a good killing shot.

She slid neatly between Ahmed and Rhys. Put one hand out, beckoning. "Your issue's with me. Let's finish it."

"Goddammit," Ahmed said, lowering the gun.

"I've got unfinished business," Nyx said. "Put the gun away, and leave it be. You need to talk? We'll talk."

Nyx gestured for Rhys to come away from the others. They walked together down the other side of the rise. The view here of the moons was spectacular. The closer she was to dying, the prettier things got. The moons didn't get much above the horizon out here, but they seemed bigger. They ate the sky.

"I know where he is," Rhys said.

"We have a shot?"

"You have a good magician."

"Ahmed is—"

"No, the woman."

"Safiyah?"

"If that's her name, yes. I saw what she did to the walls in there. Not your cell, but the hall. They've got a half-dozen magicians in there running around trying to figure out what happened."

"How'd you know she did it?"

"What, that man do it? No. He's… something else."

"What do you mean?"

"There are magicians, and then there are people who play with bugs. He plays. You can just tell."

"How is it you came out here, Rhys?"

"Came for a job. Stayed for the lovely scenery."

"Seriously?"

"I'm indentured. Hanife, the leader here, hired me on as a translator. For all sorts of sordid stuff like what you saw in there. The pay was too good to give up. So I… left my family in the south and came here. I meant to send for them, but… well, things are different."

"I don't get it."

"He bought out my blood debt. I defended myself from some of those Aadhya. The desert people. It's complicated." He sighed. "There's a war brewing out here. Hanife and his ocean people are recruiting men from the clans, giving them weapons and status and having them fight the women-led clans. It's really brutal out there. You've see what the sand can do."

"That's why those men attacked us in the hall."

Rhys smirked. "Yes, not one of your best plans. But then, half your plans never turned out very well."

"I even tried to stay the fuck away from you," she said. "See how well I did with that?"

She saw the hint of a smile touch his face. "At least this time, there's nothing you can take from me."

She was going to ask him how sure he was of that, but thought better of it. It had been a long few years. Years without Rhys always felt longer.

"What about these ocean people?" she asked. "Why are they harboring Raine?"

"I don't know. It's hard to ask around without looking suspicious. All I know is he's been here a few months, kept not far from where you were. No one's allowed in to see him. A group of people brought him in, then just… left him. Jailer says he had orders to just hold him until told otherwise."

"That's… suspicious."

"It is."

She saw him reach into his burnous and pull something out. Her eyes widened. "Is that… a cigarette?"

"You want one?"

"Bloody fuck, things *do* change." She held out her hand.

He broke the carapace of a fire beetle, and lit both their cigarettes. Nyx inhaled deep. They were laced with sen. Almost immediately, she felt the pain that had been riding with her the last few weeks begin to fade. The throbbing at the back of her head and jaw eased. She had missed sen.

"What else do you know about the ocean guys?"

"There was some split up here, they say. Some great catastrophe the magicians created. That's what made the desert. After they walled it in, there were still some people left on the other side of that wall. The Yazdani. Not a surprise they'd want to forget people they left behind, I suppose. Their ports up there are frozen most of the year, and I can't imagine they have a lot of materials for ship building. We certainly don't."

"Why the fuck would they want to take Raine that far north, though? There's no bringing him back from there. If they wanted to kill him, why not kill him?"

Rhys shrugged. "Maybe they anticipated you coming?"

"I don't like this," Nyx said.

"Who are you running this note for?"

Nyx shook her head.

Rhys sighed. "The bel dame council asked you, didn't they?"

"Fatima mentioned it."

"And you just believe everything Fatima tells you?"

"I don't take any job without questioning it."

"She didn't… Did she make you a bel dame again, Nyx?"

Nyx worked her mouth a bit, considering. "No," she said. "She offered it. I didn't take it."

Rhys studied her closely. His eyes were dark, piercing. He could always read her. She hated it.

"So you aren't a bel dame?"

"No."

"You're just doing this for fun? Not enough blood in your life?"

"I haven't had any blood in my life in near on seven years, Rhys. It suited me fine. It's not the blood I missed." She got to her feet.

He gazed up at her. "What, then? What is it you missed?"

She stared into the blackness. "I missed being useful."

"I can't imagine you never being useful, Nyx."

"I'm almost a decade older than you, Rhys. When you're my age, you'll feel it."

"No," he said, and stood, brushed off his dusty trousers. He had cleaned them of Khatijah's blood. "I don't fear peace, Nyx. There's always a place for men like me during peace. What destroyed me was this war, and the expectation that I protect my family at all costs. I was tested, Nyx, and I failed."

"Any man would have failed in your place, Rhys," she said, low. It didn't come out as nice as she wanted it to, but it was the truth.

"Is that meant to be comforting?"

"You know, Rhys, I let a whole squad of men die. Men I failed to save. I spent my whole life hearing all about how I was supposed to protect men. My brothers. My squad mates. My team. Then my brothers died, I let my squad get blown up, and I lost some of my best male partners. I lost Taite, and Tej before him. Then you fucked off too. When it all came down to it, I failed again and again. But I didn't give up like you did. I didn't walk away from my people. Not when there was something else worth protecting."

"Didn't you? You didn't just run away to the coast?"

"It was that or prison. You fancy prison?"

"You run away from your failures too, Nyx."

"So we have something in common now?"

"I wouldn't go that far." He sighed and started back the way he had come. "Peace be upon you," he said.

"Yeah, fuck off," Nyx said. She nursed her cigarette.

"Nyx?"

"What?"

"If you want to get Raine, we should probably have some kind of plan."

"Should we?"

"One condition."

"What now?"

"If you take Raine out of here, you need to take me too."

She didn't want to tell him that—Raine or no Raine—she would have taken him anyway.

39.

Breaking into Bomani was a lot easier now that they had some idea of what they were doing and a guy on the inside. Rhys pointed them to the least-patrolled portion of the wall, and provided a fine distraction by telling the guards on duty that Hanife had need of them elsewhere. The "corridor" that Nyx had tunneled her way into from the prison cell was actually something like a giant ventilation chamber. Once they slipped back inside, it was easy to move around in and connected most of the major areas inside of Bomani.

Safiyah said she could get them back to the vent they hauled Nyx out of, which meant all Nyx needed to do was extract Raine, haul him into the vent, and then get the whole happy fighting party the hell out of there.

Nyx kept Kage back at the camp with Isabet, insisting that she'd need her on point in case they came running out of the place with thirty desert men on their asses. Safiyah argued against it, insisting that Kage would be useful inside Bomani. But Nyx just didn't see that. What she needed inside was her magicians, not her sharpshooter.

They went in during the deepest part of the night, the day after Nyx's escape. The longer they waited, the more likely it was Hanife would find their camp.

Safiyah slipped Nyx and Ahmed back into the vent.

"Good luck," Ahmed said.

"Don't die," Nyx said.

"Trying hard not to," he said.

Nyx padded down the corridor, Safiyah behind her. Ahmed stayed behind to guard their escape.

"This should be it, if your little Chenjan is truthful," Safiyah said. She called something within the structure, and a neat slice appeared in the tissue.

Nyx pushed herself into the mucus-filled cavity. She went face first so she could get a look inside. It was another interrogation room, much like the one she had seen the day before. Empty.

Nyx squirmed the rest of the way in. She went immediately to the cells and looked in. The first three were empty. Had they taken him already?

The fourth had somebody inside.

Nyx pulled the bar of bug secretions from the door and opened it wide.

In the dim blue light, she saw a skinny, pot-bellied figure hunched in the corner of the room, hands and feet bound together. He squinted at her. The face was filthy, and unrecognizable.

Fuck, they had come all this way for the wrong man.

The broken old man inhaled deeply, and there was something in the eyes, then, some flicker of recognition, a sharp inhalation of breath. "Well," he said. "At least they sent their best."

It *was* Raine.

"I'm flattered," she said.

"If you will not honor me, at least show some respect with a quick death," Raine said.

"I'm not here to kill you, old man." Nyx pulled her dagger and stepped forward. He squeezed his eyes shut. He seemed so much smaller now. A grizzled old head, ragged beard. She cut his bonds.

"I'm here to save you," she said.

"Is this some kind of trick?"

"I'd like to say it was. I'd be lying."

Raine began to laugh. It was a deep, grating sort of laugh that put her teeth on edge. It reminded her of times best forgotten. As she sheathed her dagger, she thought—for the barest of moments—to stab him in the throat. End of the road. End of everything. Cutting off heads was so much simpler than saving them.

"God has a terrible sense of humor," Raine said.

"Always did. Come on. The sooner we get out of here, the less likely somebody is to raise the alarm."

Raine grunted and pushed himself forward. He had been a beefy man once. Now he was mostly sagging brown skin over knobby bones. He still had a bit of a paunch, but the rest of him was so thin he seemed terribly disproportioned, like he'd fall over. Nyx really didn't want to help him get up.

"Come on, Raine. We have a long way to go."

Raine was unsteady on his feet. Pressed a hand on the wall to hold his balance. "Let's go then, bel dame."

She was going to have to carry him. Fuck.

✚

Nyx hauled Raine down the twisting corridors, half-dragging him along. He was in no shape to walk, let alone run, but it was hurry up or die now, and she had a long way to go yet. Raine sucked in breath hard and fast. After a time, he started to wheeze, but she did not stop. The flickering skin of the corridor began to change again, and she feared what it was trying to communicate now. Was it telling the guards about them? Was this place really sentient? It wasn't the night she wanted to find out.

"Didn't think it would be you," Raine wheezed.

Nyx was sighting her way along the corridor, searching for the opening Safiyah had made in the skin, the one she'd told both Safiyah and Ahmed to wait for her at. It should be any time now. She heard a soft stirring of voices behind them. Tried to pick up the pace. There weren't supposed to be people in these tunnels, Rhys said. But Raine was lagging now. Tripping over his feet. She'd have to carry him soon. Fuck, where was that goddamn entrance?

"Thought they'd send… my mother."

"Fuck your mother," Nyx muttered.

Raine grunted.

They came to the soft pulsing opening in the skin. Nyx let herself slow down half a step. "In here," she said. She unhooked Raine from her and pushed him toward the opening.

He gulped air as he tottered toward the opening. He paused in the hall. Nyx heard more voices. She turned, drew her gun.

"Nyx," Raine said. "You should know… you should know I'm infected."

"What?" Nyx said.

He gripped one edge of the seam. "They want you to bring me home. I'm infected."

"Who wants it?"

"You wouldn't have gotten this far unless they wanted it."

"Just go," Nyx said. "Save the drama for a safer space, all right? Bloody fuck. You have no idea what fucking shit we've been through to get you."

Raine stumbled through the opening.

Nyx jumped through after him.

Safiyah was still there. Nyx wasn't sure why she was so surprised about that, but she was. The magician neatly sealed the wound. As the last bit of organic light from the hall was shut out, the voices Nyx had heard earlier got suddenly louder. She heard steps across the spongy flooring approach, then retreat.

"Cutting it a bit close, aren't you?" Safiyah said.

"I thought you loved all this excitement," Nyx said.

"I love orange-flavored popsicles. Fried maggots on toast. Sunset in Ashura. This? This, I merely tolerate."

In the semi-darkness, Nyx could see that Raine had his hands over his mouth.

"Come on," she said. "We have a long way to go yet."

Safiyah peered at Raine. "Nyx, that man is not… well."

"I could have told you that back in Nasheen," Nyx said. "Now shut up and move. Where's Ahmed?"

"Guarding our way out."

They moved down another series of sticky corridors. Safiyah led, and Nyx held the rear. After a few minutes, Safiyah stopped.

"What is it?" Nyx hissed.

"It's been resealed," Safiyah said. "A moment."

Nyx gazed into the darkness behind them. The walls oozed and chittered. Beneath her, the floor itself felt unsteady. She hated this fucking place. Like being inside some half-eaten corpse being transformed by maggots.

"There. This way," Safiyah said, and they were moving again.

They came back up in a dark hall. As Nyx stepped up, she didn't recognize it.

"Where are we?"

"I'm not sure," Safiyah said. "I had to carve out another path." She murmured something else, and a small buzzing swarm of tiny mutant hornets appeared, as if from the walls themselves. The swarm buzzed off down an adjacent corridor.

"Come," Safiyah said. "Our people are this way."

Raine limped along, still too slow for Nyx's taste. They needed to get him cleaned up and into some proper clothes. As it was, he stood out abominably here.

Safiyah turned the next corner. Nyx heard a shot. It was oddly muffled—a result of the spongy walls and floor. Safiyah's arms windmilled back. She hit the floor like a tumbling mantis, all awkward limbs and angles.

Nyx swore and pulled her scattergun. She pushed Raine behind her and pressed close against the wall.

It was hard to gauge how many were waiting without taking a look herself. Safiyah was absolutely still—far too still for Nyx's taste. Unless they'd gotten her directly in the heart or head, nobody was that still unless they were trying not to draw further attention to themselves. Nyx had seen stuff like that all the time with wounded soldiers on the field. Better to lie low and let the enemy walk all over you.

Nyx decided to just point and shoot. She shoved her scattergun around the corner and fired blindly. Heard a smattering of voices. Some squelching on the floor. Damn this place and its fucking acoustics. She could judge nothing by sound.

"Let them take me," Raine said.

"Fuck you," Nyx said.

"They won't kill me. Just turn me over to them and run. Come another time."

"You think this shit was easy the first time?"

"It will be more difficult the next time if you're dead."

"Fuck," Nyx said. She fired again into the hall. Heard the steady *squelch-squelch* of approaching bad guys. Could she take them all by herself while keeping Raine intact? She decided to risk a peek. She fired again into the hall, then ducked her head out after it. One quick glance.

She pulled back behind the corner as six more guns went off. She heard the bullets sink into the soft walls. She had counted eight figures, with more behind them. Maybe a dozen total. She couldn't fight a dozen, not even when she was twenty.

"Nyx," Raine said softly.

"Shut the fuck up. I need to think."

She closed her eyes and took a deep breath. She had been shot many times. It hurt. If she could just pass Raine off to one of her crew, she could take a few bullets—

"I'm here!"

Nyx opened her eyes.

Raine was on his feet and around the corner before she could grab him. She reached for his ankle, but he kicked away, surprisingly spry for a sick man.

He had his arms raised high over his head, little pot belly sticking out over his dhoti. He looked ridiculous. He would look more ridiculous riddled in bullets. But the shots didn't come.

The people yelled something at him. He spoke back to them in whatever language they used.

Nyx wondered if she was being turned over.

Fuck this.

She chanced one last glance at Safiyah, decided the plucky magician could take care of herself, and then bolted down the corridor where they had come from. The place was a fucking labyrinth. She ran left, always left, hoping to loop back around to something familiar, preferably the corridor right behind where the men had caught them. That was the way the hornets were traveling.

Down a short flight of steps, up a steep ramp. And then she was well and truly lost. There were no windows. No sky. No open air. She turned down another corridor only to hit a dead end. What the fuck was the purpose of all these rooms? She turned back around and tried to retrace her steps. Her breath was coming hard and fast now. The halls were getting narrower. Where were the people? Was she lost in the guts of this great beast now? Another dead end.

She faced the blank, pulsing wall. Wiped sweaty hands on her trousers. Took long, deep breaths. I'm fine, she thought. Just fine.

But the narrow space was getting to her. I just need to rest. Just need to get my bearings....

She slumped to the floor. Curled up into a ball on the floor, hugging her knees to her chest. It was dark and damp and it wasn't getting any better. She squeezed her eyes shut. Deep breaths. Calm. She needed to stay calm.

"Nyx?"

She wasn't sure how long it had been. Her heart thudded loudly in her chest. Her breath was coming shallow. The stink of the hold was overpowering.

"Nyx?"

She stared up. There, outlined in the darkness, was a slim little woman holding a rather large gun.

"Kage?" Nyx said.

"Get up," Kage said. "I know the way out."

Nyx rubbed her face. "I… I'm having some trouble, here."

"It's fine. Come. Stand up. Just take some deep breaths. Come on. I know the way out."

Nyx managed to get up on all fours. She clawed her way to her feet, using the gooey wall as leverage. Kage turned, and Nyx grabbed the back of the girl's tunic.

Kage walked through the twisting darkness like it was a bright day in the desert. Nyx stumbled along behind her.

"Here," Kage said. She slipped through some crevice that Nyx hadn't even noticed. They stepped out into the open.

Nyx gulped air.

Kage patted her back.

Nyx looked up. "Where are we?" She didn't recognize the landscape.

"The camp is on the other side of Bomani." Kage pointed. "Just go that way, back around the hold. They're waiting. I told them I'd find you."

Kage began walking, but not back around Bomani—she went north, into the desert.

"Where are you going?"

Kage glanced back. "I'm done now," Kage said.

"What?"

"I came to help with this job. The job is over. You found your politician."

"But… But I don't have him yet!"

"You know where he is. My debt is paid."

"Debt?"

"I have saved another life."

"But… he's not saved!"

"Not him," she said. "You."

"What?"

"They were not coming to get you," Kage said. "They were going to leave you. Your team. But I couldn't. You kept wanting me to kill things. But that wasn't how I could discharge my debt. I had to save people. I don't expect you to understand."

"Kage, wait—"

Kage pressed her palms together and gave a little bow of her head. Nyx had seen Drucians greet one another that way. "I can't say I like you very much," Kage said, "but I hope you achieve an end most appropriate to the way you have lived."

"Kage—"

"I must go," Kage said, "before it ends for me, too." She began to run. North. Into the desert.

The bloody fucking desert.

✦

"They've taken him south," Rhys said.

Ahmed sighed. He was getting really tired of listening to this Chenjan. First, he wanted to go back into that hive for Nyx. Now he still wanted to push her to pursue the politician. Nyx had stumbled back into camp an hour before, much to everyone's surprise. But Kage wasn't with her. Safiyah turned up a few minutes later, shaking flesh beetles from her robe and talking about how it'd been a decade since she'd last been shot.

Ahmed had to admit he was disappointed that after all the death he'd seen out here, not one of them had keeled over. And he'd lost Kage. At least Kage had been good company.

"That's all I could find out," Rhys said.

"What does south mean? Back across the bloody desert? We came all this way just to run back after them the same way we came?" Ahmed said. "Is this a joke?"

Safiyah sat on a rocky wall above them. They had left the camp overlooking Bomani and retreated further south, to a tumbledown stir of ruins near one of the massive rock pillars that soared to the sky.

"Do you know who took him?" Nyx asked.

"The same people that brought him," Rhys said.

Nyx sighed. "Of course."

Ahmed watched her stare off into the distance. She had not been the same since she limped back into camp without Kage. He had demanded to know what had become of the Drucian, but Nyx just waved him away and said she'd left of her own volition.

He half believed her. He'd been telling Kage to leave for weeks. Now every time he looked north, he wondered if he should have gone with her. Then he wondered if Nyx had actually just killed her.

"The men said they were headed south," Rhys said, "to the tunnels. I don't know what that is. Some hiding place?"

Safiyah slid off the wall and landed neatly on her feet, like a cat. Ahmed shivered. Sometimes the way she spoke, and moved, troubled him. It put him in mind of someone else he'd known a long time ago, though he couldn't say who.

"I know where they're going," Safiyah said.

"You're kidding," Nyx said.

"I wish I were," Safiyah said. "But all together, I think the lot of you will much prefer this mode of travel to the one you used to come up here."

"Oh, this'll be good," Nyx said.

✚

It was good.

Safiyah handed Nyx the specs. "And that, my precious tidbit, is the closest inlet to the Abd-al-Karim. Better known to your colonial ears as the magicians' tunnels."

"Fuck me," Nyx said.

"You're not my type, darling," Safiyah said.

"They don't go this far up," Rhys said. "They only connect key Nasheenian cities. How did you know about this?"

Safiyah wrinkled her nose. "Colonial magicians may use them to traverse cities. But First Families can use them to cross the world."

Nyx looked at her sidelong. "You mean powerful First Families with powerful fucking magicians. Even if we'd known the tunnels came all the way up here, all the entrances in Nasheen are protected. There's no way we'd get in."

"So many words. Words, words, words. Come now, we're losing the light." Safiyah strode boldly toward the mound, three hundred paces distant. Clouds were rolling in, and the wind was picking up. Nyx admitted she wasn't looking forward to the cool dark of the tunnels after Bomani.

Beside her, Isabet and Ahmed were talking in Ras Tiegan, presumably to clue Isabet into what was happening. Nyx secretly hoped she would die next, eaten by some bug or taken out by some bullet. Every time Isabet looked at Nyx, she thought of Eshe.

Safiyah stepped boldly into the mound—and disappeared. The same way Nyx had disappeared when she fell into the prayer niches at the settlement before Kiranmay.

"Gotta love a good glamour," Nyx muttered. "C'mon, let's keep up."

Above her, the sky rumbled—so close that the ground itself seemed to shudder. A jolt of lightning lit up the sky.

"Fuck," Ahmed said.

Nyx watched the desert where Safiyah had disappeared.

There was something moving near the mound.

Rhys came up short beside her.

A massive arthropod humped its way past the entrance to the tunnels.

The giant, undulating arthropod was bigger even than the one that made up the bar of the tea house back in Kiranmay. As Nyx watched, it surfaced just two hundred paces from them. Its massive head sprouted six nasty, needlelike protrusions. Then it dove back into the sand.

"Maybe we should wait this one out," Nyx said. She could have really used a sniper. Goddammit. Not that I can blame her for going, Nyx thought.

"I can control it," Rhys said.

"No you fucking can't."

He strode out across the crackling desert. The lightning storm sent jagged arcs of electricity over their heads. The whole sky was a wash of white and purple heat. And there, visible in the flickering light, was the massive segmented form of the… thing. It undulated just beneath the desert's surface, pushing up crumbled heaps of clotted sand in its wake.

Nyx wondered what exactly Rhys wanted to do with the fucking thing—ride it? Or just get it out of the way? She was content to find a fucking rock to stand on and just wait it out, but there he went, forging down into the desert like some stupid kid. We are too fucking old to act like idiots, she thought. But she pulled her sword and went after him. Just like a fucking idiot.

"Rhys!"

There was a low rumble in the sky. Then another, so loud this time that the whole desert really did shake. He's going down there to die, Nyx thought, suddenly. He can't be this stupid. He just wants to fucking die out here, and this is a way to do it.

"Rhys!"

He came to the edge of the broken desert and raised his hands. His dark arms spilled free of the white burnous. He was terribly thin and wiry, and the ghastly light flickered across what was left of him.

Another dagger of light lit up the sky.

Nyx slowed her pace, just a hundred paces distant from him now. Already, she was out of breath. She heard a low buzzing above the din in the sky. Then the ground beneath her trembled so violently that it knocked her to her knees. She gazed up just as another dart of light arced across the sky. There, rearing above Rhys like some half-forgotten bedtime monster, was a scaly arthropod the color of the night, banded in violet. Each of its undulating segments was half as tall as Rhys. As it reared above him, she counted a full six segments. It totally dwarfed him, and that was just what was visible. She had a grinding moment of primordial terror. It was the same puking feeling that had overcome her when Anneke's kids showed her the globular monsters they called fish. It was like looking at some alien thing that struck some deep note of dissonance within her.

She sucked in a breath and started to sprint toward Rhys. But the desert had other ideas, and her sprint became a slog as the crust of the desert broke beneath her. She waded forward. The arthropod wavered above Rhys for a few more moments. She made three-quarters of the distance to him, cursing and snarling the whole way. And then it struck.

The massive head drove toward Rhys.

Nyx screamed at it. At the sky. At the storm. At herself. But most of all, she screamed at Rhys.

She had gone off into the desert expecting to die to save everything she cared about. But the deeper she got into this, the more it looked like she was going to lose everything and save nothing.

And she would be the one cursed to keep on fucking living.

✚

Rhys had spent a lot time running away from things. Running away from the war in Chenja. Running from life with Nyx to start something new in Tirhan. Running from Elahyiah and his children. He ran because he believed that if he ran far enough and fast enough that in some other place, he could be some other man—someone more confident, more powerful. But every place he ran, he found that he was still the same old person. He was the man who ran away—a boy, really. He was a frightened child waiting for someone else to save him. What he had realized during these months in the north was that he was not a man who deserved to be saved. It was when he gave up, that God sent Nyx here.

He knew the arthropod was one of the mature *mauta kita*. He had seen the smaller versions back in Shaesta. The Khairians murdered them on sight. But first, they would sing to them.

Rhys ran so close to the monstrous thing that he felt the ground shake as it thundered by. Then he drew his pistols, and sang the way Tarik had taught him. Lightning flashed.

The arthropod reared up from the sand a dozen paces from him. It was a massive thing, at least four stories high, gleaming in the thundering night.

Rhys's voice quavered. He needed one good shot. Just one shot. But to get it, he had to stand his ground.

He heard Nyx yelling behind him. For once, he was glad for her age, and her slow steps. If she went in with weapons blazing now, the beast would devour them both.

Rhys sang. The arthropod undulated above him. It opened its gaping maw, showing row upon row of endless teeth that stretched back into its interior. Rhys took aim at the dark roof of the thing's mouth, just behind the furthest row of teeth he could see.

The arthropod dipped its head, preparing to strike. He fired. Four shots.

The beast drove straight at him.

Rhys broke and rolled away, and the monstrous thing crashed into the sand where he had stood a moment before.

He heard Nyx's scattergun go off. Two shots. Then six clicks. She was out.

Rhys struggled to his feet. He stared at the massive body of the arthropod, glittering in the sand a few paces away. As he watched, it spasmed one final time, and was still.

Nyx bent over, trying to catch her breath. "The fuck was that?" she said. "It sick or something?"

"They're heavily armored outside," he said. "But not inside. You have to get them to reveal themselves."

Rhys went forward. Grabbed her hand. "Let's go," he said.

Nyx stared at his hand in hers, but didn't pull it away.

She glanced over her shoulder, where Ahmed and Isabet stood on top of the far dune. She motioned them forward.

"Let's go!" she said.

Rhys released her hand, and went forward, into the tunnel entrance. The glamour shielding the entrance gave easily as he entered. It had been a long time since he traveled in the magicians' tunnels.

"Safiyah?" he said.

No answer.

It was bitterly black inside.

He pressed his hands forward, and found the familiar silky walls of the tunnels. He started walking, keeping his right hand pressed to the wall as a guide. The tunnels were known to bend and twist at strange times, sometimes even after passing a seemingly featureless wall. Rhys didn't know how they worked, and even the magicians he spoke to in Nasheen had only empty explanations. They were something created at the beginning of the world; a safe space for traveling across Nasheen when the air above still wasn't breathable.

"Rhys?" Nyx's voice.

"I'm trying to find Safiyah," he said. "It's still dark up here."

"Where the fuck is the Drucian when you need her?" Nyx muttered.

He heard more voices—Ahmed and Isabet—behind her.

"Let me get ahead, Rhys," Nyx said.

Rhys moved aside and let her pass. He knew how much it would annoy her not to lead. He used to think it was her arrogance that did it. Now, he wasn't so sure. Maybe she always had to lead because if there were bad things happening ahead, she wanted it to happen to her first.

"Safiyah?"

Finally, a response came from far ahead. "You're terribly slow. Hurry. I'm losing them."

Rhys heard Nyx's footsteps quicken. The wall next to Rhys twisted, opened, and he pulled his arm away, fearing it would get caught if the way closed again.

"Slow down, Nyx," Rhys said. "We're going to lose the others."

Ahead, he saw a pale amber light, just visible beyond Nyx's body.

"There are lights ahead," he called back at Ahmed and Isabet.

When he caught up to Nyx, she was standing in an oily, shimmering cavern illuminated by a long line of pulsing glow worms that edged the floor. The lighting cast their faces in garish shadows.

"I can track them by the pheromones they leave behind. They're playing with the chemicals as they go," Safiyah said, "Opening and closing spaces behind them. I can't tell you where they're going until we get there."

"So it could be anywhere in the world?" Nyx said.

"Yes. It could be Yazdan, for all we know."

"Why would they move him now?" Ahmed said. "The Chenjan said they'd left him alone for weeks. They weren't even in Bomani when we made the raid. Now suddenly they're back and carting him off across the continent?"

"They were always close by," Safiyah said. "There are entrances to the tunnels all over the red desert."

"Wait a minute," Nyx said. "If you knew about these tunnels, what the fuck did you need us to get you over the Wall for?"

Safiyah smiled. "Well, you know, I would have had to trek all the way back to Nasheen to enter, then pop out here. Easier to get over the Wall where we were."

"Catshit," Nyx said. "Who the fuck *are* you?"

"I recommend we address that concern at another venture," Safiyah said. "I am losing their scent. You want to find Raine, or you want a pretty story? I, for one, am interested to see this through."

Rhys watched Nyx mull that over. What more did she have to lose? He certainly had nothing. Rhys glanced back at Ahmed and Isabet. He wondered which of them would run off first. Isabet, most likely. How had she ended up here with Nyx in the first place?

"Go on," Nyx said. "Get us to wherever Raine is. Then I want some answers."

"Answers just lead to more questions," Safiyah said. "But, as you like."

She clapped her hands, and the wall next to her parted. A perfect, oily cavern opened up—a portal to God alone knew where.

Safiyah stepped inside. Nyx went after her.

Rhys looked back. The red desert and dead arthropods, or something unknown? Anything will be better than here, he thought, and stepped through.

40.

Nyx stepped into humid air. The world was awash in blue-gray dusk—or dawn?—and all around her, massive, twisted trees clawed at the sky. Their monstrous leaves dripped great globs of water onto her face and shoulders. If it wasn't so fucking cold, she would have been grateful for it after so long in the desert.

Ahead, Safiyah was struggling to get over a mossy dead tree half as tall as she was. "Hurry!" she said. "They're just ahead!" Nyx saw lights through the trees.

She ran after Safiyah, pausing to help the others over the tree trunk. Isabet was pulling leaves from the trees and dumping the water on her head.

Nyx slogged after Safiyah. Bracken and sticky flowers clung to Nyx's burnous. She batted them away, hoping none of them were poisonous. She broke through the forest cover a few minutes after Safiyah, and found herself staring over a lush, rolling valley. After so long in the desert, it was like stepping onto some alien world. A city spread below them, protected by a shimmering filter that flickered and flared like some dying thing. Someone had infected it. Nyx expected they would find great black patches of rot on it if they got closer.

"Where the fuck are we?" Nyx asked.

"Ras Tieg," Isabet said, from behind her.

+

Nyx had them camp just inside the filter under the decaying roof of an abandoned outbuilding, already half reclaimed by the wood. Ras Tiegan filters were less effective than Nasheenian ones. They permitted everything through but the worst of the bugs. The one surrounding this city was especially bad, and Nyx found a massive, cancerous hole in it as soon as they got close. They were exhausted, and in no shape for a fight. Safiyah said she could track Raine with hornets from now on, so Nyx permitted them all six hours of sleep. It turned out the sun was going down. Wherever they were taking Raine, somewhere in the city was the likely destination.

"You know where we are?" Nyx asked Isabet.

She shook her head, and said in her terrible Nasheenian. "Get closer. To see."

"Not tonight," Nyx said. They could ask the locals in good time.

Ahmed volunteered for first watch, but Nyx took it. Safiyah set out a hornet swarm. "Just a little extra protection," she said, and winked.

Nyx did not feel safer. She had three magicians and some rich Ras Tiegan kid. It meant she was the primary muscle. The thought depressed her.

She sat at the edge of the camp. They dared not light a fire. It was just eating and sleeping. No one took off their weapons.

After a time, Rhys joined her. They sat in silence, staring into the jungle beyond the filter.

Finally, she said, "You want to come back with me, when this is over?"

Rhys leaned forward. He sighed. "My first duty is to my family."

"Sure. And they aren't here. So what's the harm?"

"Do you really have to ask that?"

"Yeah. You'll ask it soon enough. Either while I'm here or when I'm gone."

"Always so certain of yourself."

"Should I be anything else? Tell me you don't want to come with me, if it's so easy."

"It's not that."

"What, then?"

"I'm married, Nyx."

"I fuck a lot of people too."

Rhys snorted. He started rolling a cigarette.

"Filthy habit," she said.

"That's what my wife says."

That made her laugh. It hurt to laugh. She pressed a hand to her chest, wondering if and when she'd bruised something.

"How is it you know exactly how far to push?" he said. He lit the cigarette, offered her a pull.

She accepted.

He said, "You know you can always take it far enough to get me to walk off. Is that what you always want? You like to watch me walk off? Because that's what happens when you treat people this way, Nyx. Maybe no one else will say it, but I will. You treat us like tools and things. It's why I loathed every moment in those six years I was on your team."

"I thought it was all the sex and liquor and—"

"No, stop. It was you, Nyx. It was everything you are."

Nyx turned and moved closer to him, her face a handbreadth from his cheek. She could feel the heat of him. He was as beautiful underneath the clothes as he was in them, if she remembered right. No, more so. But there were many beautiful people in the world. There was Ahmed, just a few paces away, and Safiyah, eerily beautiful even for Nyx's taste. But to be dead honest, Rhys really wasn't as pretty anymore. She was almost certainly uglier, and he wasn't getting younger. Was it the fucking she wanted? Would that end it, if she just convinced him to let her fuck him now, far from his wife and family, his petty concerns forgotten for just a few stolen moments? Would she be over it, then?

"You hate everything I am," Nyx said softly. "But you're still out here with me. Is that it?" She kept her tone low, the way she would if she was trying to lure some skittish bug, a shiny green beetle. "Is it that you have to take care of her out there? But out here—" she carefully moved her hand to his neck, lightly, as if by accident. It was freeing, really. She figured they'd all be dead by morning. "Out here I take care of *you*."

Rhys averted his eyes and stood. He put out the cigarette.

"That it?" Nyx said. "Rhys, hold on." She stood and went after him, took his arm. "Hey, listen. I didn't mean anything by it. It's not anything. I'm just really fucking tired."

"You have no idea what you're doing," Rhys said. He sounded out of breath.

"I'm just playing around, Rhys."

His face was stricken. "That's the problem. To you this is all just some game. A fun way to pass the time. But for me, this is about my personal integrity. Honor. You understand honor? You became a bel dame because it gained you honor, is that right? Being a man who can protect the honor of his own family is all I wanted. I was supposed to keep them safe, Nyx. I failed them. I failed God and my father when I did not go to the front. And I failed God again when I permitted those bel dames to do what they did. They took everything from me, Nyx. They took everything I was. And… fucking you in the woods is not how a moral man would conduct himself. I know what I am, Nyx. I've struggled with it, I won't pretend. But do you know who I am?"

"I think if you relaxed you'd be a better man," Nyx said.

"Elahyiah left me," Rhys said. "She took the children."

Nyx caught her breath. She wanted to fuck him there, and realized, too late, that it wasn't the right response.

She reached for him. He pushed her away.

"That's it, then?" she said.

"That has always been it. What does it matter?" He sighed heavily and rubbed at his shaggy head. "If we fucked now, what would it be like in the morning? Would you be done? And if not tomorrow, what about the next day? The next year? A decade from now? I don't fornicate with women for fun, Nyx. It means far more than that to me. Everything you touch turns to ash. And when things are bad, I always know who you will look out for. You will sacrifice every person in this world for whatever foolish goal you have. Every person here. Even Eshe. Even me."

"Don't bring up Eshe."

"Why, because it's true? He was the closest thing you had to a child, and you killed him over this."

"Fuck you, Rhys. I never sacrificed *you* for anything."

"No," he said. "Just my family. That's what you don't understand, Nyx. They *are* me." He seemed to be searching for more words.

Nyx let him chew on them. She was tired of talking. She wanted to walk off into the jungle and not look back. She had nothing to go back to.

"When I'm with you, Nyx, I don't have to try and be a better man," Rhys said. "I can uphold the barest level of decency and look like the son of the prophet by contrast."

"So stick around."

"You don't understand. I don't... have to be strong when I'm with you. I don't have to be good. But Nyx, I have to be a better man. That's what life is. It's striving to be peaceful, worthy before God. And when I'm with you, my relationship with God is much different. Do you understand?"

Nyx shook her head.

He sighed. "Think of it this way. There are two roads. A morally high road, clear and free of obstacles. And there is a lower road, filled with brambles and contaminants and festering insects. At the end of the high road is a safe but unfulfilling life. It is the life I must present before God at the end of all things and say, 'Yes, because I lived this easy life and submitted to your will in all things, I am worthy of paradise.' And that is when he says, 'How can you come before me and insist on paradise when your faith in me was never tested? Never wavered?' Then there is the darker road, the one full of obstacles and terror. The one that tests my faith. That challenges me to question God, and His will. The one that requires me to be a better man at the end than the beginning. To fight. And at the end of that road, when God welcomes me, and I prostrate myself before Him, He will see the road I chose to travel. He will see I chose not ease and comfort, but the path that challenged me to become a better man. I have committed many terrible acts, Nyx. God may forgive, but He does not forget. I will account for all my crimes. There will be a reckoning. All that remains now is to choose how I will redeem myself before the end days."

He took a breath. She still wanted to kiss him.

Rhys turned from her, and trudged back to camp to join the others.

Nyx watched after him for some time, watched him roll himself up in his burnous and turn his back to her. She wondered what it was like to live in a world where your children were something more than just fodder for a war. His old family in Chenja was rich, back when he went by some other name. They wouldn't have had to sacrifice as much. She wondered if that was what love was, knowing there was someone in your life who most likely wouldn't get torn apart.

She saw Eshe again, eight years old, his hand in her pocket; a fistful of notes. He had looked up at her with big, dark eyes in an unremarkable face, and in that moment, she had imagined him blown apart by some mine, or gunned down by a Chenjan, or poisoned by hornets. He was just a child, just a boy. But boys always met bad ends. It was the first thing she thought of—his mangled body sacrificed to a perpetual war for a God she didn't even believe in anymore.

It took a powerful belief in God to pretend that your children were not destined for something else in Nasheen. She had almost convinced herself that Eshe would live, that she had saved him from the fate she saw for him. But no, it came for them all the same, certain as a swarm of locusts in the dry season. How long had it been since she had faith in anything? Not since she burned it all away at the front.

✣

Isabet woke Ahmed well before his watch.

"I know where we are," she said.

Her face had mostly healed, though he still caught her putting unguent on it every morning. She had wept over Eshe's death, and confessed at least a dozen things in Ras Tiegan, so quickly, and sobbing so hard, they he could barely keep up. Somehow, she was pregnant, though he couldn't imagine when it was she and Eshe would have had time to fuck. Maybe the same way Eshe and I did, he had thought, and gnawed on that all over again.

She had clung to him the way she clung to Eshe, and he was annoyed by it. He missed Kage's easy silence. He would even have taken Khatijah's curt attitude over Isabet's terrified neediness.

"Where are we, then?" he asked. He rubbed his eyes and sat up. It was still a long time until dawn, but Nyx would have them moving again soon. If Raine and his captors were still sleeping, it gave them time to catch up.

"You don't understand," she said. "This is Inoublie. I think I know where they're taking him."

"What?"

"There is a man here who collects shifters. Eshe and I were tracking him."

"How does a man who tracks shifters—"

"Just listen. I'm not stupid. You all keep treating me as if I'm stupid. The reason the government never moved against him is because he's cousin to the Queen of Nasheen. She is half-Ras Tiegan. I don't think it's a coincidence that your politician is being brought to Inoublie where he lives."

"Are you sure about this? You know where he lives?"

"No, but I know someone who does."

"Who?"

Isabet glanced over at Nyx. "She's not going to like it," Isabet said.

41.

Inaya blew into her headquarters as a sea-green gale, stirring dog hair and feathers, sending coded papers and discarded napkins flying off desks and tables. The halls were filled with the dead and dying, the partially shifted, the mangled, the bloody, the mad. Inaya took them all in as she passed. Her anger mounted.

She slid under the door of the communications room, and found Michel and Gabrielle in a heated discussion with two local cell leaders. The rear door was open, so their bickering was on display for half the desperate people in the hall.

Inaya recalled herself. She pulled her disparate elements back together, and reformed there in the room, vomiting flies and red beetles.

She didn't even bother to wait until her transformation was complete before she slogged to the table on half-formed legs, trailing long strings of mucus.

She put her hands on the table and waited for her tongue and throat and lungs to come back into form.

Then she said, "What the fuck have you all done?"

"Inaya!" Gabrielle said.

"What are you doing here?" Inaya said. "You should be in Montmare. Who's running things there?"

"I had to evacuate. There have been repercussions. We expected—"

"We?" She rounded on Michel. "This was not the course of action I directed."

"Let me get you a habit," Michel said. "You should cover up."

"Move another step and I will unmake you where you stand. Our people are dying in the hall, and you care about my nudity? Are you a madman?"

Michel went very still.

"I want a status update," Inaya said.

"We have riots in all the major cities," Gabrielle said quickly. She tapped up a map of Ras Tieg on the slide. "As you instructed, we carried out operations in—"

"My instructions?"

Gabrielle glanced at Michel. "Yes, your instructions. Michel—"

"Tell me what my instructions were, Michel," Inaya said.

The two cell leaders, Alix and Juste, hovered in the door. More curious operatives peered in.

Michel cleared his throat. "This was an operation in planning for some time," he said. "You and I discussed it before—"

"Before I told you that violence would simply confirm to this country's citizens that we are dangerous animals that should be put down."

"Strength!" Michel said, and his face flushed. "We must show strength or be put down like animals. You think simply showing them our numbers would make an impression? You know what these people find very impressive? Strength. And we have shown them that."

"Indeed," Inaya said. "And now half our movement's leaders are foolishly holed up in the same space as the noose grows tighter and tighter. How long do you think it will be before they find us? If they have not been tipped off already when they followed these three?"

"Inaya," Gabrielle said softly. "I don't understand. Was this not done at your direction?"

Inaya's gaze never left Michel. "I have been in prison for many, many weeks."

"That's impossible," Alix said. "I received word from you just last week."

"Michel said you had simply gone underground," Gabrielle said.

"Oh, I was underground," Inaya said. "Yes. He ensured that. Didn't you, Michel?"

He shifted. It was not a quick process, not even for an experienced shifter. She, however, had more freedom and forms than he would ever have. She transformed her arm into the ridged leg of some massive insect, and stabbed him in the thigh with it. The shock to his body halted the shift. He collapsed, grabbing at his bloody leg with skinny arms that had just begun to sprout stubby feathers.

"Alix, get me Romaire and Aslain from security. I want Michel confined," Inaya said.

Alix ran off. Michel swore at her.

"As for the rest of you, tell me what we're going to do to fix this bloody mess."

✢

Inaya had been awake for nearly forty hours. Each time she thought she could not stay awake another moment, some other bit of terrible news came in. Three cell leaders, including Hynri, had been detained. Six detention centers had been overrun by her people, and most of the raiders and the inmates killed. There was mass looting and destruction across seven major cities. An entire district in Montmare had been burned to the ground.

She had dispatched Alix and Juste to separate safe houses far outside Inoublie. Whether or not they would get there safely, she had no idea, but it was far better than keeping them all here. As for her headquarters, she had given orders that it was to be packed, moved, and purged immediately. If the detention centers had cell leaders, it was only a matter of time before one of them gave up this place.

Her retreat was fast, but calculated. She had put this plan into place the year before. She knew where they needed to go. How she would build anything positive from the madness, she did not know. Right now, she just needed to salvage as much as possible before they were all burned out.

She was sitting at the stove in her room, burning stacks of correspondence, when Adeliz appeared.

"There's someone here to see you," Adeliz said.

"They will need to wait. Our timeline cannot be altered."

"All right," Adeliz said. She turned away.

"Wait," Inaya said. She held one of Eshe's reports in her hand, one of the first he had brought her, before Inaya insisted on sending them on undocumented. "Who is it?" she asked.

"It's Isabet Softel," Adeliz said.

"Oh, my God," Inaya said. "Take me to her."

She followed Adeliz up and into the secure reception room. Inaya strode confidently after her. Perhaps something could be salvaged, she thought. If Isabet was alive, almost anything was possible. What she and Eshe had done was of no concern. All that mattered was that they were back, precisely when she needed them.

Inaya stepped into the reception room—and stopped short.

Isabet was not alone.

Inaya had expected Isabet and Eshe, looking like children caught dressing up in their parents' clothes. She intended to pat Eshe on the shoulder and scold Isabet lightly, and then put them to work helping her pack. She believed God had answered all the prayers she sent to him through Mhari during her long confinement.

The last thing she expected to see was Nyxnissa so Dasheem standing next to Isabet Softel.

Inaya was speechless.

Isabet was filthy. Inaya realized, with a start, that the girl's left arm had been severed at the elbow. Her hair was a matted tangle, pulled back from a scarred, reddened face that was barely recognizable. And Nyx—Nyx was unmistakable, though the years had been especially unkind to her, and the last several—weeks? Months?—even less so. She saw fresh wounds, scars, bruises on her hands and face. She, too, was filthy. Inaya could smell them even from three paces away. And they were not alone. Behind them were a Chenjan man and a Nasheenian man, as well as a strikingly lovely woman who stood out all the more because she appeared to be the cleanest of them.

It took a full breath before she realized the Chenjan man was Rhys. That, too, was shocking. Her mind began to work, preparing her for the worst. Nyx only showed up when things were very, very bad. Inaya worried because she could not conceive of anything worse than her current situation. It spoke of a lack of imagination on her part, and right now, that could prove dangerous.

Inaya went forward. She took Isabet by her good arm and asked, "What has she done to you?"

"Eshe is dead," Isabet said, and her eyes filled.

"I'm sorry," Inaya said. She swallowed a spasm of grief. But what did she expect? Nyx had gotten involved. The fact that Isabet and Rhys and these others still lived was miracle enough.

Inaya pulled her away from the others. "Go with Adeliz and get cleaned up. Let me speak with Nyx."

Isabet slipped past her. Adeliz took her hand and led her back into the maze of rooms beneath them.

"You look good," Nyx said, in Nasheenian.

"How is it you took up with her again?" Inaya asked Rhys.

"I haven't," he said. "It's all very complicated."

"I can imagine," Inaya said. "To what do I owe the honor?"

"I believe you owe me a favor," Nyx said.

"A… what?"

Nyx folded her arms. "I have it on good authority that girl's not just some minor operative."

"And who told you that?"

Nyx looked back at the Nasheenian man behind her. "Let's just say I know a guy who's good at eavesdropping."

Inaya glanced behind her, to ensure no one was in the hall. Few of her people spoke Nasheenian, but she had not come this far for lack of caution.

"She's an oracle," Inaya said.

"An oracle?"

"Daughter to a living saint, a saint reborn."

"Is this some Ras Tiegan thing? I don't follow."

"We have saints."

"Yeah, your minor gods."

"*Saints*," Inaya said. "They speak directly to God, and have been chosen, touched by Him in some way. Many have been known to perform miracles. Her mother is a living saint, a woman known to perform miracles. She can cure illness, yet has no magical skill. There are… other things. And Isabet is her only daughter. The others died in the womb.

"So people listen to her? Is that what you're saying?"

"People believe she speaks directly to God."

"I don't get it. Nobody's recognized her?"

"She is a virgin, and daughter to a living saint. She only ever went out veiled. No one knew who she was."

"But you did."

"I… it was in our best interests to find a powerful religious or political figure we could align ourselves with."

"And she was young. Impressionable."

Inaya pursed her mouth.

"Oh, I get it," Nyx said. "And now you owe me a favor, right?"

"Nyx, this is not the time—"

"I can see that," Nyx said. "In a hurry, right?"

Inaya closed her eyes. God had a very grim sense of humor. "What do you want?"

"I need to get into Jolique's house. He's cousin to the Queen of Nasheen I hear."

"He is also a madman. He sends priests around to women's houses after they've given birth and buys their… unusual babies, when he's not just buying and trading shifters like dogs. Why would you need to see him?"

"I have a bounty for a man, and I think his captors took him there."

"Why would they go there?"

Rhys interrupted. "The note is for Raine al Alharazad. Remember him? He's become a very powerful figure in Nasheenian politics since the end of the war."

"Didn't you kill him?" Inaya said.

Nyx waved her hand. "Details. Can you get us in or not?"

"I can show you the house, certainly. It's on Rue Clery. But I cannot spare any people."

"I need a safe house," Nyx said.

Inaya shook her head. "Absolutely not."

"I could always go find this kid's mother and tell her where her daughter is."

"You wouldn't."

"Inaya, you have no idea what I've been through to get here."

"And you have no idea what I've been through to keep this movement together. The entire world doesn't stop for Nasheenian politics."

"It doesn't stop for Ras Tiegan catshit either," Nyx said. "Your petty rebellion isn't my problem."

"Nor is your potential one mine."

"All right," Rhys said. "Can we come to some agreement?"

Inaya said, "Rhys, you know what she breaks apart whenever she shows up."

"I don't know that things here can get any worse," Rhys said.

Inaya watched him. She wanted to know what had happened, and why he was running with Nyx again. "We have surveillance on Jolique's house. I can tell you if anyone came in recently. When would they have been in?"

"Early last night."

"Easy enough," Inaya said.

Nyx stepped forward. "Not you," Inaya said. She motioned to Rhys. "Come back and I'll show you what we have," she said.

Rhys exchanged a look with Nyx. Nyx shrugged.

Inaya stepped back into the corridor with Rhys. They walked together through the crowded halls, through coded doors, and a final filter before they reached the communication room.

"This is an impressive setup," Rhys said when he saw her activate the slide.

"It took many years to build," Inaya said. "And only a few weeks to destroy."

"Much of life is like that," he said.

Inaya called up surveillance on Jolique's house. "You're in luck," she said. "I had a check in at midnight. No one went in or out from dusk to midnight."

"We're a few hours from dawn now," Rhys said. "I suppose they could have moved then."

"Surely if they were moving a prisoner they would wait for daylight," Inaya said. "The streets aren't exactly safe."

"Then it's possible we can set up an ambush. Do you have the address?"

Inaya wrote it down for him, and handed it over.

"How long have you been with her?" Inaya asked.

"Just a few days."

"Where's Elahyiah?"

Rhys dropped his gaze. "Safe," he said. "And where is Khos?"

"The same," she said, and realized then that they had nothing to talk about. They had made their choices.

"Come," she said, "let's not keep Nyx from her bloodbath."

42.

Rhys watched the house from the rooftop of a local bakery. Jolique so Romaud lived six blocks from the church in a walled compound that Nyx had been happy to climb right into. He was astonished at the lack of filters in the city. The architecture was different from anything he'd ever seen; spires and monstrous statues and saints' niches clotted the city. Everything was built close together, practically on top of each other, with twisted, winding ways that often ended abruptly in walled-over doors. He wore a long coat and hat, hopeful the darkness would shield them all a while longer. Safiyah didn't want to risk holding a glamour and fighting with bugs at the same time unless they had to. In the daylight, a Chenjan and three Nasheenians would stand out like grasshoppers among roaches. Dark clouds and driving rain helped, he supposed. Right now, he was not particularly thankful for the rain, but knew he would be later.

A cloud of red beetles hovered just above his head. He and Ahmed kept a channel open. It was more secure than transceivers, less secure than a com, but served the same purpose.

Rhys was much more skilled with a gun at close range, but Nyx put him above Jolique's house with a sniper rifle she got from Inaya's people. It was poorly made; Ras Tiegan, not Tirhani, and he'd only had enough time to tweak the scope and fire off a few practice rounds before they needed to move. It was not his favorite weapon. He was already soaked through and shivering. The gun was slick beneath his fingers. He watched the door through his scope.

They had been sitting an hour with no movement aside from two people entering the bakery beneath him.

"How long are we going to give this, Nyx?" he asked through the beetles.

"As long as it takes," Nyx replied, her voice tinny.

Of course. Rhys sighed.

Above, the rain continued.

"Hold on," Nyx said. "Here we go. Southwest."

Rhys sighted through the scope, sweeping the alley. He saw a group of hooded figures—six large individuals, circling a seventh.

"You want me to take the risk?" Rhys asked.

There was a pause. He waited. This was when he preferred someone else making decisions. He had already told her he wouldn't kill them. She nearly put Ahmed up here in his stead, until he pointed out that even his worst shot was going to be better than Ahmed's best.

"You know I'd prefer you killed them," Nyx said.

"I'm done killing," Rhys said.

"Fine time to talk morality."

"The best time," he said.

"Remind me to buy you a packet of sen-laced tobacco when this is over."

"If you live? Certainly."

"Take them down," Nyx said.

Rhys took aim and shot out the knee of the first figure. It took far too long for him to reorient and retarget as Nyx and Ahmed stepped out of the alley just behind the group, shooting three of the figures at close range. A buzzing wall of hornets came down around the central figure. Rhys got off two more shots, crippling two more people.

He saw Nyx finish off the ones at the back. Rhys shot off the hand of another figure going for a weapon.

Nyx took hold of the one cloaked in the hornets. Rhys heard cursing.

"What have you got?" Rhys said.

"It's not him," Nyx said.

Ahmed was at the front of the pack, yanking off the hooded hats they wore.

"Shit," Nyx said.

"What is it?" Rhys said.

"He's at the front, bound. You just blew out his fucking knee."

"Better than his head," Rhys said. "Clear out of there. There's movement coming from the house. We'll have order keepers on us soon."

He covered Nyx and Ahmed as they slipped back into the alley with Raine. As they went, he sighted Raine's head in his scope, and remembered a hot room in Chenja, and the sound of his finger bones breaking under a mallet. A mallet held by the man Nyx was so keen on running across the world to save. For the good of Nasheen.

Rhys took a deep breath. He didn't have a care for Nasheen. It could be swallowed up tomorrow. But Nyx cared. It was one of the few things she still pretended to care about.

Rhys didn't take the shot.

"Don't say I never did anything to help you," he said.

"What?" Nyx said through the buzzing of the red beetles.

"Nothing," he said. "You're clear. I'll meet you back at the safe house."

43.

"We have him," Nyx said. "I need a safe room."

She saw Inaya's mouth harden as they hauled Raine into her headquarters. She motioned Nyx toward the next room. "This way. Hurry. There's a way through."

Inaya brought them down a short flight of stairs and past a few storage rooms. Curious Ras Tiegans watched from the shadows, their own faces obscured by hoods. Too many witnesses for Nyx's taste, but they didn't have much of a choice at this point.

Behind her, Ahmed stumbled, so she stepped in and took his place at Raine's left side. Rhys still trailed behind them. Ahmed leaned against a wall. She saw a long trail of blood behind him. His face seemed drawn. She gritted her teeth and focused on hauling Raine forward.

"Inaya, get somebody to help Ahmed, all right? Safiyah?"

"Coming, darling," Safiyah called from behind them. "I'll get him. Go on."

Inaya unlocked a storage room door and palmed on a light. "In here," she said.

A scattering of cloth sacks littered the floor. Nyx flopped Raine down on them. Rhys came up behind her. He was sweating heavily. She saw him wince as he drew up, and clutch at his side.

"You hurt?" she said.

"Just winded," he said.

"You have a hedge witch or something for Raine?" Nyx said. "His knee's blown out."

"I'll see what I can do. But we don't have room for you here, Nyx," Inaya said. "We're going to be out tomorrow. I can let you stay the night, but not a day longer. You understand? I can't have any more hell. Not here. Not with everything we still need to do."

"Got it, sure," Nyx said. "We just need to get patched up. I promise—we're gone in the morning."

Inaya didn't appear convinced. Nyx couldn't say she blamed her. "Come with me, Rhys," Inaya said. She gestured for him to follow.

Nyx gave Raine's face a good pat. He moaned. "Come on, you fuck. Enough people died to get you here. Wake up. I need some bloody fucking answers and we don't have much time."

"Nyx," he said.

"At least you remember that much."

"Where are we?"

"A reasonably safe place. For a while, anyway. I need some answers, Raine. I need to know what the fuck is going on."

"If I knew that, I wouldn't be here."

"Who are they, the ones who took you? Those people we attacked weren't Nasheenians."

"I thought you knew."

"I heard all sorts of stories. First Families, bel dames, Ras Tiegans…"

Raine snorted. "Oh there are all sorts. Ras Tiegans, yes. But there are bel dames involved here, too."

"No, the bel dames sent me after you."

He raised his brows. "Impossible."

"It happened. Bel dames sent me after you."

"Are you… one of them again?"

"I already told you I'm not."

"Pardon, Nyx, but I've not known you to tell the truth."

"You always said you could tell when I was lying, just like most folks. So why would I bother?"

Raine winced. His leg was still bleeding badly. Nyx sighed and crouched next to him. She unknotted and reknotted the makeshift tourniquet. He hissed. "We'll have someone in soon to look at it," she said.

"I haven't been this gutted in a long time," he said. He wheezed.

"Who is it, Raine?"

"My mother," he said.

Nyx sighed. "Alharazad. That's worse than I thought. Is Fatima with her in this? Why the fuck did she send us after you, then?"

"No, listen, it's deeper than that. You should not have come for me. I'm infected."

"You said that already. What does it mean?"

"I've been given some kind of… virus. They brought girls with us. From Ras Tieg. They were harboring some kind of… contagion. Some of them revolted, and were killed. But the rest came north with us, and they… mixed something, their magicians, in Bomani. It could all be so much catshit. I don't know. I've been carted around a long time. It was my own fault. We were finally getting a voice, enough to put them all on edge. Alharazad invited me in to speak about the new government. I took it. And they took me."

"The bel dames?"

"Yes, but they turned me over to those Ras Tiegans once we came into Khairi."

"But why here? What the hell is going on?"

"They want me infected, presumably so you'll kill me?"

"But I wasn't hired to kill you," Nyx said. "Maybe somebody in Nasheen can cure it."

"You understand it will be triggered when I'm killed? I could take a city with me. Maybe more. I don't even know what the contagion is."

"Why the fuck would they do something like that?"

"I don't pretend to know their motives. When they first told me about it, my understanding was that it would go off if I was anywhere near Nasheen. I'm not sure that's even possible, but I'm no fucking magician. And I'm… I'm just very tired. But listen. Whatever has been done… You can't take me back to Nasheen, Nyx."

Nyx rubbed her face. Of course not. That would be too easy. "Raine, I'd like nothing better than to see you rot here in some moldy little shit cell. But I can't do that. The boys back home are on the verge of all-out rebellion. They'll burn down Mushtallah if you don't come back in one piece."

"How is it they didn't object to a bel dame going after me, then? Surely they'd all think as I did, that you're here to kill me."

"I'm not a bel dame, Raine. Fuck, how many times do I have to fucking tell people that? Nobody's stupid enough to believe Fatima would send a bel dame to bring you back alive."

"Fatima… Fatima Kosan? The high councilwoman."

"You know her?"

Raine grimaced. "Oh, I certainly do."

"She not a fan?"

"She tried to have me killed last year."

"What?"

"Before the Queen started talks about the new government. She's had me under surveillance since then."

"Well… I can't say that killing you hasn't crossed my mind, either."

Raine shook his head. "I understand your grievances, Nyxnissa. I forgive you."

"You… what?"

"I forgive you. When you drove that sword through me in Chenja, I thought I would die. I had made my peace with God. I stared up at that sky and it was the most peaceful I'd been in… years. The pain… it was nothing. It just bled out of me. Fear, pain, anger… it was very liberating. There was a flash flood not long after, and it pulled me up along with it. I rode that tide for a long time. I'm not even sure how long. When I woke, your blade was still in my gut and I was still alive, washed up near a little homestead. A man named Abbas and his fourteen wives. Fourteen." He shook his head. "And you should have seen the number of children. They took me in and called for a magician. It was another day before the magician came, and I was nearly gone by then. But as I hovered there at the edge of death, everything changed for me. I saw everything in those moments. My fate. The fate of Nasheen. The fate of the world. We have lost our faith, Nyx. What we need is to set it right again. God told me we must return to the literal word of the Kitab."

"Oh fuck," Nyx said. "They were all right. You really have gone stir crazy bug fuck. God didn't talk to you, Raine. You were hallucinating."

"I'm not here to convince you of anything, Nyx, only to speak the truth of what happened and what was said to me. I knew someone would come for me. I just… God did not see fit to tell me it was you."

"For good reason, I'm sure."

He seemed puzzled. Then a broad grin lit up his haggard face. "You don't believe me," he said.

"I don't believe in much of anything," she said.

"That is your curse. I pity you. Those without belief can be taken in by anything. Without strong beliefs, well… a person could be persuaded to believe anything."

"'The way you were?"

"We've been second class in Nasheen for centuries. Fodder for an endless war. We want equality, Nyx. That's all."

"Equality," Nyx spat. "You want two years of your life at the breeding compounds? You want to be a vessel for twenty babies, all of them carted off to get blown up in some war? Then you want to give up another two years at the front, throwing your body against munitions with the boys? Come home and raise up some house boys and girls from the coast and then throw them out, too? We're just the caretakers for the fodder, Raine, when we're not the fodder. If it'd been you here at home while we fought the war, it wouldn't have been any easier. At least you had a dream of home. I was already home. I knew it was all a lie."

"I won't have a state that treats my body as a disposable thing."

"We all give our bodies to Nasheen. You're not special. You keep going on about how you want to change things for men. Surprise, Raine. The whole bloody system is fucked. Nobody else in this bloody country is any better off than you are."

"The men—"

"What's your solution? Bring the men home but keep women in the compounds? Men get back their bodies but women don't?"

"We'll deal with that when it comes. The important issue right now—"

"Is men's advocacy. Yeah, I get it. Men at the expense of women. You need to change the whole system to be free, not just improve your part in it."

"But if we started with—"

"As soon as you improve your lot, you'll fuck over the rest of us, the same way we did you. I know what people are like, Raine. Humanity is a monster you can never kill."

"The only monster I'm looking to put down is the war," Raine said. "Killing a man doesn't kill a war, Nyx. I understand politics. It's more than just blowing up a school or chopping off a head. Even if the head's mine."

"I told you I wasn't here to kill you."

"I have faith in many things, Nyxnissa, but faith in your ability to deliver a man alive to the bel dames? Let's say that undertaking this journey with you will certainly test my faith to its utmost."

"I'm sure you can write a book or something about it later."

She glanced down at his knee. It looked terrible. How he managed to natter on with a shattered knee astounded her. Always full of surprises, Raine. And now he thought he was some fucking prophet. Fatima wanted her to bring a delusional, self-proclaimed prophet back into Nasheen? One Fatima had already tried to kill once?

The hedge witch appeared in the doorway, saving her from further blathering.

"God's grace, that's a fine mess," the hedge witch said in heavily accented Nasheenian.

"You have no idea," Nyx said.

✚

"It's that bel dame," Adeliz said.

Inaya sighed. "Bring tea, please. Perhaps that will dissuade her." She stood in her communications room, wearing a long dark habit and coat. She had her traveling cap on the table, and a single pack at her feet. They would burn the rest down after them.

Nyx stepped in.

"Everyone lived?" Inaya said lightly. "That must be a first for you."

"On this trip? Yes." Nyx stepped up to the table.

Inaya tapped out the pattern that opaqued the information on the slide.

"We're leaving," Nyx said.

"And we will part right after you," Inaya said.

Adeliz came back in, bearing tea. Inaya took her cup. "Tea?" she said.

"Rather drink piss," Nyx said.

"Thank you, Adeliz," Inaya said.

"And what have you decided to do with Raine?" Inaya asked.

"He'll be staying here."

"What, in Ras Tieg?"

"Best place for him."

"I don't understand. Weren't you supposed to bring him to Nasheen?"

"That's what we'll tell them."

"Who?"

Nyx picked up the tea. Sniffed it. "What is this?"

"Jasmine."

Nyx sipped it. "Huh," she said, and took another sip. "Anyway, I need a safe place for Raine for a while. Think your people could watch after him?"

"No."

"Come on, Inaya. At least until the knee is better. He's promised me he'll stay out of your hair."

"We're burning this place after us. He can't stay."

"I know you can get people smuggled out of here safe. I can't do that and get back to Nasheen. Help me out. One last time."

"No."

"What about Khos? You still in touch with him? He'd know how to get somebody over the border."

"No," Inaya said. She thought of the last time she saw Khos, and remembered the letters. Her children would never see them now. "You know, Khos came to me when I was in prison."

"Did he? That's quite a trip. Folks have been telling me your little rebellion thing here has gotten pretty exciting."

"That's why it seemed so odd. I expected he was there to retrieve me."

"But that meant giving up your people, right?"

"Doesn't it always?"

"Huh," Nyx said. "And he didn't say anything?"

"Just the usual nonsense about going home. But… well, there was one strange thing. Maybe you know something about it. You were close to him, weren't you?"

Nyx shrugged. "We worked together."

"He said it in Nasheenian. He said, 'Look to what you devour.' I thought maybe he was telling me something in code, maybe just telling me the food had saffron in it. It wasn't terribly helpful."

"In Nasheenian?" Nyx said, and laughed. "It's slang, Inaya."

"What?"

"It's slang for when you go down on somebody, you know," and she waggled her tongue.

Inaya grimaced. "You're so crude."

"That's what it is."

"Why would he say something like that?"

Nyx gnawed on that. "There's a tavern in Punjai called the Licking

Cat," Nyx said. "Folks talk about it a lot using that phrase. It's a joke. You know, look to what you eat because… Yeah, you wouldn't get it. Anyway. There any taverns here called something like that? Make allusions to getting a good rub?"

"I wouldn't know about that."

"Oh, wouldn't you? The rebel leader with an eye on every fucked up thing going on in her town?"

Inaya considered that. They had surveillance at most taverns in the area. "I'll ask my operatives," she said.

"Come on, Inaya, say you'll take him. I promise, that tavern thing is a good tip."

"Let him stay," another voice said. Nyx knew it. Isabet.

Isabet stood in the doorway, dressed all in white muslin. Her hair was clean and brushed, bound in a simple white scarf. Even with her imperfect skin, she was a lovely thing, and Nyx could understand what Eshe had seen in her. A poor, unsuspecting little rich girl getting far too deep into matters she did not understand. Eshe always had a thing for those sorts. Nyx felt another sting of grief, and pushed it aside.

Inaya turned, and she and Isabet spoke in Ras Tiegan for a time. Finally, she sighed. "Isabet insists we help him," she said, "though I have no idea why she should feel any desire to help you."

"She's not helping me," Nyx said, "just finishing what Eshe started."

Inaya narrowed her eyes. "I'm sure," she said.

Nyx finished her tea. "As for me, I've got a bounty to bring home. Or say I'm bringing home. It's going to be a terribly fun time. I can see you're disappointed to miss it."

"I'm sure we'll have all the enjoyment here we can handle," Inaya said.

44.

Nyx stepped out into the rainy morning. Rhys waited on the stoop of the old factory that Inaya's compound was built beneath. There was a smell of smoke in the air. Nyx heard the sound of gunfire, far off.

"I'm glad this is a short trip," Nyx said.

"I'm sure you'd love to stay longer," Rhys said.

She looked off further down the lane, where Ahmed and Safiyah were buying food from one of the only open stalls. "Sure you're not coming?" she said.

"I've had my fill of bel dames, thanks," he said.

"You think you can make your way to the port?"

"Inaya's always been precise with directions. I expect I'll have little trouble finding any number of ships fleeing Ras Tieg right now."

Nyx nodded. She pulled on her hat. The hats here were like cowls, covering the neck and face with a fitted sleeve, topped in wide brims. She hated them.

"We done then?" she said.

"Good luck with Fatima."

"The words 'luck' and 'Fatima' should never be used in the same sentence. We'll see what her reaction is when we say we've brought him back. I think I can get something out of her."

"What are you going to do about the boys? The new government?"

"Raine's agreed to handle that from here. He sent out some communications last night to let people know he's alive. I had him put somebody in his place, too. Somebody to speak for him. Help with the politics."

They stood for a while longer in the rain. Nyx heard more gunfire. She knew it was time to move. Her feet were already wet. She never bought the right shoes in these cold countries. Trouble was, her feet were going to take her in a different direction from Rhys.

"I should go," Nyx said.

"Nyx?"

"Yeah?"

"When this is over, what happens?"

She shrugged. "Nothing."

"Nyx?"

"Rhys?"

"Have you ever been happy?"

She thought of Radeyah, and drunk nights at the fights. Dinner with Anneke's squalling kids. The stink of the ocean. And she remembered, during all those moments, of yearning for this one: the sound of gunfire, and Rhys's body beside her.

"No," she said.

She turned away, and started walking across the muddy street to join what remained of her team. Cutting everything up, cutting everything away. And for what? A chance at saving Nasheen from blowing itself all to hell? Some days she wondered if it was worth it. She had killed a lot of people, for nothing. Given up everything she loved, for nothing. Saved nothing.

She heard splashing behind her, and turned.

Rhys came at her.

She half thought he meant to shoot her, and stepped back, pivoted left. But he slipped his arms around her and embraced her. He pulled away before she could figure out how to hug him back.

"I have always been happier without you," he said.

"I know," she said.

He released her, and then he was off and away, through the blinding sheets of rain.

Nyx stood there for a good long while, until Ahmed tapped her on the shoulder.

"You coming?" he said.

"What?" she said.

"Come along, cat gut," Safiyah said. "Let's find some breakfast while he runs along home. Your road isn't as easy as his."

"Don't I fucking know it," Nyx said.

45.

Isabet gazed long into the polished metal mirror in the room Inaya had given her. The Fourré headquarters was strangely quiet. Just a few others were left. If she did not move now, there would not be another chance. Using her teeth and her remaining hand, she knotted a black length of cloth around the stump of her upper left arm. She took the long dagger her mother had given her from its place beneath her bed. No one had thought to search her rooms when she first joined the Fourré. She had assumed they would, and hidden the dagger the first few months she lived among them. But after a time, she realized Inaya had swallowed her story whole cloth, and the deception was not necessary. So the dagger hid in plain sight.

She sheathed the dagger at her hip and drew on her long coat. With her weapon concealed, she crept out into the hallway and made her way to the storage rooms below. She did not have much time.

Her belly felt heavy and overfull, as it had for many months. But it had never been a child she carried. A child was a prettier story. She had seen just how lovely a story it might be written on Eshe's face when he offered to marry her. She had believed, just for an instant, that together they could somehow change their fate.

But that was not what God wanted.

At the door to the prisoner's room, she paused. Drew a deep breath. She pushed the door open.

The man was asleep. His wounded leg was mostly mended, but the hedge witch had obviously given him something for the pain.

Isabet drew her knife and stepped forward. Knife poised, she hesitated.

He was just an old man. How was it one old man had the power to change everything? She wished, again, that it had not all gone so wrong. Wished her mother would have lived longer, and not sold her to Genevieve Leichner as some virgin maid. But being a virgin maid had given her the backstory she needed to infiltrate the Fourré, and to do it at far less risk than Saint Genevieve's real daughter.

Her grip on the blade eased. She wanted to turn back. Go to Inaya and cry on her shoulder and confess everything. Eshe always said that a single death could change the course of the world, if it was the right one. She had known that in her heart, but refused it until she was the last of Saint Genevieve's maids, the only one who could carry out the final judgment.

She tightened her grip.

The old man's eye popped open.

Isabet froze. Sheer terror. For one long blink they regarded one another, the would-be assassin and the old man. And then her blade came down in his throat.

Blood rushed up. He gurgled and thrashed. Grabbed her hand. She shrieked. He held her hand there at his throat, and stared deeply into her eyes. She tried to yank herself away, but his grip was firm, even as his life ebbed out over the bed. Isabet lost her resolve, then. She fell to her knees and began to sob and pray. Blood soaked her sleeve.

"I'm sorry," she said. "I'm sorry. It's the only way to stop the misborn, and what the saint has growing inside me."

Finally, his grip began to loosen. She pulled her hand into her lap. Her arm was covered in blood nearly to the elbow, and it wet the front of her habit. She sobbed and sobbed as the body beside her went still.

"Oh God be merciful," she said. "God forgive me."

God could forgive anything. Surely he could forgive this. Was there any forgiveness to be had?

The body trembled.

Isabet clawed across the floor and dragged herself to her feet. She was unsteady, a little faint. She saw black spots at the edges of her vision. She wanted to retch.

"God have mercy," she murmured. "Please, I'm sorry."

She heard a strange sound, then. Like someone gasping. Was he still alive? Isabet stepped closer, cringing at the sight of her dagger thrust into his still oozing throat. She saw bubbles of blood around the blade, as if he were still breathing. God, would she have to strike him again? Her whole body began to tremble. She couldn't do it again. She couldn't.

As she watched, the bloody flesh around his throat began to shudder. Some kind of tiny… insect? Fear choked her. Was he being invaded by bugs already? Was he turning into one?

"Raine?"

Isabet looked up. Inaya stood in the doorway, hand to her mouth. "My God," Inaya said. "What have you done?"

"He was meant for you," Isabet said. "This was all meant for you."

46.

"I know I've got an infiltrator on my team. If you're it, let's just get this done now," Nyx said to Safiyah.

They stood just inside the roiling darkness of the magicians' tunnels with Ahmed, the only light a faint glimmer from a glow globe Safiyah had spirited away from some inattentive trader. It was the safest place Nyx knew to talk about it, and the last place. Because the next stop was Nasheen, and she needed to know what she was facing back there.

"I am God's hammer," Safiyah said. "But I've not come for you. You're just the bait."

Nyx had been a lot of things, but never bait. It was kind of a letdown.

"Bait for who?" Nyx said.

"The Families want an end to the war. Your old friend Alharazad does not."

"Fucking Alharazad," Nyx said. Her fault, again, for not killing that scheming bel dame when she had the chance. How many could she have saved, with that one death? Eskander and Khatijah and Eshe, maybe Kage too. Who knew if Kage had made it across the desert on her own? Not to mention the Aadhyan women she killed. Or the men she shot and stabbed in Bomani. Or Mercia's body guards. Bloody fucking.

One life. She could have taken one life, seven years ago, and spared them all of this.

My life for a thousand, the bel dame oath went, but she hadn't sacrificed herself, had she? She'd chosen to live and eat and fuck and rebuild at the coast, the same thing she'd heckled Rhys for doing. And this is what came of it. This is what happened when bel dames went soft.

"Tell me truly," Safiyah said. "If Alharazad was the catalyst for all this madness, where would we find her?"

"How the fuck should I know?" Nyx said. She remembered the desert, the murderous crows, hauling her team's bodies across the sand. All that for nothing. All that because she had stayed her hand.

"I know you can find her," Safiyah said. "I bet a great deal on it."

"Then you're a fucking fool."

Safiyah sighed. "Child, where would *you* go if you sought to thwart the Queen's plan of shooting the aliens out of the sky and ending the war? If you wanted to steal the aliens' technology, and twist the bel dames against themselves, and seize power in the vacuum left behind as the Queen stepped down, the broederbond fought one another over Raine's death, and the bel dames were implicated in that death? Where would you go? The last place anyone would look?"

"I knew the aliens were a part of this," Nyx said. "Fuck." She considered Safiyah's words. As Safiyah had spoken things began to click into place, things she hadn't been able to fucking put together because she was so caught up in smashing into Rhys again. "I'd be in Amtullah," Nyx said. "I'd make alliances with somebody who had some power. I'd get her on my side. Then we'd open up shop in Amtullah, and wait the Queen out."

Safiyah raised her brows. "Would you really?"

It was like some map unrolling in her brain. "That's why Fatima moved everyone to Amtullah," Nyx said. "She could keep an eye on the Queen, and build up her following there. Strike when the moment was right. Seize power. Make nice with our old alien friends."

"I don't get it," Ahmed said. "If Fatima was in on this, why did she try and protect Raine?"

"She didn't," Safiyah said. "She bet your friend here would murder him. And do it as a bel dame. Then the bel dames get blamed for the death, the broederbond in an uproar, etcetera, etcetera. Someone has to fill that vacuum. Alharazad has not been a bel dame in some time. In fact, she's well known for speaking out against the current council. You colonials really are terrible at thinking through politics. I'm surprised you didn't pick all this up weeks ago."

"What, we're just going to walk up to Fatima and ask her where

Alharazad is so we can kill her?" Ahmed said.

"No," Nyx said. "I think Alharazad will come to us."

"Why?"

"I'll tell her we have Raine," Nyx said.

"You should contact your little diplomatic liaison," Safiyah said.

"You did your homework," Nyx said. "How'd you know about Mercia?"

"I wasn't wandering around in the desert with you for pleasure," Safiyah said, "though I admit I had a rather enjoyable time."

"She'll want to know what her people are doing with Nasheenians out here," Nyx said. "Unless she's already in on it."

"A possibility. But worth the risk," Safiyah said.

"So you intend to just walk into Amtullah without any explosives or weapons or… and what? Just… talk to her?" Ahmed said. "Is this the plan? Please tell me this isn't the plan."

"There's more to it," Nyx said, "but I need to figure it out first."

"Fucking mad," Ahmed said.

"One condition in all this," Nyx said to Safiyah. "You can have Alharazad, but I do what I want with Fatima. Understood?"

Safiyah shrugged. "I never developed much of a taste for politicians. The bloodletters were always far tastier."

✚

Nyx didn't believe in martyrs, because she'd been one. It was easy to become disillusioned with something others thought she was. She knew the rot at her core. It was good to know what you were before you acted foolishly. It kept things in perspective.

The first thing Nyx did when they clawed their way back into Nasheen was buy a wad of sen from a street vendor in Amtullah. Nyx got Ahmed settled back into the storefront and had him contact Mercia. Nyx preferred an area of operations far from the bloodshed. She didn't expect to come back from it. She gave Ahmed a list of people to call, and took care of some quick legal business, then locked it all away in a coded lockbox.

"I'm not back in two days," she told Ahmed, "here's the pattern for the lockbox. Take what you want and get out."

She figured he would take it long before that, but didn't mention it. With just one team member left, she could actually afford to pay him for the months he traveled with her.

"Anything else before you get started?" Ahmed said.

"Just one," Nyx said. "No matter what happens, try to keep that pretty little face of yours intact."

+

Nyx chewed sen as she and Safiyah approached Blood Hill. The bel dame novice at the gate asked their business. Nyx said, "Tell Fatima Kosan I've brought in Raine al Alharazad."

The filter admitted them almost immediately. They were led to Fatima's quarters on Blood Hill by no fewer than a dozen bel dames. Nyx thought that very complimentary.

The bel dames announced them. Nyx pushed past them before they'd finished.

And there Fatima sat behind her bel dame council desk, wearing her high council finery. Next to her, as Safiyah had promised, was Raine's mother, and the most notorious bel dame in Nasheen, the one that nobody in the country had the stomach or the skill to bring in—Alharazad.

"Where is he?" Alharazad said.

"So you figured that he'd told me you were in on this," Nyx said. "So you showed up to confirm I had him."

"Obviously," Alharazad said. "Where is he?" She spit sen on the floor. On the whole, she was much improved from the last time Nyx saw her. Her eyes were still a little bloodshot, nestled in a haggard face, but she had cleaned up quite a bit, cropped her white hair, and washed. She dressed in rather expensive maroon trousers and matching tunic with silver stitching. She had a pistol at either hip and a dagger lashed to one thigh.

Fatima set aside a ledger she had been consulting and pressed her hands to the table. An old bel dame show of respect, that—showing the person you were with that you were unarmed and come to parley in peace.

"I brought Raine home like you asked," Nyx said.

Fatima's eyes widened. "Not to Nasheen?"

"That's where I was supposed to bring him, right?"

Fatima glanced to Alharazad. Alharazad shook her head.

"He's not in Nasheen," Alharazad said.

"And what makes you think that?"

"Because we would all be dead," Alharazad said.

✚

Inaya watched as Raine's body began to burst apart. There was something… leaking from him. Not bugs or bile or blood but… sand. Gray sand.

"What did you do?" Inaya said.

Isabet was crying. She dropped the bloody dagger, and pressed her filthy hand to her face. "I'm not Genevieve's daughter," she said. "I'm one of her handmaidens."

"My God."

Inaya stepped back into the doorway.

Isabet stretched her bloody hand skyward. "I'm sorry," she said. "I'm sorry, but I am the last. Only I could do it."

"Do what?"

"She says you're an abomination. They infected all of us and brought us north. One of the girls refused. They had her dig her own grave with her hands, then cut off her hands and buried her there. I escaped, but they found me. They had another use for me. I'm sorry. I'm so sorry. If I didn't do this I'd be dead with the others in the desert. Eshe, I'm so sorry."

"Isabet, why didn't you—"

"It's my burden. If I didn't kill him, what's inside me would fester eventually. It'd kill me. I had to, Inaya. I'm sorry."

The sand slithered from Raine's body like a living creature. As Inaya watched, it leapt forward, adhering to Isabet's body. The blood on her hand disappeared. Isabet began to scream. Blood appeared at her eyes, her mouth.

Inaya ran.

"Get out!" Inaya yelled. "Get out! Out, all of you!" She sprinted down the hall, crying out at the last of her people remaining in the old headquarters. As she ran, she heard more cries behind her. And then a hissing, spitting sound, growing louder and louder.

Inaya herded the cook up. She grabbed Adeliz by the arm and pushed her toward the stairs. She glanced back once. The gray sand had become a tide, multiplied. It overwhelmed one of her clerks. He screamed. It rushed into his mouth. His body seemed to burst, then disintegrate.

Inaya yelled at Adeliz to run.

They went up two flights and surged into the open air. The rain had let up. Inaya ran ahead. Her people had darted off into different directions. She stared at the rooftops. "Up!" she yelled after them. "Find high ground!"

The door behind her burst open. A rolling stir of gray sand poured out after her. She took off again, running for the church. It was the tallest building in Inoublie. Her skin prickled, then roiled, and as she ran, she simply let go and burst apart into a misty green cloud, pouring forward as fast as the wind could carry her. All around her, she saw more shifters transforming themselves into their alternate forms ahead of the gray tide.

Inaya reached the parapet of the church and found a safe place to reform. She pulled herself back together, painfully, and shook off long strings of mucus, coughing black beetles. The air was bitterly cold against her slimy, naked skin, but she ignored it, and stared, instead, at the tide of gray flowing out along the streets. With every person it devoured, it seemed to grow larger, stronger; a gray ocean come to eat the entire city.

She saw Adeliz across the street on the opposite roof, standing with two parrots and a raven. Below, those unable to flee fast enough screamed and disintegrated under the onslaught.

Inaya stared at the wave, wondering if it would ever crest. Surely it would run out of organic matter to eat? It couldn't keep getting larger, could it? And what had Isabet meant, that this was all for her? Then she heard a terrible crackling sound, and gazed back to the factory. The sand had devoured the base of the structure, the bug secretions that had bound the base of the building together.

It didn't just eat people. It ate everything organic. Inaya raised her head and gazed out past the filter, to the lush, wild jungle that surrounded Inoublie.

"My God," she said, because Nyx had delivered them a plague after all.

✚

"Well, you're mistaken about that," Nyx said. "He's in Nasheen, and he's very much alive."

Alharazad laughed. “Don’t try and bluff me, girl. Raine isn’t coming home alive. We made certain of that.”

“Why did you send me after him if you never meant him to come home alive?”

“It was because we didn’t want him coming back alive that we sent you, you fool,” Alharazad said. “I sent you after him because you were the only bel dame we had with the guts to murder him where he stood, and you’d do it without getting the order.”

“So that’s why you wanted me to be a bel dame,” Nyx said. “So I’d kill him for you. What purpose does that serve?”

Fatima sighed. “Nyx, you are sadly behind the times.”

“Enlighten me.”

Nyx was aware of Safiyah beside her, fairly humming with anticipation. This was the deal. It was Nyx who wanted the answers this time. Safiyah was ready to burn the place down around them. Nyx wondered how that would go, with over a thousand bel dames on Blood Hill. But then, she didn’t expect to make it out of this interview.

“There’s no room for bel dames in the new world, Nyx,” Alharazad said. “I didn’t believe it, not until Fatima came to me about it. If we want power in the new order, we need to be something else.”

“‘We’? You mean you and her.”

Nasheen was about power. Having it. Wanting it. Killing for it. Without power you weren’t anything. And when you saw power shifting, you either fought for the old way or you blazed a new one. Alharazad and Fatima had decided to burn it all down behind them. And murder Nyx and Khatijah and all the rest of their bel dame sisters behind them. Nyx should have figured that.

“We need what those aliens have,” Alharazad said. “The First Families would have them shot out of the fucking sky. But let me tell you what a stronger leadership would do. One led by Fatima and myself. With the aliens’ help, we finish Chenja. We end the war properly. That’s all any of us ever wanted.”

“This is all very unfortunate,” Fatima said. “You really need to tell us where Raine is. When a man like Raine has been lost, the Queen has only one choice to avoid civil war, and that’s to disband the order that took him out.”

“How many women will die for his death? I assume you’ll blame more than just me.”

"We've chosen a suitable number," Alharazad said.

"Tell me this, then," Nyx said. "Since I'm such a fucking idiot. Why did you take Raine to Ras Tieg? The Queen's cousin? What was that about?"

Fatima said, "That was not our call."

"That was done at the Queen's request."

"To what purpose?"

"When she found out he was still alive, she asked that he be moved there to assist in taking care of their shifter problem," Fatima said. "Two problems settled with one piece. There's a rebellion there, you know. She requested that he be left there for you to dispose of. And if you didn't, well… we had an agent in place to act if you didn't."

"I—hold on. What?"

"Raine was never meant to come home," Alharazad said. "We told him he couldn't come home so he'd convince you to let him stay in Ras Tieg. You forget, Nyxnissa. I was a bel dame long before you. And a far better one. We played you from the start. And you sang beautifully."

"What agent?" Nyx said, and then she knew. "The fucking Ras Tiegan girl."

Alharazad grinned. "Not so slow after all."

✚

Inaya paced the parapet as the tide of sand lapped at the base of the church. There were hundreds of people up on the roofs now, watching as the sand bled the streets dry. The public buildings went down first. Inaya watched over a dozen people devoured as it succumbed.

She looked again to the jungle. It would spread without end, eat the entirety of Ras Tieg. And then what? The world? She knew there were contagions bred to engulf certain people, or certain areas. Had this been tailored to the city, the country, or the world?

"Mother Mhari, full of grace," she muttered. She got down on her naked knees and prayed. She thought of God's Angels, mutant shifters like her who had been trained only to hurt and destroy. She thought of her husband, Khos, and her children. She had told them she would make a better world. And instead, she had brought some spider into her house and now everything was disintegrating around her. She gazed up at the cloudy sky. No light, no signs, no miracles. Just her, naked on a roof in a tiny town at the edge of everything, with a choice to make.

She got to her feet. When she shifted, she was able to move the matter she was not using… somewhere else. It was how she moved organic and inorganic objects… like a bakkie that she needed to get across a border. She didn't know where the bits of her went when she did not need them, but she knew she could recall them at will. Or leave them, if she chose.

Now she must do something very terrible, something that could upset everything, because though she was able to put pieces of herself into that other place, she had no idea what would happen if she tried to put something like… *this* there.

Inaya drew a deep breath—

and broke apart.

✚

"We'll do with politics what we tried to do with blood," Alharazad said. "You'll see. Where's Raine?"

"You should know better, Alharazad. Nasheenian politics will always be full of blood," Nyx said. "And Ras Tieg, too, it looks like."

Fatima sighed. "The girl was just one of Genevieve Leichner's virgin maids. I'm astounded you didn't see her for what she was immediately."

No, Nyx admitted, she always overlooked people who played at being weak. She'd made the same mistake with Inaya, way back when.

"They were dispatched to infiltrate the Fourré some time ago," Fatima said. "It's not my pet project, but the Queen was very hopeful about the outcome. I told you we have been working closely with her on this. Ras Tieg has been highly unstable since the rise of the Fourré. Before then they were not much of anything. But when the Queen realized a simple trade could help us solidify our relations with Ras Tieg, she agreed."

"She traded them Raine for political stability?"

"Where do you think she's retiring once she steps down?" Alharazad said. "Not the fuck anywhere here. She's not going to be popular much longer."

"I'm sorry we kept you out of much of this, Nyx, but you understand the necessity," Fatima said. "You would have done the same."

Nyx felt numb. It was all so big that she had trouble getting her head around it. She had been used. Thoroughly, totally, and completely. She had given up everything—her home, and Anneke, Radeyah; and lost an entire team, lost Eshe—for what?

Alharazad laughed. "You look so confused. It's all right. Are you really the last one standing?"

"Can't be," Fatima said. "You'd have to have gone through the tunnels to get back so quickly. Is this your new magician?"

"Indeed," Safiyah said. It was the first time she'd spoken.

"And what are you called? Need a job?" Alharazad said, and laughed.

"I am on a job, actually," Safiyah said lightly. "Perhaps you remember me, Alharazad. Surely you of all people remember my name, and how you angered my Family when you murdered our brothers."

For a moment, Nyx didn't register the look of horror on Alharazad's face. She thought it was just gas.

But as Alharazad's mouth began to work, Nyx realized it was more than just some passing bodily discomfort.

"You," Alharazad said.

Safiyah grinned. "Me," she said.

✚

Inaya tore herself into a billion pieces. It was freedom. Complete, utter, perfect freedom. When she tore herself, she tore part of the world. Something folded. But instead of letting that piece of the world close back up, she kept it open. She bent the spaces around the tide of sand, and began to funnel it to the place where she kept herself.

There was a moment of deep resistance. Then the sand, too, began to break down, break apart. She transformed it. One moment, seething gray death. The next, inert matter broken up into its basic parts, perfectly packaged for storage in the twist she had made in the world.

She broke the weapon apart bit by bit, even as more people screamed and died around her, and the flow of sand gushed toward the edges of the filter. She began to spread herself thinner and thinner, blanketing the town, the world. She heard the caw of a raven.

As she spread apart, she was less and less aware of herself. The matter broke beneath her. She broke against it. She was losing. Something was being lost.

+

Safiyah gazed upon the face she first saw in the palms of her handler, several months past. She had enjoyed her sojourn in the desert, tracking down the one woman sure to draw this one out of hiding.

Alharazad was not an easy woman to find, or to fool. Not unless she wanted to be found. And Nyx was the sort of woman that Alharazad delighted in underestimating. Safiyah knew, because she hadn't thought much of her either, in the beginning. The colonial was slow, uneducated, and very dirty. But resilient. Terribly resilient.

Safiyah said, "What, no greeting?"

"You know each other?" Nyx said.

"In passing," Safiyah said. "It took me a time to remember your face. You were much younger when you visited me, weren't you?"

"Who let you out?"

"Oh, I'm not going to tell you everything now. Why would I do that? Simply congratulate me on finding you, and die gracefully."

The old woman tried to bolt. The bel dames around them surged.

Nyx drew her blade, and stepped further into the room. She prepared for a good fight. A final fight. Safiyah could see it in her face, and thought it very cute.

Safiyah called the ravenous swarm of flesh beetles she had kept on call in anticipation of just such an event.

The screaming was perfectly lovely. The councilwoman even retched. Any day Safiyah could make a bel dame retch was a fine day indeed.

And the troublesome retinue of armed bel dames? Well, that only took a few moments longer.

Somedays Safiyah truly loved what she was.

+

In some other life, there was a woman named Inaya il Parait. She married a man named Khos. Khos loved her all his life, but she did not love him. She loved her children. She loved her freedom. She loved the idea of being normal, and leading a normal life.

But she had never been ordinary.

And now, she was coming apart.

Inaya watched the world from the sky. She was all-seeing, all-knowing. She wondered if this is what it felt like to be God. To see all the joy and horror at once, to pick up grains of sand one by one while a great tide of destruction threatened the world. She was just one entity. Her against the world felt like too much.

She knew she was breaking further and further apart, knew that she was fading, knew that with each grain she removed from the world, it was one less piece of her that she would have the strength to pull back.

The sand broke against the filter. She half hoped it would stop, but no—it simply ate the filter. Bled through. She spread herself thinner. Consciousness floated.

There once was a woman…

And then she felt something else ahead of her. Some other entity, something like her. It, too, ate at the sand. The tide had become a wave.

The wave soon became a runnel.

Inaya began to grasp back at the bits of herself. She felt some semblance of consciousness return. As she regained control, she was able to focus on the final movement of the sand, until every last grain was broken and removed.

It was painful, coming back.

Inaya burned with the effort. She staggered into her body like a drunkard. Fell to her knees. Coughed up bloody mucus and dead beetles. She snorted air into new lungs. The ground beneath her was scorched bare. Every last scrap of organic matter had been eaten by the sand.

She raised her head.

There was another figure there across from her at the edge of the filter, a pale man. He coughed up a swarm of red beetles. They buzzed about his mucus-smeared head.

Inaya crawled toward him. Hunger stabbed her belly. She would need to eat soon.

He looked up.

It was the Angel who interrogated her—Pieter. The one from the prison. The one she had spared.

He met her look, said nothing. Then he was on his feet, running out past her, through the filter, and into the trembling jungle.

✚

Nyx stared at the pile of bones where Alharazad and the dozen bel dames had been. "I'm... I can't... what the fuck was that?"

"You asked once why I followed you," Safiyah said. "It's because I'm hoping they give me something difficult next time."

"They?" Fatima said. Her voice was faint. The beetles had picked Alharazad clean, but left Fatima intact.

"You think you are the only power in Nasheen, child? Oh no. Yours is a very new power, and you only have as much as we permit you. Don't get too comfortable, now."

"The boys—" Fatima began.

"The boys will be just fine," Nyx said, suddenly. It bubbled up from inside of her. "Because as I told you, Raine's still alive. You don't know any different, do you? There will be people here to corroborate that. He just checked in with them. Should be on the radio any minute. Raine isn't going to be found. And nobody else is going to look for him. He's retiring from politics. The bel dames are going to keep going on as they are until the new government decides what do to with them. No one's going to kill anyone. How does that sound?"

"Bloody awful," Safiyah said.

"Fatima?" Nyx said.

"I... need to think."

"No thinking. Doing." Nyx walked up to the table. "If there's a new government in Nasheen, you can bet I'll do everything in my power to make sure you're not a part of it."

"Then shoot me."

"Why?"

"Because that's what you do."

"Is it? You really don't know me at all, do you, Fatima? I'm not like you. Not anymore."

"There is no place for you in the new world," Fatima said.

"That's what I'm hoping," Nyx said. "If you had any goddamn sense, you'd hope so too."

Nyx pushed past Safiyah into the hallway. She needed to get away. Far, far, the fuck away.

"Nyx!" Safiyah called. "Come now, darling, let me buy you a drink."

But Nyx was unsteady on her feet, burning with fear. As she stepped into the hall, she was overwhelmed by the number of women around them, scurrying from one job to another. She reached for her blade.

Safiyah took her arm, quickly. "Hush now," she said softly. "Head high. Sword sheathed. We are going to walk right out of this dismal place."

"I fully expect to fight my way out. Fatima will call someone. We'll carve out bloody bel dames for spans." Nyx could see it. The bodies. The blood. The twisted young women's faces.

Safiyah patted her arm. "Not today, child. Not after the call you made."

"She won't come."

"She will."

They walked through the open foyer unmolested, and when they stepped into the courtyard, there she was, with a mixed force of order keepers and Ras Tiegan security professionals. They had already breached the filter.

Mercia stood at the head of the little army, foolishly, Nyx thought, but that was just like her. When she saw Nyx and Safiyah, she frowned. "I expected you'd be fighting your way out," she said.

"Me too," Nyx said.

"Colonials," Safiyah said, and shook her head.

"Thank you for the information. The Queen's given me leave to extradite Fatima as a war criminal for what she's done to Ras Tieg. Do you have the confession?"

Nyx decided not to tell her that the move on Ras Tieg was all the Queen's idea. The girl would find out soon enough when she watched the recording. Nyx was fond of imagining Fatima living in some moist Ras Tiegan prison for the rest of her life. It was fitting, seeing as where Fatima had put Nyx for a year of her own life.

Safiyah took a locust from the deep sleeve of her burnous and passed it to Mercia. "My bugs see and record all."

"You going to forgive me about the bodyguards, then?"

Mercia's face was unreadable—the perfect politician. "I'm keeping that note in my ledger."

"Fair enough," Nyx said.

47.

Ahmed waited for Nyx at the rented storefront. He wiped himself clean with water pooling in the sink and a durable bar of yellow, scentless soap. It was not a proper bath, but it was the best he'd felt in a good long while. He caught his reflection in the cracked, opaqued windows at the front of the office, still hung with Nyx's sign, though she had turned it inward, so her advertisement for a "bug killer" was visible only to him. He kept the windows opaqued, glad for the privacy, and dressed.

Outside, Amtullah was a city on the brink of change. Whether that was civil war or not, he wasn't certain. There were large protests in the main square, and the night before, no one had obeyed the curfew. The word at the taverns he stopped in was that Hamza Habib had finally communicated with his people, and negotiations with the new government would continue in his name by a man he had designated.

"God the compassionate, the merciful, has willed that another be my voice in the movement during these months of my exile," his recorded voice said over the radio—Ahmed was shocked the government channels were covering it—"and until my return to Nasheen I designate Dawud al Bassem as leader of the men's initiative to restore Nasheen to its former bounty, God willing."

Ahmed had never heard of Dawud al Bassem, but he expected he would be hearing a good deal more of him in the future.

He went back into the gear room and set out what he had left. Two pistols. One that seemed to be forever clogged with sand. A broken knife.

He had kept it for the metal. It might be worth selling. He had no plan, no purpose. He half hoped Nyx would keep him as a part of her new team. Would she open up the storefront and take up bounties again? It wasn't great work, but it was work, and the only sort he seemed to be good at.

As he cleaned his weapons, he became aware of a faint sound in the outer room. He paused to listen. Nothing. There was a good deal of noise on the street, and it was bleeding into the storefront.

He turned.

A woman stood three paces from him, a long dagger drawn. She was young, perhaps twenty, and she wore loose crimson trousers and a dark burnous.

Ahmed had already emptied his weapons to clean them. The dagger was broken. He could wield it if he must, but not well. He had never been good with knives. He preferred words. And looks.

They regarded one another for a long moment. He pressed his hands to the table.

"There's no life for a man in Nasheen, is there?" he said.

"Plenty of room for men," she said. "Just not criminals."

"And we're all criminals to you, aren't we?"

She stepped forward.

Bel dames never gave up, no matter how far you ran or how many politicians you saved.

"Make it quick," he said.

"Let's not make it at all," Nyx said. She entered from the back door. Her face was haggard. She watched the little bel dame.

"How long have you had the note?" Nyx asked.

"A month. Another sister passed it to me."

"I bet she did," Nyx said. She walked up to Ahmed and put a hand on his shoulder. Oddly comforting. He understood what the Chenjan liked about her. "I just came from speaking to Fatima Kosan," Nyx said. "Rumor has it you're all going to be out of a job soon."

"What are you talking about?"

"Who was your first?" Nyx asked.

The girl firmed her mouth.

"That young, are you?" Nyx walked toward the girl. "Let me tell you a secret. They forgive you when you let your first one go. There are boys out there threatening to riot. There's a new government to put together. A whole country to run. A world to fix. And you're fucking around in here swinging a knife at a war vet. There are no more deserters, honey pot. There's no war. We're just people now. You get that?"

The girl stared at her knife.

Ahmed held his breath.

"Go home," Nyx said. "There's been enough blood spilled in Nasheen today."

In another life, Ahmed would have lost his head. He could see it, staring back at him from the floor.

But as Nyx put her hand on the girl's shoulder, the girl's expression crumpled.

"It's all right, Nyx said. "They'll be another one."

"You're Nyxnissa so Dasheem," the bel dame said.

"Yeah. No note on me either. I checked."

The girl pulled a red letter from her burnous and handed it to her. "I pass his note to you," she said. "I don't give up notes either." And she walked out.

Nyx held the red letter. Sighed.

As Ahmed watched, she tore up the red letter and threw the remnants onto the floor. "I'll tell the bounty office it was passed to me. Even if it's not wiped clean, well, it's mine now. And I'm retired."

"I thought you weren't a bel dame anymore."

"I'm starting to realize it doesn't much matter what the truth is, only what people think is true."

Ahmed took a breath.

"Don't go thanking me yet. I can't pay you any currency. I'm flat broke. But I hope you'll accept that instead."

"I will," he said.

"Pack your things," she said, and opened up the safe. She passed him what was inside.

It was a train ticket to Mushirah, and a government-stamped land deed made out to a woman named Bakira so Dasheem, passed to Kine so Dasheem, then Nyxnissa so Dasheem, and then Eshe al Khazireh. The final name, scrawled in at the bottom and sealed with a shimmery organic stamp, was Ahmed al Kaidan.

"I've been holding onto that a long time," she said. "My sister fought for a decade to get our mother's farm back from the government. Maybe you can make some use of it."

Ahmed felt his throat swell. It was the kindest thing anyone had ever done for him. "Thank you," he said.

She shrugged. "Find yourself a nice boy to settle down with, and raise something worth a damn in this fucking desert. That's thanks enough."

He opened his mouth to deny it, but realized the time for deception was done. There was some relief in that.

+

Nyx leaned back on a wicker chair on the roof of the storefront, feet up on the edge of the parapet, gazing out over the city. She was drinking whiskey, and it had never tasted so good. Safiyah sat next to her, legs crossed beneath her billowing robe, hair pulled back from her creepily lovely face.

Nyx rubbed at a smear of blood on her trousers, wondering what injury it had come from. Most everything still ached, though the whiskey was dulling it now. In the distance, Blood Hill was lit up like a torch as order keepers and Ras Tiegan irregulars set up camp as temporary investigators.

"Think the bel dames will ever get it back?" Nyx asked.

"Of course they will," Safiyah said. "You should know that better than I. But of course, they still have Bloodmount."

"Just figured you'd have more experience with them than me."

"I have seen bel dames do many things. Play many roles. But the bel dames I once knew and the ones as they are now…" She smirked. "They are far different people."

"You talk about it like you remember when they ruled the world. Not like you read it in a book."

Safiyah sipped her drink. It was some gross fruity thing. Nyx could smell it. Safiyah gestured up at the bright light in the sky—the alien ship locked in orbit around Umayma. "Have you ever seen a ship shot out of the sky?" she asked.

Nyx gazed up at the light. "Never happened in my lifetime. They say we lost the ability."

"Not lost," Safiyah said. Her eyes were bright. "Just dormant. Saving it for when they truly needed it."

"How old are you, Safiyah?"

"Old enough."

"How's that possible?"

Safiyah sighed. "We were all long-lived people, once. Nashins and Senyans. We were from different worlds, it's true, but related ones. We had a shared religion, shared culture. Shared genetics, even. For a good long time, the richest were like immortals. Lived for centuries. On Umayma, that changed. Mutations happen faster here. They are difficult to correct, and nearly impossible to control. But we found that if we kept a few bloodlines very pure, we could maintain some of those genetics. You should have seen the things our conjurers could do, even in my time. But those skills are degrading. The bugs are mutating faster than we are. I worry that someday we may lose our hold on them all together. And the shifting… Well, the shifting is getting worse. Sometimes I think we're fighting the bold truth that what the world really wants to do is change us to fit it. We keep trying to change the world to suit us. I don't think that's the way—ah, there it is…"

Safiyah pointed back up at the sky.

Nyx followed her gesture, and saw a brilliant blue burst of light puncture the night from the direction of Mushtallah. It roared across the darkness, into the atmosphere, fast as a comet. It left a misty trail of debris in its wake, like a spent burst.

Nyx watched the light change, grow smaller as it ascended. Then, a bloody eruption of light: purple and blue, tinged in orange, ringed in green. For a moment, it was as if a small star had exploded in the sky. Then bright flares broke apart from the mass and rained down from the atmosphere. It was like fiery hail. The end days from some bloody book.

Nyx took a drink. It was one of the prettiest things she ever saw.

Safiyah sighed as the rain of debris flared, darkened, and died in the night sky. After just a few minutes, the residue from the explosion had all but dissipated, leaving just a few misty trails of aurora-like folds in the sky and gaggles of awed spectators on the streets.

"Not as dramatic as I hoped," Safiyah said.

"Did you shoot down the Drucians, a thousand years ago?"

Safiyah sipped her drink. "There were still a few of us alive, then. We could afford to be more dramatic. Their ship was bigger, too. A proper colonial ship, not a military vessel like that one."

"Military?"

"Oh yes. You think your queen would tell you the truth of anything? That was a military vessel, Nyxnissa. They didn't wake me up just to kill

Alharazad. Certainly not. They wanted to know if I could still protect us from those expansionists. They have wanted to eradicate our kind for millennia. There was once a filter over this world, did you know? It protected us for nearly two thousand years, until some bloody expansionist came by and tore it up. It took every resource this planet had to beat them back. After that, the Caliphate fell and the wars started. There was only so much left here for us. Few resources means the ones with the most control over them will survive. So when the Drucians came, yes, I blew them out of the sky. There was not enough here for us, let alone half a million more."

"Half a million?"

"Oh yes. At least that many."

"You murdered half a million people?"

"Would you rather it was our people I murdered? You of all people understand that we must make choices, Nyxnissa. Half a million aliens to save millions of our own? Absolutely. I still consider it a fair trade."

Nyx shook her head.

"Are you shocked?" Safiyah asked.

"About which part?"

Safiyah shrugged. "Oftentimes, when I tell colonials, they cannot comprehend it."

"I've seen a lot of crazy, surprising shit in my time," Nyx said. "Long-lived mutants blowing shit out of the sky is the least of it." She thought of the massive organic atmosphere machines, and the creature that had attacked Khatijah.

Safiyah polished off her drink. "Well, that should be all for the sky theater tonight," she said. "I'm back off to my masters. There's apparently been some disturbance in the old derelicts beneath Mushtallah, ever since that business in Ras Tieg. No doubt crawling through that muck in search of the disease will keep me busy."

"Who is it who polices somebody like you?"

Safiyah smiled. "Oh, now, you don't think I'm going to tell you all my secrets, do you? What I've learned about this world over the centuries is that just when you think you're starting to understand the full puzzle, something pops up that forces you to rearrange the whole picture. Stay on your side of the divide, Nyx. It's simpler and easier that way."

"I like it over here," Nyx said.

"I do as well. It's a shame, really." She watched the sky a moment longer. "Good night, Nyxnissa so Dasheem. I do hope we can work together again someday."

Nyx raised her glass.

Safiyah left her.

Nyx sat on the roof a good deal longer, refilling her glass until the bottle was empty. She wondered how a person was supposed to sleep at night, knowing the kind of shit Safiyah did. But was it really all that different? Killing a hundred people or a million? After a while, they all blurred together. Oh, sure, there were some you thought about more than others. The boy from Radha who screamed for three hours for his mother after Nyx threw an acid burst into his garret window. The pretty girl from Barsa who Nyx killed as she lay between her naked thighs. Just reached up and pushed two thumbs into her eyes, fleshy jelly. Nyx had been drunk and high on some military grade narcotic then, so that memory was milky and distorted with the memory of the three other times they fucked. And then there were the twin boys who had taken an entire textile factory hostage in Aludra. When Nyx finally got in, she found nothing but bent, twisted, bodies. Charred and bashed in, ragged clothing. But it was not the female workers who had drawn their wrath. No, the women had gotten out the back. All that was left when the twins came in were half a dozen young boys, twelve to sixteen, not one of whom had done a day of combat training. They were frail, skinny, pretty little things—what was left of them, anyhow. Nyx found the boys upstairs, sobbing over the last two bodies. These ones were mostly just melted flesh. They had run out of bullets, and used acid on them.

When they stared up at her, Nyx wasn't even so certain the boys knew what they had done. Slitting their throats was clean and easy, but when it was over, she sat exactly where they had, staring down at their bodies as they bled out and blood pooled around her sandals. She wondered what somebody else might think, coming upon her that way, surrounded in a factory full of mangled bodies. She half hoped they might kill her.

Now, Nyx sighed and stood. She took one last look at the sky. For the first time in a very long time, she believed there was another world on the way… a world that had to be better than this one. Cause fuck knows it couldn't be any worse than the one she knew.

She understood, now, why she and Safiyah got along so well.

48.

Inaya walked into a tavern called the Lapping Cat. It was at the far eastern edge of Inoublie, the half of the city left blessedly untouched by the devastating sand. She walked to the bar keep, who appeared more than a little surprised to see a woman wearing a modest habit and wimple enter his tavern.

"Is there a message here for Inaya Khadija?" she asked.

He raised his brows. "There is, Madame. One moment." He walked to the back and returned with a sealed envelope.

"Thank you," she said.

She walked outside and went to a nearby café to open the letter. Inside was a picture of her children and a train ticket to Shirhazi, the capital of Tirhan.

Inaya stared long at the photo. When she last saw her children, Taite and Isfahan, they were six and three. That made Taite thirteen and Isfahan ten now. They were serious children, more serious than she remembered. They stood together on a balcony overlooking Shahrdad, the salty inland sea in Shirhazi. Isfahan covered her hair, and Taite's hair was already tangling into dreadlocks like Khos's.

She wept there at the table.

The serving girl came to her table with more tea, but said nothing. Inaya expected they had seen a great many weeping people here the last few days.

She placed the photo on the table and stared at the train ticket. It should be so easy to go home. She remembered life in Tirhan, before the bel dames came, before she realized everything she lived there was a lie. The streets in Tirhan were safe. She left her garden door unlocked. She could walk anywhere she wished, be employed wherever she wished. The festivals were colorful; the people friendly, the food plentiful. It was like a dream of a place. And the reason it existed was because the rest of the world was like this. The people there could live that way because they sent weapons to countries like hers, and dared them to tear each other apart.

Inaya tore up the train ticket. She finished her tea. Took the photo from the table.

"Madame?" Adeliz said.

Inaya glanced up and saw her waiting in the doorway. "Yes, I'm coming," Inaya said. She pushed the photo into her pocket and placed a few chits on the table for the tea.

"There is a message from Alix," Adeliz said as they stepped onto the street.

"And what is that?" Inaya asked.

"She says the bakkie's waiting."

"Then we best not keep her waiting," Inaya said, and buttoned her coat against the cold.

49.

Rhys sat in his new home in Bahreha, in Chenja, unpacking boxes of linens from Tirhan. He had always preferred Tirhani clothes. Better made, more beautiful. For so long, he had thought himself as a poor nomad, a drifter—he had forgotten what it was to build a home. The terror of losing it again had cut too deep to risk that loss again.

But the alternative…

He imagined Elahyiah singing in the other room. Heard Rahim's wailing. But it was all fantasy.

He had no family now. No path. No purpose.

The first thing he did on his return was send half the salary he had received from Hanife that week to Elahyiah's parents' address in Tirhan. He'd left Bomani before Hanife had him pay it back. He did not know if Elahyiah ever received it. He still had a few friends in Tirhan, though, and they told him his wife and children were safe with Elahyiah's family. It was enough to know that his resourceful wife had done what he could not—bring their family home. But it was no thanks to his words or deeds. He knew that, and the knowledge threatened to devour him. All he had left now was God.

Outside, he heard the call to prayer start at the center of the city. It had been some time since he was back in Chenja proper, and the first time he had been back as a man and not a criminal. What remained of Hanife's money had rented him a proper house in a decent part of town. His uncle, Abdul-Nasser, lived not far from here, and though his uncle was a bit scattered in the head, he was a good ally to have as Rhys settled in his new life.

Rhys had started work at the local madrassa, teaching the Kitab to young children. Despite some disapproving noises from the madrassa's elders, his request that girls be allowed to attend classes as well was approved. He would teach nothing to boys, he said, that he would not teach his own girls. His girls… the ones he let die, and the ones Elahyiah had taken from him. He could hate her for it, he knew, or release her. A man who could not fix himself, who did not know his own path, was not fit to be a husband. He knew that.

He had come home to find his path.

The end of the war had meant the end of many things in Chenja. There was an opportunity for change here, and he intended to be part of it.

He uncovered his pistol box from a stack of belongings that had come with him from his temporary apartment. He imagined going upstairs, past Mehry and Nasrin's room, where they would be playing with a collection of dolls and toy bakkies he had bought for them in Heidia, one of the ports of call on his journey home. He had never been the best of magicians.

But instead, he had the dolls and toy bakkies here, in a sad pile beside his pistol box. The two things could not exist together. He knew that. Had known it back in Tirhan, but fought it.

He put the pistol box into his pile of things to sell.

Someone knocked at the door. The Mhorian woman who came in to cook and clean for him, Rahel, answered it.

Rhys carried the clothing upstairs. The house was still very sparse. Perhaps it always would be. Some men could start over, he knew. Pretend they had never failed. But he was not that type of man. He would live with his mistakes, even if he did not know how to fix them.

"Patron?" Rahel called from the bottom of the stairs.

"Yes?" Rhys said.

"Pardon, patron, but this man says he's your father."

Rhys took a deep breath. He had known it was a possibility for his father to find him. People would talk. Especially his uncle. "Let him in, please. Prepare some tea."

Rhys walked to the window in his study, and gazed out into the dusty landscape outside Bahreha. He imagined a day when his grandchildren would play in the parks there, and his children would rebuild the roads and the fountains and sponsor the theaters. He imagined a whole world on top of this one, better than this one, a thousand years of peace.

Perhaps even a world he could be a part of.

He only thought of Nyx once, when he heard his father enter the sitting room. Heard his distinctive voice speaking softly to Rahel. Rhys had fled his home a coward. What would his father have to say to his cowardly son? He wanted Nyx beside him then, wanted her easy confidence, her surety.

Instead, he recited the ninety-nine names of God. Then he went to the basin on his side table and performed the ablution, as if for prayer.

When he gazed into the mirror, he saw a face he had thought forgotten, long dead. But as he straightened, he saw that it was Rakhshan Arjoomand, not Rhys Dashasa, or Rhys Shahkam, who now prepared to face the consequences of everything he had fled.

He walked downstairs.

A tall, thin man stood at the door, wearing a beautiful green shalwar khameez stitched in gold. His head was shaved, but a neat white beard clothed his handsome face. The man had his long, slim hands folded in front of him. He gazed up at Rhys; an old man now, much smaller than Rhys remembered.

"Rakhshan," the man said.

Rhys held out his hands to greet his father.

50.

The season had turned. Cloudy skies and misty days had given way to partial clouds and drizzle. Nyx hadn't lived on the coast for the weather.

She drove down the long, dreary drive to the coastal compound, past the towering trees, comforting as minarets, and parked next to the ruin of the compound wall. Got out of the bakkie.

The compound wall had been imploded. As had the compound itself. It was just a heaping pile of rubble and weeds now. Nyx knew how it would go because she had been the one to design the blast and set the charges. She had taught the kids how to make eighteen different kinds of mines and shown them exactly how to set them.

It's why she didn't hesitate, now, to walk over the ruined wall and into the overgrown garden as the rain misted her face. She tracked each and every charge with her eyes, checking that they had blown successfully. From the look of the damage, every mine had gone off as planned. She had been a sapper, once. It was nice to know she was still good at it.

Nyx settled on the remains of the porch. The damp soaked through her coat. With the wall down, she had a good view of the ocean, and a bruising violet sunset that she had to admit was kinda pretty. The heap of rubble behind her that had once been her home was less pretty. That was all right. She never blew a place with the intention of it looking nice afterward.

Nyx pulled a bottle of whiskey from her coat pocket and broke the seal. Stared at the ocean. Drank.

She remembered Fatima putting that paper in front of her and telling her she could become a bel dame again. It had been tempting. Take up the old bel dame title. Throw it around like she really was somebody great. Somebody important. Somebody the world would remember. An honorable woman because she could kill well. But when she looked at that paper, she thought of all the other stuff that came with it. She thought of Radeyah's scars, and her dead brothers, and how her mother had died in the breeding compounds. Being a part of the old world meant being a part of the system that created all that shit. In her own way, she had supported it all, hadn't she?

Nyx took another pull on the bottle. Without God or the bel dames, she wasn't so sure what she was anymore. Maybe that was all right.

In the end, she refused Fatima's offer, then called Anneke and told her it was time to blow the place. But when Anneke and the kids ran, they couldn't tell Nyx where they were going. Nyx knew that when she called. When she set it all into motion. She knew she'd give up her home, the kids, Radeyah, and everything she built, and kill a good many people besides, when she took this note.

But it wasn't taking the note that was so bad. Or calling Anneke, or even giving everything up. Even trekking across the desert, bleeding out magicians, killing women, watching Eshe die, no… that was all just what you had to do to survive. The worst part of a fight was always afterward, when you could hear the screams of your injured opponent, and the snarling crowd; when you felt your own chest filling with fluid, and snorted great gobs of coppery blood. The worst part was when you realized it was all over, but you weren't dead yet.

Nyx took another pull.

She heard a coughing sound above the gnashing of the sea, and saw a bakkie coming up the drive. It was a smoked-glass bakkie, the sort used by security forces in Nasheen. She set down the bottle and pulled her scattergun from her back. Placed it in her lap.

The bakkie had been following her since Sameh. She half hoped it was some rogue bel dame come to end it all. But she supposed it could be some other person—Anneke come to take her back, Radeyah to forgive her, or maybe, just maybe, it was Rhys, giving it all up to… no, it probably wasn't Rhys. Whoever it was would be somebody with nothing to lose. She thought of Mercia, and wondered if she'd come out for another round between the sheets. Wouldn't that be something?

The driver cut the juice to the bugs. The coughing and hissing in the cistern stopped.

The driver's door opened.

Nyx gazed out toward the horizon, and weighed her options. There was a lot of thinking a person could do, in the long pause between what was, and what could be. She remembered the starship, bursting apart in the sky. She had done her part to usher in twenty years of peace. What Nasheen did with it was up to Nasheen.

Now, she figured she'd either have a good tumble, or go down blazing. Either way, it was a fitting way to end things.

The rain stopped. A pity. She'd been hoping for a storm.

"I'm retired," Nyx said—to the ocean, to the air, to Nasheen, to her visitor—and took her last drink.

++

ACKNOWLEDGEMENTS

Writing these books has been a bizarre rollercoaster ride.

It turned out that *Rapture* was a far more exhausting book to write than I anticipated. The realities of deadlines and day jobs kept me in front of the computer and research books for long stretches—sometimes fourteen to sixteen hours a day. It was not always fun, but it was necessary. Thanks to Jayson Utz for all the support during various deadline crunches.

My first readers this time around worked with a very tight deadline as well. Thanks to Miriam Hurst, Julian Brown, David Moles, Dave Zelasco, and Alec Austin for fast, detailed notes, suggestions, rants, and the occasional rave. After all those hours in front of the damn computer, I barely knew my own name, let alone what weapon anybody was carrying or the proper way to gut a corpse.

Many thanks to team Night Shade throughout the life of these books, as well—my editor, Ross Lockhart; Jeremy Lassen, my acquiring editor; Marty Halpern, my copyeditor; and Liz Upson for marketing support, as well as Tomra Palmer for fast turnaround on annoying new author questions.

Thanks as well go out to my agent, Jennifer Jackson, for making the tough phone calls.

My parents also remain among my top fans and supporters—thanks for cheerleading me on throughout my career.

Finally, thanks to all the readers, bloggers, book club participants, and fans who took a chance on these books. It's because of you that this book exists at all. Keep passing copies around, and I'll see you again for the next one....

The Big Red House
Ohio
Summer, 2012

ABOUT THE AUTHOR

Kameron Hurley currently hacks out a living as a marketing and advertising writer in Ohio. She's lived in Fairbanks, Alaska; Durban, South Africa; and Chicago, but grew up in and around Washington State. Her personal and professional exploits have taken her all around the world. She spent much of her roaring twenties traveling, pretending to learn how to box, and trying not to die spectacularly. Along the way, she justified her nomadic lifestyle by picking up degrees in history from the University of Alaska and the University of Kwa-Zulu Natal. Today she lives a comparatively boring life sustained by Coke Zero, Chipotle, low-carb cooking, and lots of words. She continues to work hard at not dying. Follow the fun at www.kameronhurley.com.